SO-BZO-539

THE WHIRLWIND IN THE THORN TREE

Book One of
The Outlaw King
Edited and Formatted

S. A. Hunt

Published February 2013 by S. A. Hunt
ISBN: 9781482615555
Visit S. A. Hunt's official website at
http://theusualmadman.net/
for the latest news, book details, and other information

Copyright © S. A. Hunt, 2013
Cover Art: S. A. Hunt

This book is a work of fiction. Names, characters, places and
incidents either are products of the author's imagination or are
used fictitiously. Any resemblance to actual events or locales or
persons, living or dead, is entirely coincidental. All rights reserved.
Except as permitted under the U.S. Copyright Act of 1976, no part
of this publication may be reproduced, distributed or transmitted in
any form or by any means, or stored in a database or retrieval
system, without the prior written permission of the publisher.
Fan fiction and fan art is encouraged.

Hunt, S. A. (2013-02-21). The Whirlwind in the Thorn Tree (The
Outlaw King, Book 1)
Print Edition

The Betrayal

HE CREPT TOWARD THE house through cold blue beams, the wash of the moonlight dancing across the forest under his feet like a handful of silver coins. He was there to be the dealer of death, but he wasn't loaded for battle; indeed, there was only one pistol in his gunbelt and only one bullet in it.

It was a small house, a two-story half-timber cottage set back deep in the trees, up the hill from the main grounds. If you weren't looking for it, you wouldn't even realize it was there. A small wooden platform served as the front porch roof, accessible by a door that opened in the middle. Next to the front door was a small table, and on that table was a wooden game board.

The man had never heard of the game before the house's occupant had foisted it on him fifteen years ago, on one of their few meetings. The rules were labyrinthine and the pace was nerve-wracking; they would sometimes go days between moves.

He climbed the front porch, careful to avoid the always-creaky second step, and tested the doorknob. It was locked.

He was never one for picking locks. He went back out into the front yard and looked up at the widow's-walk on the second story, sizing it up with a veteran eye. He rubbed his hands together and leaned on his knees, gauging and making mental calculations.

With four quick steps, he ran at the house and stepped on one of the columns holding up the platform, launching himself up at the ledge. It was a challenging jump, three meters at least. He caught the ledge with his fingertips and flexed his arms, kicking both feet up as he did so, and pulled himself onto the widow's-walk. The railing became a ladder that he heaved himself up and over.

The night was a living thing out here in the wilderness, a soul-painting crawling and crying with the dark paint of a thousand creatures. The man paused, squatting next to the door to avoid being seen, to make sure he hadn't woken up the man inside.

He listened to the frogsong and the fiddling of the insects, his heartbeat settling. Still water. A telescope bolted to the railing focused a speck of moonlight onto the boards.

Satisfied he hadn't been heard, he tried the door and found it unlocked. He eased it open, slipped inside, and pushed it against the jamb.

He squatted there in the darkness of the bedroom as his eyes adjusted to the grainy, colorless environment. Some enormous sort of artwork dangled from the ceiling, a giant paper tube that coiled around the room once. If he hadn't entered on his haunches, he would have ran right into it.

The owner of the house lay asleep on the bed in the middle of the room, snoring softly. The intruder lingered in the shadows, watching him sleep. He didn't *think* the fat bastard was faking it, but he knew better than to trust such a canny son of a bitch.

He crouched there for a long time, twenty minutes maybe, long enough for the sleeper to get bored of pretending and look to see what was going on.

Nope. He went on snoring, oblivious to his fate.

The man stood up and drew his pistol from the leather jackass rig under his jacket; it was a well-polished seven-shot breaktop revolver, too big to qualify as a hidden piece. He was only wearing the jacket to muffle the holster's tack.

"I'm sorry," the man murmured, and fired a slug into the back

3

of Ed's head.

At first, he thought the round had vaporized the sleeping man; the instant the pistol had discharged, the muzzle-flash lighting up the room and icepicking his eardrums, Ed had vanished. He didn't get up and run, he simply *ceased to exist,* and his assassin couldn't understand what had happened. In a strange fit of pique, he had the bizarre notion that he'd popped Ed like a balloon. Ed was a big guy, almost three hundred pounds. Maybe all that flab was nothing but hot air.

The killer stood there, the gun still pointed at the bed, trying to wrap his head around the results of his premeditated murder, when snow began to fall from the ceiling: great big goosedown flakes that waltzed to and fro as they fell, twirling in the air.

Still bewildered, he looked up and opened his other hand, catching one of the flakes in his glove. It was a feather from the mattress.

A tearing, a deafening pain whickered through his mind and he dropped the pistol on the duvet, sinking to his knees, his fists over his temples. Both ears were ringing and he felt like all the blood had drained out of his skull, leaving him wall-eyed and out of breath. The room centrifuged like a zoetrope.

"Guhh," he said, his forehead ground against the intricate carpet. His brainpan felt like it was being emptied and washed out. "Nnnnggghhh, ffffggg . . . leave me be, for the love of the gods. I've done your deed."

The voice in his head was corrupted by his resistance, but its message was still clear. MY SOLDIER. YOU ARE NOT FINISHED.

The man floundered on the floor, his fingertips twitching, searching; he found the bedpost and hauled himself to his feet. His cheeks were cold; he touched them and realized that he was weeping.

4

He picked up the smoking revolver and put it back in its holster, and sat down on the hope chest at the end of the bed to collect himself.

"No," he said. "I don't want to do for you no more, devil."

His downcast eyes swept over the familiar shape at his feet. He leaned over and picked up the gunbelt that had been lying at the foot of the bedpost. It was empty of all but the rounds.

A cursory search uncovered the pistols lying on the nightstand, in easy reach of the bed. The man picked them up, put them in the gunbelt, and slung the gunbelt over his shoulder like a gentlemen's jacket. It was an easy, jaunty look, but he felt sick to his stomach and not at all jaunty.

On the way downstairs and out the front door, he paused at the typewriter sitting on the desk and typed a few meaningful words, then walked out onto the porch where he half-expected to see a squad of lawmen waiting to gun him down as he left the house.

There was no one. A surge of grief and anger filled him up and burned away quickly, leaving only regret in its place, tempered by shame. Perhaps he only *wanted* there to be someone there to punish him for what he'd done.

He raked the pieces from the game board in abject rage.

*   *   *

The sound of gunfire startled him awake, but instead of his bed, Ed found himself underwater. A dark and subtle landscape of undulating blue, red, and green materialized from the nothing. The cold water threatened to take his breath away.

Ed pushed the slimy stones with heavy hands and rose against the water's surface, feeling it glass smooth and round over the top

5

of his head. It seemed to happen in slow-motion; he couldn't get enough air into his burning chest, the water wouldn't stream out of his beard fast enough. It clung to his face like melting ice and blurred his eyes.

He gazed, bewildered, at the dead fingers of the evening forest through a curtain of crystal.

Then the water was gone and he fell away from it, collapsing on his back at the stream's edge as it coursed over his numbing feet. He sat up and barked a gout of water from his lungs, panting in ragged gasps, the pain sawing at his throat with every breath.

In that clarity which is so common to the dying, he looked down and marveled with grim eyes at the little sores all over his naked shins, calves, and feet. The diabetes was eating his legs, but today, today was the last day he'd ever have to worry about it again.

Out of the chilling rush of the autumn water, the bullet-hole howled anew and Ed fell back again onto his elbows, growling.

"Get to the house," said the voice, echoing in his head, and he realized it was all he could hear. His head felt like it was wrapped in foam. As he had done so many times before, for so many years before, for so long to his benefit, Ed heeded the raspy words.

He rolled onto his side and pushed himself up again, struggling to his feet. The world swam again, as if he were underwater once more, and dimmed, and he bent over and grasped his knees until he could regain his faculties. He took one step, then another staggering lurch, then stood a bit straighter and continued onto the house.

It waited, lurking huge and fat in the forest, a rundown old white plantation house in the middle of ten thousand winter-stripped trees.

He made it to the back door, and leaned against the splintery rail at the bottom of the stoop to muster up another round of fortitude. He snatched the door open and ordered himself inside.

When he got into the kitchen, he heard someone tapping an impatient foot on the linoleum, but when he looked around in confusion he realized that what he was hearing was the sound of his blood dripping on the floor. The sight of it astounded him, made him reel again; he leaned on the island as he passed it, and started toward the living room.

His shirt, already filthy and soaked through, began to greedily drink up the crimson leaking out of the shredded hole in his neck, spreading it across his chest and shoulder, letting it run down his coarse-haired back.

He couldn't stand anymore. He went to his knees with a thunderous weight that made the dishes in the sink clatter, and fell over onto his side, causing the grill shelf inside the oven to buzz. Ed lay on his back in his own kitchen, his gray eyes staring up at the horrid popcorn ceiling and the overhead light that had stopped working when his boy was still in diapers.

This isn't how it was supposed to go, the old man thought, and he could feel the life running out of him from second to second. *This isn't how it was written.*

Silent feet approached him from a dark corner of the room and someone knelt over him. "Where is it? What did you do with it?"

With what? Oh, I know what you want. Ed's mouth worked, but he couldn't get the words out of his throat. The world was falling away, he was dropping, dropping through a trapdoor into oblivion, looking up at his oldest friend's face as it dwindled to a point high above. He could hear the soft rustle of arrow-shafts in a quiver.

I'm sorry, old friend. He'll find it. He'll do the right thing.

"Where did you put the key?"

Your turn, kid, thought Ed, as the world came to an end,

7

narrowing to a bright point like an old television.

Good luck. You're gonna need it.

My Ithaca

I AWOKE TO THE lights of home, jostled from sleep by the Greyhound bus as we rattled down an offramp. I peeled my face away from the windowsill and sat up, pulling the fleece cap off my eyes and looking around. Lexington scrolled past the glass, greeting me with an urban smile I hadn't seen in a year.

I tugged the hat down over my eyes again and savored the feel of the tires grumbling on familiar surface streets.

The bus pulled into a parking lot, waking me up again. I grabbed my backpack and sidled off into the cool night air. The driver opened the sidewall compartments and helped me pull my bags off onto the asphalt: a black gym bag, a green canvas duffel bag, and a camouflage rucksack, all of them stuffed to capacity.

He grunted as he dragged the rucksack out and it hit the ground with a soft thud. I caught a glimpse of the tag the airport baggage handlers had put on it. It was a picture of a stick figure bending over with a lightning zigzag coming out of his back, and the words "TWO MAN LIFT".

"There we go," he said. "Gonna be alright? Got somebody to pick you up?"

"Yeah," I said.

He hesitated for a moment, wiping his hands on his pants, glanced at me, then got back on the bus and started writing on a clipboard. I took off my backpack, then knelt and hoisted up the rucksack, shrugging into the complex strap frame. I put my backpack on my chest, then squatted to pick up the gym bag and duffel, and shuffled away.

I felt like an astronaut in my rucksack and heavy boots, just returned from a journey to an alien planet.

I made it across the parking lot of the pizzeria next door and was halfway across the next when I had to put the bag and duffel down and rest. Cars shushed past on the four-lane, oblivious white-eyed roaches scurrying back to whatever hidey-hole they lived in.

I panted, my breath a billow of white in the late fall air, and listened to the droning buzz of the sodium mast-light overhead. Exhausted by almost a week of constant travel, I was starting to sweat in my uniform.

I hefted my stuff again and resumed my shuffling quest.

The stark lights of the restaurant were a welcome sight. It wasn't too busy; there were a couple of families eating supper, kids playing in the enclosed jungle gym, a young couple in a corner booth. An old guy in a threadbare jacket was standing at the front counter.

I squeezed in through a side entrance and crammed the duffel, gym bag, and backpack into a booth and sat down next to my rucksack. My crap and I had pretty much occupied an entire booth.

Once I'd caught my breath, I took out my cellphone and turned it on. I dialed Tianna's number and put it to my ear.

"Hello? Ross?"

"Hey," I said. The plastic bench felt slick and strange against my fatigues. "Yeah, it's me. I'm home."

"Where are you?"

"The Burger Queen on New Circle Road."

"Okay," said the voice on the other end of the line. "I'll be there in a minute."

I hung up the phone and went to the counter to order something to eat, feeling self-conscious in my rumpled regalia. I could feel eyes on my back as I waited for my food, unconsciously toying with the wedding band hanging from the chain around my neck. The world around me felt unreal, an elaborate prank.

I sat back down with my boothful of fat traveling companions and dug into my cheeseburger and fries.

I thought it would be an orgasmic experience after so long eating NATO chow like raw cabbage, beat-up fruit, and rabbit stew, but it tasted . . . *grungy,* for lack of a better word. Dirty, greasy, heavy. It tasted like the junk food it always was.

My first meal at home was a distant memory by the time I saw the pickup truck pull into the parking lot an hour later. I got up and reassembled my astronaut getup, then carried it all outside to where the Dodge sat, idling.

My wife got out and watched me load all my stuff into the back.

"Hi," she said.

"Hi."

We stood there for a long moment, and she stepped forward and we hugged. I wish I could tell you that it was a passionate reunion like the movies, with lots of feverish pawing and kisses, but I'd be lying to you, and I don't quite want to get into tall tales just yet. There will be plenty of unbelievable things recounted later, believe me.

The embrace, brief and stiff, broke off and she stepped back. She gave me a vague, wistful smile through the hair the wind was blowing across her face.

I tucked it behind her ear and she said something I couldn't quite hear. "Hmm?" I asked.

"I said, I missed you."

"I missed you too."

She got into the truck; I slid into the passenger seat and rubbed my hands together, savoring the blast of hot air from the heater vent. We pulled out of the parking lot and merged with traffic, my hands warming on the dash.

The silence was uncomfortable, but I didn't have enough time to get wound up over it and turn on the radio, because our house was only a few minutes' drive away. We climbed a steep curve, slipping through the looming oaks of the neighborhood night like a snake through a tunnel. The headlights washed up the driveway and over the front of our home, a sprawling 1970s ranch house.

My teeth started to hurt and I realized my jaw was tight. We pulled up into the carport behind my Mercury Topaz and Tianna put the truck into gear. I got out and took my stuff out of the back, carrying it inside.

I loved that house; the groovy-dude architectural taste made it into a work of Brady Bunch art. It was like a bargain bin Frank Lloyd Wright creation—the whole foyer was visible through a floor-to-ceiling glass window with the front door in the middle of it. Not very secure, but for the rent we were paying, it was Beverly Hills on a Podunk budget.

Almost every wall had a window in it looking through to the next room, and was filled with either plate glass or shelves laden with knick-knacks—or, would have been, if the knick-knacks were still there. As I came in, I realized that the walls were bare and the closet in the foyer was empty.

I carried my stuff into the living room and saw that while my TV, recliner, and the shelf my mother had given us were still present and accounted for, everything else was missing: the sofa, all the pictures, tables, and lamps, the dresser that contained all the vinyl records for the turntable I'd bought her last Christmas, and the big mirror that had been hanging over it.

13

I went into the bedroom. The bed and dressers were gone. The closet was empty of everything but my own clothes.

The linen closet was empty and so was the bathroom medicine cabinet. I went into the kitchen and opened all the cupboards. The pots and pans were gone, the dishes, the blender, the Foreman were gone. My quesadilla maker was still there. The fridge had nothing in it but a bottle of margarita mix, a squirt-bottle of mustard, and a half-stick of butter.

I came back outside. She was standing next to the Dodge, which was still running.

"Do you have everything you need?" she asked.

I still don't know if I was actually confused or just playing dumb. Perhaps I only asked what came out of my mouth next because I didn't want to accept the truth.

"Everything I need?"

Even though her voice was low and soft, the silence of the fall evening made it easy to hear her. "Yes."

I just stood there, as my mother was wont to say, 'like a bump on a log'. I didn't know what to say. I don't know what I had expected, but it wasn't this. It wasn't an empty house. Concessions, maybe. Reconciliations, arguments, reassembly, repair, patchwork. Me sleeping on the couch for a while. Awkward breakfasts. Getting to know each other again. Apologies. Not using pet names for a while.

Not this.

I looked down at my feet, at the desert dust still ground into the rawhide of my boots.

I wouldn't need food. I wasn't hungry. I wondered if I would ever be hungry again.

I sighed and said, "Yes."

She opened the door, but didn't get in. I was a deer in the

headlights, literally and figuratively, on my feet in the washed-out white of the truck's low-beams. I had enough time to think about asking her to stay, to think about asking her *why* she wasn't staying, to ask her where the dog was. Our dog was not in the house, not in *our* house, the dog was not home. *Where was the freaking dog?*

I opened my mouth to speak, but didn't. She stepped up into the truck and sat behind the wheel.

A few minutes later, my wife closed the door, put the Dodge in gear and backed out of the driveway into the street, slowly put it in drive, and drove away.

I remained there in the dark, a shadow and piece of the night, standing next to my car listening to the distant sounds of the city.

When I got tired of being cold, I went into the house and turned the heat on, then went into the living room and sat in the recliner. The acrid smell of burning dust from an unused heating unit filled the house.

I looked up and saw the blinds over the living room's big picture window. I had put them up on my mid-tour break seven months ago, when we had moved into the house. It had been a massive pain in the ass but I'd done it for her—they were too big and I had to redo the brackets several times, but I had been happy to do it. I was happy and looking forward to coming home for good.

Home. It was my home. My house. My name was on the lease and the address was on my Army paperwork. I was paying the rent. But I had never lived in it.

I sat in my armchair looking at the lights of the city, ignoring the stink of baking dust.

After a while—maybe an hour, maybe three hours, I'm not sure—I got up and stood in the middle of the living room for a bit, my mind beginning to whirl. My eyes had become adjusted to the darkness, turning the house into a monochrome labyrinth, a mausoleum wallpapered in dingy yellow.

I sniffed. Looking down, I saw the shelf.

My mother had given it to us as a house-warming gift, a five-tiered curio shelf about four feet tall. It was made out of particle-board with a wood-grain veneer, and as fragile as a carton of eggs. Our wedding photos used to stand on it, in a large frame that was made to look like an open book. It also once displayed two music boxes and a backless clock inside a bell jar.

I picked it up, carried it out onto the carport, and slammed it against the cement floor with everything I could muster. It exploded into six pieces.

I picked up the biggest piece, a half-shelf with a leg sticking out of it, and used it to club the rest of the debris. A chunk of the board broke, bounced off my face, and twirled into the darkness. I ignored it. The end of the leg broke off and hit the ceiling.

I threw the piece of wood in my hand and stood shivering with rage, trying to think of something else I could break. The laundry room was immediately to my left through an exterior door. I opened it and turned the light on.

I was looking into a small space with a washer and dryer inside and garden—no, the gardening tools were gone. That was probably a good thing: we had a "Garden Weasel" that consisted of a long handle with three spiky rotors on the end of it and looked like some sort of medieval death-hammer.

The washer and dryer were coin-operated; our last landlord had given them to us when he replaced the machines in the apartment complex's open laundry. I'd had to pry the quarter boxes out—and to use them, you had to reach down into the mangled timer's housing and pull a lever. An inconvenience, but worth it for a tough, high-capacity machine.

As I went to close the door, I saw something written on the wall in pencil.

It was very small and gave me chills every single time I saw it. We had discovered it the day we moved in, as we were installing the dryer. At the time, we called it our 'good luck charm'.

Someone who had once lived here had scrawled, *This was a very happy home. 11/26/88*

My throat closed up and I held the top of the dryer like a little kid on a boogie board because I could feel it coming. I knew it was there lurking in the dark, cold house, when I saw the blinds, but when I—quite literally—saw the writing on the wall, I felt the top of my heart crack.

As I slouched there gripping the dryer for dear life, the entire thing broke into a thousand pieces.

*   *   *

I was still sitting in the recliner when the first rays of Kentucky sunlight came over the trees, golden spears tracing long arcs across the wall and kitchen door, solid and heavy with snowlike dust. My right knee was bouncing and my eyes were raw and grainy.

My cellphone rang. The opening bells of Ray LaMontagne's "Gossip in the Grain", tinny but always beautiful, resonated in the morning stillness. *Ding ding ding . . . ding . . . ding.*

It rang again. My hand came up off the chair's arm and I wiped my wet nose with a paper towel, a piece of Bounty, because there was no toilet paper.

Ding ding ding . . . ding . . . ding.

I picked it up and looked at the screen as it rang again, in my hand. The digital readout told me it was 7:12 AM. I pressed the Call button and put it against my ear.

17

I could hear someone breathing. I finally said in a listless voice, "Hello."

"Ross?" It was my mother Caroline in Georgia. "Are you home yet?"

I swallowed and tried to speak. My vocal chords didn't kick in at first, and I had to stretch the word out.

"—Yes."

"Are you there? Hello?"

"Yes," I said, "I'm home. I got home . . . last night."

"Oh," said my mother. "I'm so sorry. I'm so sorry."

I blinked. How did she know? I sat up, slowly, like a mummy rising out of the sarcophagus, and huddled on the edge of my seat, hugging myself with the phone against my head. "What about?"

"Your dad."

"My dad?" I asked. Like my voice, my thoughts seemed to be coming to me from some faraway place, as if I were listening to them on a shortwave radio. I felt as if I were on the airless moon, thousands of miles away from everything and everybody. I breathed, watching the motes of dust orbit my face. "What about my dad?"

This wasn't about the first shoe. This was the second shoe dropping.

My mother sighed. Her voice was slow and measured and sympathetic. "He . . . I'm so sorry you had to come home to this, son. I'm so sorry. He had a heart attack yesterday. He was . . . . Ed's gone. Eddie's gone. His agent Max found him."

I listened to the birds outside. I hated them. "Goddamn," I said.

My mother didn't respond, but I could feel her confusion.

"She left me," I said, looking at the floor. "All her stuff was

18

gone when I got home. She's gone too."

"Ohh, son. I'm sorry. There's—there's not really anything I can tell you that'll make you feel better. Maybe it's better this way, baby. Maybe you're better off."

Knowing someone was listening to me ruptured whatever control I had developed during the night. I started sobbing. She listened to me as I struggled to maintain myself. When I had settled enough to listen, she spoke.

"Why don't you come home? Get out of that empty house for a little while and come to the funeral. They're doing it in a couple of days. I hear there's going to be a few of his fans there. It'll be good for you, you'll have somebody to talk to. You won't be alone."

I said, "Okay."

After I got off the phone with her, I took a dose of melatonin, swung out the chair's footrest, and took a nap for a few hours. When I woke up, I put a couple of outfits in my backpack with my laptop and left. If I'd known then what I know now, I would have taken *all* my clothes, because that was the last time I ever stepped foot in that house.

Oriensligne burned around him as Pack lay in the dust by the well. He had managed to drag his father's heavy corpse away from the fire before it had spread too far, but by the time he'd returned to the house, it had engulfed his mother and sister. They were black, peeling-bubbling figures, withered phantoms, sleeping in the inferno.

His tears made tracks in the dirt on his face, landing on the glossy chrome of his father's antique pistol. Pack held it now, as he curled protectively around his father's body. He held the gun against his face and reveled in the smell of the oil and the familiar scent of his father's hand on the sandalwood grip.

He pretended that the gun was the last surviving part of his father, and that it represented a place where he could never be hurt again, where nothing could ever be taken from him as long as he lived. He went there, now, the flames rippling across the polished, scrollworked surface. He went there and slept.

He would never come back.

—The Fiddle and the Fire, vol 1 "The Brine and the Bygone"

Cats, Cradles, and Comic-Cons

I WAS STANDING IN my shitty hotel room alone, adjusting my tie when it hit me that I was about to go to my father's funeral. I suppose like any child, I must have assumed he was going to live forever.

In a way, he will, I suppose. They say that the only immortality that can be achieved by mortal man is through the act of creation. My father managed to accomplish both of these feats in his lifetime.

I finished straightening myself and left. My junky little car took some coaxing to start, but purred like a garbage disposal when I got it running. I pulled out of my parking space and took off across town, driving a little slower than usual. I wasn't looking forward to my destination, and that had little to do with seeing my father dead in a box.

Speaking of my father, I'd like to introduce you to Vincent Edward Richard Brigham.

Yes, that's four names. Born in June of the year of our Lord 1951, Ed survived your usual Southern childhood: church every Sunday and fatback ham with turnip greens and black-eyed peas on a regular basis.

In high school, he started tinkering with the medium of fiction, and in the middle of his first year of law school, Ed discovered what he was meant to do and then he did the impossible: he started making a living writing fantasy novels south of the Mason-Dixon line. As you can imagine, passing the bar was

22

no longer of any concern.

Over the next forty years, my dad made a name for himself in the hearts and minds of bookworms everywhere with his novel series *The Fiddle and the Fire,* a fictional biography of a man's life in pursuit of vengeance across a fantasy-western world.

We lost track of each other somewhere between that second and third decade, so to speak, but he went on to become a semi-legend in the entertainment world . . . not exactly a name on the lips or scripts of Katie Couric or Mary Hart, but whispered to each other over dusty paperbacks at the neighborhood book shop and doggedly tracked down on Amazon. He was like the American god that he turned out to be, ubiquitous but invisible.

I barely registered the drive to the chapel and before I knew it, I was there. Unfortunately, I was nowhere near as invisible as Ed used to be.

The teenager at the podium, who had just given his own personal eulogy, was wearing a polished revolver like the ones from my dad's books. I hoped that the gun wasn't real, as he stepped down from the podium at the front of the funeral party and returned to his seat.

Following him back to his pew, I locked eyes with a pretty girl a few rows back, on the other side of the room. Her big, bright eyes, platinum-blonde hair, and serene expression made her look like a rock-chick version of a young Joanne Woodward. She waved daintily at me with a hand clad in a fingerless black glove.

I looked away. A heavyset girl dressed like a cross between Annie Oakley and a valkyrie stepped up to the podium, and gave her name as Judith Raske. She began to give a very sincere, heartfelt eulogy that I couldn't quite pay attention to.

The man in the casket had no blood relation to anyone in the funeral parlor except for me. I sat in the back, wedged into a narrow space somewhere between schadenfreude and disappointment. I knew that Ed had managed to squeeze out enough of his fantasy series to amass a cult following, but none of us had expected to see almost two hundred people crammed into this tiny chapel.

The mourners considered themselves members of an extended family to three-time Hugo Award nominee Ed Brigham, the deceased fantasy novelist now resting on the dais at the head of the room.

I couldn't believe I felt like an interloper at my own father's funeral.

Most of them had the good sense to show up in their Sunday finest, but many of them wore ratty jeans and T-shirts with ancient, unintelligible decals peeling off of them. Those people who had the money, the guts, and the knowhow to craft quasi-medieval costumes were inspired by the finery my father had described in his book series. They were resplendent in their hand-crafted chain mail, their wide-brimmed hats, their leather long-coats and rich red tabards.

To my right, beyond my mother, was a churlish-looking, shaven-headed buffalo in biker leathers (LIVE TO RIDE, RIDE TO LIVE). In front of me, a very attractive woman in a conservative business skirt. To my left, across the central aisle, was a crater-faced youth that looked like Scottish Death in a *Dropkick Murphys* T-shirt, a black kilt with tactical pockets, and black combat boots. I saw several older women that clustered together in their pew, looking for all the world like a genteel country knitting society.

I could see the waxy white bald head of my father's literary agent Max Bayard where he sat in the front row, his impeccable suit the soulless gray color of an office carpet.

I tuned back into the proceedings just to catch the words I dreaded hearing.

"—And although our good friend E. R. Brigham is now in—ahh—a better place," Judith Raske was saying, "—we were regrettably left without closure to his long-running fantasy series, *The Fiddle and the Fire*. For those of you that might be unfamiliar with it, this was a string of novels that followed their protagonist from his childhood as the boy Pack, growing up on his father's plantation, through the massacre of his parents at the hands of the Redbird bandit Tem Lucas, and on into his adult life as the gunslinger Normand Kaliburn.

"The final novel Mr. Brigham began was *The Gunslinger and the Giant*, which went unfinished due to his sudden and unfortunate passing this year. It was to recount the Battle of Ostlyn, the outcome of the war, and the conclusion of Normand's vendetta against Tem Lucas. It saddens all of us to see this long-told tale go uncompleted."

I felt my heart quicken. Frozen mice scurried through my veins. Bayard looked over his shoulder at me, the windows glinting on his eyeglasses.

"I would like to take this opportunity to inform everyone assembled about—ahh—a petition that was started on the online *Fiddle* forums soon after this terrible news reached the internet fan community," said Judith.

I was very aware of this petition; it was the source of my current anxiety. She adjusted her glasses, bumping the microphone with the Batman-style swordbreakers running down her bronze gauntlet. A muffled thud reverberated throughout the room. "Excuse me. It started slowly, but soon reached over twenty thousand signatures."

If I was drinking something, I probably would have spewed it all over the person sitting in front of me.

"This petition began half in jest, according to the man who put it together, Sawyer Winton," the girl said, then paused, squinting into the congregation. "Sawyer, could you come on up, please?"

Someone stood up behind me; I turned to see a slim young man in a sweater and cargo pants. His black hair curled rakishly over one piercing gray eye, and he had the scratchy beginnings of a handsome Jack Sparrow goatee. His healthy, clean-cut look gave me a sense of maturity that would give him conviction and purpose.

My father's agent saw it too, and I expect he also saw the weird feathery quill that Sawyer was carrying, some sort of ridiculous ostrich-feather pen. He was also carrying a little camcorder, a GoPro. He was actually filming the funeral.

"You know what they're gonna want," Bayard had said on the phone. "What do you think about it?"

"I think I'm in big trouble," I had replied, which was the absolute truth.

Winton stood beside the girl. To my alarm, his voice was confident. "Thank you, Judy."

Judith continued. It struck me that she looked rather old to be wearing such an elaborate costume; she had to have been in her thirties or early forties. "But once it caught on, it burned like wildfire. What this petition requested was that continuing authorship of the *Fire and Fiddle* series be passed onto another writer, one particularly familiar with Mr. Brigham, as well as his style and subject matter. That writer would of course be Mr. Sidney Ross Brigham, his only son, a notable author and artist in his own right."

I experienced something not unlike being sprayed in the face with gasoline mid-cigarette. As soon as her scripted speech finished, everyone turned to admire my now-crimson face. I managed to smile, although I suppose it might have more resembled the snarl of a cornered timber wolf.

"Mr. Brigham?" Judith indicated, and as I rose from my seat, I felt like a helium balloon slipping a toddler's grip. I approached the podium through a chaos of applause, feeling a bit lightheaded, shaking their hands when I got there.

Sawyer leaned toward the podium, tugging the mike closer to his face. "We feel that your father would have wanted you to finish his magnum opus, and we as fans of his work hereby request authorship to be passed down to his son, so that the series can end on a proper note. Or, perhaps, even continue if need be."

If need be? I was beginning to feel like a virgin sacrifice on his royal bamboo sedan being carried up the mountain to be offered to the tribal volcano god. Sawyer Winton held up the ostrich feather like a trophy goose and thrust it in my direction. I resisted the crazy urge to stick it in his throat like Nicholson's Joker and accepted it, taking Judith's place behind the mike.

As she turned to leave, her broadsword scabbard bumped one of the full-length candlesticks standing next to the casket and set it metronoming. I slid into place and grabbed the candle, settling it before it could fall over into the fake spray of flowers around Ed's casket and start an open-casket cremation. I could just see the headlines in tomorrow's paper.

"Hello, everybody," I said, way too close to the microphone. My muffled voice erupted from the speakers flanking the dais. "First, I would like to thank you all for coming. From what I understand, my father loved all of his fans from the bottom of his heart and put every drop of blood, sweat, and tears he had into telling his stories for you guys.

"Second, I'm going to admit that I'm no good at public speaking whatsoever, and I have a very limited imagination, so in lieu of a visual aid to help me with my stage fright, I'm going to have to ask all of you to remove your clothing."

No one laughed. My face felt like I'd been bobbing for ice

cubes.

"I've actually been following the progress of the petition since not long after its inception," I said, "—and I am deeply moved by your dedication to my father's life's work."

I turned and glanced into the coffin behind me. My father lay face-up in the box, against his lifelong wishes, his hands pressed around the handle of a quicksilver broadsword, his eyes closed (thank the stars), dressed in an incongruous white robe. I realized with disconnected bemusement—and a vague horror—that he looked like Gandalf Lebowski, ready for entombment in the catacombs of a bowling alley.

I faced the crowd again, biting my lips to keep from laughing at my own imagination.

Ahh, the Inappropriate Laugh.

Most of them were looking at me with sympathy except for my mother, who I was glad had the restraint to keep from hurling her purse and sensible shoes across the room at my face. I took a second to gaze at the floor and compose myself again. "However, I regret that I must inform you: I was not remotely as familiar with his fantasy series as you, his eternal fans.

"Some of you may be aware that I was very young when my parents separated, and although he was awarded visitation custody, I did not see my father very much at all. Indeed, after a couple of years, my mother Caroline had to move up north for business, and I only saw my father Ed on holidays," I said, staring down at the novel on the podium.

"Which I don't suppose inconvenienced him very much, because after the move, the few times I ever spoke to him was when I sought him out myself. I'm not sure that he was aware of my birthday at all, nor did he acknowledge me on Christmas. Or Easter. Or Thanksgiving. Or Yom Kippur. Or even Kwanzaa. He didn't even come to my Army graduation or come see me when I

28

got home from deployment."

The resentment made me brave. My voice seemed to carry farther than it had before, rolling out of me on wheels greased by bitter memories. "In fact, I'm not one-hundred-percent sure that my existence registered in Edward Brigham's mind at all after 1986," I said with a shallow sigh, opening the book. On the title page, my father had written *To Judy Raske — To The Bounds of Behest and Beyond!*

"So, I must admit that I may not be the most suitable replacement. I am deeply, deeply sorry that I must tell you that I have to decline the inheritance of E. R. Brigham's series *The Fiddle and The Fire.*"

The entire gathering seemed to freeze in time, and each of the one hundred or more people I could see from the podium bore the expression of the proverbial "deer in the headlights". I flinched at the sight of the near-instant transformation of the hundred-odd people before me from bereaved mourners to astounded lynch mob.

It's also when I noticed the cameraman and his news correspondent standing next to him, standing in the back of the chapel, nestled in amongst the other attendees, ready and waiting to make sure the revolution would be televised.

The longer I studied their shock waiting for pitchforks and torches, the darker their faces got, until they were all murmuring to each other and glaring at me as if I'd changed the formula for Coca-Cola. This entire vignette, by the way, seemed to stretch on for three hours, but it in fact persisted a mere twenty-five seconds.

"Really?" asked Judith, her eyes wide and bright in the window-filtered afternoon sun.

"That—kinda sucks," said Sawyer, and I watched the joy drain out of his face. The mild satisfaction I was feeling at cracking his boy-band confidence faltered, and the result of my insolence pierced me to my core.

"Look," I said, sighing, "I apologize for the reaction, everybody. I really do. My father and I just really weren't on the best of terms to put it mildly, and I don't know a whole lot about his series. I read some of the first book when I was in the Army, but with work and everything over there, I never really got into it. And after that, well—I pretty much missed the boat, I think."

Bayard got up and joined us on the dais. "We knew this was coming," he whispered to me, cupping the microphone with one bear-paw hand, leaning into my face, filling my nostrils with his coffee breath.

I could see my own honey-colored cornered-wolf expression in the reflection of his 70's bicolor glasses. It struck me that he looked like Hunter S. Thompson if Thompson was thirty pounds heavier and given to picking out ties to wear to Olive Garden.

"And you have no idea just how much this is going to blow up if you agree to step into your father's shoes," he was saying. "This could be the next big thing with this Comic-Con crowd. To that end, I've been working on a little something in my spare time. A little deal. Something to sweeten the pot."

"What would that be?" I asked. "Max, you know I'm an artist first. I haven't written anything worth a crap in ages other than that ghostwriter project, for the climber guy that got stuck in the Colorado mountains a couple years ago. I got a couple graphic novels and advertising jobs on the table."

"HBO wanted to talk about doing a *Fiddle* TV series before your father passed. Nerf wants to license foam swords and dart revolvers. I'm even getting word of a video game. Of course, you would only see a fraction of it—but this all would make your residuals from *Bear With Me* look like hobo change."

I felt a hand on my shoulder. It was Sawyer, and his eyes were like scalpel blades. "I've read some of your stuff, man. You're not as bad as you think you are."

I studied Bayard's rubbery face and considered his intel, then stared down at the ostrich feather until the world around me faded to gray.

Once I'd had enough of pretending to think about it, I looked over to Sawyer and Judy, staring straight into Sawyer's camcorder, and said loud enough for the microphone to catch, "You know, they say you can do anything if you put your mind to it. Let me sleep on it, okay? Let me catch up on the series, and I'll see where we can go from there."

They both grinned. A few people in the funeral party applauded softly; I scanned the people before me and saw quite a few more beaming faces than just a few minutes prior. Even the teenagers that looked like they woke up in a cave and came straight to the funeral were glowing.

Sawyer leaned into the mike and said, "We won the battle, guys. Here's hoping we win the war!"

I smiled back at them. Their enthusiasm was infectious; I felt a little excited to be part of this. And then the enormity of the task before me came rushing back in a blast wave of fear.

Ravens and Writing Desks

AFTER THE VIEWING, I stood alone at the side of my father's coffin, looking down at his aged body with a growing sense of sadness that threatened to eat at my edges. Conflicting emotions warred with each other.

Regret, at never bothering to get to know him better, at never closing that gap he created himself. Anger, at myself, for just writing him off as a reclusive hack. Anger at him for disappearing from my life until now. Satisfaction at having an opportunity for achieving something wonderful thrust onto me.

A cool, hollow void where a great weeping sorrow should have been at losing my father.

"I don't think for a moment that talent is genetic," I told the man in the coffin. "I'm no writer! At least not the kind of writer that twenty thousand people sign a petition over. I am definitely not my father's son. What the hell am I going to do?"

My father said nothing, of course. The broadsword he clutched in his spotted hands gleamed bright, blinding bright, in the dusty light of the octagon window in the back wall where the slopes of the roof met. I turned around to what I thought was an empty viewing room and Bayard was standing there with his hands in the pockets of his suit jacket.

He stepped toward me and hugged me out of sympathy. I surprised myself by being grateful for it. He took off his rose-colored Thompson glasses and hung them by one stem from the collar of his shirt, and regarded me with ancient eyes. The ponderous bags under his watery hound-dog eyes made him look thirty years older.

"When I was a kid," Bayard said, with a vague, wistful smile, "I came walking out of the town library and saw something big and black in the grass next to the sidewalk. I went to go see what it was and it turned out to be a raven, lying there on his back, looking up at me and cawing. I guess it got hit by a passing car and knocked onto the median.

"Well, that big dumb bird let me pick him up and carry him home. He had a busted wing and a broken leg. My dad, he was a doctor, he had a little clinic in Ohio, he helped me put splints on that raven."

I smirked in spite of myself. "Does this story have a point?"

Bayard took a box of Camels out of his pocket and started packing them against the palm of his hand. "Walk outside with me."

We hung out in the funeral home carport. Golden rays of sunlight filtered through the filthy washrag clouds and lit up the green leaves of the dogwoods flanking the driveway. The listless hiss and roar of oblivious traffic passing on the street down the hill was soothing in its detachment.

The literary agent lit a cigarette, took a deep draw, and blew the smoke across the carport in a thin stream. "A couple months later, that fat-assed raven was one hundred percent back to health. I didn't want to, but my dad made me take him outside and let him go.

"No matter what I did, he absolutely would not leave. I shook the shit out of that dumb bird trying to get him off my arm. He knew he had a good thing and he didn't want to leave. I took him out every day that week trying to let him go and he refused to do it."

33

I gave him a Clint Eastwood squint from the corner of my eye and folded my arms. "Are you about to tell me that that bird never forgot how to fly and if I just believe in myself and quit resting on my laurels expecting the world to hand me a living, I can fly too?"

"A few days later he got ahold of my brother and tore him up, so my dad had to take him out and shoot him," Bayard said, flicking his ashes onto the carport floor. "I'm telling you that if you don't start flying, I'm going to shoot you."

I laughed and he took a deadpan drag off the unfiltered Camel.

"Those things will kill you," I said.

"World War II didn't kill my dad, and neither did Camels, and if my wife couldn't do it, this Camel ain't gonna do it either."

We stood there a minute, listening to the traffic. "I always wondered how Carl got that scar on his neck."

"Well, now you know. So what are you gonna do, Ross?"

At that point, it hit me that over the course of my life, I'd probably seen more of this man than I had my own father. The idea stunned me. I managed to say, "Not sure. I guess write the damn book."

"Attaboy. What made you change your mind?"

"Those people's faces."

"Very commendable. You sure it wasn't the money?"

"No. Maybe that Winton guy's right. Maybe I'm not so bad. Maybe I can do it. I don't owe them anything, but . . . what kind of guy would I be if I didn't even try?"

"It wasn't the fame? Not even a little bit?"

"No. I just don't—well, I guess I don't really want to let them down after all."

"You're a damned liar."

"Okay, okay," I said, smirking at him. "Maybe the fame. Just a little bit."

"Attaboy."

*   *   *

My mom, Bayard, and I were the last ones to leave—or at least I thought we were. On the way out, I passed the doorway into a little kitchenette and spotted Sawyer Winton sitting at the table inside, drinking a cup of coffee, his camera off and lying on the table.

As soon as he saw me, he spoke up, "Hey, Mr. Brigham!" and started to get out of his chair.

I told my companions I would be out in a minute and ducked into the little break room. "Don't get up, Sawyer," I said, settling into a chair myself. "And you can call me Ross."

"Okay . . . Ross," said Sawyer, sitting back down. But when he saw the expression on my face, he tensed up again. We sat there for a long moment like this, staring at each other. He pretended to fiddle with the camera, turning it on; he put it back down at an angle that captured both of us. No doubt some sort of documentation, experience footage, for YouTube.

At long last, Sawyer blurted, instead of whatever he had meant to discuss with me, " . . . What? What is it?"

"I'm a wee bit pissed," I said. "What possessed you two to bring up the petition in the middle of my father's viewing? Call me up in front of my dead dad and put me on the spot in front of my mother and God and everybody? That reporter? Did you both lose your minds? What the hell, dude."

"Yeah," he said, looking down at the table as he picked his fingernails. "I guess that wasn't the most tactful thing to do, yeah, maybe. I guess I just thought something like that deserved some kind of—I don't know, ceremonial feel, you know? A couple of the others thought it was kinda bad form, too. I'm sorry, Mr. Brigham."

"Well . . . I know you meant well."

I let the moment linger for emphasis, then added, "So what did you want to talk about?"

"I just wanted to thank you for considering the book, and to let you know that I'm always available if you have any questions about the lore and canon of the series. I've been a lifelong fan ever since I read the first book when I was in third grade. I'm gonna be in town a couple days visiting with a few of the other fans while I'm here."

"Third grade, huh?" I said, taking out my cellphone. "What's your cellphone number?"

He gave it to me; as I entered it into my contacts list, Sawyer said, "My teacher, Mrs. Kirby, was reading it; she gave it to me when she was done with it. I finished it in like, a week or two, and she was so—impressed and stuff . . . that she went out and bought me my own copy of the second one as soon as it came out, later that year."

"That's cool."

"Look, uhh . . . Ross," said Sawyer, taking something out of his jacket. It was an elderly, dog-eared copy of my father's second book, *The Cape and The Castle*. The pages were yellowed, the art on the paperback's cover was faded by time and sun, gone green-blue. The picture of my father on the back depicted a much younger man, his hair and beard lush and dark.

"I . . . I know . . . you didn't really have a good relationship with your dad. And I know you couldn't give two damns about his novels. My dad died in a car accident and left me and my mother when I was seven, so I can understand, maybe. You just sit in your room and you think and think and think and you just wanna know—you just wanna know *why*, right?"

I studied my hands as they rested on the table in front of me, and glanced over at the accusatory eye of the GoPro camera.

"This series is what kept me company, man. You said you didn't see much of your dad. Well, I never saw my dad ever again," Sawyer said. "I would lie up at night reading your dad's books until I got sleepy. Then for Christmas one year, my mom bought me the audiobook for the third book in the series. You know, the one Sam Elliott did in '95.

"At the time, I didn't know who he was, so I pretended it was E. R. Brigham reading to me. Like . . . a bedtime story, I guess. It probably sounds weird, but in a way, I liked to think of him as a— as a sort of dad. Those times. Since I didn't have one."

When I looked up, Sawyer was gazing intently into my face. "That's why I want this so bad. He did something very special for me, even if he didn't know it. And I want to give back, y'know? I want to see his dream get finished. And after reading the stuff you've done—the autobiography about the dude in the mountains *Bear With Me*, the comic book you did a few years ago . . . I even caught the play in Chattanooga you cowrote with Marshall Davies right before you went into the Army."

"Really?" I asked. I didn't bother asking how he knew I'd been in the Army. Most readers knew at least the largest events of my life. "What were you doing in Chattanooga?"

"I was on my way home from college and my layover got cancelled. The snow."

"Oh, right. That was a fun night."

"Mm-hmm," nodded Sawyer. "I actually went hoping your dad would be there, but no such luck."

"Yeah, he didn't get around to my things. He didn't go to my graduation from Basic Training, either. Nobody did."

"That sucks. I'm sorry, dude."

"No big thing. What's your email address?" He gave it to me and I entered it into my phone with his number. "This way if you need to send me large passages of text—or vice versa—you can," I said, standing up. "Hey, I gotta go. Gotta catch up with my mom. Talk to you later."

"Yeah," Sawyer said. He picked up the camera, but didn't turn it off.

When I got outside, everybody was already in the car, my mother driving, the Pontiac idling. They were listening to the latest pop music fad song on the radio, at such a low volume I didn't realize there was anything playing until I walked up and leaned on the window. The car was spotless but still smelled of the agent's cigarettes.

Bayard glanced at me over his shoulder. "Hey kid, you gonna be in town for a while?"

"Yep. I want to look through my dad's working notes and take a look at some of his old haunts. See if anything inspires me."

"That sounds like a good idea. I'll be heading back to California in the next day or two myself."

The clouds were darkening again, threatening the green birches and pines of Blackfield with warm, dirty rain as they danced their swaying tango, flickering paler shades of money green in the cooling September breeze.

"Thank you for doing the right thing," she said, tucking a lock of her graying, once-auburn hair behind her ear. "Agreeing to at least attempt the book really made all the difference. I was back there and heard the sweetest things they were saying to each other about you. They're all excited, son."

"Kid, if it makes a difference, I can send out one of my other guys to help you. I'm sure one of them will be more than happy to collaborate on the final *Fiddle* book," said Bayard.

I was beginning to feel introspective and morose. If this was a movie, I'm sure the poignant, haunting, minimalist piano score would have started playing around the time I had walked up to the car.

"No," I said, "I think this is something I have to do on my own. My dad did it alone."

All alone, I thought, gazing out at the scenery, the aging country storefronts, the gas stations, the mom-and-pop restaurants, the dead and dying commercial vestiges of yesteryear—drugstores, craft knick-knack shops, local-owned department stores—and seeing none of it.

*   *   *

I sat in my motel room, watching the darkness gather between the curtains, until the only light I could see by was the ferocious glow of my laptop screen. I felt as if I were floating in a black void without end or beginning, my last remaining anchor the blinding empty-white rectangle in front of me, like some window in the wall of reality that opened onto the featureless wasteland of my brain. I wanted to reach through, pull the words out by the neck, and shake them until a story came out.

I turned on the lamp. On the table next to the laptop was one of three boxes of my father's notes on the *Fiddle* series.

I had been looking through them in the hour since I'd gotten back from the funeral, but nothing was registering. All I could think of was the sight of my father in the coffin and how *old* he'd looked. That was the point in which it had struck me just how long it had been since I'd seen him last.

I'd never even gotten the chance to say goodbye, and what dug even deeper than that was the epiphany that until now, I had *always* had the opportunity, I hadn't cared about taking it.

"Why didn't you call?" I asked the box.

I got up and went out, putting on my shoes as I fled the question.

* * *

A few minutes' walk from the motel was a burger joint named Jackson's, staffed by local college kids. Blackfield is a school town, so just about everywhere you went your transactions were handled by children, the vast majority of them as slender and attractive as the cast of your average cable TV teen drama. It was like living in Neverland.

When I walked in (pulling open a door that had a baseball bat for a handle), it felt as if I'd walked into some sort of cave overgrown with a strange green fungus.

Once my eyes acclimated to the dim interior of the dive, I realized that the walls and ceiling were wallpapered with dollar bills. They were taped, glued, and stapled to every structural surface in eyesight, and signed with everything from Sharpies to ink pens.

I took a booth in the very back of the L-shaped restaurant, by the restroom, out of sight of both the front door and the bar, where a television was touting a football game at top volume. After a few minutes of ogling the dollars on the walls and wondering what the insurance policy on the place could possibly be, a waitress approached me and took my order.

As soon as she left, I opened my laptop on the table and stared at the blank word processor. The icon in the corner told me that there was wireless internet coming from somewhere, and lo

40

and behold, it was unlocked. According to the name—"Cap'n Pacino's"—it belonged to the coffee shop two doors down. I logged on and busied myself reading the news.

The media's half-assed coverage of the funeral was on a few lesser-known aggregators and social news sites. Fark, with a "Sad" tag and a comments section full of thugs and geeks flinging epithets and threats at each other. Reddit's literature communities.

They were replete with apoplectic debates over the quality of *The Fire and the Fiddle* and comparisons with Tolkien, Saberhagen, King's *Dark Tower* series, G. R. R. Martin; outrage at *my* outrage, outrage at my initial refusal to pick up my father's mantle and please the masses; threats and promises to murder me outright both if I *did* and if I *didn't* continue the series.

I ordered a hamburger, but I don't remember eating it.

As the boy trickled his way down the hillside, picking his way among the rocks, he saw a woman hanging laundry on a line. "Blessed be!" she wailed when she saw him. "Where have you been? I've been worried sick! I thought you'd fallen somewhere or got ate up by a wild dog."

"I was just nappin. I fell asleep waiting for the train to come in and I missed it," said the boy. He was wiping his eyes; he had obviously been crying. "Pah's not gonna be riled at me, is he?"

"No, I spose not. I'll talk to him," she said, flicking a towel at him. "Get on in the house and get ready for dinner."

"Yes'm."

"Save my heart, I swear, I thought for sure you were dead, son. Don't scare me like that again!"

—The Fiddle and the Fire, vol 1 "The Brine and the Bygone"

Prologue

I WENT BACK TO my room and put the laptop back on the table, then started filling the bathtub. By this time it was a little after 9, prime time for a good hot soak. I dug through the bag I'd come back with and mixed a Black Russian. Call me all the names you like, but I'm a fool for coffee, and beer is the most disgusting thing I've ever put in my mouth. Well—maybe the second most. I've had to eat some pretty nasty things.

I sat on the couch staring at the box of crap on the table, sipping my drink, listening to the bathtub fill with hot water. "Why did you have to die and leave this shit for me?"

Splatter, splatter, sip, sip, feel sorry for yourself, rationalize, splatter, splatter, angst, angst, sip, sip.

I put the drink down and picked up a notebook. Flipping through it, I found page after page of intricate pictures and unintelligible text.

Complex sketches filled entire pages; there were drawings of grim-faced men and women—young and old, hideous and beautiful—in dark armor of industrial make and artisan design, with rippling chain-mail shrouds and dozens of insectoid, overlapping segmented plates. Exploded diagrams of firearms of all shapes and sizes, with gruesome and inventive ammunitions, and decorative etchings of mythical beasts.

There were also bizarre, baroque conveyances that reminded me simultaneously of futuristic hovercrafts from old Johnny Quest cartoons and illustrations of Captain Nemo's Nautilus from *20,000*

44

Leagues Under the Sea. Likewise, there were pages that were nothing but articles written about hundreds of different subjects, filling the paper from margin to margin, with footnotes scribbled against the edges.

There were words that made no sense, exotic names and terms in some curling, sinuous handwriting of a language I was wholly unfamiliar with. It was a vast compendium of what amounted to multimedia glossolalia.

There was a small planner-style journal; it looked like it had seen twenty miles of rough road. I picked it up and began to leaf through it, turning each onion-skin page as if I were a Vatican historian examining the Dead Sea Scrolls. After a few minutes of reading, I realized I was looking at some sort of creation myth.

"When time was young, the universe was not so different.

"Stars drifted, without origin or destination, in a never-ending void while the laws of nature fell into place like stones settling on the bed of a stream. This was the period of first-birth.

"Slumbering in the womb of the void was the wolf-god Oramoz—the true name of Measure and Order itself—and She was an ancient and powerful creature. She was luminescence and righteousness and distance incarnate, Her slender body stretching across the Universe, held together by a million points of light.

"Her husband the dragon-god Angr'manu--the true name of Time, Chaos itself—was a wrathful being in an eternal state of flux, sleek and obscure, whose driving essence was to destroy and sunder and scatter. He was made of darkness and hours, and was everywhere at once, infinite and absolute, without measure.

"Oramoz was deeply familiar with the workings of the universe; Her soul was intertwined with the basic structure of nature as it matured and developed. She was there to witness the creation of the rules, and She knew how to manipulate them. The Dragon Angr'manu—Her husband since birth—knew nothing of this important structure around Him; He was a belligerent glutton answerable to no one. Thus the wolf-god Oramoz felt that it was Her inherent duty to maintain order in the cosmos.

"Every morning, the dragon-god Angr'manu devoured Himself tail-first, second by minute swallowed whole, turning the Present into the Past, Now into Then, and while Oramoz slept in the evening, She dreamt of the coming Future, thus ensuring the survival of Her husband.

"To allow Time to devour itself entirely would be folly. To allow Angr'manu to swallow himself meant the end of time.

"The Wolf gazed into the darkness in which She drifted, and became restless. Her dreams had gone awry, and She had seen herself dozing in deep valleys of lush green forests under the rays of a warm golden sun, supping Her fill of oceans sparkling blue.

"The beauty of the place She saw in Her dreams was so endearing next to the cold and unforgiving abyss, She decided to form it out of the very fabric of the Universe.

"And so, taking a part of Herself and a part of Her husband, Oramoz crafted the elements—Fire, Water, Earth, and Wind— from darkness and light, and used them to build Her paradise while Angr'manu slumbered. It took a long time, long even for gods.

"She made Her mistakes in the process, churning out worlds of barren rock and freezing winds, poisonous air and boiling water. These Oramoz set aside as raw material.

"Finally, Oramoz succeeded in devising a habitable world.

"She shaped it into a perfect orb and named it Behest. With Her claws the Wolf dug the valleys out of the land, and the piles of earth She put aside became majestic peaks. A nearby point of light kept it warm as She worked, Her sweat seeping into the stone underfoot, glowing red and flowing hot.

"Almost done, the Wolf looked over what She had made and appreciated it; then, inspired, She formed the creatures of the world out of the four elements in the forge of Her love, for it was as strong as the hardest metal, as bright as the hottest star.

"Man sprang from Her heart and populated Behest in multitudes, praising their creator in scripture and song. The years were like days to the immortal people of Behest, untouched by the oblivious Time.

"When Oramoz finished, She rested.

"By and by the Dragon awoke, noticed what the Wolf had made, and came to see. He saw the hope and delight in ageless mankind, and wept in His anger at what She had done behind His back. While the Wolf slept sparkling in the night sky, Angr'manu forgot to consume Himself and instead began to devour the world.

"Men withered and died; mountains crumbled, oceans evaporated, and Angr'manu grew and grew as Oramoz unwittingly dreamt Him anew. Eons passed while the Wolf slept. Civilization developed; nations rose and fell. Oceans swelled and sank. The world slipped into the eager jaws of entropy.

"This was the end of the first age.

"Angr'manu had grown hoary and long by the time Oramoz awoke, and fat on the meal He had made of the corroded iron-and-glass world of Behest.

"The Wolf, incensed by Her husband's mischief, flew into a rage and cut Him in twain in a battle that shook every universe. The world of Behest, lodged in the gullet of the Time Dragon, split as well—into two separate worlds divided by a gulf of time and space: Zam and Destin. It was a great, ferocious duel that raged across the sky for half an age, and in their fury the bloodshed of the Dragon and of the Wolf mixed.

47

"After the great sundering, Oramoz lay on the the shore, covered in blood, and wept over what she'd done. Her tears trickled down and filled that great Void, and became the Sea of Dreams, Vur Ukasha, the ocean from where all stories flow.

"During the battle, a nomad by the name of Ahan Lith, who was the daughter of the daughter of the son of the first woman, Chawah, happened upon a drop of this mixed, tainted blood as it hurtled from the black sky one evening in the emerald wilds. This holy droplet fell into the lake from which Ahan was filling her water-skin; drinking of it, she was filled with the power of Oramoz and Angr'manu alike.

"Sitting in the shade of a palm tree, Ahan achieved perfect understanding. Thus the first true enlightened came into being, blessed with the knowledge of the secret workings of the universe.

"Ahan Lith possessed a righteous soul and bore herself with grace and charity. She was canonized by the clergymen of the religion of Oramoz and became a holywoman, rising into a status of the highest nobility. She married, and begat seven children, almost all of whom continued in their own lives and are detailed in dozens of hidden gospels long lost to time.

"Their descendants are known as the Etudaen.

"In time, a certain fungus began to grow by that vaunted lake, drawing life from the waters and swelling with the knowledge and power of the Wolf and of the Dragon. It still grows there, serving as a doorway into true understanding of the self, and bestows the possessor with the ability to alter both space and time. It is called the Acolouthis, and it is the sacred secret of the longevity and prowess of the warriors of Destin, the Gunslingers and the Grievers."

I tossed it aside and picked up another notebook to be presented with the same sort of fish-eyed madness. Reams and reams of dead tree-flesh littered with the artifacts of a lost world that never existed. The sheer Lovecraftian absurdity of it all made me laugh.

As I took up my glass of vodka again, I had a race of adrenaline that singed my heart with a tongue of flame and I kicked the box off the table, scattering its contents all over the boring green carpet.

I got up and shut off the bathwater, and laid in the tub for a while until I had finished the Russian, savoring the feel of my skin tightening from the heat and the cold air on my face.

When I was done, I dried off, poured another Russian over the sink, and came back to a very cold motel room. Instead of turning up the heat to combat the early autumn chill, I put on a pair of pajama bottoms and a hoodie pullover with the Harper's Ferry flintlocks embroidered on the back of it. Thus armored, I set to the task of picking up the journals and notebooks and putting them back into the box.

Under the final notebook was a bronzy little house key, its teeth worn from use.

* * *

My father's house stood back from the road, a dark-eyed sentinel almost invisible in the woods. As I pulled up in the driveway, the headlights of my ancient Mercury Topaz wheeled across the hulking shadow and transformed it into a white two-story plantation house. E. R. Brigham's green '86 Chevy Nova was still sitting where we'd left it this afternoon when Bayard and I had come to fetch my father's *Fiddle* material.

The windows of the car were filmy with dust. I walked up the drive and pointed my cellphone into the backseat. To my relief, no one was sitting there.

My cellphone's glow washed over the unseeing eyes of the house. My father had inherited it from his father, who had inherited it from his father. Corinthian columns supported the roof like a Greek temple, screening the face of the building from the outside world like a mask. Their long, tall shadows capered west and tumbled off the end of the porch as I stepped up onto it and pulled the key from my pocket.

My face fell when I discovered that it didn't fit in the deadbolt or the doorknob. I used the key on my keyring to open it (given to me by my mother this morning), and let myself in. To my chagrin, the power bill had been due when my father passed, and so it went unpaid and now the electricity was off.

I was standing in the foyer, a cavernous front room where a flight of stairs curled along one wall to a balcony overhead.

I swept the cellphone over the accumulations of an old man's lifetime as I forayed deeper into the house, walking past an antique grand piano into the living room. The faint smell of habitation came to me, the camphor of cough drops and the dank, sweet yeast of age. There, a sofa with an avocado-green linen slipcover tempted me with its soft embrace.

I refused and kept moving, past my grandfather's roll-top desk and the Magnavox boob-tube with foiled rabbit ears. I went into the kitchen, passing between bookshelves crammed with names.

Simmons, Lumley, Barker, Koontz and King epics and haunters. Ragged decades of National Geographic, appliance manuals. Ludlum, Grisham, and Clancy thrillers. Obscure horror and fantasy from the 70s and 80s. My light passed over the spines of the books and a wistful frisson marched up my spine at the sight of so many recognizable pseudonyms.

The kitchen was spotless in relation to the rest of the house; the air was pungent with an acrid citrus aroma. My mother must have cleaned it after I'd left. Dry dishes were piled in the drain, silverware gleaming in my searchlight.

The fridge was empty, the door ajar.

There was an open padlock on the cellar door, installed years ago to keep me from taking a header down the stairs (as a child, of course). The key didn't work on it, so I opened the door and made my way down the creaky steps into the damp darkness of the basement.

The floor was painted with some gray sealant that kept the cellar dry and clean, so there wasn't much of an odor. I turned this way and that, looking for locks that might perhaps fit the key now resting in my pocket. A chest freezer stood open to my immediate left, devoid of contents, dry and warm.

I felt a small twinge of guilt at not participating in the clean up, which I would have done, had I gotten to Blackfield soon enough. I continued investigating the cellar, wondering who my mother had gotten to help.

In a back wall, beyond a minefield of heirlooms, furniture, and dubious appliances, was a padlocked door. I picked my way through the silent forest of chair legs, cheap paintings, space heaters older than the kids working at Jackson's, and shuffled between a decrepit bookshelf and a very dirty armoire until I stumbled into a small space littered with dead pillbugs and cottony cobwebs.

The key did not work on the padlock. I sighed in disappointment. What was I even doing? What made me come looking for a lock, anyway? What was I looking for?

Was it some Great Secret, some hidden inspiration, some foul and lurking deed that my father had hidden away from the world for decades until I came along and dragged it screaming and kicking into the light of day? My deformed twin brother, locked in some dank oubliette behind a bag of Christmas decorations and my father's teetering collection of funk vinyl and issues of Hustler 1987-1994?

I sneezed, bracing myself against the door, and noticed that the padlock wasn't locked, just inserted into the hasp and rusted solid. I twisted it, jerking it this way and that, until it broke in a shower of corroded brown steel. An eldritch breath of cold, wet air seeped through the crack like fog creeping over the ground in some old-timey vampire movie.

I pulled the door open and shined the cellphone inside.

A crawlspace full of white mildew, dirt, and rotten material. I could see the underside of the front porch and the retaining wall that ran the exterior length of the platform overhead. I forced the door shut and turned around, and screamed like I'd been goosed.

I was not prepared for the shock of turning around and finding myself standing face to face with Hugo Award nominee Ed Brigham.

Old Goats and Indian Chiefs

I JERKED BACKWARDS, SWEARING and falling against the door, sliding onto the concrete floor in surprise. I pointed my cellphone at the silhouette in front of me, and discovered I'd scared myself with a cardboard cutout. It was an old promotional stand-up from my father's last big book tour, covered in a fine layer of dust and paled from sun.

The man in the picture was smiling wanly, holding up a thick hardback copy of the fourth novel; his hair wasn't entirely gray yet, and he was a good thirty pounds lighter. He still looked like a particularly weatherbeaten Kevin Flynn.

"Ya dirty son of a bitch," I said, getting to my feet.

I slid between the bookshelf and armoire, and hiked back to the stairway, where I brushed the dust off my clothes and thumped back up the stairs like a tired sasquatch. I came back out into the kitchen and looked around, half-expecting to get jumped in the dark.

Nobody was waiting for me, so I opened the back door, trying the key on the deadbolt and doorknob on the way out to the back yard.

Outside, a chill wind told me that winter was coming, and it brought with it the soft, innocent trill of crickets and the susurrant cackle of a deep brook down the hill to my left. There, a waterwheel mill three times older than myself lurked at the limits of my light, a squat building made of river shale and redbrick.

I could see from here that there was no door in the doorway to be locked. I played the cellphone glow across the Wilderness, and saw a woodshed standing at the treeline to my right.

There was a spotty old padlock on it, and the key didn't work, so I tried my keyring. It turned out to be the last one on the ring; when I got the door open I pointed the light inside and saw a work table with a modest array of tools lying on it and a C-clamp gripping the corner of a sliding closet door panel. Dried wood glue oozed out of a crack where the clamp was pinching it.

To my left, a canvas tarp covered some large and lumpy object the size of a sofa.

I pulled off the fabric and uncovered a 2002 Indian Chief Roadmaster with an aqua top and cream belly, leather seats and saddlebags.

I swore under my breath and sat on the machine, my shoes crunching on the oil-spotted refrigerator carton underneath it. It was a work of art. I remembered something my mother had told me about my dad buying a bike several years ago, but I had no idea it was this fantastic. He had kept it in mint condition; probably came out here every day to tinker on it and clean it.

I was ambushed by a longing for the old man. Just to see him again. To talk to him again. What was I thinking?

"You only have one dad," I said, holding the handlebars. "Sorry I didn't come see you, you old goat."

I looked down at the gas gauge, feeling like the lowest of the low. "Why didn't you come see me?" I asked the motorcycle, buttoning the top button on my thermal shirt. "Why didn't you call? Did you not want me around? What gives?"

The sound of a twig snapping outside made my heart jump.

I froze, my ears straining to catch the furtive movement of a stranger. My eyes leapt from tool to tool until I looked down to my right and saw a woodaxe leaning against a stack of firewood that lined the wall. Too heavy.

Lying next to it was a hatchet; I grabbed it and got up off the motorcycle, creeping toward the door.

I got there just in time to look up at the house and see the back door swing shut. I resisted the urge to sprint across the yard and still made it to the back door in record time. I threw it open and stepped inside, but I couldn't bring myself to run through the kitchen and up to the second floor.

"Hello?" I called, yelling into the suffocating silence.

No answer. "Is anybody here?"

Same as before. I tightened my grip on the hatchet, but made a detour to the kitchen sink, where I pulled a carving knife out of the dish drain and stuck it in one of the pockets of my cargo pants with the handle sticking out. My heart was pounding and all I could hear was my anxious breathing and the soft ripping sound of my shoes on the linoleum floor.

I went into the living room, leaping through the doorway like a TV show cop and turning back and forth as I landed. The shadows reeled in dizzying swoops as I aimed the cellphone's light around.

No one lay in wait for me. I continued on to the foyer.

The piano was unoccupied. As I moved past it, I very much knew that as I did so, it was going to reverberate with a deep, dissonant *THUNNNNNG!*, but luckily, I was proven wrong. Even so, I stared at it until I was halfway up the staircase curving along the wall to the landing overhead.

I stepped onto the second floor and brandished the hatchet at the corridor leading to my left and right.

In front of me was a huge framed print of the cover art of the first book in *The Fiddle and the Fire* series, a picture of a cowboy hat dangling from the top of a weathered fence post somewhere on a grassy prairie. A young boy was visible in the background, a thin, ragged-looking spectre, looking up at the hat.

"Hell*oooooo!*" I yelled into the reaches of the house.

I looked over my shoulder at the glass chandelier hanging over the foyer, now eye-level with me, and the massive windows in the face of the house that looked out on the magnolia trees in the front yard, feathered goliaths hissing in the night breeze.

The wind outside was blowing so hard I could hear the faint chuckling of the teardrop crystals in the chandelier. "Helloooo, who's in here?" I shouted. "Whoever you are, you better come out, cause I got an axe, and if I find you, I'm gonna *fuck you up!*"

The corridor yawned before me, a tunnel of dingy, florid wallpaper and old hardwood, studded with gilded paintings and wall sconces draped with the same teardrops as the chandelier. My eyes began to burn and I remembered to blink.

A bathroom lay to my right; I checked that first, kicking the door open and jabbing the cellphone inside. I stepped in and felt a chill at the sight of myself standing there, my face underlit by the soft blue luminescence of the cellphone. The shower curtain was closed, but it was still rustling in the wind from the door flying open.

Steeling myself, I reached out and snatched it open.

There was nothing inside. I exhaled in relief, and left the shower curtain pulled out of the way to eliminate the blind spot.

Back outside, there was a meaty *bump* down the hallway to my right, like someone dropping an orange.

My head snapped in that direction and my heart roared in my chest. I debated fleeing the house, but the hatchet in my hand drowned out the instinct of self-preservation. *Someone is in my dad's house,* I thought, my fingers writhing on the axe's handle as I

57

prepared myself to swing it.

A territorial little voice in the back of my mind said that this wouldn't do, no, it wouldn't do at all. I kept making my way into the depths of the house and came to the upstairs guest room. I shoved the door open with the end of the hatchet and stepped in with the axe raised high, like some kind of Viking policeman, my upper body on a swivel.

I looked in the closet, but there was nothing inside but a cluster of hangers hanging on the pole. When I opened the door, they clattered together with a musical jingle. On my hands and knees, I lifted the bedskirt and peered under the box springs.

No one lay underneath the bed.

That's good. I don't know what I would have done if there was. Probably shit my pants.

Nothing left but my dad's bedroom at the end of the hall. The door was open when I got there, just a crack, just enough for me to see a sliver of darkness beyond. I eased it open and my all-revealing light pushed inside.

Ed's bedroom was just as cluttered as I expected it to be. It wasn't filthy, but it could use a definite once-over. As I stood there in the dark, surveying the room, I remembered that this was where they found him.

He had been lying on the bed, with blue lips. Maxwell Bayard had been the one to find him, he had come to talk to my dad about the plans HBO was cooking up for the book series and discovered the body here in this very room.

God, I had been such an inconsiderate, selfish son of a bitch, I thought, looking down at the bed. It had been neatly made—probably by my poor mother.

I noticed that the topmost blanket was the brown goat-hair throw I'd bought in Afghanistan and sent to my dad for Christmas.

I'd wondered if he'd even appreciated it. I wondered if it had been on the bed already, or if my mom had put it on when she made it.

Next to a nasty ashtray full of mashed butts, there were a few books on the nightstand, some of them reference books about firearms or medieval warfare tactics, some of them novels. The windows were covered with blackout curtains that night-shifters put up to help them sleep during the day. A pewter candle-stand was also there, that seemed to be a statue of a voluptuous nude holding up a squat green candle.

There was a noticeable lack of fantasy collectibles in here. I figured Ed would've been the type to fill his house with plates and statuettes and figurines depicting various figures from movies and books. Ceramic wizards and dragons with pewter claws and staves, scrying the future through glass marbles meant to be crystal balls. Leggy painted faeries with child-like faces.

None of that was in here; to be honest, it could've been the nest of any average middle-aged man, if not for the lack of sports paraphernalia. If anything, it looked like he'd been a research nut.

His laptop sat on a white TV tray by the bed, a two-legged affair that stood on the floor or collapsed to sit across one's lap. It was several years old, but immaculately kept. I got down and looked under the bed. There was nothing there except for a few old electronics boxes. I tapped them with the axe; they were empty.

I stood up, confused. I knew I'd heard something in here earlier. *Something* had come into the house, through the back door. I just knew it.

I turned to leave and saw the closet door on the other side of a folded-up card table and a vacuum cleaner. I picked up the vacuum and moved it, slid the table out of the way, and opened the closet door.

Jackets, sweaters, and other winter clothes hung there, reeking of years and boric acid. Tweed, thermals, leather, the thick cotton of sweatshirts, an aging quilt I remembered seeing on my parents' bed when I was a kid. I shuffled through them, though at this point I wasn't sure what I was looking for anymore.

Was I looking for an intruder, or something else? Was I looking for something that could connect me to my father? I shoved a heavy coat aside and caught a glimpse of a goatish horn, and snarling teeth in a pink face.

A hand took hold of my wrist, a claw wrapped in leather, with black, hook-like talons.

Terrifying yellow eyes blazed at me.

Normand stumbled across the vast Emerald Desert, his mouth a puckered, dry pit full of sticky teeth and a leather tongue. The flaky, glittering dust-sand made an epic chore of breathing. It got into his eyes a dozen times and cut his whites, irritated him beyond belief. After an hour of trying to watch where he was going, he couldn't take it anymore. He closed his eyes, pulled his hat down over them, and walked blind.

They had double-crossed him. The sons of bitches. They'd ran with the whole take and left him for the Kingsmen. He still couldn't believe he'd escaped with nary a scratch. It had been a nasty chase.

He stepped on a rock the size of his head and stumbled, pitching headfirst down a steep slope of shifting green sand. When he finally rolled to a stop at the bottom, Normand rested for a moment, upside-down and exhausted, his feet pointed up the hill. The first thing he did was check his droplegs to see if his father's gun was still there.

—The Fiddle and the Fire, vol 3 "The Rope and the Riddle"

Crazy Pills

HALFWAY DOWN THE STAIRS, I slipped and went head over heels, tumbling the last seven steps and sprawling in a stunned heap on the wood floor. I knew I'd be a wreck in the morning, but at the moment, my adrenaline made me invincible.

I shoved the front door open and sprinted into the front yard. When I got to the Topaz I ran around to the driver's side and slid in the wet grass, coming down hard on my left shoulder.

I'm still amazed that I never fell on the knife.

I wrenched the door open and crammed myself into the car, cranked it, threw it into Reverse, and did a J-turn in the driveway, spinning out in the mud and flinging gravel all over the Nova and into the trees. I came out of the driveway and into the highway going sideways, and almost lost control of the car.

I pulled out my cellphone, trying to keep from doing a header into a culvert. I could hear the mud clattering against the car's undercarriage. I was thumbing through my contacts before I realized I had no idea who to call. Who would believe me? Who would care? Who could do anything about it?

I was going seventy-eight miles an hour. I took my foot off the accelerator as my heart-rate sank toward normal. What the hell was in that closet? *What the hell grabbed me?*

I shook my shirt sleeve down and turned on the dome light with a *click* to look at my wrist.

There was nothing on it; no slime, no cuts, no bruises, no

burns. I glanced into the back seat, turned the light off, and continued driving.

The car slowed to an acceptable speed and I could feel my grip on the steering wheel relaxing. It occurred to me that I was no longer carrying the hatchet; somewhere in the back of my mind I wondered where I'd left it. I found the carving knife in my pocket and tossed it into the passenger seat.

I came to the end of the road, a T-junction in the middle of nowhere, and slowed to a halt, my headlights illuminating a bright yellow bidirectional sign across the road.

I put the car in park and sat there for a moment, trying to calm myself and gather my thoughts. The red STOP octagon to my right wobbled in the wind. The dark forest surrounded me with ominous shadows, shivering limbs that looked like hands out of the corner of my eye. I watched the woods for unnatural movement.

Maybe it was someone trying to mess with me.

Who would do that?

Maybe it was one of the kids that had come to town for my dad's funeral.

But how had they gotten into the house?

They'd waited until I'd unlocked the doors to sneak in.

How did they know I was coming?

They didn't.

Maybe they were looking for a way in when I got there, and waited until the door was open. Then it hit me that I'd left all the doors unlocked. Dammit!

I looked into the rearview mirror, then peered over my shoulder. I could see the road behind me and the dead grass around the asphalt, limned in the red of my tail lights. There was no devil chasing down the car, no cloven-hoofed demon pursuing me. I wondered if it were safe to go back to the house.

63

To hell with that.

I pulled up the contact list on my phone again and rang Sawyer Winton. I got his voice mail. "Hey. This is Ross. I need to talk to you. Please call me back."

*　*　*

I was sitting in the parking lot of a gas station drinking a beer when Sawyer called me back. As he picked up, I could hear uproarious laughter in the background. "Hey. What's up?"

"Was that you at my father's house?" I asked, skipping any pretense.

"Huh?" Sawyer said. "I was up there a couple days ago with Noreen and Judith, helping your mom clean. Is that what you mean?"

"Helping my mom clean?"

"Yeah. We'd went to Mrs. Brigham looking for you—to ask you about the petition—but she told us you weren't in town yet. Then she told us that she had to go, that she had work to do, and when we asked about it, she told us she was going to your dad's house to clean, so we offered to help."

"Oh. Anyway, I was just up there. I went up there to get something. Something . . . " I paused to put the next part together in my head. "Something happened. I saw something. I don't know what it was. I thought it might have been you or maybe one of the others."

"Not sure I understand, Chief."

"There was . . . I was out back in the woodshed and saw someone go into the house. I went inside to look and found something hiding in one of the bedroom closets. I don't know what the hell it was. I thought it might have been one of you in

64

some kind of costume. It scared the hell out of me. I swear on . . . I swear it looked like a—like a *demon*."

I struggled to illustrate my point, shaking my other fist, pressing the phone to my temple. "Like Satan or something. I ran right out of there and jumped in the car and hauled ass."

Sawyer sounded either unimpressed or as if he were talking to a mental patient. "A . . . demon?"

"Please don't patronize me," I said. "It touched me, *nnnngh!* It reached out of the closet and grabbed my wrist! It had these—claws, like a goddamned hawk. Black talons. Skin, raw pink, like a nasty sunburn. It had short little horns, and when I saw it, it was looking at me, with these bright yellow eyes, like a cat's eyes!"

"Hey, calm down, man," said the voice on the phone. "Nobody's talkin' white jackets just yet, okay? We're on the same side, here."

"I need to know, and I need to know right now. Was that you or somebody you might know, Sawyer? Because if it was, I swear on a stack of Bibles that if it was one of you, I'm going to my motel room right now and I'm going to burn every box of my dad's notes in there. You will not see—"

"Woah!" Sawyer interrupted, "Let's not get crazy here. It wasn't me, Mr. Brigham."

"Don't call me Mr. Brigham, Sawyer," I reminded him, my voice exasperated, "We're almost the same age."

"Oh. Yeah, I guess you're right. Look, Ross. Are you sure you saw what you think you saw? Maybe some kind of animal got into the house and you mistook it for something else. It was dark, I'm sure, and I'll bet you've had a long day. And maybe—maybe your dad's death is finally hitting you. I know when my grandmother died a couple years ago I didn't cry at all. I thought something was wrong with me.

65

"All I could do was wander around at the funeral making sure my family was okay. I thought I was some kind of robot, but I guess death hits everybody differently. I was screwed up for a couple weeks after that. I thought I actually saw her ghost at one point."

"Maybe you're right about my emotions, or whatever, *but I know what I saw. I know what *reached out of the closet* and *grabbed me.*"

"I believe you, just don't hurt me."

I snorted at that one. "So I guess we're both in agreement that I'm crazy."

"Yes."

"Okay. Okay. Look. Uhhh—all right, so I need you to do me a favor."

"Anything, man."

"I ran off and left all the doors unlocked. If I'm going back to that house to rectify that, I need backup. I need a wingman."

"Whatever you saw really scared you, didn't it? Are you serious?"

"As a heart attack. Sawyer, I was holding an axe and I had a knife in my pocket when I opened that closet door. I'm sitting at the Kangaroo down the road, and I have no idea where the axe is, and I'm sitting here drinking a beer. I hate beer."

"I like beer. Beer is good. Especially craft beer. There's this place near where my brother lives that has *peanut butter beer.* Ain't that righteous?"

"Totally tubular. Can you come out here or not?"

"Yeah, sure. I'll be down there in a minute. The convenience store down the road from your dad's house, right?"

"Yep. And bring a weapon if you have one."

The glass bottle banged into the inside of the dumpster as I trashed it, Sawyer's headlights washing across me like surf-crash. He was driving a red 1988 Toyota 4-Runner with the hardtop shell off, and it was meticulously clean. As he got close, he turned down the heavy metal he'd been listening to at rocket-engine volume.

"We'll take the Yota," he said as I got in. "It's got a little more power if we need to make a quick getaway. That Ford you're driving looks a little . . . depressed. And that leopard-print furry steering wheel. Woof."

"Hey, don't talk about Agnes like that," I said, glancing at my boxy, cream-colored Mercury Topaz.

Sawyer pulled out of the parking lot and started down the road to what I was now thinking of as The Devil's Den. I noticed that his camera was mounted on the dash, recording our conversation. "That's the only wheel cover I could find that would fit. The steering wheel was sticky when I bought it and I couldn't clean it off."

"Agnes?"

"Yeah. I look at the car and I think, 'If that car was a person, it'd be a chain-smoking little old lady named Agnes.'"

Sawyer chuckled. "Yeah, I guess I see what you mean."

I looked down and saw a ball bat in the floor board. "That's your weapon, then?"

"Yep. I got carjacked once a few years ago, so now I keep it in the car with me. I guess there's not much room to swing it, maybe, but you ever been poked in the face with a ball bat?"

"Can't say I have."

"It hurts."

We rode on in silence, and then I made an attempt at small talk. I think after the last hour or so, I needed something normal. "So what're you up to around here? You said earlier that you were visiting with some fans, or friends, while you were in town?"

"You'll just think it's silly," Sawyer said, nodding dismissively.

I said, "I doubt that. I've participated in some fairly silly things in my life."

"We were having a sort of mini-convention for *The Fiddle and the Fire* at the Hampton Inn. We were all getting drunk and acting out scenes from the novels wearing our costumes. It was a lot of fun."

He took a deep draught of a soda wedged into the console. "Barry managed to do the entire soliloquy from King Fairbairn's siege in a really . . . *really* bad Scottish accent. I mean, it was hilarious. You shoulda seen it. We're talking about making it a yearly thing. We just . . . come down here for the weekend in costumes and get loaded."

"Maybe if we survive the night, I might join you. I still have a lot of catching up to do before I can start writing."

"I'm sure the others would appreciate the chance to thank you for agreeing to finish the book. Have you thought about continuing the series?"

"I don't know," I said, truthfully.

"I understand."

"We'll see how this goes. The main thing I am concerned with at this point is doing the original series justice."

"Now, I've only been out here once," Sawyer said, peering through the windshield at the road ahead of us. "And it was during the day. You might have to let me know when we get there."

"It's the fourth mailbox after you get on Tollemache Road. The next driveway. Here we are." The 4-Runner crackled across the gravel as we pulled into the country driveway alongside the Nova. Even in the relative darkness, I could see the divots in the lawn where I'd carved ruts in the grass as I fled in terror.

"Shit," said my wingman, looking over me out of my window at the destruction. "I'm getting a little nervous now. I'm bowed up like a Halloween cat."

"You? I'm the one that saw it."

"You said it looked like a devil or a demon or something?"

"Uhhh . . . yeah. Like . . . you remember that movie *Clash of the Titans*?" I asked, making sword-stabbing motions. I'd been thinking of appropriate analogies since I'd called Sawyer earlier, and finally came up with something close enough to what I'd seen. "With Harry Hamlin and the little mechanical golden owl?"

"How could I forget? That's a seminal piece of film history. Right up there with *Krull*, *The Neverending Story*, *The Beastmaster*, and *Conan the Barbarian*."

"Remember the ugly dude with the curly hair and funky skin? Maybe his name was Calephebas or Calibos or something. I think Harry Hamlin cut his head off at some point and carried it around in a bag. Anyway, that's what I saw in that closet, except it was bald and had pale pink skin."

Sawyer's big bright eyes gazed at me, sparkling in the eerie green light from the dashboard. "No offense, Ross, but that's scary as shit. I think I might be regretting coming out here with you."

As I got out, Sawyer was digging under the seat and I heard him swear under his breath. He jumped out of the truck and we walked through the damp late-night chill to the front porch, where the front door was standing wide open.

I looked over at Sawyer and saw that he was carrying his baseball bat and the camera. There was no visible light emanating from it, but I could see on the screen that it was in nightvision

69

mode, the viewfinder screen displaying the world in shades of mint green.

The house was still as dark and silent as I'd left it. I started up the stairs to the second floor, beckoning to Sawyer to follow me. He trailed behind, sneaking almost cartoonishly, gripping the bat with a white-knuckled fist as it rested on his shoulder.

I could hear a faucet dripping as we crested the landing and I looked at Sawyer. He was biting his lips in anticipation.

I stepped in and turned the handle as far as it would go, cutting off the leak. As I did, I noticed something odd: the shower curtain was closed again. I used the tip of the knife to pry back the edge of it and peer into the tub, my heart thundering within me.

To my relief, nothing awaited me.

I lingered momentarily in the soft green light of Sawyer's camera, trying to remember if I'd left the curtain drawn when I'd come through the first time, but I wasn't willing to stand around in there staring at my spooky reflection in the mirror.

When I came out, Sawyer was standing guard, looking up and down the hallway, the bat at the ready. I tapped him on the shoulder and felt him jerk in surprise; I nodded toward the back bedroom.

He pushed the door open with the end of the baseball bat and I rushed in SWAT-style with my knife, waving my cellphone around. My foot struck something and a loud clatter scared me bad enough to make me shout. Sawyer was beside me in an instant, ready to start swinging; I have to give him credit for that.

"What?! What is it?"

I picked up the hatchet I'd kicked and showed it to him, then jabbed the tip of the knife into a fat, yellowed Nora Roberts paperback lying on the dresser, so that it was standing up. I left it there and I pointed at the closet, hefting the axe, preparing to defend myself.

Right there, I mouthed at Sawyer, my face a ghostly green in the display on his camera, my eyes gleaming with an oblique light like a telescope lens. *That's where I saw it. Get ready.*

The door was still open. I cat-stepped toward it, too aware of the floorboards shifting under my feet, every creak and click amplified to deafening levels, a stage upon which I crept and fretted, sure that at any time, I was about to be disemboweled by some horrific spectre from the dirty, black, root-veined underside of the earth.

I slid the axe-blade between the clothes hanging inside, slowly, and then swept the hatchet back and forth, chuffing out loud in a high voice of fear and certainty.

A frigid thrill erupted at the base of my neck and turned my hands and face into numb cadaver parts, and my hair prickled at the sight of a silhouette crouching in the back of the closet, waving something menacingly at me in the weak glow of my cellphone.

I froze, muttering, *"Aaaa—*aaaah!"

"W—wait a minute," Sawyer said, leaning over my shoulder to gaze into the abyss that was staring back at me. I thrust my cellphone toward the jackets and shirts and realized that I was looking at a floor-length mirror, leaning against the back wall of the closet.

Sawyer relaxed. "You have got to be kidding me. It's a mirror. It's a goddamned mirror. You saw your own reflection in a mirror that was in the back of the closet."

I whirled on him. "What I saw earlier, that was *no mirror.* Something reached out of there and grabbed me. *Don't even go there.* I'm not crazy, and I'm not stupid, and I'm no coward. I *saw* what I *saw* and I *felt* what I *felt.*"

"What *I* feel is freaking stupid," Sawyer said, walking away. He turned off his camera and looked at his watch. "It's midnight . . . I'm getting out of here and hitting the hay."

What I felt right then was the suspicion that someone had been grinding up crazy pills and stirring them into my dinner.

I saw no sense in trying to explain, or excuse, or rationalize any further, so I just gave up and let him leave. I followed him back down to his truck, both of us traipsing through the moonshadows. The fear and trepidation were disspelled by the strange mix of disappointment and relief, oh, great waves of relief coursing through my system, leaving me spent and dull-witted.

We rode back to the gas station in silence, but my mind rocketed through plans on a red-hot wire, powered by the last dregs of adrenaline in my brain. I would be back tomorrow, and I would see in the heartless blaze of day, just what was so special about that mirror.

White Lightning

THE AUDITORIUM WAS PACKED with people I'd never met; they'd all shown up to see people that I'd never meet again. I stood on the basketball court floor, my Oxfords just as polished as the boards under my feet, looking up at them, scanning the crowd for someone I might know, hoping someone had come to see me.

I was alone in the thunderous pandemonium of that screaming standing ovation. My green wool uniform made me sweat in the harsh glare of the studio lights overhead, reflected by the gold buttons on my lapels and the medals on my chest. Hundreds of beaming faces regarded me from the stands, none of them familiar, none of them clapping for me.

I closed my eyes. Silence fell in a sequential rush from the back to the front like a late summer shower, until I was an island in an ocean of soundlessness.

When I reopened them, my breath caught in my throat.

The stands were empty, but I was no longer alone. My father stood in front of me, holding a six-shooter at arm's length, a Colt Single Action Army .45, pointing it at my forehead.

When I didn't move, he flipped the gun around with a flick of his wrist and offered it to me, saying, "You don't know where you're goin', son, 'til you can see where you've been."

I looked down at the revolver and the pink, black-taloned hand holding it.

I awoke with a start, and opened my eyes to cold iron light seeping between the hotel room curtains. I felt like I'd been twisted and wrung out by a Greek god. Every joint in my body was radiating heat and my left tricep felt like someone had taken a baseball bat to it. I tried to shake off the grainy-eyed remnants of the melatonin I'd taken to fall asleep.

I've never been able to sleep in hotel rooms, for some reason. I don't know if it's a mental block, or the highway noise, or the unfamiliarity, or what. As I lay there under my warm blanket reassembling my brain and gearing up for another day, the phone rang.

I picked it up. "Hello?"

"Morning," said Maxwell Bayard. "I'm going to grab something to eat. You game?"

*　*　*

I slid into the booth across from Bayard and ordered us coffee. The IHOP was packed with people; luckily, they were all homebodies still recovering from a night's sleep since it was half past eight and the workaday crew was already on the clock. Everything was relatively quiet except for the clinking of silverware, and the occasional snippet of a mumbled conversation. The P.A. system softly howled George Jones's "White Lightning".

My dad's agent had picked up a newspaper from the box outside; he took the top section and I took the funnies. The rain sheeted down the restaurant's windows; the drizzle that had been going on all morning had progressed to a downpour, and rushed against the safety glass in staccato handfuls, blown by the wind.

Bayard must have caught me watching it with a worried expression on my face, because he picked up another section of the paper and showed me the day's weather. "It's not supposed to stay this bad all day. It should taper off around the time we go down for the burial, at least to a mild shower," said Bayard.

George Jones punctuated it with a "Pbbsshh—*white-uh lightnin!*"

The waitress came back with our coffee and to take our order. I grabbed the funnies and tried to read the rest of them, but I couldn't concentrate on them long enough. I looked at the newspaper Bayard held, and saw a headline I'd seen far too much of that year: 13 KILLED IN GUNMAN'S SCHOOL RAMPAGE.

I dug in my pocket and pulled the top of the agent's newspaper down, showing him the enigmatic key I'd gone around testing last night. "Would you happen to have any idea what this goes to?"

He seemed to think about it, and said, "Afraid I haven't a clue."

"I found it in one of the boxes that had my dad's stuff in it."

"Maybe it's an extra house key."

"See, I thought it might be, but I went to my dad's house last night and tried it on every lock I could find. It doesn't go to any of them."

"Strange. Well, you know how people collect junk over the years. I myself have quite the impressive junk drawer. Drawers. Okay, a *garage*."

I twirled the key this way and that, studying its dull, tarnished surface. That's when I noticed a scratch on one face. Two scratches. Someone had used an engraving pen or something to carve a + on the key.

"What do you make of this?" I asked, showing it to Bayard.

76

He examined it up close, looking down his big nose at it through his bifocals.

"French toast and sausage," said the waitress, putting a plate on the table. Bayard put aside his newspaper and gestured to himself. She put my omelet down in front of me and deposited a ramekin of pancake syrup and one of salsa. I took a sip of coffee and stared at the key, willing the secret to out itself; I began to feel like Don Quixote, chasing windmills.

Bayard grinned over my shoulder and boomed, "Hey, look what the cat dragged in. Come sit with us!"

I turned in my seat to see Sawyer Winton and the rock-chick Joanne Woodward I'd made uncomfortable eye contact with at the viewing. She was ruffling the rain out of her short pixie hair; Sawyer was folding an umbrella.

They came over and we made room for them; the waitress came back and took their orders. Sawyer was carrying the camera again, but it wasn't running and the lens cap was in place.

The girl beamed at me. "It's nice to finally meet you in a place that's not quite so somber, Mr. Brigham," she said, proferring a hand. I shook it. "My name is Noreen, Noreen Mears. I've been a fan of your dad's books for as long as I can remember. I wish I'd gotten to meet him while he was alive. It's a lot of lore to catch up on, isn't it?

"I don't envy you—but maybe I do, because you're getting to experience the series from the very beginning. Oh, it must be so exciting! You've got a wonderful journey ahead of you, Mr. Brigham. I'm so jealous that you get to read all of your father's notes, I bet he has an amazing collection of material built up over the years—"

"Three shoeboxes' worth," I interjected. "And I haven't even looked at his laptop yet, which as I understand, might take some time—"

"Is it locked? I bet it's got a really hard password. Would you like me to take a look at it?"

"No, that's okay," I said, as the waitress got a word in edgewise, and took their orders. "I think I can manage. Thank you for the offer, though. Oh, and just call me Ross—we're almost the same age."

"Oh, right."

I was relieved that Ms. Mears was not drinking coffee. I put the key in the breast pocket of my jacket, but Sawyer had already noticed it. Thankfully, he didn't mention it, or our trip to the Brigham estate yesterday.

I picked at my omelet, ate a few bites, and said, "You're all coming to the burial today, then?"

"Wouldn't miss it for the world," said Sawyer.

Noreen looked me in the eyes, which again made me feel as if I were staring into the sun. Her eyes were a high, cold cerulean, and as piercing as any sword. I was fond of her smoky cowgirl voice. She sounded like she'd done a lot of yelling in her life. "Are you doing okay, Ross? How are you holding up? You look a bit less—"

Callous?

"—mellow than you did at the viewing."

Like you've seen a ghost? I glanced at Sawyer, but his face was impassive.

"Yeah," I said. "I guess it's finally hitting me." I looked down at my food, and speared a bit of green pepper with my fork. My throat felt dry, like I hadn't had anything to drink all morning, and the words had to climb to get out of me. "I guess it's occurred to me that . . . I don't know. I should've made more of an effort to connect with him."

"You don't know what you've got until it's gone," said Sawyer. He sounded genuinely sympathetic.

78

"Yep," said Noreen. "Well . . . if it's any consolation, you may have lost your father, but you've gained hundreds of friends."

I regarded them both, and Bayard was smirking, his eyebrows arched. I agreed. "That I have."

I abruptly took out the key and held it up where everyone could see it. "Everyone, I'm having a bit of a difficulty trying to figure out what this key unlocks. I would be highly obliged if one of you would perhaps take a penny for your thoughts on it."

Bayard choked on his french toast and coughed. The fluorescent lights played across the key's worn brown surface, glittering in the etched +. Noreen leaned closer for a look at it and asked, "Where did it come from?"

"I found it in a box of my dad's things."

"Have you noticed the cross somebody scratched on it?"

I nodded. "I have." And then I paused. "Cross?"

"Yeah," Noreen said, turning the key in my fingers so that I could see the +. Indeed, as she said, as I studied it, the lowest arm of the + did seem to be almost imperceptibly longer than the others. It did in fact resemble a crucifix, and now, I could not unsee it.

"You could be right."

"I'm sure it's nothing," said Bayard, tucking back into his breakfast. He had methodically cut off and now chewed a bit of sausage, speaking to us as he did so. "You are—you are imagining—there is nothing to it. You are simply having trouble adjusting to your father's death and your new obligations. I'm positive this key is just a spare house key, or perhaps it goes to an old storage locker somewhere."

He swallowed, gesturing at the key with his fork, "In fact, I think I recall your father saying something a few months ago about having to give up a storage locker that he had been renting. He was

79

keeping his motorcycle in it until he could get the shed in the back of his house cleaned out."

I humored Bayard and let the subject drop. I caught a look in Noreen's eye, however, that told me she was hooked on the mystery.

*   *   *

The remainder of the meal passed in good-natured conversation about everybody's jobs back home, and their immediate plans, and how they thought the continuation of *The Fiddle and The Fire* should proceed: how the plot should wrap up, how the characters should find closure, what kind of tone the book should end on.

Obviously, I didn't know much about the series, so I didn't have much input to offer, but I enjoyed it vicariously through listening to the others' enthusiastic discussion.

I have to say, the discussion rejuvenated my creative energy. I was beginning to look forward to taking on the project; it was nice to be a part of something larger than myself again. I was getting the same feeling of responsibility I'd felt on deployment, thrust into a locus of tasks the likes of which I'd never had to deal with before.

If there was one thing I'd learned from war, it was that, surprisingly, I enjoyed having big things expected of me. Responsibility was motivating, empowering, and exhilarating, emotions I had never expected to experience.

As we were coming out of the IHOP, I told Bayard I was going to ride with Sawyer and Noreen. His reticence at deducing the key's origin and purpose had made me wary of his motives. To me, the agent had seemed all too ready and willing to write it off as nothing but a coincidence, or something completely innocuous altogether.

There was something about the key—and the agent—I just couldn't shake.

I approached Sawyer and Noreen as they were getting into Sawyer's 4-Runner. "Hey, you guys mind if I ride with you? I don't really feel like heading back to the motel just yet."

"You're not a very good liar, Ross," said Noreen, squinting at me with suspicious eyes. The rain had lessened to a misting again, and it pebbled in her hair like diamonds. "You've got an idea about that key, and you want to drag us into your sordid, shadowy conundrum, don't you?"

I paused. "Well, I—ahh—"

Sawyer smirked. "Get in the truck."

As we roared down Main Street, I leaned close to the back of Noreen's passenger seat, trying to get closer to the heater's blast. She turned to me, holding the collar of her jacket shut with one white-knuckled hand, and raised her voice to be heard over the rumble of the Yota's tires and the paper-bag bluster of the wind coursing around us.

"So what is this clue you've got in mind, Scooby Doo? Where is the Mystery Machine going?"

"I got to thinking about what a crucifix could mean," I said, "—and I thought, well what about the church my parents got married in? I don't know why my dad would have a key to it, but I couldn't think of anything else."

Noreen made a grand gesture through the windshield. "Make it so, Number One."

Pack leapt out of his chair at the lowing of the carnyx. "What's going on?" he asked.

The mercenary dumped the rest of his soup into the fire, dousing the embers. He drew both of his revolvers and ordered Pack into the tent, where he crouched by the tent opening. The boy clawed handfuls of laundry out of the trunk at the back and climbed inside, pulling the lid down over his head.

He pulled out his father's gun and folded himself up in the cramped box, trembling in fear, peering out through a thin slit.

"It's Wilders," said the mercenary. Pack heard gunfire crackling out there, and a strange and horrifying hooting and snarling. "Stay quiet. We'll get through this."

With that, the man ran outside into the chaos. Pack never saw him again.

—The Fiddle and the Fire, vol 2 "The Cape and the Castle"

The Preacher-Man

IT TOOK US A good hour to find the place, as it wasn't quite where I remembered it. The church was a little red-brick affair tucked back in a subdivision on the road out of town. A illuminated letterboard sign out front read, "You Think Your Bad? Job 37:18."

The grammar error made me wince as I ducked, jogging through the rain to the front door of the church. There were no services taking place, so the front was locked. I tried the key, but it wouldn't even go into the doorknob keyhole; the deadbolt accepted it, but it wouldn't turn.

I shook my head at the others as they sat in the Yota (Sawyer was pointing his camcorder at me), and went around to the back door, tried it.

No such luck.

When I came back, I noticed that the passenger-side mirror was missing from Sawyer's truck. Noreen let me in and I collapsed into the back seat with a sigh. "No dice, team. Didn't find anything."

"Now what?" asked Noreen, staring out at the rain pattering on the windshield. Crystal rivulets snaked down the glass, scattered by the wipers whipping back and forth.

"I don't know," I said. "Let's just go get ready for the interment. I'm sure we'll think of something later."

*   *   *

The rain tapped listlessly on the canvas tented above us on aluminum poles, providing a dissonant backbeat to the proceedings. I panned my gaze across the small sea of faces. It appeared that many of them had gone home after the viewing, reducing the number of attendees to about thirty.

I was glad to see that none of them had decided to wear their costumes. It was one thing, I think, to wear them to the viewing, on private property, inside a building . . . but I figure it was even beyond them to stand around a man's burial dressed in a costume, outside.

The grave was at the top of a hill, at a cemetary only a few minutes' walk from the commercial district. From where we stood, we could see just over the treetops of the oaks that populated the grass medians running through the city of Blackfield.

Taller buildings loomed over even these; in the farthest distance, bleached pale by the rain's vapors, was a twelve-story bank building whose top three floors had been gutted by fire several years ago. Several other structures rose from the leaves and fog, faces streaming with water.

"'Do you see a man skillful in his work?'" said the preacher, a tall and lanky black man in a much-too-large jacket. His gravelly, powerful voice belied his fragile frame, and carried easily in the soft crash of falling rain, even over the faraway noise of traffic, even though he had to be in his eighties or nineties.

"'He will stand before kings; he will not stand before obscure men.' That is Proverbs 22:29. I have to admit that I am not familiar with E. R. Brigham's fantasy series, but from what I gather, he was a skillful man. Skillful at something that I believe serves to fulfill that most basic and sacred of requirements for what constitutes a man.

"God created man in His own image; God was a creator, and

may it be said that—just short of childbirth—in literature does man find his destiny most intertwined with the original Creator.

"Because from the mind of the writer springs forth entire worlds full of creatures and continents, plots and pomp, and memories and also man. Man with a capital M, Mankind in all its features and flaws, Men full-formed, that walk straight out of the imaginations of these great luminaries and onto the page, where we may love or hate them like any other.

"Exodus 35:31-32 says, 'And he has filled him with the Spirit of God, with skill, with intelligence, with knowledge, and with all craftsmanship, to devise artistic designs, to work in gold and silver and bronze.' Matthew 25:16 says, 'He who had received the five talents went at once and traded with them, and he made five talents more.'

"And much it works the same way as for writers, even as it does for artists, and even, indeed, as it does for us bound by the holy Word," said the old man. "By virtue of his creativity and the power of his generous talent, Mr. Brigham made loaves and fishes with the flour of the written word, and his talent multiplied itself through inspiration of those who would read his works and be motivated to create their own worlds beyond these."

The preacher thrust one of his gnarled old fingers at the crowd, "I daresay there are some of *you* here today to see our dear friend into Paradise."

I appraised the people around me again, and saw the glitter of tears in most of their eyes. I knew that they probably didn't see my dad as of much of a father figure as Sawyer Winton did, but I knew they still loved the man in the casket for taking them to worlds they would most likely rather live in, and introduced them to people they would have given anything to personally know.

I glanced at my mother, who stood by my side, a whole foot shorter than I; her eyes were dry, but I recognized the expression on her face as one of genuine loss and pain.

"My friends, you may not know who I am," said the preacher. "My name is Moses Atterberry. I am the pastor over Walker Memorial Church. When I began my career in the Lord's light, the Brighams were one of the first families to become involved with church charity functions in the neighborhood, and I saw them on frequent occasions, so I came to know the teenaged Mr. Brigham personally.

"Even then, I knew he was a very talented individual.

"It would be several years before he wrote the first book in his fantasy series, but that did not stop him from using his prodigious way with words to entertain and educate the boys and girls in our Sunday school class every week with his own brand of parable, full of dragons and knights and so unlike those you might find in the Bible, but valuable and enviable nonetheless.

"It saddens me greatly to see a man so good-hearted cut down in the prime of his career," said Atterberry, his voice weakening with emotion. I felt my own eyes burn when I saw the pain cross his face with a heart-breaking grimace. The rest of his words were choked by the threat of tears.

"I hope this most untimely death reminds you all, everybody standing here today, that chasing your dreams is one secret of life that is of utmost importance," he said, pressing a indicative fingertip to the casket hanging in front of us.

"And if you are going to catch them, then by God and all his heavenly host of angels, do it, *do it*, because only God knows when you are going to run out of time."

I was absolutely wrecked. My eyes unfocused, and I let them drift over the old man's shoulder into the trees. I realized my hands were in my pockets, looking for something to keep my hands busy, and as I absent-mindedly rubbed the key in my pocket, I noticed the steeple of Walker Memorial Church spearing up out of the carpet of green.

When I looked back to the podium, Sawyer was there.

"The Buddhists had it right," he said. "The impermanence of all things is the key to contentment. Nothing lasts forever. The only constant is change. Why pull your hair out over something when it will be gone a week from now, a month, a year from now? Nothing in your life, nothing you do is written in stone, not the books you write, not the movies you make, not the mountains you climb. You and your name are written in magic marker.

"Your job is to write your life as big as you can, and bear down as hard as the marker can take it, and have fun doing it. Life is a bumper car arena. Drive the hell out of it until the man at the control panel turns your car off."

*　　*　　*

I went back to the motel for a little while to get out of the rain, get some lunch, and dry off. Since Noreen and Sawyer drove me back, I invited them in to hang out before I revealed my next destination to them. I figured they might appreciate a few minutes with my dad's notes, and I was right.

They each took a notebook and took turns making noises of awe and recognition, showing each other pictures and especially resonating articles.

"So that's what he intended the Swordwives to look like," one of them would say, or "I had no idea the political structure in Ain was so complex," or even such enigmas like "What the hell is Obelus?" and unfortunately, the conversation was a labyrinth of terms to me.

I contented myself with paging through whatever they weren't engrossed in. Sawyer's camera lay on the table, passively recording them.

I envied their curiosity. To put so much emotional stake in something must have been fulfilling; I could not remember the last time I'd felt so damned enthusiastic about anything except for the key. While my motivation to work on the final book of *The Fiddle and The Fire* grew by the hour, I couldn't turn my back on the mystery of the key.

Even if it were just a junk key, a spare or an obsolete original, why would it have been in a box of *Fiddle* material?

I sat on the bed, eating the other half of my gigantic hamburger from last night's visit to Jackson's, watching the Discovery Channel, listening to Noreen and Sawyer discussing the notes, indulging my own inner monologue, realizing just how empty and tired I was.

It was beginning to dawn on me just how unlustered my life had become. One long parade of self-denial, self-loathing, boredom. Not for the first time, I felt gratitude that I wasn't a heavier drinker, like my father had been in his hey-day. He had been the Hemingway of genre fiction, a booze-fueled Tolkien.

Maybe I was afraid of taking on the series because I thought on some level that I wasn't good enough. Oh, who was I kidding; I *knew*, openly, that I wasn't good enough.

Maybe it was my tiredness that was making me morose. Or maybe it was the burial.

I put down the hamburger, looked down at the notebook open on the bedspread in front of me, and realized that it wasn't going to happen this way.

If I was going to get the gist of the series, subjecting myself to the unfiltered contents of E. R. Brigham's head, exploded and disarranged like exotic car parts, wasn't going to do me any favors. I was going to have to read the series end to end, witness the assembled Maserati in action, and immerse myself in the lore that way.

"I guess I need to get a copy of the first book in the series," I said, half to them and half to myself. "This chaos just isn't going to cut it. I need to read the series."

"Good luck on that one, Chief," said Sawyer. "The first book was printed in 1973. I don't even know if you can get a paperback of it these days without one hell of a scavenger hunt."

"Really? I guess I'll have to head up to the house later and see if my dad has any copies."

I called Bayard on my cell to see if he had any copies of the first book; he didn't, at least, not on him—there was a first edition on the bookshelf in his office. He promised to mail it to me as soon as he got back. I hung up and massaged my aching left arm.

"Hey guys, when you two get done, I wondered if you want to go with me to check out a lead I have on the key."

"Walker Memorial?" asked Sawyer.

"Yep."

"I figured so, from the way you were looking at it earlier."

They looked at each other and Noreen winced. "Actually, I have to get back home pretty soon. I have a hell of a drive and I have work in the morning. I'll see you when you get back, I gotta go pack."

Sawyer shrugged. "I have all this week off," he chuckled. "I told my boss there was a death in the family. Which, now that I think about it, wasn't too far off the mark, I guess. So I guess I'll go with you."

I stood up, rolling my shoulder, and turned my computer off. "I hate to cut it short, you two, but I want to get down there before it gets dark. Sneaking around churches at night trying locks might fly on TV, but in the real world, they call it trespassing."

"What do they call it during the day?" asked Sawyer, wallowing his way out of the Queen Anne chair and slipping into his jacket.

I put my motel room key in my shirt pocket and smirked. "Seeking guidance."

Sawyer and I piled into my car. The rain had tapered off to another misty drizzle and the gray sky was an unending wool blanket, turning the world into a Cezanne painting. I sat there for a moment, letting the inside of the car warm up, watching the vapors outside bead up on the windows.

The windshield was clear by the time Noreen opened the door and slid into the back seat. I twisted in my seat to look at her. She was putting on her seat belt. "Just shut up and drive."

I grinned. "By the way," I said to Sawyer, "Where did you dig up that little speech you gave at my dad's grave?"

"It was in the afterword of his last book," he said, looking out the window.

Too Many Heebies and Not Enough Jeebies

THE CHURCH TURNED OUT to be an imposing structure; Walker Memorial was a tremendous, sprawling castle of a building made of some sort of pale yellow stone that made it look like a cross between a Germanic monastery and Alexander the Great's desert fortress. I couldn't count the number of times I'd driven past it in my life, as it was directly on the main street in town; so I was familiar with it by sight, but I'd never bothered to learn its name.

All three of us were gazing up at the belltower out the windows as we approached it and pulled into the parking lot out back. There were a few other cars here; as I parked, I wondered whose they were. It was late afternoon, so I didn't have much room to speculate. The clergy had every reason to still be here.

When we got out of the Topaz, the subtle majesty of the church made itself evident. Sidewalks were protected by corridor battlements held aloft by flying buttresses. Whimsical tavern-style mullioned windows perforated those elevated hallways. The towers, each side sporting two narrow archers' windows for each floor, were peaked with sharp steeple points. Each steeple except for the bell tower ended in tiny onion minarets.

There was no one in sight as we walked toward the nearest door, an ornate, heavy-looking wooden door at the base of one of the corner towers. Sawyer poked me in the arm with a finger; when I turned to address him, I saw that he was aiming the GoPro at me and he asked, "What do I say if someone catches me nosing around?"

"Tell them you're looking for Jesus."

"Okay. What do I do if I find Him?"

"That means it's your turn to hide."

Noreen burst out laughing. I took the key out of my pocket and walked right up to the door. It was the moment of truth. I held my breath, and looked back at the other two. Noreen was crossing her fingers at me in a conspicuous gesture of good luck, but Sawyer had his hands on his cheeks and he was pulling on his face in mock exasperation over the suspense.

I turned around, oriented the key in my hand, and thrust it slowly and dramatically toward the lock.

It was an antique pin-tumbler lock, the kind that took a large rod-style key. The keyhole was big enough to stick my little finger in.

"Well, that was anti-climactic," said Sawyer.

Noreen stepped between us and pulled the doorhandle. The door opened with a soft ripping sound as the draft flap brushed across the threshold, and it sounded heavy with destiny, like Howard Carter opening Tut's tomb. Or, at least, so I thought.

She stood aside, ushering us in with a sweeping gesture. "Age before beauty."

We both gave her a look and stepped into the church.

We were at the end of a long hallway, carpeted with a lush red runner. Gold pinstripe wallpaper and dark wainscoting ran the length of the walk into darkness; somewhere in the void, I could hear a vacuum cleaner rhythmically roaring in and out of earshot. Someone was talking, every so often. I stood there a moment listening before I realized it was someone singing.

Sawyer took the lead, bulling headlong into the depths of the tabernacle, rolling his feet as he walked, moving silently on the balls of his feet. Noreen and I followed suit. The grandiosity of the building made me feel like a secret Allied agent sneaking through an Axis headquarters.

We came to an open door with no light on inside. Sawyer peeked in, saw no one, and we continued. There were several other instances of this before we came to a junction where an orange drop-cord was snaking back and forth on the rug; we could hear the vacuum around the corner.

I made it to the intersection first and leaned out just enough to see a man in a pair of slate-gray coveralls dancing, having made his own Grace Kelly out of a decrepit Eureka. He was breathing heavily, white earbuds in his ears, and murmuring to himself as moved. "One two three four, one two three four . . . ."

His back was to us. I beckoned to the other two and we twinkle-toed across the open space to the adjoining hallway. From there it was only a few steps to the nave itself. The coast was clear, so we walked right in and stood in front of the altar, looking up at the giant golden-brown effigy of the Christ Himself. I felt a vague dismay at the sight of such an agonized figure, pinned up there on a huge cross made of what looked like old railroad ties. What a condition to be immortalized in.

I heard a sigh and turned to see Sawyer pointing the camera up at the representation of the Son of God. "We found Him. Now what?"

"Now *you're* It," I said, examining the nave around me. I noticed a small gray metal box lying on a nearby pew. I tested the key on it and was relieved when it didn't work, since it looked like a cash box and felt empty. Other than that, I didn't see anything else to use the key on.

Noreen broke off and went to the other side of the room, strolling casually through the darkness under an overhanging part of the far flank wall. I could see the shadowy shapes of hymnal shelves and paintings there. Sawyer went to the opposite side, where I could just make out his blue sweater and pale face against the brown-black. I heard a clatter as he kicked something and swore to himself.

Since there was nothing in the middle of the room to inspect, I went straight to the narthex, where two huge wooden doors served as the front entrance to Walker Memorial. Smaller doors to either side led into areas flanking this small space.

I chose the one to the right and tried the key on it. It didn't fit, but when I turned the knob the door opened and I was bathed in a soft light from above.

I leaned inside and saw a very steep staircase leading through a hole in the ceiling. Closing the door behind me, I climbed it and found myself in another, smaller space. A ladder in front of me led through another hole in the ceiling full of daylight.

At the top of that I pulled myself up out of the hole and discovered that I'd climbed into the apex of the bell tower. A pigeon was startled at my presence and flapped squealing into the canopy.

I surveyed the town of Blackfield around me, watching traffic motor by through the branches of the oaks and maples that dotted the grass median running up and down Main Street. Of course, there was a bell here, a grand and thunderous-looking thing that had obviously not been rung in many years. Instead, I espied a pair of loudspeakers bolted to a nearby wall, the crotch between the two horns crammed with a handful of pine-straw and hair.

Finding nothing of interest, I began the dirty and laborious descent back down the rickety ladder and the nearly vertical staircase. As I made to open the door, I could hear talking from the other side.

I strained to hear it over the noise of the traffic on the street. "—Very nice to receive visitors here—as always, of course—but I must say that this is awfully late in the day to crave salvation. To

95

what do I owe the honor of this unexpected visit?" said a voice I recognized to be that of Moses Atterberry.

Sawyer: "After hearing you talk about E. R. Brigham growing up here at the church, we wanted to see it for ourselves. Maybe absorb a little of one of the places that must have inspired Mr. Brigham so much."

Noreen: "Yes! This church reminds me so much of one of the castles in his books. A man named Seymour lived in an old monastery damaged by the war; he raised crocodiles in the moat and let the villain in book six feed political prisoners to them in exchange for letting him stay there."

Atterberry: "That's certainly a macabre reason to visit a church. But I'm glad you're here anyway."

I couldn't hear the awkward shrug from Sawyer, but I could see it, as by then I'd opened the door just a crack. They were standing and talking in a loose triangle just in front of the altar, Noreen and Atterberry facing away from me. I knew Sawyer couldn't see me behind the door, so I came out of the bell tower anteroom and waved at him, creeping across the narthex to the other side; he only vaguely acknowledged me, averting his eyes from the movement.

Luckily, Atterberry didn't notice, and he nearly did, when I almost ran into a candelabrum because I wasn't watching where I was going. I pulled the key out, boogied over to the other door like a ninja running the last five yards of a game-winning touchdown, stuck the key right into the old deadbolt lock, and turned it.

There was a faint *click!,* and my heart leapt in shock and fear.

I peered over the top of the rearmost pew to see if anyone was looking at me. They weren't, so I turned and opened the door only to find myself face to face with a most opaque darkness. I literally could not see *anything* beyond the door's threshold.

So, I walked right in and eased the door shut behind me.

*   *   *

The musty void I'd hurled myself into threatened to consume me with dread. I knew only that I was standing on a staircase because the floor was extremely uneven. If I hadn't been so nimble, I might have taken another tumble down the stairs, and those never end well.

I rotated slowly, feeling my way with my toes, and took my cellphone out, shining it all around me, illuminating my surroundings with an eerie blue glow. The walls of the stairwell were simple red bricks, dusty and draped with buntings of cobwebs that looked like black cotton candy. The stairs were ancient-looking and wooden, jostling side by side like an old man's teeth.

Several steps down, they veered to the left and continued downward into a space under the nave. I followed them, creeping sideways, ready to charge back up the stairs at the first provocation.

I descended into some sort of a dirt-floored cellar. Tiny cockroaches scattered from the glow of my cellphone. I looked up at the ceiling just a foot above my head, and crouched out of fear. A few fat spiders lurked in the spaces between the joists of the narthex floor overhead.

I duck-walked away from them and saw an opening in the dirt wall to my right that continued deeper into the floor under the nave. I gazed inside; my phone's sorry shine did nothing to reveal anything beyond a ten-foot length of narrow tunnel.

Abandoning my senses, I ventured inside and stoop-walked down the length of it.

I came out into a roughly-hewn room about twenty feet square. The walls of it were a smooth, unbroken stone comprised of what seemed to be the same material making up the bricks that were used to build the church. Above me, I could hear Atterberry and my friends talking to each other, their words muffled by a layer of carpet, probably some insulating layer, and wood flooring.

I did some quick mental math and decided that I was directly underneath the altar and the big brown Jesus. The walls to my left and right were broken into bold white stripes. I approached them and found that there were wide swaths of canvas hanging from the walls like tapestries, with unfamiliar words and phrases scrawled on them in black.

I noticed something jutting out of the stone wall over the hole I'd entered from, so I stood up and got close with my phone. Someone had hammered what appeared to be a railroad spike into the wall's surface near the ceiling, leaving only about an inch protruding. It angled downward almost imperceptibly, as if having supported a great weight for many years.

The dialogue overhead tapered into silence, and I heard footsteps making their way off to my right. A door closed.

Something moved behind me.

I spun and thrust the cellphone out, flooding a nearby corner with light. My relief at not finding anything there immediately turned to anxiousness, and I made my way back to the staircase, hunched over and loping like Quasimodo. On the way through the first chamber, I recoiled at the sight of the spiders again and jogged up the stairs.

When I eased the door open, I was still holding the glowing cellphone to my chest, trying to still my heart, and as a result, my face was illuminated from beneath. I scared the hell out of Noreen, who just happened to be standing next to me.

She punched me in the arm. "Where did you go? Did you find anything?"

"The key works on this door," I said, excited. "I opened it and went down some stairs into some kinda burrow with a big nail in the wall. I think something used to hang there."

"Curiouser and curiouser," said Sawyer, shutting the camera's viewfinder screen. "Come on, let's get out of here. I got a huge case of the heebie jeebies."

*   *   *

It was raining in earnest again, and the water was beginning to accumulate in the culverts by the road, making for large puddles of standing water that roostered out from the car's flanks. I took Sawyer and Noreen back to the Hampton Inn on the other side of town where they were staying and I stayed long enough to see her off.

"It's too bad you can't stay a couple more days," said Sawyer, leaning into her car window. "Gonna miss ya."

"You've got my email address?" she asked.

"Yep."

"You've got my cellphone number?"

"Yep."

She pulled him inside the car by his collar and gave him a long, sensuous kiss. They broke off and Sawyer just looked at her, dazed, still stooped over with his head in the car.

"We'll see each other again," Noreen said, smiling. She turned the engine over, putting on her seatbelt, then put the car in gear and eased away. Sawyer watched her dwindle away to nothing. I just stood there, too, letting the moment linger. Life is a series of moments like this. They are what make us who we are. I'd be a rude friend to take this one away.

Once the spell had worn off and the girl was gone, he turned to me and sighed, giving me unspoken permission to intrude. "I know, buddy," I said, and tossed my arm around his shoulders as we walked away, giving him a commiserating pat on the back.

I treated him to dinner at a mom-and-pop seafood joint down the street from the Hampton. The sky was still a river of nickels, but the rain had ceased for the time being. The water standing on the street turned the headlights of every passing car into long-legged neon spiders that hissed and crashed past the windows.

I panned Sawyer's camera away from the pale indigo evening and put it on the table. "So what do you do back home?"

"I used to think I was going to be a computer programmer, but a career in tech support didn't quite agree with my sense of patience, so I'm going to film school at Full Sail."

"Really? That explains the camera. I wondered what you were up to. I knew it wasn't just vacation video."

"Yeah. I'm making a sort of YouTube documentary about E. R. Brigham, but things are getting a little more . . . interesting, I guess you could say."

"I guess you could say that."

"I'm thinking of doing something a little more cinematic with it. So what are *you* doing back home?" asked Sawyer. "I haven't seen much about you since you enlisted in the Army."

"I used my G.I. Bill to go to art school. Right now when I get home I'll be doing freelance art, and working for a little design shop in Kentucky that does things like T-shirts for ball teams, promotional office equipment for companies, coffee mugs, hats, that kind of thing."

"That's cool."

"So you say you're putting this on YouTube?"

"Yup. That *is* okay, right? Shit, I didn't even think about a privacy waiver. I am such an asshole."

"I don't mind."

We ate in silence for a few minutes, and then Sawyer spoke up, leading with a sudden inhale, a hesitation, and then, "So what was it like? I mean, if you don't mind me asking."

"It was . . . different," I said, talking as I ate. "One of the most incredible experiences of my life. You probably don't want to get me started; I'll talk about it for hours."

"I don't have anywhere pressing to be at the minute. What did you do?"

"Logistics. I picked up quite a bit of Italian while I was there, and even a bit of Dari."

I loved explaining what I did. I loved it every time someone asked me. "I may not be as public as my dad was, but in my honest opinion, I accomplished things just as important as his fantasy series. I made sure shipments of food and crop seeds got to the people that needed it, and I made sure that people that got hurt got to medical care. I heard a call to the medevac team one day about a farmer whose head was stepped on by a cow."

"Did you—*umm*—see any 'action'?" Sawyer seemed ashamed to ask, unsure of what word to use.

"My camp was attacked several times. Mortars, rockets. I was in the shower one night and heard something explode down by the airfield. It turned out to be a mortar . . . it left a pretty big hole out there. I was walking back to my chu late another night and saw a mortar hit the local police station; it looked like a Fourth of July bottle rocket in the air."

"That's crazy."

"There were a couple weeks we were on total lockdown, because of a rumor that the Taliban was trying to infiltrate the camp in disguise," I said through a mouthful of fish. "*That* was

101

crazy. Oh, man—speaking of crazy, you should've seen the blizzard we had over the winter. I had no idea it would snow so hard there. I've got pictures on my laptop if you ever want to see them."

"That would be cool. So it snows over there?"

"*Oh* yeah. Well, we were a couple thousand feet above sea level, too. But yeah, it snowed so hard several of our tents collapsed overnight."

He cracked open a lobster claw. "So now what, Scooby?"

"I want to get my dad's laptop and see if it's got a lock on it." I said, polishing off my orange roughie. "First order of business beside getting to know the series, is recovering the draft he was working on. I can't finish what I don't have."

"Fe-fi-fo-fum," said the strange, gentle voice, echoing throughout the city. The god, or whatever it was, spoke at him from some place Normand could not see from where he lay under the metal carriage. The ground shook rhythmically as the god-giant came up the road, his armored hips and shoulders brushing the buildings around him.

Pieces of masonry fell, knocked loose by his passing, and shattered on the ground. "You're not supposed to be here. This is a restricted area. Don't you know that? Can't you read the signs, silly-billy?"

The gunslinger tipped open his remaining gun and checked the cylinder out of habit. He already knew there were no cartridges left. The god-giant stepped on one of the other carriages, crushing it flat and grinding it into the street. Two of the wheels came off and rolled away; the fuel inside squirted out of the reservoir.

Normand could smell the fuel's astringent fumes. He had to find safety, and fast.

—The Fiddle and the Fire, vol 7 (unfinished) "The Gunslinger and the Giant"

Run or Die

THE DAY WAS STILL alive as we pulled into my father's driveway again. In the cold light filtering down through the gray sky, the house seemed to have lost a great deal of its monstrosity. When we walked into the foyer, it seemed docile, diminished, tamed somehow, like a lion reduced to cowering in the corner of its cage.

Perhaps it was just the watery daylight sighing in through the white shroud curtains, sucking the mystery out of what had been a legitimately disturbing place at night. Now it was what it had always been: the last vestiges of an old man's life, a home abandoned of laughter and warmth.

I stood by the piano, my arms folded; I didn't realize I was staring into space until Sawyer got my attention. I climbed the stairs, feeling stiff and old, and went into the master bedroom, where I found the Compaq computer quietly gathering dust.

I eased it closed, and as I was gathering up the power adapter, I looked up and saw my reflection in the closet. The sight startled me, but then I remembered why I was seeing it. I lifted the mirror away from the back of the closet; it was surprisingly heavy. I walked it out and stood there looking down at it.

The frame was made of some dark, weighty wood—perhaps mahogany or ebony, I'm no wood expert—and was carved with reliefs of strange pictographs or calligraphy I didn't recognize, unintelligible writing with elaborate swoops and tails that resembled the writing I'd seen on road and shop signs in the Middle East. I counted nineteen of them.

Attached to the back was a thin metal cable, looped around a pair of fixtures screwed into the frame. It was obviously meant to be hung on the wall.

"I should've figured you'd be in here fooling around with that old thing," said Sawyer. I glanced at him over my shoulder; he was standing in the doorway, leaning against the wall.

"It *does* look pretty old. Where do you think it was hanging?" I asked him, pulling on the wire to show it to him. "There's a wire on the back of it."

"Beats me," he said.

I hefted the mirror over my head with a grunt and felt a twinge in my back, and immediately put it back down.

"What are you doing?" asked Sawyer.

I stretched. "I want to take the mirror too."

"Why on earth would you want this thing?"

"I just do," I asked, but I wasn't entirely sure. I just knew that it belonged in my care, and my conviction grew stronger as I stood there holding the thing. "It's probably pretty valuable. I should take it with me and keep an eye on it."

Sawyer blinked. "I guess that's a good idea," he said, his voice taking on a peculiar monotone.

I looked at him; his eyes seemed flat and listless for a moment, but then the life so common to them returned as I watched.

Even odder was the feeling in my head of certainty at what I was doing, at odds with the vague confusion at the smooth ease at which I made the decision to take it. My father would've wanted me to have it, I was sure. If I didn't take it with me, someone could break into the house and take it, and it was obviously a priceless antique.

I gestured with my head, gripping the mirror with both hands.

"Here, help me grab it. We'll put it in the back of my car."

We were hauling it down the stairs by the time I thought about it again. It was heavy. Why did I want the mirror so badly, again? Oh, right. For safekeeping.

I stopped and propped it up on my knee so I could open the back passenger door of my Topaz and put the mirror in my back seat. When had we carried it out of the house? I honestly couldn't remember even locking the door.

"Hey, watch the road," said Sawyer, touching my arm. The sound of my tires growling across the rumble strip embossed into the roadside forced me to focus on what I was doing, which was driving my car.

I realized I was about to come to the two-way sign at the end of my dad's isolated country road and jumped on the brake a little too hard; the tires barked and Sawyer grunted against his seatbelt. "The hell are you doing, man? Did you leave your marbles back at your motel room or something?"

I apologized, staring out the window at the traffic on Main Street. "Sorry about that, man. I'm a thousand miles away today, I think. Maybe I didn't eat my Wheaties this morning, huh? I didn't drink my V8." *Wait, Main Street? The hell am I doing on Main Street?*

The light overhead changed from red to green and I pressed the accelerator, slowly surging forward with the cars to either side of me like a rank of Confederate soldiers charging the line at Gettysburg in slow-motion. The man in the car to my left wheeled gradually into a side street, his station wagon falling away and out of sight. I shook my head, sensing a strange sort of fuzziness I couldn't quite clear.

A voice droned, muddy and indistinct. "I think I want to see what ol' Moses Atterberry is up to," it said. I strained to make that out, and realized it was my own voice. I glanced up at my face in the rearview mirror; my lips felt numb, like I'd been anesthetized at

106

the dentist's office. It took effort to make my eyes focus on my reflection.

"Okay," said Sawyer. He was staring straight forward.

"What the heck," I mentioned, casually. It was a question, but it didn't sound like one. I elected to forget I said it.

"Sounds like a good idea to me," said Sawyer, and he pointed out the window at a passing strip mall. "Maybe after that, we can stop at this place over here and get some frozen yogurt. How does that strike you? Do you like frozen yogurt?"

"I would love that," I said. I looked forward to going back to the church, but I wasn't sure quite why. Then it hit me: perhaps Atterberry had the key I needed. *What key?* I thought, and reached into my pocket for the key I'd used in the nave. It was still there, soft-edged from years of use. What purpose did it serve? Why did my father have a key . . . that opened a door . . . in a church . . . he had no business being in?

"I love frozen yogurt," I slurred. The road slid under the Topaz like a tablecloth being whipped out from under a seven-course meal. "Especially the chocolate kind."

"Chocolate is freaking awesome," said Sawyer.

"I had a white chocolate mocha gelato once, at the camp where I worked overseas," I said, flicking my turn signal. "Good shit. Why do I feel like I'm high? Did you slip me something, man? Did you slip in something?"

"White chocolate mocha gelato," said Sawyer, staring out the window. "Mocha choco-lato. Gelato vibrato. Mocha choco-lato vibrato gelato. Whatta latta chocka-latta!" he chuckled, and started talking in a bad Italian accent, making gestures with his hands as if he were carrying something huge, or massaging big breasts. "I gotta so mucha chocka-latta, I dunno what to do widdit all-a."

I stopped the car and put it in park. We were sitting in the parking lot of Walker Memorial.

"You gotta eata lotta chocka-locka," I said, and I giggled, almost dropping the mirror. We were carrying it across the asphalt toward the back door of the church. I propped it on my knee again so I could open the door and I backed inside, slowing down so Sawyer could find his footing on the steps of the stoop outside. "I eata chocka-latta formosa my life-a."

"Mamma mia," Sawyer laughed. "This thing is heavier than a dead preacher."

Big Brown Jesus looked down at us with his judgemental, agonized stare. I apologized to the Son of God for Sawyer's irreverence. "Sorry about this, Jesus," I said, pronouncing it *Hey-zeus*. "Just passing through."

"Hot soup, make way for Hey-Zeus."

"Hey-Zeus is on the loose," I said, almost stumbling down the cellar stairs. "He's got the juice in the caboose." I didn't remember opening the door in the narthex. I took out my cellphone to light the way, laid it on the mirror, and continued backing down the crooked stairs. The cheap cell slid back and forth like a ball on a billiard table. "The junk in the trunk. I thought we came here to talk to Atterberry."

"Nah," said Sawyer. "We came here to hide the mirror down here in the cellar. Nobody would think to ever find it here. Nobody can steal it here. Down in the dark with the roaches and the spiders and the little man in the moon. Little Miss Muffet sat on her tuffet, eating her curds and whey, the cow jumped over the spoon."

"Good idea," I told him. We duckwalked down the tunnel into the room underneath the altar. "Now what the hell do we do with it?"

"Here, let's hang it on this nail. It's got a wire on the back of it."

108

We stood the mirror up and held it vertical in the air with a grunt, dumping my phone off onto the dirt floor. We inched forward in the dim light, and the back of the mirror thumped against the spike driven into the wall over the opening where the tunnel came into the room. We eased it down until the wire was supporting it and let go; now it was hanging neatly across the tunnel opening, and to get back out, we'd have to move the mirror out of the way.

We backed away to appraise our placement of the thing. Hanging there over our only exit, the mirror's frame made it look like a doorway. It reflected only darkness.

"Picture perfect," I said, stepping forward to readjust it.

"Why did we just do that?" asked Sawyer.

I cut my eyes back at him in confusion. "Do what?"

"Hang—*WOAH!*" Sawyer shouted; I turned my head again to look at the mirror.

A horned demon grinned at us from the mirror, his eyes burning yellow in the glass.

I snatched my hands away from the mirror's frame and leapt back with a cry of surprise and terror. The demon immediately faded into the shadows reflected in the mirror; my eyes darted around the cramped room, trying to figure out where it had gone. I pointed at the silvery glass.

"I told you, dude! I *told* you I saw a demon up there in the closet! That was it!"

"Well, I totally believe you *now*," said Sawyer. He had pressed himself against the stone wall at the back of the space. "What the hell are we even *doing* down here?"

"We came to talk to the preacher, didn't we?"

"He's not even *down* here!" cried Sawyer. "This is screwed up! Why did you bring me down here?"

109

"You thought it was a good idea too!"

"I agreed to come to the church and talk to Atterberry, not *this!*" he said, thrusting an accusatory hand at the mirror. "What the hell were we talking about, chocolate and shit? It's like I wasn't even paying attention to what was coming out of my mouth."

He stormed over to it and grabbed the frame without fear, trying to wrench it to one side to facilitate his escape. It did not move. He ripped and yanked at it again, to no avail. It seemed fixed to the wall around the opening. Then, he seemed to calm, or, from where I was standing, it looked like he had gone catatonic or something. He was just standing there.

I came up behind him and looked over his shoulder, steadying him with a hand on his back. "What's goin' on?"

He glanced down at me (as he was several inches taller than myself), and then back up at the mirror.

Then I saw it.

"We don't have a reflection," said Sawyer.

I blinked, and swallowed. My mouth tasted like I'd been licking up dust. I couldn't think of anything to say. I realized that I was gripping my friend's shirt—I had twisted my fist in it, to be precise—and let go. I felt like a vampire trying to find himself in his gothic looking-glass. "What the hell, man. What kind of mirror is this?"

Sawyer reached out to touch the mirror, but his fingertips never met a surface. He leaned, reaching, and put his hand into the empty space inside the wooden frame. There was no glass at all. We were staring into what had somehow become a doorway, on the threshold of a narrow tunnel filled with a close and placeless darkness.

I picked up my cellphone and shined its meager, sickly glow into the opening; I succeeded in only illuminating a little way inside,

110

making it look for all the world like something I'd seen on a Discovery Channel special once about the opening of an Egyptian pyramid, dim fiber-optic images of a remote-control robot trundling down a dark sandstone shaft. I felt like Howard Carter again.

I could feel an inky coldness seeping from the space beyond, and it was very obviously not the way we'd come; instead of a low-ceilinged burrow carved from the dirt under the nave, we were looking at a taller corridor with brickwork walls and floor, the latter strewn with what appeared to be sand. Debris was littered underfoot at the limit of my light.

I looked back at Sawyer; he had backed away from it all and turned on his camera. "To hell with that," he said. "I didn't sign on for this Plan 9, Stephen King, Movie of the Week shit."

I glanced into the tunnel, and back at him. "It's not like we have a choice. We can't stay in this room forever, and we can't move the mirror out of the way. We have to do this."

"I wish I'd brought my damn baseball bat."

I stepped over the frame and into the mirror-tunnel.

*   *   *

I moved from the close, damp air of the church cellar to an arid and odorless place. My shoe crunched on the grit of sand, echoing into the tunnel with a flat, metallic crackle. As soon as my head entered the space beyond the mirror's frame, my ears popped; the air pressure had changed. A cold breeze washed over me, sending a chill across my skin that made the hair on my legs and arms stand up.

I looked back at Sawyer, who was watching me in silent fascination, his eyes wide pools of liquid fear and awe. I shrugged without speaking. My new friend put one foot over the mirror's frame as well, exploring the floor, and then thrust himself into the unknown with me. I saw him roll his jaw to compensate for the ear-pop like I'd done.

"Gotta do what a man's gotta do," he said, hugging himself protectively against the dry, bracing air.

I turned and began leading us into the dark depths. It occurred to me that the grit under our shoes wasn't sand, but on closer inspection it turned out to be some sort of fine silt, or perhaps cornmeal. When I knelt to examine it, I realized that there was a deep, continuous rumble emanating from the stonework floor. Once I'd noticed it, I couldn't deny it, and now I could even feel it through the soles of my feet. The faint, deep vibrations even seemed to permeate the very air.

As I looked up, I noticed that the ceiling was wooden.

"Do you feel that?" asked Sawyer.

I nodded.

"Sounds like machinery."

I stood and kept walking. The farther down the tunnel we went, the louder and deeper the rumbling got, until the floor trembled so hard my feet began to itch. I put my palm against the wall, knocking loose tendrils of fine silt that smelled strangely of tortilla chips as they sifted toward the floor.

I looked down and saw thin drifts of the white dust piled against the walls, and it hit me that I was looking at cornmeal. My suspicions were confirmed when we emerged into a larger space where a millstone, a great stone wheel the size of an automobile, was slowly grinding in an endless circle on a round stone slab.

We had come out of the storage area of a millhouse. We stood there for a moment, trying to piece together the reality of what we were seeing. A bucket on a rope dangled through a nearby hole in the ceiling. Bags of flour or wheat were piled in the corner, chewed open by vermin; grains were all over the floor under them.

I examined the screen of my cellphone and saw that I had no signal whatsoever. I glanced at Sawyer. "Where on Earth are we?"

"I have no idea," he said, and pointed into the darkness with the camera. On the viewfinder screen of his GoPro, I could see the angular, faint green skeleton of a ladder. I went directly to it, seeking it out with my cellphone's glow, and climbed upward into a smaller room, where a log the size of a tree-trunk was turning in place, running the millstone downstairs.

I could hear the distinct creaking of a windmill's vanes somewhere overhead. I did not recall seeing a giant fan turning over Walker Memorial Church.

Weak blue light filtered through the slats of a wooden door. I opened it and stepped out into a narrow alleyway, surrounded by more tall sandstone buildings, whose archer windows stared lifelessly down at me with dark holes where eyes used to be. Gauzy white curtains billowed from those sockets, fluttering in the breeze.

I felt as if I were standing in some replica of an Italian village built by Egyptians. Directly overhead, a black, unmoving river of stars filled the narrow canyon framed by jagged, damaged roofs.

I was speechless with horror and confusion, and judging by the expression on Sawyer's face, tinted green by his camera screen, he was as well. He was slowly, fearfully, rotating in place, pointing the GoPro in a wide arc across the alley.

A loud *BANG!* startled both of us as the door of the millhouse blew shut.

I jumped; Sawyer swore out loud, ducking, looking up and down the alley as if we'd been shot at. I tugged at his sweater. "Come on, let's get out of here. This place is creeping me out."

We walked down to an intersection and found a slightly larger corridor. Stoops of three and four stairs led up to doorways hewn roughly into the sides of the alley, flanked by unseeing portholes with rotting shutters that hung unsecured, swinging free.

I began to understand that we were in some sort of primitive village; for some reason, our surroundings looked familiar. Most of the windows were mullioned, but the glass was gone out of almost all of them. Out here, too, the stonework pavement was gritty, but outside the millhouse, it was sand. It piled coarse grains against the walls, sifting toward us in low, ghostly movements that contributed to the illusion of walking against the current of a pale river muddy with gold dust.

I gazed up at the windows as we passed them, fearing the sight of some guarded, unwelcoming, half-glimpsed face, and whispered to Sawyer. I took a picture with my cellphone. He was pointing the camera at the windows.

He walked over to one of them and reached upward with the camera, holding it over his head so he could aim it into the narrow hole; it was at least a couple feet taller than he. Satisfied, he came back, pointing it at me, collecting my terrified face in the green netherworld of its nightvision mode.

"I have no idea what's going on," I admitted, beginning to panic.

"Yeah," said Sawyer. "Me neither."

At the end of this watchful, shadowed lane, we emerged into a spacious plaza bleached white by moonlight. A large fountain dominated the center of this somber area, long devoid of water. Sparse clumps of dead wheatgrass reached up out of the sandy cistern with rustling golden skeleton fingers. We were surrounded by a towering council of two and three-story sandstone villas, cleft into a dozen blocks by slender alleys that tapered into darkness at every angle.

Buffering us from those swarthy cracks were old marketplace

stands, draped in tattered canvas in faded shades of a thousand colors. They displayed worthless wares: tiny animal bones picked clean by scavengers, threadbare rugs, dry and withered husks that must once have been fruit, pottery scoured smooth by windblown sand and lying broken on the ground.

The sky was an unbroken dome of deepest black velvet, strewn with a billion glittering diamonds through which pulsed a constant slow beat of twinkling luminescence. Perching in the western half was a giant bone-white moon three times the size of the one I'd come to know, its pockmarked china face foreign and unknown to me, a stranger dressed in my brother's clothes. Another, smaller orange moon hung in front of it like a mask. The orbs were either so large or so close that I could see individual craters and valleys on their surfaces.

I crept closer to one of the stalls, and found a rack of tarnished jewelry. Some of it was scattered across the counter; I let my hand rake softly over it, my fingertips brushing against semiprecious stones I still had trouble believing. I saw no deep blue minerals, none of the gold-flecked lapis lazuli I had become familiar with in the desert the previous year.

I was surprised, however, when my rumination was interrupted by the shock of cold gunmetal. Lying underneath the necklaces and earrings was an ancient revolver.

I picked it up and opened the cylinder, relieved to find cartridges in four of the six chambers. "I found a gun," I told Sawyer, hurrying to show him. When I tilted it so that he could see it, the pistol's polished flank reflected the moonlight in a flash of cold white that blinded my right eye for a second. The afterimage had a strange shape in it; I took a closer look at the nickel-plated surface and saw a tiny coat-of-arms behind the cylinder, below the hammer. "Look at this weird shield on the side of it."

Sawyer nodded, panning the camera around. "Keep it ready,

man. This place, it's . . . there's something here. Somebody is watching us. We're not safe. We're not safe. We're not alone."

I eased back the hammer until it caught, and held it in the three-point stance I remembered from my MP days carrying a nine-millimeter Beretta. It'd been years since I'd had anything to do with a sidearm, but standing there holding it brought back the feeling as if it had been just yesterday that I was taking my place at the firing line of the M9 range on Fort Leonard Wood, Missouri. *Move your selector switch from safe, and watch . . . your lane,* said the range safety in the back of my mind.

I sensed movement in the corner of my eye and my head jerked to regard it, but the window I'd noticed, far above the street, was only a black hole. Something else made me turn and point the six gun at an empty doorway.

An electronic *bink* told me that Sawyer was doing something with the camera. His face, limned with pale green, gradually fell as he stood there, replaying the video he'd been recording since we brought the mirror to the church. His features flashed from anxious clarity to astonished fear. He rewound the video, then wordlessly turned the camera around and pointed the viewfinder at me.

On the screen, we were creeping down the alley again; the camera hovered here and there, rising to higher vantage points for a quick peek into the windows looking down on the thin space. The video-Sawyer approached a window and held the camera over his head. The windowsill sank out of sight and the lens was thrust into a blackness that resolved into a blur of green, which focused until I could see the interior of the room beyond.

Inside was a table, set with bowls, cups, and dishes, ostensibly arrayed with food long since rendered decrepit. A painting hung on the wall, one corner ripped and dog-eared. A dusty bookshelf stood to the left, littered with the detritus of a life of memories: framed

116

photos, figurines. The video was too grainy to make out any meaningful details from the pictures.

The camera panned to the right. I immediately noticed something in that corner of the room, on the other side of the table.

A man-like figure lurked there, hunched over, nearly shapeless, a ghost made of cobwebs.

As the infrared light of the camcorder's nightvision illuminated it, the shape slowly turned to look at the camera. It was dressed in the deteriorating remnants of some sort of linen robe. A chill shot through me as it began to creep toward the window before video-Sawyer walked away with the camera.

I checked the pistol again and slapped the cylinder back into place.

"I think I might know what that is," said Sawyer. "And it's not good."

"What is it?" I asked, my eyes canting in his direction. There was a white-faced figure standing behind him.

I raised the gun and pointed it over his shoulder; Sawyer must have thought I was aiming at him, so he dove out of the way. As soon as he hit the ground, he started scrambling away from the creature. It was clad in a gauzy shroud, and had a pale face that resembled a white hockey mask, only with a long nose and crowned with large, triangular ears. I thought of plague masks I'd seen doctors wear in pictures of medieval Britain during the time of the Black Death.

It studied us with lifeless, yet intense black eyes; simple markings had been fingerpainted across its cheeks and brow in some dark ichor.

"It's a Wilder," said Sawyer, getting to his feet and hiding behind me, pointing the camera at the thing. "One of the Bemo-

117

Epneme. You're not going to believe why, or how, I know that."

"What?" I asked, backing away as it came closer.

My hand, and the gun in it, was beginning to tremble. The "Wilder" continued to move toward us on nimble feet, gliding-floating like a spectre. As it drew near, I could hear the being behind the mask breathing, hissing venomously. Ice crashed through my veins.

I caught a flicker of movement in my peripheral vision. I looked up and saw that more of them were easing out of the windows of the buildings around us like paper Halloween ghosts. They looked like barn owls, staring at us with those horrible black eye sockets.

"These creatures," said Sawyer. "They're from your father's books. I have no idea why we're here looking at them. And that gun ain't gonna do us any good. There are way too many of them and only two of us. We gotta *run*."

I looked over my shoulder at him.

Sawyer roared, his voice reverberating in the hollow plaza, *"Run! OR DIE!"*

A Wilder Shade of Pale

I FIRED A SHOT into the face of the Wilder coming toward me, but he sidestepped it in a deft, casual way, as if he were simply making room for a passer-by. He didn't even flinch or cry out, he just kept moving toward me, soundless, a murder-minded shark. My heart thundered in my chest as Sawyer pointed to our nine-o-clock and hissed, "That way!"

I glanced there and found a break in the incoming phalanx of ghosts.

We fled, cutting through a stall arrayed with a display of rotten clothes that flagged in the wind. Ripping through the shrouds, we found ourselves in a black space that funneled into an alleyway.

We took that and ran.

I held out the cellphone and the pistol at arm's length, aiming them both from side to side. Sinewy, bestial claws rose out of windows as we passed them, long, corded arms that pulled white-faced spectres from inside the hulks looming over us. They spilled into the night air in our wake.

"This way," said Sawyer, cutting right.

I assumed we could make it back to the millhouse this way, but a sheer brick wall blocked us. It turned out to be a hook in the path and we ran to the left, bursting out into a small sitting area where two stone benches faced a collapsed merchant stall.

One of our adversaries was crouching on the pile of garbage, and as we passed it, it reached into the folds of its cloak and drew a dagger, leaping at me. I put a deafening bullet in it at about seven inches.

It dropped at my feet, but was immediately up again, slashing at me with a ferocious blade.

"Keep moving!" screamed Sawyer.

By now, he had abandoned trying to videotape the situation, and was pumping both arms, sprinting at full power, no doubt sending the image on the camera into unintelligible fits.

Dark, silent ghosts were emerging from every shadow and hole as we ran, curious and lethal.

We came into a T-junction and cut right. Before we made it to the end of the alley, I looked behind us and caught a glimpse of a dark shape standing motionlessly at the other end, holding something long that looked like a sword.

I could hear footsteps that were not our own. The shape was chasing us.

We rounded a corner, Sawyer flailing to keep his balance, and ran into a dead end.

Without hesitation, he threw one leg up and breach-kicked a door open with a hollow *crack*—*"Eeeyah!"*—then disappeared into the dark doorway like a rabbit into a burrow.

I followed him into a jet-black nothingness, tripping over the threshold, fumbling at Sawyer's sweater, almost tumbling. The sound of soft, running footfalls came to me from somewhere, and then the sound of a bootsole gritting across a rooftop overhead.

Someone broke a window, and a loud *thump* from the ceiling sent a paroxsym of panic through me. I barked my shin on a chair, hit a table with my hip, dishes crashed unseen to the floor.

I slipped on the pieces and righted myself, brushed against threadbare fabric. A vicious snarl ripped the air right in front of me. I could see Sawyer's nightvision camera glowing to my left.

121

I pushed away from the table, ran my shoulder into a doorway, almost knocking myself down.

"Here!" I heard him growl. Another startling *bang* was followed by a flood of moonlight from a rectangle in front of me. A shadow ran through it and I followed it into the night.

We were in a dead, enclosed garden. Strips of white cloth dangled, tugged by the air, tied to stakes driven into lifeless, plowed rows. The buildings directly around us were low, only one story tall.

The shadows of the windmill's arms passed over us at regular intervals; I could hear the canvas flapping with a throaty *crump-crump, crump, crump-crump*. Sawyer ran toward a wooden crate and meant to hurdle up it to grab the eaves, but when he put his foot on it, it disintegrated, swallowed his leg to the knee with a dry crunch.

I helped him up, panting, struggling to speak, "Somebody following us."

"I know—over there," Sawyer said, and ran away.

Another of the ghost-faced figures was coming out of a nearby window, perching nimbly on the sill like a buzzard on a fencepost. When it saw me, it called loudly, its piercing, metallic scream reverberating in the valley of shadows and mudbrick.

My blood tore through me in fear, frozen rocket fuel in my veins. I could hear my heart hammering in my rib cage, driving spikes into my dry throat.

I found Sawyer leaning a table against a wall at the back of the garden. He ran up it and lifted himself onto the roof, but when he pushed off he splintered the wood.

As I attempted to use it as a ramp myself, it broke and sent me sprawling shoulderfirst into the wall below.

"Shit!" I said, landing on my back. An open hand thrust down

at my face as I got up; Sawyer had clipped the camera to his belt and was reaching for me. I grasped his palm, put the revolver in my pocket, and he grunted as I began to try to billy-goat up the wall. I looked over my shoulder.

One of the masked creatures was no more than a meter from my back, his tattered cloak billowing around him like stormclouds.

I started to scream, but there was a strange, sibilant *shick* sound, accompanied by a spray of red across my legs. The Wilder's head spun free of its torso and twirled into the dust; the rest of it collapsed at my feet and lay still.

Standing behind it was a slender figure, draped in a dark cranberry-red hooded cloak, a sheer veil concealing his face. A leather crucifix bisected the veil.

He flourished the blood from his strange long-handled broadsword and feinted at me.

I flexed my arm, reaching up, clawing at Sawyer's shoulder, fighting up onto the roof. Sawyer fell backwards and I on top of him.

I rolled to my feet and looked down at the swordsman standing in the garden ruins.

He looked up at us; I could see the lower half of his face in the moonlight. *"Kah t'vam!"* he spat in some plosive language, the childlike voice of someone not quite yet a man. "Keem a-tra agama-nam!"

And then, as we watched, the swordsman disappeared in a diffusion of matter, a silent explosion that scattered him to nothing. He wasn't there anymore. It was like he'd simply stepped out of reality, ceased to exist.

We ran. Sawyer took three steps and the corrugated tin roof collapsed with a horrendous crash; he bounced off of the top of the wall underneath and I almost made it to the other side before a rafter broke and sent me sailing into a dark hallway below.

A nail scratched my back as I fell. I landed in a hail of cloudy dust beside Sawyer, who was coughing, the breath knocked out of him.

I kicked, wrestling with the debris, stood up, helped Sawyer stand. He was grunting, keening like a dying calf, trying to breathe: *"Hhhhhnnnnngh!"* I saw a sliver of moonlight and kicked at it. A door shattered, flying into grey-blue light and I pulled Sawyer through.

We were in another alley. Sawyer was drooling, holding his stomach. "You okay?" I asked.

I quickly checked him for injuries; nothing was protruding from his gut, but there was a rivulet of blood running down one arm. He nodded, staggering a bit, waved me off.

We kept running and six seconds later we were in front of the windmill, facing two more members of the Bemo-Epneme that were coming toward us from the other end of the way.

I snatched the door open and shoved Sawyer inside with my body, then spun and slammed the door shut.

"My father's books?!" I said, overturning a table. I dragged it in front of the door and started throwing bags of cornmeal behind it. "You said Dad's books?"

Sawyer was bent over, his hands on his knees, wheezing. "Yeah," he croaked, and straightened up. His face was red. "Books."

I grabbed his sweater and dragged him toward the storage bin at the back of the millhouse.

"Ah, Jesus," I said, when we got to the back.

We were staring at a blank wall. There was no doorway.

I took out my cellphone and shined it at Sawyer. He had tears in his eyes that threatened to come tumbling out, and he was holding his left arm. I went to pull out the revolver and realized my pockets were empty. I'd lost the gun somewhere; probably in the roof collapse. I swore several times and kicked the wall, producing a deep thud.

"No gun!" said Sawyer, crawling over to the corner of the bin. He squeezed into a ball and hugged his knees. I joined him, and put a finger to my lips. "Shh."

Pale shafts of moonlight fell through the cracks in the wooden ceiling, made solid by the meal dust. It was a bisected bin lid that opened in the middle and hinged out to either side. Soundless shadows coursed back and forth overhead, sending the beams of light flickering in epileptic mania.

I heard footsteps in the front of the millhouse. Someone was walking toward us.

Sawyer shook bodily, trembling harder than I'd ever seen anybody tremble.

A pale bald head came into the moonlight, crowned with a pair of goat horns. Sloping lavender shoulders came into view, and fiery yellow eyes flared to life, regarding us with amusement.

Clayton thanked the girl and closed the door on her. She was winsome, he gave her that, but he dared not lay a hand on her; not even to help her out of a pit of snakes. The Grievers were nasty customers and would brook no transgressions on any of their number, no matter how slight.

He crept over to the edge of the fire-lit platform and strained his eyes to see down the dark tunnel to the left and the right. The catacombs clattered with the distant echo of falling water, making it hard to get his bearings in the gloom. He sat down and felt with his toes, trying to find purchase, and slid until there was no hope of pulling himself back up.

At the point of no return, his fingertips slipped and he fell into the water like a log, touching bottom and bobbing back up. The bitch was down here somewhere, he thought, as he clasped the airtight waterskin with his pistols inside. He would swim all night if that's what it took.

—The Fiddle and the Fire, vol 5 "The Blade and the Bone"

Muffins

I OPENED MY EYES. I was in darkness, enveloped in some soft, binding material. Visions of giant spiders and cotton-candy cocoons filled my mind, exacerbated by a terrifying, buzzing, obnoxious screech from somewhere to my right. I threw an arm in that direction and hit something hard.

The screeching stopped. I sat upright.

Weak daylight streamed in around heavy drapes, diffused by diaphanous curtains. I slid out of the bed and ripped the curtains open, revealing another gray day in Blackfield.

The interstate traffic poured past, coursing down the freeway, a river of raw nerves and subsonic steel. The sky was a dark, pendulous iron belly, once again threatening to unleash on the people below.

There was a family in the parking lot loading their minivan for the next leg of their journey, and their youngest, a chubby little girl in pigtails, was screaming her desire for pancakes. I blinked in confusion, unable to form any coherent inner dialogue except for that which came naturally to the front of my mind. *The whole thing was a dream?*

I was still wearing yesterday's clothes. I found my cellphone lying on the bedsheet. It was dead. I plugged it into the wall charger, but nothing happened; I couldn't even turn it on. I thought about using the room phone to call Sawyer, but I couldn't remember his number without looking at my phone's contact list.

I stood in the parking lot, my fists on my hips, and sighed. My car was evidently still at the church, because it wasn't here at the hotel.

How the hell did I get back from the house?

Did we even *go* to Dad's house?

This was going to be a hell of a walk, especially if it started raining. I went back to the room and got my jacket—no, in case I was gone too long to renew my room, I got all my stuff and took it to—ahh, shit, no car.

I tightened my rucksack's straps, pulled my hood over my head, and started walking.

* * *

Cap'n Pacino's Coffee Cafe was busy this morning, but not packed. It was a classy place, if a bit kitschy, with booths that resembled the seats in a dinghy and a bar that looked minimally like the bulwark of a galleon, festooned with a faux-aged rope. The whole thing had a sort of art-nouveau nautical theme like a waterfront pirate tavern, if pirates were known to plunder Seattle in the year 2040.

There were sleek white life rings and stylized green anchors on the walls, along with dreary expressionist paintings of storm-tossed seas and lonely lighthouses and riotous scenes of pirate bacchanalia, and everything was done in shades of tan, bottle-green, and driftwood-gray.

There were at least three laptop screens glowing in the booths as I pushed the wooden door open and humped it inside with my over-stuffed rucksack like some kind of backpacker Santa Claus.

I went to the counter and ordered the strongest mocha I could find on the chalkboard over the bar. I was going to need the energy to make it all the way to the Hampton Inn on the other side of town. I was standing around waiting for my coffee when I heard a familiar voice chirp behind me.

"Ross?" It was Noreen Mears. She was sitting by herself in a booth, watching the news on a flatscreen bolted to the wall in the corner, her pull-behind suitcase on the booth seat next to her.

I collected my mocha and crammed my pack into the booth, sitting next to it.

"What are you doing here?" I asked. "I thought you took off for home."

"I got about six miles out of town," she said, and sipped her own drink. I could smell peppermint. "My transmission ate shit. I had to get a tow back here, and I had to sleep in my car overnight because with the repair bill, I didn't have enough money for another motel room. Can you believe it took the tow truck three hours to get out to me? Is that not some bullshit?"

"I agree. Hey, if you need a place to stay tonight, I'll spot you."

"Oh, thank you. I hate to put you out, though."

"It ain't no thang," I said, burning my tongue with my coffee, which had apparently been extracted from the center of the earth. I coughed, making a face, and Noreen chuckled. "Hot?"

I sucked air, and stared at her hands thoughtfully, noticing that she was a nailbiter. Finally, I said, "Something happened last night."

The girl tilted her head, smirking, her brow furrowed. "That sounds ominous. Do I want to know?"

I gave her a reproachful look and traced the rim of the cardboard sleeve with my thumb. "No, something really, *really* weird happened, and I'm not entirely sure it was even real. Hell, the last few days have been a little bit unreal, to be honest."

It occurred to me that I'd never said anything to Noreen

130

about the demon I'd seen in the closet, and now had seen in the mysterious millhouse and the gilded mirror. I told her about what had happened that first night, when I'd gone by myself to Ed Brigham's house and saw the horned man, and, later, Sawyer and I delving into the mystery and coming up empty-handed.

She seemed skeptical. "Maybe you're just really stressed out from your dad's funeral. My sister used to see shadow-people when she had throat cancer."

"Really?"

"Yeah, but I think it was because she didn't get much sleep, with the pain and the chemo making her sick all the time."

"I believe it. Sleep deprivation can do that," I said, and scalded myself again with a wince. "But I don't think that's the case here. For one thing, Sawyer saw it too. What happened last night, we were side-by-side for. We *saw* some shit."

I sounded like a Vietnam vet. *We saw some shit, man, it was rough out there, Bubba.*

"You'll have to get a little more specific than 'shit'," Noreen said.

"*Crazy* shit."

"Woah," she interjected, "Too *much* detail. Just the facts, ma'am."

I chuckled. "Well, after you left yesterday, me and Sawyer— we went back to my dad's house to get his laptop, and I ended up dragging the mirror out of the closet so I could look at it."

"The demon closet?"

"The very same. And then . . . something happened. I don't know what. It was like . . . we were on auto-pilot. Like we'd been hypnotized and we started sleepwalking. I don't even remember thinking, *we need to take the mirror out of the house,* it just—happened. I was standing there with the mirror, and the next thing I know, we

131

were putting it in the back of my car, and then we were at the church."

"The church?" asked Noreen. "Walker Memorial?"

"Yeah. And then we were taking it down to the cellar. I don't know why; it was like the whole thing was our idea, but it *wasn't*, too. Does that make sense?"

"Not one bit. But continue."

I recounted how we discovered the mirror door, and the abandoned city beyond.

"You guys know how to get your hands on the good stuff," said Noreen, with a sardonic smile. "Your dad must have had one hell of a stash."

I shook my head. "I don't do drugs, you goon. Anyway, these creepy people—"

"People?" asked Noreen. Her wiseacre skepticism had started to transform into genuine concern.

"I don't know what they were or if they were even human, but Sawyer said he knew what they were. He said—and I'd swear on a stack of Bibles—that he knew them from my dad's novels. He called them *Wilders*."

Noreen's eyebrows shot straight up. *"Wilders?"*

"Yes. We ran from them and there was somebody there chasing us." I told her about the swordsman chasing us, and the goat-horned man in the grain bin.

"What about Sawyer? Have you talked to him?"

"No," I said, showing her my dead phone. "I don't know his number."

Noreen took out her own phone and dialed Sawyer, then put the phone to her ear and listened. "Hey, sweetie. Call me back when you get this message. Thanks," she said, and immediately got up out of the booth. I understood without having to be told.

*   *   *

We were marching down the sidewalk a couple blocks from Cap'n Pacino's, warming our hands with hot coffee cups, when Noreen said, "That person with the sword that you said you saw; I don't think that was a man."

"How could you possibly know that?" I demanded, but I knew the answer as soon as the question came out of my mouth.

"Well, you told me that you saw Wilders there, wherever you were. It doesn't make a bit of sense, but if I completely abandon all remaining semblance of tangible reality here and take what you've told me at face value, then according to *Fiddle* lore, the person you saw was a Griever, or a *swordwife*, in the book's more casual slang."

"The hell is a Griever?" I asked, stepping onto a redbrick planter-wall built out front of a law office. I tightroped down it beside Noreen as she ate up the sidewalk, walking and talking, pulling her suitcase behind her on noisy wheels.

"You haven't really read any of the books, have you?" she asked. "They're kinda like nuns, except they're like Amazon warriors. Look, in book five, *The Blade and the Bone*, your dad established that certain women are enlisted specially to fight No-Men."

"Certain women?"

"Widows," she said. "The House of the Forge sends emissaries around the world of Destin to find and indoctrinate war widows into their culture. The House was established as a way to mobilize those that lost loved ones to the war to rid the world of the ones that killed them. It's a bit of a cross between a Ladies' Auxiliary and a kung-fu monastery."

133

"That's crazy as hell," I said, hopping down off the end of the planter wall.

"Not as crazy as the main subplot of that book. You see, when widows are brought into the fold, they're trained in the ways of swordsmanship. The only way you can end a No-Man is with a blade. So all the widows are trained in swordfighting and then, at the end of their training, they have to forge their own sword in a ceremony not unlike marriage. Basically, they're remarried to the sword they create, and they never, ever take another lover for the rest of their lives.

"It's an unbreakable bond, punishable by imprisonment in the catacombs underneath the House. There are rituals after that, for other things, but the sword ceremony is the true dividing line that you could say separates the girls from the women."

"So you said the subplot was crazy. What happened?"

"Are you sure you want the spoilers?"

"Yeah."

Noreen took a deep breath, "Well, in *The Blade and the Bone*, the Kingsmen found out that Ancress Bachelard was secretly ordering the murder of dozens of men in a concerted effort to fill the House's ranks and create an army she was going to use to overthrow the King.

"She was defeated and killed by Normand Kaliburn's squire Clayton Rollins at the end of the book, and now they're all knights-errant, like *ronin* samurai, wandering Destin looking for No-Men to eliminate and killing other horrible things and devious people for pocket money. They're basically bounty hunters now. After the Ancress's betrayal, they're not exactly popular, but they're treated a hell of a lot better than the Redbirds."

"I'm starting to wish I'd read the series now," I admitted.

"I'm starting to wish you'd read it too. I don't know what's going on, but regardless of whether you both had a serious mental break, or got baked on some top-shelf grass you found in your dad's house, or the two of you walked through a magic wardrobe into E. R. Brigham's dark-fantasy novels, this is some profoundly messed-up shit."

I heartily concurred that this definitely qualified as quote-unquote *messed-up shit,* although I was a bit offended at the wardrobe jibe. "It was a mirror, not a wardrobe."

She gave me a sharp look.

"You keep mentioning 'No-Men'," I said, grabbing at a change of subject. "Who—or what—are they?"

"It's a long story. Honestly, you'd be better off reading the books."

"Let's say, hypothetically speaking, that I'm a terribly impatient man."

We kept walking for a little while in an artificially cool and uncomfortable silence. I could sense her assembling and arranging the information in her mind. Finally, she looked over to me and said, "You're going to ruin it for yourself."

"I'll survive. If you don't fill me in, I might not."

She sighed and said, "I'll start with the basics, give you a Cliff's Notes version of how the series started. The Antargata k-Setra—affectionately referred to as 'K-Set'— is where the bulk of the *Fiddle and the Fire* series takes place. A couple of generations before the beginning of the first novel, a large medieval nation— the country of Ain—began to send explorers to the farthest reaches of the world of Destin looking for new territory and resources.

"With seventeen large, well-provisioned ships, the explorers embarked on an expedition from the western shores of Ain across the massive Aemev Ocean. Nearly a year later, the final remaining

135

ships finally reached the shores of what the remaining crew called 'the Undiscovered Continent'.

"By this time, the survivors were only a fraction of the initial party, having dwindled from around five hundred and forty to just a little under two hundred men and women. When they landed, they were astonished to see the ruins of tall, slender buildings in the distance.

"See, the Undiscovered Continent held the very last vestiges of an ancient and very advanced civilization, isolated from the rest of the world by the ocean. No one really knows anything about them, and no one can read their language."

We stopped to wait for a traffic light to change. As the cars trundled by, their music fading past in disconnected snippets of noise, Noreen continued to talk.

"The 'Wilders' you saw are a nomadic tribe of humanoids that inhabited K-Set long before the people of Ain began to attempt to colonize it. They call themselves the *Bemo-Epneme*. At first, the Wilders were leery of the explorers from Ain, but after several months they were trading with each other.

"That's when Ainean expansionists began to send scouting parties into K-Set, looking for resources and places to establish new settlements and outposts. As you can imagine, the Wilders weren't too happy with these strangers overtaking parts of their territory, so they started attacking the expansionist parties."

The traffic slowed to a stop and Noreen and I jogged across the street. When we reached the other side, we passed in front of a deli getting ready for the day's business, filling the air with the smell of baking bread and roasting meats. The aroma made my stomach knot up in anticipation.

"By the time the colonists left Ain for the voyage to K-Set, Ain had invented firearms and crude machinery, like clockworks and steam engines. Guns were the deciding factor in the new war

136

against the Wilders; in several years, the colonists had penetrated the mainland of K-Set and built several towns and farms in a free-homestead expansion.

"It was a war of attrition. Basically, if you could take it and survive on it, it was yours. There were some Aineans, though, that sympathized with the Wilders, and broke away from colonist society to form adversarial groups—some of them actually began to cohabitate with the Bemo-Epneme, even stepping into the more primal lifestyle of the Wilders."

"Is this ever going to get to the No-Men?" I asked with a smirk.

"Be patient, you jerk," she said. "So, it turned out that the Wilders worship a god called 'Obelus', an entity that was responsible for the destruction of the civilization that had ruled over K-Set centuries before *The Fiddle and the Fire*. They prayed to this god, desperate for salvation from the invaders, and finally, one day, Obelus answered them.

"At the end of the first book, *The Brine and the Bygone*, a large expedition of settlers were slaughtered by something at the farthest frontier of Ainean territory. Only two people survived the attack: the boy Pack and a settler named Aarne Hargrave. Pack escaped unhurt to a far-flung sympathist fortress where the second book, *The Cape and the Castle*, took place.

"Aarne made it back to their camp three days' march away, where he died of his injuries, but not before warning the Kingsmen captain there of what devastated them. The captain asked him if the attackers were men, and Aarne's last words were, 'No . . . they are no men.' It stuck.

"As for what they are, your dad never really went into much detail about them—he always portrayed them as mysterious lurking giants, never really showing the 'face behind the mask'. In the second book, Pack gets a good look at a dead No-Man while he's

137

imprisoned by the Wilder sympathists.

"He describes a 'monolithic golem made of some strange metal he couldn't identify; a heavy, vaguely human figure all draped in the overgrowth of the ruins'."

My coffee cup was cold and empty when I saw the spires of Walker Memorial reaching over the trees. The cars on Main Street whooshed past us in an endless multicolored stream of steel and lights as we approached the church.

I bypassed the building itself and went straight to the parking lot, where I spotted my car right in the place I'd parked it the previous afternoon. I cursed when I saw the white square on the windshield, but it turned out to be nothing more than a promotional pamphlet for an upcoming street festival, turned spongy and sloppy by the condensation on the glass.

I scooped the wet paper off and unlocked my car, put my rucksack inside. I was going to head into the church to check on the mirror, but Noreen had already climbed into the passenger side of the Topaz and was sitting there, her arms folded, her mouth pursed tight.

I got in and started the car. We were pulling into traffic when she said, "If he's not in his room, I'm going to—gonna—I don't know what I'm gonna do."

*   *   *

I caught myself doing sixty twice on the way across town; the entire path was a forty-five zone. It's a wonder I never attracted the ire of the local police. I pulled into the parking lot of the Hampton so fast that the ass-end of my car scraped the pavement as we crossed the frontage.

Noreen was already climbing out as I parked the car and

turned it off. I fell out of the door, putting my hand in a rain puddle, and ran to catch up to her. We nearly sprinted through the lobby, where the desk clerk started to ask us about our reservation, and went directly to the elevator.

Noreen jabbed the up-button a rapid-fire ten or fifteen times. I could hear the cab inside moving, but it simply wasn't fast enough. She walked away, shoved the door open to the stairwell, and ran up the stairs, throwing her coffee cup into a nearby trash can.

Two flights of climbing later, and we were beelining down the third floor hallway toward 312. Noreen pounded on the door with one tight fist and waited.

Silence.

She beat on it again, faster and harder. "Sawyer! Are you in there?"

"Sawyer—?" I called, kicking the door lightly a few times for deep thumps that echoed down the lushly-carpeted corridor.

Nobody came to the door. Noreen stepped back as if she were going to try to kick it open, and thought better of it. *"Goddam it!* We need to get a key and get this door open," she said, obviously starting to panic. There was a wild look in her eye. "We need to get this door open!"

I jiggled the doorhandle in desperation. It was definitely locked.

Noreen turned and stormed past me in the opposite direction, and then stopped short. I turned to follow her and paused as well.

Sawyer was standing at the corridor intersection, clad only in a pair of jeans and socks, his hair wet and spiky. "What's all the yelling about?" he asked. "I told you I was in 321, you crazy-people."

Noreen ran at him and embraced him so hard she almost

139

knocked him down.

"Woah," he said with a smile. "Nice to see you too. I thought you left?"

We followed Sawyer back to his room and I started searching it, shaking out the clothes that were lying around and peeling back the bedsheets. I was looking through his bags when Sawyer interrupted me.

"Hey there officer, do you have a search warrant for that?"

I sat back and exhaled. The room was warm and swampy, and from where I was sitting, I could see that the bathroom mirror was foggy. "Where's your camera?"

"I dunno," he replied. "I guess I left it at your dad's house last night. The hell did we get into? I don't remember any booze, but it must've been something strong. The last thing I remember is going through the stuff in your dad's bedroom, and then I was waking up in my bed wearing all my clothes."

I sighed.

Sawyer shrugged. "And for some reason, I was covered in flour or cornmeal. Did we get drunk and bake something? I don't remember muffins. I would definitely have remembered muffins— maybe not *bran* muffins."

"Why didn't you answer your phone, you asshole?" asked Noreen, shoving him lightly. It was more of a pushing slap.

He shrugged, and picked up his phone, checking the screen. "Like I told you, I woke up gross. I guess you called me while I was taking a shower."

I sighed. "No proof at all. I look like a psycho."

"Proof of what?" asked Sawyer, knuckling one eye. "You don't need proof to look like a psycho."

"Proof that we walked through a mirror under the church and into the world in my dad's books, that's what!"

140

Sawyer's eyes got as big as silver dollars and he dropped his phone. The battery cover popped off and it slid under the bed. "Are you *shitting me?*" he asked, getting down on his hands and knees to look for it. "I had a dream about that. Are you telling me I didn't dream that? That happened *for real?*"

"Hell yeah, it happened for real," I said, squatting next to him.

He found his phone and put it back together. Once he'd turned it back on, he stared at it for a moment in thought, then looked up at me. "Didn't you take a picture with your phone?"

(I gazed up at the windows as we passed them, fearing the sight of some guarded, unwelcoming, half-glimpsed face, and whispered to Sawyer. I took a picture with my cellphone.)

I nodded. "I remember doing that, but my phone is dead," and blinked. "Why isn't yours?"

"I left it in my room when I went with you to Ed's house."

"Oh."

"Well," said Noreen, throwing Sawyer a shirt, "Now that we know Sawyer's non-phone-answering ass is okay, I think we should hie thee to the church and see if that mirror is still there. You two have me crawling with curiosity."

141

A Heart-to-Heart

I DID NOT EXPECT to find the church locked up tighter than a—
"Tighter than a hooker with lockjaw," said Sawyer, coming around
the corner to join us. We had been all around the perimeter of the
sprawling church and found no entry whatsoever. Noreen and I
both froze mid-step and laughed at him. He came toward us,
shrugging it off.

"Got any more bright ideas, Columbo?"

Noreen looked up at the castle-like church and let her arms
drop to her sides. "You guys really had me going. Were you telling
the truth about what happened? Are you playing a prank on me or
something?"

"I wish I could say I was," I said. "But as far as I can tell,
unless both of us are having identical hallucinations, it really
happened."

I let my hands drop to my sides, consternated.

"I have to admit, this is getting a little weird," said Noreen.
"I'm not sure what to think anymore."

Sawyer shrugged helplessly. I felt like a fraud; no, worse, I felt
like I might actually be losing my marbles after all. I couldn't deny
how crazy it all sounded, and even now I was having trouble
reconciling the surreality of the previous night myself. I looked
around at the parking lot; we were the only ones that had a car
here.

As I thought about the situation, a sensation of warmth

142

spread across the back of my neck; when I turned back around, the morning sun was breaking through the clouds. I was momentarily blinded by a force of golden light.

I shielded my eyes against the searing glare and canted my head away—and saw it.

"Look," I said, thrusting a finger. "There's a window open on the third floor. You see it? There, behind that—the—"

"The buttress?" said Sawyer.

"—Yes, the buttress. Up there."

We assembled at the base of the wall. It was a sheer vertical drop of thirty, maybe forty feet from the window to the ground. The sand-colored bricks used to construct the building were easily as large as any cinder block, if not larger; they seemed to have been mortared so that there was a horizontal gap of an inch or so between layers.

The face of each block was rough and uneven, presenting ledges and crags here and there along the wall surface.

I glanced back at the others and wedged a couple of fingers into the gap between the bricks as an experiment. Then I hopped up and put a foot on a thin ledge that protruded just enough to catch the edge of my shoe.

"Oh, I know you're not doing what I think you're doing," said Sawyer. "Are you seriously going to climb that?"

"I've climbed worse," I said, hugging the wall and reaching up to another gap.

I hopped down and rubbed my hands, and took off my jacket, handing it to Noreen. It was a nice one, a recent purchase, made of coffee-colored leather, and had a gray hood sewn into the lining that made it look as if I had on a sweatshirt underneath. "I need some kind of dust. My hands are sweaty and they're only going to get sweatier."

143

"You're in luck," Noreen said, but took two steps in the opposite direction and threw her hands in the air, making a frustrated noise. "Never mind, I don't have my talcum powder with me because I don't have my *car* with me."

"Why do you have talcum powder?" I asked.

Sawyer made a snipping motion at his scalp with his fingers. "She cuts hair back home in Florida."

"Oh," I said, after a beat, and started climbing the wall anyway. There were walls to either side of me; we were in an alley deeply between two parallel walls, so I wasn't too concerned with being spotted by police officers that might take offense to me breaking into a church.

I forced my fingers into a crack and hoisted one foot onto a ledge. A thought occurred to me and I spoke over my shoulder, "Do either of you know how to pick a lock?"

A beat of silence, and then a simultaneous, "No."

"Then onward and upward it is," I said, and continued climbing.

I stood, lifting myself onto the bottom-most windowsill. I braced myself inside the windowframe and sat on the flat stone, then pulled my legs up, planting my feet on the narrow platform heel-to-toe Egyptian hieroglyph-style. That gave me a solid base to push off the inside of the window behind me and stand up, crouching like a gargoyle in the window.

I reached over the arch above me and found a new grip, then kicked my right leg up and found a new place to step, used it to lift myself. I traded hands and reached upward.

"This is crazy," reiterated Sawyer below. "What if you fall and get hurt? I'm guessing you probably don't have insurance."

"I figured you would catch me if I fell," I grunted. I was now just above the bottom window, clinging to the wall, a giant spider in a shirt too thin for the weather.

"Thou dost assume too much," he replied.

I made it to the second floor window and grasped the sill edge with both hands, preparing to pull myself inside like I'd done with the first one; as I began to drag myself upward, my foot slipped and my heart roared in my chest. My face grew hot with the rush of adrenaline as I dangled from the rim of stone. I gasped, scraped my left cheek hard across the rough brick.

The edge of the sill dug painfully into the tendons of my flexed fingers.

"Shit," said Noreen, her voice echoing faintly off the walls around me. "Watch out, I'm not taking you to the hospital. If you fall, you're fired before you hit the ground."

"Thanks, boss," I said, my shoe regaining traction on the wall surface. I clambered slowly into the second window and perched again. This time I stopped to rest, and as I turned to regard the church's back parking lot, I was nearly overcome by the vertigo of height.

From here, I could see into the residential neighborhood one street removed from Main Street. The narrow mouth of the alley only afforded me a view into the side windows of two houses, but that was enough. I could see a man standing at a kitchen sink washing dishes. At the other house, a teenager bundled in a heavy blanket was curled tightly in a bay window reading a book by the wan light of the cloudy day. She squeezed her nose with the wadded tissue in her free hand.

I shut my eyes tight and leaned my face against my own window behind me, calming my nerve with the shock of the wind-chilled glass. It was colored a dark bottle-green, which made it easy to see my own pallid expression.

"I can't believe this," I said to myself. "What am I doing?" *Do*

145

I really want to go back there? Back down into that dirt cellar, maybe even back through that mirror? A faint thrill of terror flared inside me as I considered it.

Suddenly, I wasn't sure if I was more afraid of falling, or getting caught breaking into a church, or of going back to that dark pueblo-city of weird ghosts.

I looked down, which was a mistake, and closed my eyes again.

"I can see my house from here," I called down, my voice breaking.

Sawyer swore long and low. "Be careful. This grass ain't as springy as it looks."

I reached over my head and grabbed the keystone again, and pulled myself up. My mind reeled back to my days as an MP, climbing up and down the obstacle walls on Fort Leonard Wood, and to the several months I spent on Fort Hood the year before I deployed, climbing the false wall at the gym down the street from the Transition Barracks.

I envisioned my grasping hands and feet on the pods screwed into the faux rock wall outside the basketball court, looking so much like giant wads of chewed bubble gum pressed onto the stone.

I surprised myself by sweating; it was so cool outside. A trickle of moisture crawled between my backbone and hip. My feet were freezing, my toes like icy monkey paw fingers in my shoes, slick with sweat and chilled. My fingers were raw and felt like the gnarled claws of Death.

As soon as the topmost windowsill was in reach, I grabbed it and scrambled toward it. I almost lost my balance at the last second, and I felt my center of gravity slide backwards, but I found the lock-handle on the inside of the windowpane and caught

146

myself.

I could hear the pane's hinge groan under the strain, but it held until I could lift myself into the window.

Immensely relieved, I sat on the windowsill as if it were a park bench and exhaled a slow stream of vapor-smoke, feeling for all the world like a dragon gazing out of his aerie.

"I made it," I said, and scooted backwards into the third floor of the church.

I was in some sort of office; luckily, there was no one in it other than myself. I stood behind a richly-appointed cherrywood desk with a calendar blotter on it, scribbled with various dates and short scripture passages. A clergy office, though which one, I had no idea. I wasn't even sure if Atterberry was the only clergyman in Walker Memorial, nor was I sure how it all even worked, to be honest.

The room was spacious, with walls and wainscoting the color of snow, and a dark red carpet. An American flag stood in one corner next to an ancient green filing cabinet. I checked the nameplate sitting on the desk: *Pastor's Assistant Janice Evers.*

The name made me feel even guiltier. I got out of there in a hurry.

Atterberry's office was next door, but I didn't go in, had no reason to. I went straight down the long hallway, past doorways labeled with positions like *Music Director, Educational Ministry Assistant,* etc. The Berber carpet under my feet muffled my steps as I moved into silence, isolated from the outside world and traffic by so much stone.

The wallpapered walls were lined with framed reproductions of what were probably historical architectural sketches from the county clerk's office, as well as landscapes and portraits of previous clergy. They eyed me from under their bristly brows as I walked, rolling my feet to stay silent.

At the end of the corridor was a creaky old wooden staircase. I jogged lightly down to the ground floor and came out next to the nave; instead of going down to open the door for Sawyer and Noreen, I succumbed to the temptation of curiosity and went into the nave to see if the mirror was still in the cellar.

The nave was virtually unchanged from yesterday except for the angle of the sunlight limping in through the stained glass; it was slightly darker, which in my solitude made it ominous and agoraphobic, especially when I looked up at the Big Brown Brooding Jesus looming over the altar.

He stared straight ahead with his dead, colorless Roman bust eyes, somehow oblivious and judgemental at the same time.

In this cavernous chapel, gutted hollow by the guilt and listlessness of a million parishioners, even my carpeted footsteps seemed to echo.

I went straight to the door in the vestibule. I wasn't surprised to see that it was locked, which I remedied with the key in my pocket. I stepped inside, and as before, I turned on my cellphone—or, at least, I tried, and remembered that it was dead. I stood there in the shadows for several seconds, confused about how to proceed, feeling like an idiot—worse, a *blind* idiot.

When I went back to the nave, I was walking slowly up the center aisle toward the altar, wondering where I could find a candle in the church (and something to light it with), when I heard a deep, eloquent voice from the darkness at the far end of the pews.

I spun to discover a man sitting in one of them, barely visible in the gloom behind the soft beam of sunlight. His feet were kicked up on the back of the pew in front of him. I squinted into the light to make out his features.

It was Maxwell Bayard. "Kid, I think we need to talk."

Naturally, I was shell-shocked, locked into place by indecision and confusion. I eventually said, "What are you doing here?" which sounded completely stupid as it came out of my big dumb mouth. My face burned with embarrassment and anticipation at being caught trespassing.

"Come here and sit down with me, amigo," said my father's agent. "I had a feeling I might run into you here."

I went over to his pew, my legs wooden and loose, and took a seat. My hands were shaking.

"Atterberry called me yesterday, told me he thought he'd seen you and that Winton kid in here after services," he said in his nasal, gravelly Kojak voice from the heavens, and paused for emphasis.

He was smoking a cigarette, and the blue curls of his smoke hung motionless in the air around his head like the rings of Saturn. "Now, to anybody else, that might or might not look shady, but luckily, as it goes, I might know a thing or two about why you might be in here. And why you're here now. How did you get in here, anyway?"

"I climbed in through a window in the assistant's office," I said, my voice barely above a whisper.

"Damn," Bayard said, his brow arching, frowning like an old catfish. "Third floor? That must've been a hell of a climb. I didn't even check up there. You're a tougher man than I thought. Chip off the old brick."

I heard a knock on the front door; Sawyer's faint voice came to us from outside. My new friends wanted in.

"They can wait," said the old man. "What I've got to talk to you about, they may not be too inclined to hear."

I blinked.

He seemed to be searching for the right words. "I'm guessing you're here looking for what your father called 'the Burrow'—a

149

door to another place. Would I be wrong . . . or would I be right?"

I didn't know what to say—so I told him the truth. "Yes."

"Hmm," he said, nodding. He took a drag off the cigarette, held it, and let the smoke ease out of his mouth and up his nose, then tilted his head back and blew it back out again like an enraged bull from a Looney Tunes short. "What convinced you to come here to begin with?"

I produced the key to the cellar door. "I found this in one of my dad's boxes. It opens that door over there."

"I'm not even going to question the dots you connected to get from Point Nowhere to Point Church. Your father was prone to similar jumps of logic," said Bayard. His head lowered again and he regarded me with those heavy-lidded hound dog eyes. "You share a lot with him, you know. You two have a lot in common. Moreso than you think."

I put the key back in my pocket and folded my arms, letting my silence urge him to continue.

"It took about a decade for your father to admit to me his . . . clandestine trips to this church, after I took him on as a client. It was another several years before he eventually decided to let me in on his secret. Or what I should say he thought was his secret.

"That there was, in fact, a secret door underneath this building that led to another world that he claimed was real. The world that he'd been writing about for half his life."

The old literary agent looked at me sadly and took a little Maglite out of his jacket pocket. "Come with me," he said, and rose to his feet. I heard something in him crackle as he put his hands on his knees and stood with a soft groan. "Indulge an old man."

We headed for the front area; as we walked, he said, "I was afraid—however improbable—that it might come to this. Atterberry's phone call yesterday confirmed my suspicions."

150

"What suspicions would that be?" I asked, and was answered with silence.

Bayard opened the cellar door and descended the stairs into the fierce white glow of his flashlight beam. When we got to the bottom, the low ceiling forced him to stoop and crane his neck sideways, his head just missing the rafters. He squinted in his cigarette smoke and stubbed it out on the dirt floor.

I found it hard to empathize with his discomfort, or really even pay attention, because my eyes were transfixed by the wall of the dirt cellar.

There was no tunnel.

Normand flinched as the huge sea-creature plucked Bennard Koila from the gunwales of the lifeboat. The man screeched like a scalded cat; the massive jaws closed over his torso and lifted him high into the air and left him there. He tumbled end over end for a long moment, then fell into the Saoshoma's open maw as it slammed shut like a gull snapping up a catch.

Clayton opened fire with his pistols, but the rounds simply bounced off its impenetrable hide. "Die, you poxy bastard! Why won't you just die?!"

—The Fiddle and the Fire, vol 4 "The Truth and the Trial"

Ramma-Lamma-Ding-Dong

THERE WAS NO WAY into the little room where we'd left the mirror the day before. I stared in disbelief. "I don't know—" began Bayard, and I realized that he was attempting to be tactful. "I don't know if you might have picked it up from his notes, or what—but your father believed that there was a door down here at the end of a tunnel that linked this world to another one. He claimed that when he was a little boy, he was exploring the building after dark when he was approached by a being that he called a *silen*.

"He said that the Sileni were a race of beings from outside of time, ancient mariners from a place called the 'Sea of Dreams', in the 'void-between-the-worlds', where concepts and creativity flowed and ebbed like water. An ocean of stories." He pronounced Sileni as if he were saying *silent-eye*.

I heard Sawyer knocking on the front door again. "The Vur Ukasha," I said.

"You've done your homework. Yes," said the agent, and he sat on the cellar stairs.

The flashlight illuminated his face from below as if he were telling a ghost story by the campfire. He looked as if he were a thousand years old. "Ed came to my house late one night in 1989, looking like he'd been up for days, I think it was March—April, maybe. Looked like shit, to be frank. Sat me down and told me the whole story sitting by my fireplace, nursing a glass of brandy . . . so it might behoove you to take everything I'm telling you with a grain of salt.

154

"According to him, at the beginning of time the Sileni made a deal with God. In exchange for the gift of immortality, they would scatter themselves to the wind, and seek out those worthy of receiving the waters of the Sea of Dreams. They were, in essence, *muses*," he said, making air quotes with his fingers.

"*The* Muses, in fact. Living tributaries of the Endless Story, the Vur Ukasha, the only ocean that deepens as you drain it, forever carrying away its waters to keep it from disappearing. One of them found your father deserving of the water and became his muse. Remember what I said about jumps of logic?"

"Ayuh," I said.

"Your father told me that the silen could put ideas in your head. Could make you do what he wanted and make you think it was your idea all along."

"That makes sense, being a muse. That—" I said, and abruptly cut myself off.

Bayard's head tilted, a questioning gesture.

"I wonder what made him come to you with this," I said, changing the subject. "This is some pretty crazy stuff."

"*Crazy* is what we thought, too, which is why I contacted your mother and told her that your father was having a breakdown. This was about the time he was trying to get over the sauce. He was—if you'll excuse me—fucked up beyond mortal limits. The shakes, hallucinations, the works."

I became more and more grim as he spoke. "If you're trying to say I'm having similar delusions, I've got a few epiphanies for you. Mainly, there's the fact that I'm not an alcoholic. The other is that when I found the door yesterday, Sawyer Winton was with me. And third, we had a camera with us."

"Was he?"

"Yes."

"You're positive."

My hesitation spoke volumes. "Yes."

"And the camera? Where is that?"

"We're not sure. I think it's at my dad's house, maybe. But I know we took it to the other world."

"To the *other world?* Listen to yourself, kid," Bayard said, his New York accent thickening; he was actually starting to talk out of the side of his mouth. The more he talked about the door, the more he began to resemble a skinny Rodney Dangerfield.

"Look, maybe this is something hereditary, some psychological thing that gets passed down on the paternal side, I don't know. But what I do know is that whatever it was, it was suckin the life out of your father year by year, bottle by bottle. And now that I see *you* might be sufferin from this delusion too, I can't let you push yourself down the same road he went down."

He paused and locked eyes with me. "I want you to forget finishing Ed's last book."

"*What?*" I amazed myself by being appalled at the idea.

"You heard me. I want you to drop it. I'm not going to stand by and watch you obsess over it like he did. I thought—well, I *hoped*—that a sober pair of eyes on this fat fucken thing would make a difference, but apparently it doesn't. I'm cutting you off. I don't want you in the same boat with him, on the bottom of the fucken lake—*forget it!*"

I loomed over him, and replied, "*You* were the one that talked me into taking the project on—" and he startled me by jumping— jack-knifing, nearly—up off the cellar steps and getting in my face, fists clenched, shaking a finger at my nose.

He was so close I could smell his hand and the sleeve of his wet tweed jacket, a curious combination of pipe tobacco and petrichor, and I could see my reflection in the reading glasses hanging on the collar of his sweater.

The sight of such an older man becoming so animated out of anger was a fundamental surprise, and it startled the hell out of me. "I don't think you understand who you're talking to, Ross!" he bellowed. "I'm the man that handles this goddamned property, and *you'll back off of it!*"

I recoiled at Bayard's sudden rage, speechless. He seemed to regain his bearings, evidently having taken himself aback as well. He tugged the lapels of his jacket, standing straighter, a vague look of impropriety passing across his thick features. He smoothed out his hoary salt-and-pepper beard, his thick, rubbery lips making an O.

"I'm sorry I lost my temper there," and then he added, staring at the floor, "Your father did not die of a heart attack, Ross. He was murdered. Nobody knows who did it."

He tugged back the sleeve of his jacket, looking at his Bulova wristwatch, and ran his hand over his balding pate. Before I could assemble a response, he turned and went back upstairs. I followed him at a distance, unable to find my voice.

When he opened the front door, I could see a confused Sawyer and Noreen on the other side of it, dappled in pale sunlight.

As he walked out, the literary agent turned to speak.

"I have a plane to catch," he said, his steely eyes softening with concern, and he jabbed the brim of his tartan trilby at me. "Stay away from this. Your father paid the price. That was a check your ass can't cash, and I'm not going to let you."

I took the vague threat at face value. He disappeared and my friends poured into the church with alarm on their faces. "What the hell was that about?" they asked, in unison.

"I'll tell you about it later," I managed to say, brushing past them and marching out the door.

157

*　*　*

We drove back to the Hampton so Noreen could renew her room, but when we got there, Sawyer came to his senses and offered her the bed in his room. I must have looked shaken, because neither of them spoke to me on the road.

"A little confident in yourself, aren't you?" Noreen asked Sawyer, depositing her suitcase in front of the closet.

"I'll be on the couch."

I took the opportunity to use the bathroom in Sawyer's suite and compose myself. I looked at my reflection in the mirror, wincing in the bright lights and horrifying myself with the crow's-feet on my face. My shaved head was beginning to grow out, no longer rough to the touch, and I needed a shave.

I leaned closer and examined my amber eyes, surprised to find that they weren't bloodshot. I noticed one silver hair in my fledgling beard and ignored it. The crew was waiting for me when I came out, feeling tired but distinguished. "So what the hell is goin on, Scooby?" asked Sawyer.

"The tunnel is gone."

"What?" asked Noreen. Sawyer simply looked at me as if I'd grown a third arm right in front of them.

"When I came downstairs, my dad's agent was sitting in the chapel. He took me down to the cellar and showed me the wall where the tunnel used to be. Then he told me a weird story my dad told him back when my dad was in rehab, a story about Dad's muse, this thing called a 'silen' that I would imagine gave him the *Fiddle and Fire* series."

I told them what Bayard had told me, their eyes growing larger and larger, and then I dropped the punchline: "He told me

158

my dad was murdered."

"*Murdered?*" they both said in unison, getting up off the couch at the same time. "By who?"

"Nobody knows. Also, get this: Max wants me off the series. He says I'm going crazy like my dad did."

"That's garbage," said Sawyer. "I don't care if it was a dream or if it actually happened, but we saw the same thing, and that's got to count."

I lifted my shirt to show them the scratch on my back. It was long and thin, but it was scabbing over. "I think it actually happened. This is where I got hurt falling through the roof in that other-place. If it didn't actually happen, then where did this come from?"

"Maybe you did it at your dad's house? Maybe—" Noreen said, and interrupted herself.

Sawyer folded his arms. "You don't really think we got wasted and made it all up, do you?"

"I don't have any idea what to think," she said, shrugging. "I mean, it does sound pretty far-fetched, right? Seriously. This kind of thing only happens in Hollywood. Real life is not *He-Man,* or *Beastmaster 2.*"

"Tish," said Sawyer, taking her hand in his and kissing it. "Ti amo! You know what it does to me when you talk cheesy 80's fantasy movies."

"Gomez, not in front of the children."

I rolled my eyes and went to the door. "Well, you guys want to get some lunch while we figure out where to go from here?"

"Sounds like a plan, Stan," said Sawyer, and we left the room.

As he closed the door behind us with a soft clunk, I noticed a strange flicker in the corner of my eye, as if I'd poked it with my finger. I rubbed the bridge of my nose and wrung my face with my palms, pressing my cold fingers against my eyelids to soothe them. We sauntered down the corridor past silent suite doors, our footsteps quieted by the plush berber runner.

Stepping into the elevator, Sawyer pressed the button for the first floor. "So what are you guys thinking? Mexican?"

I noticed the black spot again, and winced. I noticed Noreen doing the same thing. She squinted and looked up at the cab light, saying, "Yeah, that sounds fine."

"I must be hungrier than I thought I was," said Sawyer. "I'm getting a headache."

I leaned my head back and listened to my stiff neck crackle, relieving a dull pain I hadn't noticed until he brought it up. "Me too. How much sleep you think we got?"

"Not enough."

The door slid shut and a second later, the elevator cab shifted, and began to move toward the lobby. A soft chime told us we were passing the second floor. My mind wandered as I studied my distorted features in the brushed-steel surface of the elevator wall. I grinned and the horrible, blurry face bared its teeth back at me.

Suddenly, I had an epiphany. "Sawyer, what if the thing my dad talked about was the guy with the horns?"

"The silen?"

"Yeah."

"I can believe it. You know, that puts yesterday into perspective. When we carried the mirror to the church, and we were talking all kinds of weird shit, ramma-lamma-ding-dong, or whatever. You said it can put ideas in your head, that's how it became your father's muse."

Noreen made a face, turning to look at us. "What are you talking about?"

"Yesterday," I said, as the elevator made that *ding* noise again.

160

"I told you about it, earlier. When we went to my dad's house yesterday, me and Sawyer took the mirror and put it in the car. It was like we were sleepwalking."

"So you're saying that devil thing made you open a portal to another world?" she asked. "Do you guys have any idea how messed-up that sounds?"

Sawyer bit his bottom lip, sucked on it for a second, and said, "Yep."

"I don't know if—" said Noreen, and stopped herself, a look of mild confusion flashing over her features. Or perhaps it was concern. She faced the door again, clasping her hands in front of her waist as if she were praying for the door to open. "I . . . think I'm going to call the mechanic and see how long it's going to take to get my car back."

Sawyer's face fell. Noreen's voice was a husky murmur. "You guys are kinda starting to scare me."

Ding.

"I understand," said Sawyer, and leaned against the back of the elevator cab. "I don't really know what to say. Other than, well, we're not crazy. And we're not on drugs."

"And if we could ever find that video tape, we could prove it," I added.

Noreen spoke over her shoulder, not turning around, "It's a little convenient, ain't it? That it suddenly came up missing?"

I heard a *tap* noise from somewhere, but ignored it. My eye caught the digital floor readout over the door, a black box with a red number inside. It was slowly flashing the number 1.

As I stood there watching it, I heard the cab chime again. *Ding.*

I glanced over at Sawyer, but he was still pining for Noreen, staring at her with worry in his eyes. I could tell that he was feeling

161

trapped by the situation. He flinched, and reached up to wipe at his cheek, looked down at his hand. A heat-prickle of fear wormed up my spine, made my hair tingle.

We both looked up at the ceiling. Water was leaking through the light fixture, dripping on us.

"Uhh. Guys?" said Noreen.

She backed away from the door; a thin rivulet of water was running out of the top of it, streaming onto the floor, now pouring, welling around our feet. My heart pounded at this surreal turn of events, and my eyes rolled in their sockets as I began to see more water, dribbling through cracks and crevices into the elevator cab, gurgling down the gleaming surfaces.

I gasped, lurched backwards; my pants were soaking it up, chilling my feet, infiltrating my shoes. We migrated to the back of the tiny brushed-steel room and pressed ourselves against the walls of the box.

Ding.

The lights sparked with a gunshot-like *CRACK* and a shower of stars, which sizzled, leaving us in darkness.

The door opened with a casual *hiss-clunk*, letting in a faint blue light . . . .

And a hell of a lot of water.

A Thousand Miles from Nowhere

THE WATER WAS ALREADY up to my waist by the time I realized what was happening; all I could see was a dim blue-black rectangle, glassed over by a deluge of freezing-cold water, which, as it splashed a mist of droplets into my face, I tasted and recognized as salt-water. All three of us began to panic in terror and confusion, screaming and trying to scramble backwards up the wall to get away from it.

It came in at a roaring rush, sweeping our legs out from under us with its force.

Somehow, I sensed that the room was tilting backward, so I began to crab-walk up the wall. The water surged up around us, filling the cab with a crackling liquid darkness. I could see tiny fish darting around in it, shiny silver knives shooting back and forth in a frenzy.

At the final moment before we were totally under, the three of us shared our horror, glancing into each others' eyes. We all took a deep breath of stale, hot air, and then we were swallowed up. An instant later, there was a gargantuan metallic *thud* as the elevator cab came to rest on some soft surface.

Sawyer was the first toward the door, leading a contrail of bubbles, kicking me in the elbow as he went.

I followed close behind, pulling Noreen by the jacket. Her purse scooped water at her side, constricting her movement, a little leather satellite that spat out the bits and pieces of her life. I ripped the strap from her arm and let it fade into the black.

164

Sawyer turned, reached in, grabbed Noreen's arm, braced his feet on the doorframe, and dragged her out of the elevator as if it were a grave.

I pursued them, pulling furiously at the water, my lungs beginning to cramp.

The room continued tilting as we burst out of the door, and I could hear the faint boom below me as it slammed dully onto its back. I chanced a look between my feet and saw it in the gloomy deep blue, a hulking dark cube with steel cables noodling out of both ends like a fist full of licorice.

We were in some enormous body of water.

A dark nothingness yawned below; a rippling silver curtain undulated overhead, pierced through by a chain that snaked downward into a never-ending void. A great white crescent hovered beyond the silver, and some part of my consciousness registered it as the moon.

My muscles shrieked in agony, alarm bells going off in my head as my mind howled for oxygen. I fought against the water, trying to reach the surface before I could give in. A strange, melodic sort of apathy crept in around the edges, suffusing me with calm.

My chest, my ribs began to quiver in anticipation of air, flexing, trying to draw breath.

I fought the urge to suck water as the ceiling of mercury came at me, shredded by trillions of tiny bubbles. Beside me, my friends clawed for salvation with reaching hands, time and again, their hair clouding around their heads in billowing tendrils.

My lungs threatened to cave in, I couldn't do it anymore; I finally let a little of the heavy sea-water into my mouth.

It wouldn't be so bad to die, I thought, the sea bellowing in my ears.

My chest raged like a trapped animal within me, begged to be filled with water.

The brine—so much like blood on my tongue—gushed into my throat as I put my hand out one last time and touched the sky. I broke the surface and shotgunned the ocean from my mouth in a blast of vapor.

The others did the same; we floated, gasping, transfixed.

Soaring above us was a night sky unlike any we had ever seen, even more lustrous than what I remembered from the city beyond the mirror. A black deeper and richer than any obsidian filled the heavens from horizon to horizon, salted with uncountable stars, pinpricks of light that rippled like music.

It was a serenade gilded with ten thousand shades of ten thousand colors, more brilliant than any diamond on Earth, unfouled by the lights of any city.

Even as starved as I was for air, I couldn't help but forget to breathe.

Tears laced my eyes as I drifted, in awe at the omnipotent majesty of the sight of it. The same pale moon loomed ominously in the center of the abyss, masked by the same orange orb as before, both of them scarred from rim to rim, every mile.

"Ohhhh . . ." moaned Noreen, her jaw shuddering as the cool wind stripped her face of heat. "Ohhhh . . . my . . . *God.*"

Sawyer threw both fists into the air and gave a loud whoop. "I told you! I *told* you! Ha-*haaaaaa! Yeah!*"

I tore my eyes away from the spectacle and gave them a wide grin. I felt a hot tear trace the curve of my cheek. We bobbed for a little while, marveling over the incredulous view. A voice brought me back from my reverie.

"Hey, over here," said Noreen, and we swam over to where she was clinging to a strange sort of buoy made of wood. It looked like some sort of simplistic Viking funeral pyre, a tall tripod of slender driftwood logs nailed to a small platform about four meters across to a side.

We clambered onto it and huddled, shivering, inside the tripod.

"So cold," I said. I was shivering so hard I probably looked like I was being electrocuted. "Where the hell are we? I mean, I'm guessing we're back in the other-world."

"Destin," said Sawyer. "We're in Destin. It's actually real. I can't believe it."

Noreen took off her shirt and jacket and squeezed the water out of her top. Her white bra glowed against her skin in the light of the moon. "I believe we're somewhere in the Aemev. This looks like a waypoint buoy."

"That means we're near a ship lane," said Sawyer.

I wrung out my own shirt, as did Sawyer. Noreen put hers back on and curled into a ball on the platform.

"I assume that's a good thing," I said, putting my shirt and jacket back on. The leather kept me protected from the wind, but it did nothing for my soaked cargo pants. My legs were chilled to the bone. I jogged in place, trying to get some circulation going.

"It's a very good thing," Noreen said, and added, "Providing there's a boat coming sometime in the next several months."

"Well, if we haven't t-t-t-time-traveled—is that even a thing?—if we haven-n-n't traveled back in time, then we sh-sh-should be in a point after the final book in the sssseries has taken place," Sawyer said. He hugged his knees and draped his black overcoat over his shoulders like a safety blanket.

"So we shouldn't have to wait too awfully long. By the end of the latest book, Ain and the settlers on K-Set had established a trade route with regular runners. They were talking about building a railroad, but it was too expensive to build more than one track that far."

"That sucks," I said. "If there was a track bridge, we could start walking."

"Yeah."

Noreen sneezed. "I wish I'd brought my suitcase on the elevator."

"I don't think you would've been able to get it out and get topside with it," said Sawyer. "It looked like you were having a little trouble with that pocketbook."

"Oh, yeah," she said, reaching over and slapping him on the arm. "Thanks for taking my purse away from me, you asshole. Now I have to cancel my debit card and get a new driver's license."

"Hey, that was Ross, not me. Besides, I don't think you're going to need *any of that* here," Sawyer said, and we all laughed. *"Whatsoever."*

The night tapered into near-silence, broken only by the sound of the waves slapping against the sides of the buoy-platform. I began to dry out, which only marginally lessened the chill of the wind.

"I hope my boss doesn't fire me for not showing up for work in the m-m-m-morning," said Noreen.

I heard Sawyer move, trying to cover more of his body with his coat. "I just hope we can get back hom-m-m-me at some point. I'd hate to kn-n-n-n-now we were stuck here forever this t-t-t-time."

"I think the silen sent us back the first tim-m-m-me. He was the last thing we saw before we woke up on Earth," I said. "Whatever he is, I believe he might have the ability to go b-b-b-back and forth . . . between the two worlds. I think we're going to have to track him-m-m down if we want to get back."

Sawyer coughed, his breath misting in the air. "I don't even know where to b-b-begin looking."

"First things first: we have to get off this rrrrrraft. What are these things here for, anyway?"

Noreen stirred. "They're here ffffffor people that go ooooverboard or ships that capsize. So they have somewhere to g-g-go, to get out of the water and wait for rescue."

"Wait a minute. D-d-don't these rafts have signal braziers?" said Sawyer, unfolding himself and rolling stiffly to his feet.

He jumped, took hold of the driftwood tripod, and climbed it like an upside-down squirrel until he could see into the point where the ends of the logs were tied together together in the middle. Where the logs were crossed, someone had tied down a primitive sort of hurricane lantern.

He fished through his pockets and produced a Zippo, using it to light the wick. To all our delight, the lighter was dry enough to spark, the wick caught, and a tiny tongue of flame began to burn the oil inside the reservoir.

He hopped back down and curled up next to one of the brazier's tripod legs again, bundling up in his jacket.

I could finally make out their faces by the weak flicker of the lantern. "Now . . ." I said, shivering, ". . . we wait."

As I lay down and drifted into unconsciousness, I remember thinking about how sluggishly cold my face felt, and the next thing I knew, I was struggling up out of the frigid bonds of sleep, awakened by the cold and the sound of Noreen shuffling across the platform to huddle next to Sawyer.

I swore in my head, and tried to fight my way back under, and finally managed to doze off again.

The rumors of sun finally irritated me back out of my cocoon, lighting up the world in my dreams until I couldn't keep my grainy eyelids shut any longer. I rolled over onto my back and stretched, painfully peeling my limbs out of the stiff dead-bug position I'd slept in all night.

I squinted up at the potential of a sunrise lighting up the horizon with a sickly, motionless maelstrom of green and red. My feet were like the unfeeling claws of a dead bird, cadaver-cold and stricken with rigor. I looked over my shoulder; the moon was a dome of white disappearing over the opposite edge of the world. I rubbed my numb face and found a runny nose.

There was nothing to be done. For the next several hours, until the golden glow of the rising sun shot an arrow of light into my eyes, I simply lay on my side and pretended to sleep.

The week coursed over my mind like troubled water over a bed of river-stones, worn smooth by worry and confusion.

I was too cold, too tired to form conclusions, to puzzle over clues . . . I simply replayed scenes and conversations, over and over, ad nauseam, until they lost all meaning and simply became trite scripts that the people in my head acted out like puppets on a stage again and again.

Semantic satiation, I thought in a mild delirium, waking up again. I thought about putting on a pot of coffee.

That's what it's called.

I opened my eyes. Sawyer was sitting up, gazing eastward as the white-hot orb grew into sight, burning away the shrouds of the night, warming the world and willing the life into it for another day.

I rolled over and unfolded myself again, trying to ignore the cramps.

An hour passed, and then two, as the sun rose ever higher, and seared away the chill. Soon, I was sweating in my leather jacket; I took it off and hung it on one of the knots protruding from the driftwood tripod, then climbed up to the oil lamp and cut it off.

170

When I landed back on the platform with a *clunk,* I winced at the shock to my knees.

Noreen rubbed her eyes and said, "I feel like crap."

"Yeah, me too."

The sea around us was an infinity of dark blue, broken into hillocks of wind-shoveled water that threatened to overtake the buoy. The breeze grew stronger with the sun until the raft was bobbing in great slow swaying arcs, straining against the chain that anchored it to the sea-bed.

As the waves came underneath it, the platform would cant heavily to one side to climb the surf, and then after teetering for a split second, slide into the trough like a half-pipe skater.

I scrambled to the edge of the raft and spewed bitter bile into the spray.

*   *   *

"I am seriously regretting my enthusiasm right now," I said, lying on my back with my arm over my eyes, nursing a headache. Noreen was the only one of us with a watch, but it had stopped a long time ago, now displaying the time it had been when we'd stepped into the elevator at the hotel: 11:21 AM. Sawyer's cellphone was dead, and mine was somewhere on the ocean floor below us.

The white sun was at the apex of the sky, burning down on us with the intense directional heat of a bonfire.

Sawyer had taken his shirt, shoes, and sweater off, and was standing on the edge of the raft wordlessly staring into the horizon. The blinding white wood of the raft felt as if it were scorching the inside of my skull.

I could kill for a cup of coffee, I thought, and licked my chapped

171

lips. *I could kill a wolf. With my bare hands.*

"I'm still trying to figure out what to make of this," said Noreen. She was leaning against one of the poles, hugging herself, with her jacket pulled over her shoulders like a shawl. Her voice sounded impaired, wet, as if she was having trouble breathing through her nose. "I think I've gotten past the I-might-be-crazy part, but I'm still having a little trouble warming up to the idea that I just walked into a fantasy novel."

"How are you still cold? It's like, a thousand degrees out here."

"I don't feel good. I think I might have gotten sick last night."

"I'm sorry."

"It's not your fault."

"Really?" I asked. "You really don't think I dragged you into this?"

"No, Ross," she said, with a weak, yet comforting smile. "You didn't. I'm actually half-tempted to think it was fate."

"You think so?"

"Maybe. Do you believe in fate?"

"Nah. Well, I don't know. Sometimes I wonder. Whenever I think luck's going my way, it steps up and kicks me right in the balls. I've found that if you leave fate alone and do your thing, and let it do its thing, it doesn't kick you so hard anymore. Damn. It's too hot to be asking me philosophical questions when I'm starving; I'm looking at you and it's like a Looney Tunes cartoon, you look like a hot dog with a face."

I peeled my arm from my sweaty face and sat up. The world blinded me with brilliant shades of washed-out green that became the deep, fervent blues of ocean and sky, and the bone-white of the raft.

Diamond knots punctuated the wood at organic intervals, and

it was lashed together with—surprisingly enough—some sort of plastic-coated cord, like the power cord of an appliance. I blinked. "Hey, I thought you guys said my dad's books were a fantasy series. What's this power cord doing here?"

Sawyer looked down at the raft.

"The Antargata k-Setra was home to an advanced society, remember? Well, there's very little working power grid in most of K-Set, and a lot of the ruins were scavenged for materials and resources. Most cords like this were taken and used as waterproof rope."

"Oh," I said.

"There's actually electricity on mainland Ain, though. They were at least smart enough to reverse-engineer electric lights to use windmill power."

We lingered in silence for a while. My listlessness grew by the hour until I had whipped myself into a lather and exhausted all available mental topics. I stood up and started pacing slowly back and forth, counting the logs as I walked across them, feeling my stomach knot up tighter and tighter with hunger.

After puking over the side earlier, my appetite had finally returned with a score to settle, and it was piling on the punishment. I wished I had the first book in the *Fiddle* series in one hand and a huge piece of pizza in another.

Just the thought of pizza made my mouth water.

I found myself imagining the smell of marinara and olive oil, and pepperoni, the crunch of the toasted crust, the mellow tang of pineapple—

"I think I see a ship," said Sawyer.

I joined him at the edge of the raft. Sure enough, there was a speck in the distance, an atom of white on the edge of the known world. I resisted the urge to start screaming and jumping up and down. "Figures we'd see someone during the day, when our lantern wasn't lit."

"They'll be coming near us," rasped Noreen. "The waypoints are meant to guide travelers across the Aemev too."

"There's a whole line of them," Sawyer said, and he seemed to relax. He went over to Noreen and knelt next to her, resting the back of one hand on her forehead. "You sound horrible, baby. You must really be sick. You're burning up."

"Do ships on the Aemev usually have doctors on board?" I asked.

Then something occurred to me. "Are there pirates out here?"

"Not really," said Sawyer. "Merchant ships are heavily protected by contractors, and there aren't many ships on the coast of Ain that don't belong to the royal fleet anyway. Not enough trees on the coast side of Ain for it, and most people can't afford to move the lumber from K-Set or the east side of the Ainean continent."

The dot drew closer and closer until it resolved into a tall, smoke-stacked steamship, pulling a long white contrail, followed by two more ships. I couldn't quite make out their flags yet, however, nor their crew.

I thought I saw a strange movement out to the west of the incoming boat. A long, dark scratch, faint and sinuous, was undulating through the air, like an earthworm on a glass window pane. "Besides," he was saying, "—nobody likes to stay at sea for very long in Destin. There are dangerous things living in the Aemev, Ross."

"Like what?" I asked, watching the black line trace a slow, jagged path along the whitecaps toward the ships. Whatever it was, it looked like it was at least a mile long.

I glanced back at Sawyer; he spoke without turning away from

Noreen. "The Saoshoma."

"What is that?" I asked. "Would you happen to know what it looks like?"

"A sort of sea serpent. The coastal Wilders worship it. What makes you ask that?"

I grabbed Sawyer by the shoulder, pulled him around as gently as I could, and pointed at the scratch on the horizon. I was extremely discouraged by the way that every bit of the color immediately drained out of his face.

The men buried his father while he ate. He'd gone without food for so long he wasn't even hungry anymore; his ribs and distended belly made him look like a great big horrible frog in the afternoon sunlight.

He choked and gagged; his stomach threatened to purge itself. The woman took hold of his wrist and said, "Slow down afore you get sick."

Once he'd gotten one of the eggs down and had some water, a trapper came into the tent and knelt by the boy's cot. "Who did this?" asked the man, burning into his eyes with an intense gaze. Three months ago, Pack wouldn't have recognized that gaze, but he'd seen it in the broken mirror in the black shell of his house so many times it was like looking at himself now.

"He called himself Tem Lucas," said Pack, and it seemed like an incantation as the words came out of his mouth. "He had a red bird tattooed across his eyes." As if summoned by magic, his hunger ripped into him like a wild animal and he picked up the drumstick and biscuit, taking a bite out of each. A bestial snarl came out of his guts.

—The Fiddle and the Fire, vol 1 "The Brine and the Bygone"

Wonder and Lightning

THE SAOSHOMA GLIDED OVER the waves, a terrible force of nature that snaked smoothly on billowing lateral membranes, reminiscent of photos I'd seen of sea-slugs, flat-worms, cuttle-fish. The way it moved, the dragon-like animal reminded me of the ribbon-dancers I'd seen at the Olympics: long, thin, sibilant blades that curved gracefully in broad arcs and corkscrews.

As the ships neared our waypoint, the "serpent" accompanied them. Soon we could see its blotchy mustelid hide, like velveted leather swirled with iridescent colors. At times it was a breathless shade of pale green, and then the feverish, electric indigo of a late sunset.

It was easily almost twenty meters across, including wingspan, and as it dove toward the water, I figured it to be at least a kilometer long. The water thundered under our feet as the goliath creature pierced the surface, throwing a tall plume of spray, and slid into the ocean with a continuous rumble.

It fed itself into the depths until it had vanished.

"Holy Jesus," said Sawyer. "Everybody get down and pretend you don't exist."

He didn't have to explain it again. We lay on our bellies in the center of the raft, shoulder to shoulder, gripping the logs. I peered out at the ships and recognized the icon on the lead ship's flag. It was the same shield-style coat of arms I'd seen etched into the gunmetal of the revolver I'd found in the ghostly Wilder village.

178

The ocean swelled under us, and Noreen said, "God in heaven—!" as a great black shadow passed below, dwarfing the waypoint raft. We could feel the current of its wake pulling the anchor-chain, strumming it like a guitar string.

The Saoshoma cut through the blue deep for several minutes and eventually faded away; when it did, the beast carried the raft with it. We rode the wave back down and strained hard at the very end of the chain, filling me with fear that it would break and send us sailing free, deeper into nowhere.

The lead ship approached us as the sea calmed. Several men leaned over the side; all of them but one were dressed in sleek, vespine green armor. The man not wearing any of that tossed a rope over the side and yelled something; it sounded vaguely like English, but was so heavily accented I couldn't understand it at this distance.

I got the gist of what he wanted, though. The rope hit the raft with a clatter and I picked it up.

"Can you guys bat-walk up the side of the ship with this?"

"Bat-walk?" asked Noreen.

Sawyer joined me, looking up at the men on the ship. "I think he's talking about like what Batman and Robin used to do on that old TV show with Adam West."

"Oh, okay," she said. "I'm not sure I can do that. Not right now."

"Oh yeah, you're sick," noted Sawyer.

Someone on the ship shouted in fear. I understood the word "Saoshoma", though as they said it, the term sounded like *SOH-she-ma*.

"Konyay clamb peah far de Saoshoma bebbok?" demanded the man with no armor. His long, wavy black hair rustled in the breeze. "Nao, ef yedunna maind! Needa roonda stairm spare!"

179

Sawyer and we shared an instant of confusion.

I shrugged and said, "You go on up, and I'll carry her. Get going."

"To hell with that," he said. "This is my gig, Scooby. *You* get *your* ass up there, and we'll be right behind you."

I looked at Noreen; she seemed to nod vaguely, as if to reassure me, her expression an exhausted combination of resolve and bemusement.

I took up the rope and stepped into the water, reeling myself closer to the hull of the ship. Once I reached the pitched boards, I bobbed, planting my feet on them, and began to walk and pull, walk and pull my way up the ship wall Batman-style.

It took a bit more time and a bit more effort than I expected, but once I got within reach, the unarmored man leaned down and pulled me up. "Cammen," he said, as I hopped down from the bulwark. "Dear go. Bour yer fran doonther? Gone make toop."

I realized that I was beginning to be able to understand them. He *was* speaking English.

What about your friend down there? he was saying, *Gonna make it up?*

It was oblique—no doubt flavored by the culture of a parallel world—but there was no mistaking the language: a strange, mellifluous combination of the tight-wound trill of British-Irish brogue and the laconic, tropical drawl of Jamaican. I resisted the urge to ask him to repeat himself and joined them at the starboard side.

Noreen was climbing onto Sawyer's back, wrapping her legs around his waist and her arms around his chest.

He rolled his shoulders, cracked his neck, and stepped into the water with the rope in his hands. The instant the two of them were submerged, the ocean surface exploded in a mist of vapor, and the

180

Saoshoma breached a quarter of a kilometer away.

An overwhelming chill of terror rippled up my back at the sight of such an enormous, intimidating monster.

It hesitated as it rose, giving me a better view of its long, thin face, an alien amalgam of selachian and eusuchian features, somehow both shark and crocodile.

The Saoshoma's three feline eyes reflected the sunlight like spheres of flaming copper, the center orb the largest, a rolling yellow globe in the bridge of its snout. It stared down at us with all the unfeeling emotion and empathy of a Greek statue.

I looked down at Sawyer; he was about a fourth of the way up the side of the ship, standing on the hull, the veins on his arms standing out, brow furrowed, mouth locked in a grimace of pain and determination. Noreen was as tight around his body as a vest, her ankles locked in front of his crotch, her face pressed against his back.

Sweat or sea-water ran down his forehead and cheeks in sheets. A knot of emotion welled in my throat with a surge of adrenaline. I barely knew the man, but this was the proudest I'd ever been of anybody in my life. *"Come on, you can do it,"* I screamed over the rushing chaos of the sea-dragon rising from the water.

I was so entranced, I didn't notice the hairs on my arms were standing up.

"You got this! You're almost *there!* Ten more feet!"

At the sound of my voice, the towering beast in front of us turned, ceased to breach, and faced the ship. Its snout was easily the size of a school bus.

The cavernous maw opened with the sluggish motion of sheer size, revealing two jaws of teeth like the serrated edge of a saw. The space between the sawbands bristled with baleen, and slopping from the opening of its narrow throat was a tongue, obscenely pink

181

and muscular, tipped with a barbed lance of bone.

There was a strange electric trilling from my left that rose to a crescendo and faded out with a whine.

Out of the corner of my eye, some large object standing on the poop deck lit up from back to front, and discharged a white tree of light into the Saoshoma's mouth. My heart surged as a deafening whip-crack turned the very air into a twelve-ton punch to the lungs.

The electricity arced, crackling like fireworks as it went, and forked throughout the animal's fleshy mouth in a series of bright flashes. The Saoshoma immediately drew back in pain.

I recoiled from the bulwark, frightened and disoriented. For a moment, I was blinded; I stared dumbly at the monster through an afterimage that looked like a maple branch.

Everyone nearby moved at once, and it struck me that Sawyer was near the railing. I fought through the knot of men, shouting, tearing sailors out of the way until I was standing next to the unarmored man. We both reached down and took hold of one of Sawyer's arms, hauling him up and over the side.

As he stumbled onto the deck, I could see the sunlight glowing behind his arm-hairs as they stood straight up.

The Saoshoma shook its head, flinging sea-water across the ship in a mist of rain, and lunged again. In that instant, other than Sawyer, Noreen, and the unarmored man, all I could see was the inside of the thing's mouth, hollow and bleeding, a panorama of teeth and tongue.

Another flash of light and the lightning-cannon ripped the wind in twain, shooting another salvo of white-purple electricity into the beast's mouth. The following slam of thunder hit me like a brick and I flinched, swearing out loud.

The unarmored man glanced at me.

I felt a sense of disconnected shock when I noticed that he had *recognized my face.*

I took my friends' hands and led them away from the Saoshoma, cutting through the crowd of men staring up at the monster in astonishment. I got the feeling that many of the young men had never seen it before, from their wide eyes and the hushed tones they spoke in as they made signs of genuflection in a bid for divine protection.

We ran up the first staircase we saw, which happened to be the officers' way to the upper level, and ran through the first doorway into what turned out to be a richly-furnished office.

"We're in the captain's quarters," said Noreen, slamming the door. "We probably shouldn't be in here."

"We'll tell them we just ran in here to get as much structure between us and the monster. Do you really want to go back out there?"

"Sounds like a plan, Stan," said Sawyer, and he ran to the bay window in the back of the room, pressing his face to the window in an attempt to see the beast. Below the window, the steamship's gigantic propulsion combine rolled over and over with a dull roar.

He didn't have to wait long. There was a terrifying peal of sound that reverberated throughout the ship, a piercing wail of agony, and the entire room fell dark as the Saoshoma whipped right, crashing headlong into the ocean behind the ship. The resulting tide washed against the glass panes like the soapy spray of a car wash.

Sawyer jerked away from the window as it crackled under the stress.

The monster dove under, pouring itself back into the sea, and soon, with a whip of its tail, it was gone. A grand ovation erupted outside on the deck as the men cheered and applauded the

Saoshoma's escape and their own survival. They chanted something over and over, but I couldn't decipher it.

"I must be losing my mind after all," said Sawyer, relaxing on the cushioned windowsill. "I could swear I heard those guys speaking English."

"You're not the only one. I heard it too," I agreed.

The unarmored man stepped inside and closed the door, his longcoat swirling at his calves as he did so. He turned to assess us, giving me the first chance I'd had to examine him at length.

He was a lean, handsome, swarthy man; his jet-black hair cascaded in lank, sensuous curls, framing an expressive mouth and honey-colored eyes as sharp as the tip of a sword. His dark olive complexion made him hard to pin down—he could have been Italian, Asian, part African.

The overcoat was something of a thin leather kimono . . . its huge sleeves were tied up at the shoulder, freeing most of his arm to move. He was wearing canvas trousers and a vest, but just about everything else was made of unfinished leather, which gave him the aspect of a samurai and a barbarian simultaneously.

He shrugged his right arm out of the overcoat, which was cinched with a belt at the waist, and flexed his fingers.

The empty sleeve dangled down his back. Hidden in the folds of the coat, a polished sixgun glittered in the holster strapped across his chest. His slender, bare arm was a study in musculature.

The gunslinger peered at me and spoke in that obscure flavor, his voice dusky and low.

"We meet again, murderer. This time you do not leave my sight alive."

The Two-Faced Man

I SAT IN THE CORNER of the tiny brig cell, on the floor, hugging my knees. Sawyer was in the opposite corner with his legs crossed, cradling Noreen in the pit of his lap like a baby, her face buried in his shirt. His arms were wrapped around her, his fingers interlaced behind her back, and his lips rested on her head.

I could occasionally hear him mumbling words of comfort into her pale blonde hair. They were sitting on a primitive, stained mattress, which lay on the floor. The sine-wave motion of the ship, nearly imperceptible, kept me in a constant state of mild nausea.

"I'm sorry I got you guys into this mess," I said, staring at the wall.

They offered no reply; I wasn't sure whether to feel worse about that, or relieved. I glanced over at Sawyer. His expression was one of quiet despondency, his features tight and severe, his unfocused eyes locked on the foot of the mattress. A fly zipped around the room, finally lighting on my wrist. I waved it away.

After a few minutes, I got up and stood at the door; we were in a small hardwood room with an entrance made of wrought-iron bars. If I pressed my face to the bars and cut my view to an extreme left angle, I could see down the hallway, where one of the armored sailors was leaning against the wall.

"Hey," I said. "Hey, guard. I don't know who you think I am, but I'm not. Come here and talk to me, and I'll explain everything."

He ignored me.

I gripped the bars and fought the urge to shake the hell out of them, rattle them in a blind fury, scream demands and threats at the man. Demonstrating a capacity for violence would probably not play out in my favor; I just went back to my corner and sat down again.

Sawyer cleared his throat. "Don't apologize. We came on our own accord. In for a penny, in for a pound."

I shrugged. It felt like my heart was somewhere underneath my stomach.

"Besides," he said, "I get the feeling we'll be okay. I'm not much of a betting man, or a churchy kinda guy, but I don't think this is the end."

Noreen turned to regard me, squinting against the light. Her face was puffy and pale. "Yeah . . . I have faith. This is all a big misunderstanding, and these guys can't be so hard-ass they'll just ignore what you have to say. They're Kingsmen, Ross: good people. A long line of good people."

"I hope you guys are right," I said, and leaned against the bulkhead, closing my grainy, tired eyes.

When I opened them again, I sensed that an hour or two had passed, as the hot light of the sun was no longer streaming into the brig at an angle, but falling straight down onto the windowsill above me, and onto my cold scalp. Sawyer and Noreen were fast asleep, sprawled on the mattress, Sawyer on his back and she huddled against him with her head on his stomach.

I reveled in the warm sun and relaxed, stretching my legs.

I didn't have long to luxuriate in the sunbeam, though, because the drumbeat of bootheels came down the hallway and the unarmored man appeared in the doorway. My friends stirred, but didn't awaken.

The man beckoned to me, and I obliged simply out of

187

curiosity and a desire to settle what I was convinced was a misunderstanding. He showed me the handle of the sixgun in his crossdraw holster and produced the key to the cell. "I'm going to let you out," he muttered. *Aim gwan lechu-ut.* "You try anything foolish, and you'll be dead before you hit the floor."

I put my hands up by my shoulders in surrender. "Hey, your wish is my command, *kemosabe.* I'm not here to cause any trouble. I'm on your side—I think."

He unlocked the door and opened it with a faint squeal, and I stepped out, taking care to keep my hands visible at all times. With a suspicious eye, he turned away and strode down the hallway, leading me past the guard, who gave me a glare just as accusational.

We passed into a longer corridor that ran perpendicular to the hull, crossing between what turned out to be the galley kitchen and the crew's quarters. The crew bay was a long and spacious room that fully occupied a level of the ship from starboard to port and from amidships to where I was standing.

Hammocks were tied to the support beams at regular intervals, rolled up and secured during the day. The darkness was only broken by oil lamps that swayed pendulously back and forth on chains, and sunlight that crashed down through a grate in the ceiling.

We cut to the right and went through the kitchen, where two men in kilts were standing around chatting and peeling weird vegetables that looked like potatoes with skins like apples.

As we walked into the room, they stopped talking and stared at me.

My escort said something to them in his rapid-fire accent, and they reluctantly went back to their task. We went into the pantry, a long and narrow space lined with shelves on either side. They were sparsely stocked with canned food, narrow boxes labeled with words I couldn't decipher, pickled eggs and vegetables in glass bottles, and sacks of grain.

The unarmored man closed the door and locked it with a little hook. "Sit down," he said, pointing at a nearby crate. *Set doon.*

So I did. The man stood there, looming over me with his fists on his hips, and then shrugged out of his overcoat and let it drape down his legs from its belt. He was whip-thin outside of it. It hit me that he looked like an unkempt Middle-Eastern version of Nils Asther.

"I don't know what to make of you," he said. "At first, I thought you were the assassin of Lord Eddick, attempting to use the sea to flee the justice of the Kingsmen, but your manner . . . and your words, they confuse me. Then I decided that you *are* Lord Sardis, but you sought to disguise yourself by feigning ignorance, taking on a strange affect and style of dress."

"I don't even know who those people *are*," I said.

"And the irritating thing is that I might believe you. You seem honestly without guile. Even clever Lord Sardis could not play the part of an imbecile so well."

"Thank you for your—*what.*"

"Besides, you are alarmingly pale and as soft about the middle as an infant on the teat," he noted, much to my mortification. "So if you aren't he, then who are you? The resemblance is uncanny, although I must admit I see less and less of it as I note the aspects of your unfortunate appearance."

"People always tell me I remind them of somebody."

"Perhaps," said the man. "You *are* quite plain-faced."

"Can you answer a question for me?" I took the man's silence as permission and continued, "This is Ain, isn't it? Or, the Aemev, rather."

"What fanciful hell do you live in? Of course it is. Where else would you be? The Kingsmen have no more ships that can travel

189

to the moons."

"You used to have boats that went to the moon?"

"You *are* an imbecile, aren't you, stranger? I was speaking blithely."

I sighed as he continued to study the look of frustration on my face. "So if you are not Sardis, then what *is* your name?" he asked, sitting on one of the shelves. He leaned forward, his elbows on his knees, and fixed me with his piercing green eyes. "And what is your business—I mean, other than being stranded on a raft in the middle of the Aemev?"

"My name is Ross. Ross Brigham. And I'm not sure you'd believe me if I told you."

At that, the man stood up, visibly startled. "Brigham? Are you by any chance familiar with the name Bridger?"

The world seemed to jigger in the frame, jarred by unreality. "No . . . who is Bridger?"

"The King's scribe, the late Lord Eddick Bridger."

That had to be more than a coincidence. I got the distinct feeling that I'd found my father's other-life. "That must be my father, the man I've come to mourn."

"Strange. I was not aware that the scribe had more than one son. Are you here to take revenge, then?"

"Revenge?" I said, and the notion dazzled me. I hadn't really even considered it, even after what Bayard had told me. I guess I was still too blown away by the whole thing to get ideas of retribution when I didn't even have all the pieces to the puzzle. "No, I guess I figured the authorities had handled it."

The man smiled. "It might please you to know that I am Walter Rollins," he said, drawing the revolver in his chest rig and spinning it by the trigger-guard. This he did a dozen times, at multiple angles, reversing it, transferring it from hand to hand, tossing it over his shoulder from the back, and finally twirling it sharply back into the holster.

"The Deon of the Southern Kingsmen and son of Council Chiral Clayton Rollins—the Hero of the Widowforge, and the secondmost legendary gunslinger in the territories of Ain. And I am the leader of the investigation into your father's disappearance."

I rubbed my face. "I understood a couple of those words."

"What part of it eluded you, stranger?"

"Everything but the pronouns."

"I feel I must resist the urge to either check your skull for injuries, or give you one. Are your friends as dull-witted as you are, or have we been allotted our full contingent of water-logged simpletons?"

I wanted to punch this man, but I had the notion that he would shoot me if I tried.

"None of us are dull-witted, but my friends are more knowledgeable about your country and customs than I am," I said, and decided to go the Clark Kent route: "I'm not from Ain. We are from an isolated, far-flung settlement deep in K-Set."

It felt like bullshit coming out of my mouth, but Walter didn't seem to be fazed much by my pathetic attempts at being coy.

"You say you are the son of Eddick, yet you are from the farthest reaches of the colony?"

"I am . . . an illegitimate child. My mother and I were exiled from Ain before my birth to spare my father the grief. I heard of his death and came to pay my respects, but on the way over, we were knocked overboard by a storm."

"Oh, a bastard. How charming," said Walter, ushering me back into the kitchen.

The galley sailors that were leaning against the panel trying to listen to the conversation leapt away from him and went back to

191

peeling the odd-looking potatoes. I noticed that one of them was simply whittling a vegetable that had already been peeled.

"I believe that in light of this new information, we shall seek an audience with your fellow castaways."

*   *   *

Walter opened the cell door and I went back in; Sawyer and Noreen were awake. He was still lying on the bed, her head on his stomach, and he was languidly stroking her hair as I appeared.

"I have good news and I have bad news. And then I guess some good news again," I said, sitting on the bed with them. "You were right about them. Nobody's going to shoot us. The bad news is, this guy here, Mr. Rollins, thought I was an assassin that killed some guy named Lord Eddick, but I convinced him that I'm not. And then he assumed I was here to avenge my father. Unfortunately, I'm completely ignorant about nearly everything, and now he just thinks I'm a bastard idiot that fell out of a boat. The good news is, he doesn't think we're dangerous and he wants to talk to you guys."

"Told you, you should have read the books," said Noreen. Her voice was unusually raspy.

I turned to Walter. "Do you have a doctor on board the ship?"

He shook his head. "Most of us know how to dress wounds, but there are no seplasiaries onboard, no healers, no tussicular medicines. To your fortune, however, we will reach the shores of Ain within a few days' time, and there your companions will be able to find succor of some measure."

Sawyer visibly relaxed, but his face still depicted concern. He leaned forward and spoke in a hushed tone. "Someone killed Lord

192

Eddick?"

"You know who that is?" I asked.

"A member of Normand Kaliburn's traveling party," he explained. "He was a minor character in the last several books—a nobleman author tagging along with Normand to write his biography. It's always been common opinion that Eddick was how your dad wrote himself into his series as wish fulfillment. Sidekick to his own protagonist."

Walter stepped inside and nodded deferentially to us. "I must admit that . . . my initial assumption of your nature may have been a hasty assessment. I can see that in spite of your strange manner of speech and odd garments, you are of no consequence to the Kingsmen and you have been rescued from certain death. Consider this my—"

He almost seemed to have to force himself to utter the next part, "—Sincerest apologies. Until we reach our destination at Salt Point, please consider yourselves my guests. You may rest in the crew cabin, if you like. The accomodations in our brig are . . . less than hospitable."

"Thank you, sir. My name is Sawyer Winton, and this is our friend Noreen Mears. We're—"

"We're grateful for your generosity, Mr. Rollins," I said, glancing meaningfully at Sawyer. "We were just talking about how we were coming all the way from the farthest settlement on K-Set to mourn my father Eddick."

"Yes," said Sawyer. "It's been a long trip. Did you say Mr. Rollins?" He looked up at the gunslinger. Even Noreen was looking up at him with a certain amount of queasy fascination.

"Aye, that's me. Walter Rollins, Deon of the Southern Kingsmen, at your beckon."

"Would you happen to be related to Clayton Rollins?"

"That's my father, he is," said Walter. "Taught me everything he knew and some things he dint."

"Very nice to meet you, sir," Sawyer said, and he made an odd sort of genuflective gesture that consisted of balling his left fist and bowing gently over his forearm like a French waiter. An expression of surprise flashed across Walter's face and he echoed the salute. "This man is the son of the companion of Normand Kaliburn . . . and evidently the leader of the gunslingers of the South Territories."

"I'm relieved to see at least one of you is prone to fits of intelligence," said Walter. "Are you here to make sure the scribe's bastard doesn't accidentally talk his way into a grave?"

Sawyer and Noreen got up off the bed, stretching their stiff limbs, and we vacated the brig.

"Nahhh," smirked Noreen. I sensed a faint trembling as she walked between us, and it evolved into a hard cough. "We just kinda fell in with him along the way."

When we got to the crew cabin, we took her to the nearest hammock. The ropes were coarse—to the point of bristling with tiny prickles—but there was a narrow feather cushion wedged into the curve of the ropes, redolent with the faint scent of vinegar and age.

Noreen lay down on these, and I offered her my jacket to cover up with. She pulled it over her shoulder to where you could only see her face from the nose up, and curled into a fetal ball, hugging herself. Sawyer sat on the floor next to her, holding the rope, a worried look on his face.

I asked the Deon if there were any possibility of scoring something to eat at the galley before he left us alone, and with his assent I went and fetched what I could.

This late in the voyage, they were low on provisions, but I

managed to bring back a few slivers of strong cheese, very chalky biscuits, a pickle that we cut in thirds, and some dried meat that looked like the pig-ears you could buy at pet stores back home.

Sawyer and I glanced at each other in trepidation, but tucked in nevertheless. He gave his third of the pickle to Noreen and busied himself feeding pieces of the rest of his ration to her. He was barely touching it himself, giving her the lion's share.

"Eat more," Noreen murmured from her nest, rocking with the motion of the sea. She coughed, another dry, ragged bray. "Mm go sleep."

Sawyer nibbled at the biscuit's edges, savoring the crusty, greasy rim. I sat back against a pole, my feet flat on the floor and my elbows on my knees, and watched him for a while until I could hear the girl's breathing slow. I spent the time slowly and methodically eating my pieces of cheese and pickle in tiny bites, watching the sunbeams from the ceiling grate sway back and forth.

"What was that thing you did back there?" I asked, mimicking the salute.

"It's how they shake hands here," said Sawyer. "It comes from the days before guns were invented, and the Kingsmen carried shields and spears. See how it looks like I've got a shield on my arm? Back in the old days, they bowed to each other from behind their shields as they passed on the road."

I nodded. "Ahh, okay. I get it. What's a *Deon?*"

"A Sheriff, basically, but he's m—"

"ON THE DECK!"

The sudden exclamation from every sailor in the room almost made me drop the remainder of my cheese and pickle. I leapt to my feet and looked around in a weird sort of terror; Sawyer's eyes were as huge as if he'd been shot at.

I realized what had happened when I saw a man coming

195

toward us from the front of the bay, accompanied by Walter. Sawyer got up as well, and as they approached, we gave them the shield-bow, which they returned in kind. "Friends, this is the captain of the *Vociferous*," said Walter, motioning to the man, "Thom Cuevas. Thom, these are the castaways we took on."

"May it be," said Sawyer.

"May it never end," said Cuevas. He was a surprisingly small man, with ruddy hair and beard paintstroked with silver, and a large head that made the rest of his scarecrow body look gawky. He was dressed in a similar manner to Walter, wearing no armor, but he was wearing corduroy trousers and there was a pocket watch in his vest. In all, he looked like an Irish whaler.

I was glad to see that our clothes weren't as outlandish as I had been afraid of; from what I'd seen so far, Ainean fashion was rather similar to turn-of-the-century Earth clothes, albeit with much more leather.

"Sera Ross, I hear you are related to the presumably late Lord Bridger," said Cuevas. "My condolences. I understand that the Deon has been applied to the mystery at hand; I suspect that he will deduce the scribe's whereabouts—or murderer, should it come to that—in short time."

I nodded to him in gratitude.

"Also, I'm glad we could be of use in rescuing you from a very long and protracted death at sea. That is, of course, if the Saoshoma hadn't eaten you first."

"Impeccable timing on your part," said Sawyer. He did the shield-bow thing again, and introduced himself. As he spoke, I noticed that the Ain accent had begun to creep into his speech. "My name is Sawyer Winton, captain; my lady and I were accompanying Mr. Bridger here on his voyage. I was visiting relatives in K-Set, and on my way back, I fell in with these two."

"*Fell in*, 'e says," remarked Cuevas, chuckling to the Deon. "That you did! Well, no need to explain yourself any further. These things happen, and you are among friends. All that matters now is that you're safe and dry, and we're only a few days out. You will be our guests until we make land. We don't have much in the way of provisions, but make yourself at home as best you can. There is a seplasiary in Salt Point that can help your ill companion."

"Thank you," I said. Sawyer did the same.

"Boys, I've got to get back to it," said the captain, rocking on his toes. He clapped the gunslinger on one bare arm and bustled away, giving a salute to a sailor that happened to be standing behind us. "Ensure that our new friends do not fall off of this boat as well, Deon?"

197

Normand was sitting on his cot sipping cool water when three men came in and stood in front of his cell. They stared at him, assessing his sun-blistered face and red eyes, and his filthy clothes, tinted green by the mica sands. "May I help you, gentlemen?" is what he wanted to say, but his throat was a raw tube of parched meat and he was too sullen for pleasantries anyway.

"I hear tell they gonna hang you in the morning," said the man in the middle.

"I suppose so," said Normand.

"I hear you and your boys have been knockin over coaches out on the border. That's why they gon' hang you."

He put up his hands, giving them an awkward, supplicating half-smile.

The men looked at each other, then back at him. The middle one addressed him again. "I also hear you're the wiliest, and most versed trapper out in the K-Set. Is that right? And you're the first Ainean to ever survive a siege from them whatcha-callit—Beam-o Ip-nimmy fellas?"

Normand's face slowly broke into a grin. "Ayuh."

"Congratulations, asshole," said the middle-man. "You've just been drafted."

—The Fiddle and the Fire, vol 3 "The Rope and the Riddle"

The Bright Side

THE NEXT SEVERAL DAYS passed at a glacial pace. We were full steam, but after a life of fast cars, jump-cut action movies, and the instant gratification of the Internet, it seemed as if we were sitting dead still. The second half of the first day and the entirety of the day after were spent exploring the ship, marveling at the ship's intricacies and the efficiency of the crew as they went about their business.

I also learned quite a few nautical terms from the crew, earned a few pieces of Ainean currency (called "council talents"), and got a better look at their strange segmented armor.

The armor looked like a dark-green version of the Batsuit from the Christopher Nolan *Batman* films, only it had no cape or cowl. It was not crafted by any Ain or K-Set blacksmith; according to a sailor named Gosse Read, the thin green plates were artifacts left by the original inhabitants of the Antargata k-Setra, the Etudaen.

He took one of the gauntlets off and let me examine it; the material visually resembled the shell of a June bug, but it was completely impervious, as Read demonstrated when he scared the hell out of me by attempting to break my arm with an oar.

I also got a chance to examine the lightning-gun the crew of the *Vociferous* had used to stave off the Saoshoma. It was also an artifact from K-Set. The lone engineer-bosun hired to maintain it had a rudimentary understanding of how it worked, but had no more idea of how to reproduce it than I did. He told me that it was salvaged and repaired by a scientist named Atanasije that had gone missing in the war against the No-Men.

He didn't have the insight I did, coming from 21st century Earth; I could plainly see that the turtle-shell "protective dome" he so proudly demonstrated to me by firing a musket ball at it was in fact the solar-panel array that powered it. I told him that if he kept damaging it, the "storm spear" (as Walter had described it) would no longer work.

I looked underneath the shell to see if there was any other damage. I got a glimpse of a strange, familiar icon stenciled on the body of the machine . . . a stylized eagle, wings spread and head in profile. It was barely visible, worn away by age. Something was underneath it—it looked like words—but they were so deteriorated they were illegible even if I had been able to read the language.

He told me to "shite yerself and away with ye, smart-arse".

While I was roaming the *Vociferous,* Sawyer held constant vigil over Noreen as she became more and more ill. It was beginning to look like more than a simple cold, as the coughing had worsened. Everything after the evening of Day Two came in disjointed episodes, as I had elected to sleep through the rest of the trip in one of the rope hammocks.

To my chagrin, I found that it is nearly impossible to lie face-down in a hammock without breaking one's back, so as I lay curled on my side, I faded in and out of consciousness. At one point I woke up to the smell of honey and lemons; Sawyer was administering some sort of steaming-hot fragrant mead to Noreen.

"If you can keep this down," Sawyer was saying, "we'll try the soup again."

The next time I awoke, it was to the sound of shouting. We had made landfall.

Sawyer reluctantly left Noreen in her hammock and came

topside with me to watch the ship come into port. We stood at the starboard bow bulwark, as the crew brought us in at a slow angle.

Salt Point was a pleasant surprise, a bustling seaside metropolis that wouldn't have looked out of place on an island in the Mediterranean back home. Tall chalk cliffs overlooked the bay, arrayed with layers of chiseled terraces; these were clustered with half-timbered houses with green saltillo roofs.

The streets were a fine lacework of narrow cobblestone pathways; towers and battlements of older pedigree speared upward from the maze. They were joined by squat gothic towers constructed of grim gray stone and capped with tall steeples, their tips streaming long red pennants.

I could even see a gravel path winding out of town into the scrubby highlands, where the jagged ruins of a lighthouse held dominion in the skyline with tufts of desert brush and a sail-armed windmill. A flagpole on one of the towers flew a banner with the now-familiar Kingsman symbol, an elegant shield with a pair of sixguns over a stylized wolf-face.

I got the general impression of a medieval German village that had been transplanted into Mexico.

I smiled at Sawyer as armored sailors scurried around us, preparing to dock.

"How does it feel?" I asked.

He couldn't help but return the grin. I could feel him restraining the joy of finally seeing the land he'd vicariously grown up in. "It feels fantastic, Ross. This is . . . unbelievable. If I had to do it all over, I'd step right into that elevator with you again."

That did all but eradicate the guilt I'd been feeling at bringing them into this world. "Is it anything like you imagined?"

"I don't know. So far, it's more than I ever thought it would be. The Saoshoma was a thousand times scarier and more

202

incredible . . . . I mean, it was mind-blowing. That thing was downright majestic . . . for a sea serpent."

As we drew near, men began to assemble at the edge of the dock to receive us, ropes coiled over their shoulders.

"I've been wondering something."

"What?" Sawyer asked, his eyes fixed on the wharf.

"Destin . . . did my dad make it up, or has it always been here?"

"Like, did he write it into existence? Or did he discover it, and wrote about it?"

"Yeah. I can't make up my mind."

"For what it's worth, I think it's always been here. Like the story Bayard told you, the silen came to tell Ed about it, to 'slake the thirst of imagination' with the waters of the Sea of Dreams," he said, elaborating the phrase with a grand flourish of his hands. "But who really knows?"

"We've got to find the silen," I said. "I want to find out who killed my dad, and and I want to know why the silen brought us here."

"I wonder if Normand knew about your dad's life in our world. They were pretty close at the end of the last book your dad published; Eddick Bridger was serving as Clayton's steward, housesitting the Rollins estate in Maplenesse while Clayton and Normand went to fight in the war."

"I don't know. Do you think he's still alive?"

"We could ask Deon Rollins."

"Ask him what, pray tell?" said Walter, strolling leisurely up behind us, twirling a leather chupalla on his finger as a nearby sailor stepped past us and flung a coil of rope off the side of the ship. The Deon whipped the hat onto his head and tugged the brim down.

Sawyer took the reins of the conversation. "Did Normand Kaliburn survive the war?"

"Survive it?" laughed the Deon. "He didn't merely survive it; after King Fairbairn was slain by the Redbirds during the Battle of Ostlyn, Normand was appointed as his replacement by the Council, in gratitude for avenging Jude Fairbairn's death. You lot have really been out of the news, haven't you?"

"Yeah," said Sawyer. "Way out in the ass-end of nowhere."

As he spoke, I saw a light come on in his eyes and I turned to find Noreen standing behind me.

"How are you feeling?" I asked. She made a face and shook her head. I could tell she was still cold, as she was clutching my jacket tightly around herself like a shawl, even though the afternoon was comfortable to me even in my shirtsleeves.

"I feel absolutely horrible. Wow!" she said, cutting between us to lean against the rail and take in the stately beauty of the timber-frame buildings now looming over us.

Walter asked me, "Where do you plan to go after leaving Salt Point?"

"I've been told that my father was serving as steward for your father when the war began," I explained. "I'd like to go to Maplenesse and talk to Clayton about Lord Eddick, if possible, and to see if my father left anything that could be of use to the investigation, or of sentimental value to me."

Walter screwed up his mouth in empathy for delivering disappointment. "I do loathe to be the bearer of luckless tidings, but my father the Chiral is in Ostlyn with the King and the Council. He more or less lives there now, and he's left the ancestral manse to me.

"However," he said, "I would not be averse to accompanying you to our estate so you can visit your father's house. I will be departing for home without my contingent and would be glad of the company; it's a long and lonely journey when one has none to banter with."

"I like the sound of that," I said. "I've never really been to Ain, and I'm a bit lost."

"I'm assuming your father sired you in K-Set and you've lived in the colonies ever since."

"That would be correct."

"Well, then!" exclaimed the Deon, throwing his arms wide, as if to encompass the glory all around us. "Welcome to the land of Ain, traveler!" he said, then promptly walked away and down the gangplank, sidestepping a soldier carrying a heavy crate. "Come fetch me once you've seen to your friend; I will be feeding my most hideous indiscretions at the Vespertine."

*   *   *

We were left to roam Salt Point, looking for somebody that could sell us what we needed to help Noreen. We had to get it cracked before it turned into a deadly-serious issue. As we marched up and down the cobblestone streets looking for signs that indicated the shop of a "seplasiary", the Aineans paused to assess us and went back to their business with little more than disapproving headshakes and sidelong glances to their companions.

Most of them were coming home from wherever they worked, their spouses doing a bit of last-minute cleaning, their kids playing a odd version of hopscotch in a gamespace of fifteen concentric rings, like a target. They hopped toward the center, yelling and pausing, laughing every so often.

Like I mentioned before, our fashion wasn't so far removed from theirs; we could have simply been ahead of the style curve, so

205

to speak. Luckily, none of us were wearing shirts with Earth-culture pictures on them.

I was wearing a gray henley shirt, tan cargo pants, and my trusty dock shoes, Sawyer had on a blue sweater, a pair of corduroys, and Doc Martens, and Noreen wore jeans, Plimsolls, a colorful sundress that looked like an African dashiki, and my leather jacket. Not quite the linen and wool suits, ponchos, and petticoats the Aineans were wearing, but not *too* anachronistic . . . at least, that's what I told myself.

We still stuck out like sore thumbs; it behooved us to find something more appropriate to wear, before people started asking too many questions.

After a little while of wandering through winding alleyways, we came into an open marketplace, populated by dozens of stalls, kiosks, and shops. The street was long and straight, running between two-story buildings along the back side of town, and choked with traffic milling in both directions. Gravel crunched and crackled under our feet, and the air was chaotic with the voices and street-music of a hundred or more people.

I was grateful for the crowd, because it cut down on our visibility and ironically made it easier to move through Salt Point unnoticed. All thought of subterfuge, however, went out the window when I saw the wares for sale.

There were tables arrayed with a collection of things made of some honey-colored stone, a beautiful translucent gem shot through with veins of dark, sparkling green. Vases, statues and figurines, flutes, dishware, chalices, hinged jewelry boxes, cameo pendants, tiny scale models of castle towers, spheres that looked like bowling balls and billiard balls made of amber. It was inlaid into the long necks of lutes and fiddles, and framed the striking surfaces of tall bongo drums ribbed with bones.

We also saw garments in many colors and styles, from wool

three-piece suits in earthy shades, to frilly velvet skirts trimmed in snow-white lace, and also pieces of the sleek green armor salvaged from K-Set. Intricate, embroidered linen tunics, hide vests, finished and unfinished leather overcoats, silk robes in a hundred dazzling colors, and even the blood-red cloaks worn by the Grievers.

We passed a table with a great many revolvers, glittering like polished silver in the afternoon sun, accompanied by oiled leather gunbelts and cases of brassy cartridges. Laid out beside them was an assortment of wicked-looking knives and swords of many shapes and sizes.

A few stalls had cages containing a veritable menagerie; one cage held a huge black parrot with brilliant green eyes that was methodically picking apart and eating one of the potato-apple vegetables. In another was a pair of tiny yellow birds with black crests on their heads that made them look as if they were wearing wigs. I even saw something that looked like a skinny red koala with a pendulous, flaccid nose and ears that flapped like those of an elephant.

As we passed each display, the men tending them called to us in friendly, eager voices, trying to wave us into their space. Even miserable Noreen couldn't help but marvel.

Once or twice I accidentally caught one of their hands when they offered it and was led into a stall to my friends' amusement, where I had to pretend to be interested, and then excuse myself. "I'm sorry. No, I'm sorry. I don't have enough money! Maybe later. Thank you, though! They're very nice. Thank you. I'm sorry."

Sawyer and Noreen had spotted a shop across the street with a huge collection of colored bottles in the window. The sign over the door was in bizarre lettering none of us could understand, or at least I couldn't; I'm sure they had some degree of familiarity with Ain written language.

A shirtless man sat on the sidewalk outside, playing a steel lap guitar and howling nonsense lyrics at the top of his lungs. I couldn't understand him, but I could've stayed and listened to it if I had time.

We ventured inside and found a rather dark, rustic shop only illuminated by the furtive flames of a candle on a back shelf, and the sunlight coming in through the entrance and the colored glass bottles. The floor was floured with sawdust and creaked as we walked on it.

An old man stood up from behind the counter; he was wearing a vest and shirt with arm-garters and had a goatish beard— and hair just as long and bushy. I felt like I was looking at a bookie that took bets on gator wrestling in the Everglades.

"What can I do for ye?" he asked, taking in the sight of us over the rim of his glasses. He was missing several teeth, which made him whistle a bit as he spoke.

I took out the money I'd won back on the *Vociferous* for singing and showed it to him. "You are the local seplasiary?"

"I am, I am. You don't seem the sort to be shopping for perfume, so I guess you're here for something a touch more medicinal?"

"You are correct. Our friend here fell in the ocean last night and got sick."

The seplasiary came out from behind the counter to appraise Noreen. He ordered her to open her mouth; he looked down her throat, and then in her ears, manhandling her head as if it were a cantaloupe. She looked rather bemused by the examination.

He wrote something down on a notepad. "I expect it's a touch of the sea-plague. Your friend's got a day, two at the most."

"What?" we all said in unison.

"That was a joke," he said, going to the shelf to sort through the vials there. He spoke over his shoulder, "It takes a clever man to understand my *geeeen*-ius brand a' humor." He took down a couple of bottles and a paper envelope and brought them over to the counter, where he picked up a clipboard and checked them off on an inventory ledger.

He handed it to me and said, "Just sign here."

I found a fountain pen by the cashbox and picked it up, figured out how to use it, and was about to put down my signature when a thought hit me. "Just what's *in* these bottles, anyway?"

"Oh, you know," said the seplasiary. "The *usual.*"

"What's 'the usual'?"

"How the hell should *I* know?" he said, throwing his hands up in a shrug. "I'm just watching the place while the shopkeeper takes a piss. I don't know nothin' about any of this stuff."

"Are you serious?"

"Why *hell, no!* Just sign your name, ya dodder—afore I die of gray age." And with that, he picked up a nearby vial, popped the top, and took a long swig of the dark green contents. Sawyer made a face as I signed the ledger. The seplasiary burped.

I put the brassy "council talents" on the counter. They looked measly next to the bottles. "Is this enough? It's all I have."

"I'll be damned," said the man, lifting his glasses to look under them at the money.

"What?"

"That's just about exactly what you needed," he said with a wink, and put them in the cashbox.

Sawyer took the vials and put them in his pockets. I lingered at the counter for a second, thinking, and finally the old man seemed to snap out of it.

"Oh, right. *Ahem.* The slightly yellow long-necked phial," he said, indicating it with one knobby-jointed finger, "That there's your tincture of astragalus. Put a few drops of that on your tongue every day. The envelope is tea leaves for *cham*-o-*meel*. Does a body *goooood*," he crooned through his teeth, puckering his lips. "The big bottle is coconut oil. You can just gulp that down any ol time. You can even put it in your hot bathwater."

I uncorked the coconut oil on the way out the door to smell it. It was repulsive and sickly sweet.

"That bad, huh?" asked Noreen. "He said the magic words, guys: *hot bathwater*."

"No! It's *greaaat*," I said, though I'm sure I was less than inspiring. Sawyer elbowed me. "Where'd you get that money?"

"Oh, I earned it back on the steamboat on the way here."

"Oh yeah? How'd you manage that? You don't strike me as a cardshark."

"I taught a couple guys Monty Python's *Always Look on the Bright Side of Life*," I said, and almost dropped the bottles when they both thumped me in the shoulders.

Dirty Dead Arse

THE VESPERTINE WAS A honky-tonk, if fantasy worlds had honky-tonks. As we approached the saloon on the edge of town, we could hear the talking and music down the street, even over the ebbing noise of the dwindling crowd outside. It didn't have the batwing door I anticipated, and there wasn't a hitching post outside, but there was an upper balcony overlooking the street, and a few people were relaxing there in the dying bronze light of the day.

I suddenly realized what I hadn't seen since we'd arrived in Salt Point: horses. There were none to be found. I was about to ask Sawyer about it when one of the shadows on the front porch detached itself and came out into the sunset's caress to greet us.

It was Gosse Read, the man that had shown me the green armor on the steamship. Read was without a doubt in the world one of the biggest men I had ever seen in my life. He looked like someone had ripped down a piece of the night sky and draped it over a tree.

That's a funny thing, too, and I'll mention it here: back home on Earth, you'd occasionally see Africans with skin so dark they seemed to have a green or blue tint; I saw men here that were actually intensely dark shades of moss-green, with brilliant green eyes and dark limbic rings. The man looked positively mythical.

There was no one here you could reliably refer to as "whites" or "blacks" or "Asians". That's not to say there weren't racial physical differences, though. Most of the people were like Walter, with olive-mocha skin, tall and thin. There were also those similar

212

to Read, broad and mossy-brown.

I also saw short, slender people with sloping shoulders and large triangular heads, their skin a faint two-tone gradient of sky-blue, like a fish. I even saw several women with pale brown skin that bore dark, ragged striations that reminded me of drawings I'd seen of the human nervous system.

"I thought I would catch you before you met up with the boss," said Read in his impossibly deep voice. He was a Kingsman gunslinger too, although he didn't carry a six-shooter. He had a fearsome-looking shotgun strapped to his back as long as a broom-handle and twice as thick.

He blocked us from going into the Vespertine and ushered us to the end of the front porch, where we could speak alone, in confidence. I felt like a child; he was at least a foot taller than myself.

"What's going on?" asked Sawyer.

Read screwed up his mouth and glared at us from under his heavy brow. He spoke fast, an elaborate, enunciated tumble-string of words. "You think you are clever, but you are *not.*"

I felt my face grow cold. "I'm not sure what you mean."

"You say you're from the back *end* of K-Set, but that is a hard, and mean, and lonely place," he said, pausing for emphasis. "It does *not* make people like you. It makes people like myself. I know what I am looking at, and it is not a man accustomed to life on the frontier. You and your unusual companions are from elsewhere."

Noreen coughed. Sawyer shook his head, waving the question off with his hands: *that's enough, this is going nowhere.* "Look, Mr. Read—"

Read tapped on Sawyer's chest with one beefy finger. "I don't know . . . *why* the Deon is takin it so easy on you, because it is not too *difficult* to see you are not what you say you are. He is not a

213

stupid man in the least. He must have gotten something obscured up his sleeve. He might have a . . . trying personality, but his *heart* is in the right place.

"Also, he is perhaps one of the smartest men I've ever had the fortune to introduce myself to. But as for myself, I'm the sort of individual that likes to see the truth on the street, and I don't. Abide. Liars. Or. Obfuscators."

"You wouldn't believe us if we told you."

"Try me."

"You sure about that?" asked Sawyer.

"I've seen a lot in my time here in this land. I've, I've seen a woman go from one place to *another* with nothing in between . . . and cut through six inches of steel like it was warm butter. I've seen a giant as tall as this saloon step on a man and crush him like a bug. Once I saw Walter Rollins himself put a pistol bullet through a man's head at four hundred yards. I've seen ghosts, phantoms, and ghouls. I'm primed to take in just about anything at this point."

Sawyer glanced at me, and we both looked at Noreen, who shrugged.

"All right," I said, and asked Read, "How well did you know my father Lord Eddick?"

"The scribe? Not that well, I suppose. I met him a few times before the war, but I never really got very personal with him."

"You're familiar with how Destin was created, aren't you?" asked Sawyer, using his hands to detail the bisection and the two results, "How Behest was created by the Wolf and swallowed by the Dragon, and was cut in half by the Wolf to create the dual worlds Destin and Zam?"

"That is an accepted rendition of the story of Creation, yes."

"Ross, his dad, Noreen, and I—we're from Zam," he said, indicating his left fist. "We were transported here by an

214

interdimensional being called a *silen*. Now we're on a quest to find out who killed Eddick, and to find a way to get back to our world."

Sawyer's explanation actually made a sideways sort of sense to me. I think I felt my sanity slipping loose, like an ill-fitting sock. Read seemed to be processing this new information, staring right at my forehead, his nostrils flaring.

Read's eyes twitched. He blinked, looked over my head into the middle distance, casually remarked, "Aaaawright," and walked away into the Vespertine.

*   *   *

The saloon was almost exactly how I pictured it would look. Rich, dim light from the grimy electric sconces on the walls cast a warm glow on a dozen round pub tables. Scores of people sat in circles, drinking and chatting and playing cards. The bar was a glossy cherrywood spotted with white mug-rings and carved graffiti, manned by a hulking bald bartender with bushy red muttonchops.

The shelves behind him held a great and varied collection of bottles in a dozen different hues, and one fat wooden keg that didn't linger untapped for more than a couple minutes at a time. The air was heavy with the smell of fried food wafting in from the kitchen behind the bar, and I heard a growling wolverine in my guts.

I found Walter Rollins, Gosse Read, and another Kingsman sitting at a table in the corner, and went over to sit with them. They were drinking in a sullen silence, hunched over mugs of some dark beer.

"We're here, yo," I said, and Sawyer shot me a look.

Walter sat up sharply, his hands on his thighs, and he thrust an offering hand in my direction. "So you are. Have a seat."

215

There was only one chair. I let Sawyer have it; Noreen sat on his lap and folded her arms protectively. I stood over them in an awkward silence as they brooded over their beers, waiting for someone to say something.

Eventually, Read said, "You're looking a little peak-ed. I don't suppose you want anything to eat?"

"Don't have any money," croaked Noreen.

"I didn't ask you if you had any money," he said. "I asked you if you wanted something to eat."

"Sit down, bastard; you make me anxious," said Walter.

"Yes, we're hungry as hell," said Sawyer, as I attempted to obey the Deon and take a seat. "What's good here?"

I looked around for a chair but saw no nearby empty ones. I briefly debated the wisdom of carrying one from the other side of the Vespertine but decided against it.

I tried to take a knee on the floor but felt weird doing it, and stood back up. I put my butt on the back of Sawyer's chair but it was too tall, attempted to lean my elbow casually on the table but it was too low. I finally settled for squatting next to Read with my hands on the edge of the table to steady myself.

Walter was looking at me as if I'd lost my mind. He said to Sawyer, "The cheese and spinach pie is the best thing here for your coin."

Sawyer wrinkled his nose. "I'm not too hot on spinach. Is there anything else?"

"*Pohtir-nyhmi*," said Read.

"What's that?" asked Noreen.

"A large horned beast of the fields. We ride them."

The Deon nodded, scratched his head, and said, "And they smell like dirty dead arse."

"I have suddenly developed a taste for spinach."

While they discussed the merits (or not) of eating livestock, I surveyed the saloon.

There were many rough-looking people here, in a variety of conditions and outfits, from many different dubious backgrounds and equally shadowy occupations. It struck me that it was an incredible experience—efficient, even—to be here, to be immersed in the culture and world of my father's books.

Would I even have the opportunity, I wondered, to return to Earth (née Zam) and attempt to write the last book in the series? That raised the issue of what I should—or could—even write. Did I even have to make anything up? Here lay the world of Destin before me, its plots and contrivances physical, emergent, and at my beck and call. I made up my mind that, if I were going to be stuck here for a while, I should begin finding out what I could about what had transpired since the events of my dad's latest novel, so that I could transcribe them.

I realized that this must have been how he had written the series: by coming here and seeing the events and places in the novels firsthand, by recording its history, and weaving it into a tapestry of prose. He had been a biographer.

The atmosphere loosened as we sat there having dinner, and we conversed about ourselves and each other, about our accomplishments and failures, our experiences, amusing anecdotes—tempered, of course, by judicious censorship of anything that pegged us as outsiders (outside of our clothes and accents). We'd told Read where we'd come from, and he didn't seem too fazed by it. I was glad of that. I hoped Walter would be an equally easy sell.

I must have been getting over my initial shock at being brought here, to such an alien place, in such a startling way. It was nice to have time to rest, warm up, pack away a good hot meal, sort

217

through the situation, and get to know each other in a place that wasn't making me seasick. The more I learned about our friends the Kingsmen, the more I made up my mind to bring their history and adventures to life back on Earth.

I must have been a quiet, introspective dinner guest, because my mind—fully ensconced in our circumstances by now—was finally beginning to spin up to operational velocity.

By the time we were getting ready for bed in the Vespertine's upstairs accommodations, I was positively vibrating. I lay in the simple four-poster bed staring up at the ceiling, contemplating, listening to a headboard thump against the wall in an adjacent bedroom as Sawyer administered Noreen's medicine in the bed next to mine.

This must have been how Edward Richard Brigham/Lord Eddick Bridger felt when he first came here.

The thumping eventually subsided; my friends went to sleep, and I rolled over, hugging my musty down pillow to my face, excited about tomorrow's prospects. It hit me, as I tried to drift off, that I was effectively taking his place. I hoped that I wouldn't join him in the grave the same way.

The size of the thing was dismaying in and of itself, inspiring despair and dread just by existing.

The giant No-Man moved with a fluid gravity, stepping over the rampart of junk without even disturbing the crenellations, or the men standing on them. Pack's heart leapt in shocked fear when he realized just how woefully under-prepared Harwell's men had been, and how close he'd come to dying every time he'd perched on the wall after joining the Lord on his morning rounds.

The boy ran, not hiding or fighting, but simply away from the commotion. He hoped that he could put enough landscape between himself and the thundering monster before either the sun went down and he couldn't see, or the thing chased him down and killed him. He pushed his way through a throng of people paralyzed by fear, and clambered up a ladder.

When he got to the top, he paused just long enough to look back at the great silhouette looming over the village, and wonder if they ate people.

—*The Fiddle and the Fire, vol 2 "The Cape and the Castle"*

There's a Catch

MAXWELL BAYARD RELAXED AS American Airlines Flight 4276 rocketed down the runway and eased into the air. He could feel the weight of the plane's belly take over, the wheels leaving the tarmac, the floor almost seeming to droop under his feet.

He checked his watch again, and took off his hat, combed his fingers through what was left of his hair. He held out that age-spotted hand and saw that it was trembling.

He was nervous. He'd taken thousands of air trips across the States in his career as Ed Brigham's literary agent. Hurtling through the sky at four hundred miles an hour in a four-hundred ton metal box never bothered him before, but today he was definitely beset by unease.

It wasn't because he was afraid Ross was going to get caught up in Ed's shenanigans—he had enough confidence that he'd intimidated the boy out of prodding further into the circumstances of his father's death.

Maybe he shouldn't have illuminated the fact that Ed was killed, and hadn't died of a heart attack as the world was led to believe, but he figured that was the price to pay for using the revelation to scare Ross. He hadn't told Ed's son how he had discovered the writer in a puddle of his own blood on his kitchen floor, a gaping bullet wound in his throat.

Besides, he contemplated as the world outside the window spiraled down out of sight, there was no way to get into Destin without the door under the church, and somehow, the Sileni had

220

closed it off from the other side.

And that meant Ross would be safe here on Earth.

To pat himself on the back, Maxwell had enjoyed the couple days of vacation he'd given himself in Chattanooga before heading home, visiting the aquarium and treating himself to some top-shelf Thai cuisine. He'd been through Chattanooga a thousand times, but he'd never gone to see the Tennessee Aquarium. What a shame.

The Sileni hadn't needed to talk him into covering up the murder; the prospect of being richer than his wildest dreams had been enough to goad him into talking the kids out of following Ed into that other world, as well as abandoning the *Fiddle and the Fire* franchise for good.

He reclined the seat, toed his loafers off of his feet, stretched his cramping legs, and closed his eyes.

When he opened them again, the plane was at cruising altitude, somewhere over the Midwest. He'd been awakened by the silvery burning in his bladder that told him he had to piss, and he had to do it soon or face the consequences. He unbuckled his belt and shuffled sideways down the aisle to the lavatory, where he found that it was occupied.

He sighed and leaned against the wall.

A flight attendant sidled past him toward coach. "Excuse me, sir, but we're about to serve refreshments. I just thought I would let you know in case you end up waiting a while."

"Thank you," he said. He followed her pert little ass with his gaze, and accidentally locked eyes with a woman that had been watching a movie, earning an angry glare. Embarrassed in spite of himself, Max Bayard turned his head the other way, and that's when he saw something that validated every last one of his fears.

He forgot about waiting for the toilet and traveled back across

221

the business class section to the cockpit door, glancing back at the people sitting there. He noticed a powerfully-built man in a cheap suit giving him a look that would wither cabbage.

"Can I help you, sir?" said the air marshal.

Maxwell smiled, though it felt like more of a wince. "I'm just waiting for the lavatory where I won't be in the way of the drinks cart."

"Your seat is closer."

"Yes, well—" Max was about to say something about having to tie his shoes, but he wasn't wearing any.

"Sit down, sir," said the air marshal.

Maxwell was in no position to argue, but the passengers and the marshal couldn't see the little horned man standing by the cockpit door, whispering to the pilot on the other side, his moving lips an inch from the panel's surface.

If Max pointed it out, that wouldn't have helped the situation in the least. The silen was invisible, and the only person on the plane that could see him was the literary agent, even if he only materialized as a pale, ethereal shadow, his face the last truly solid part of him.

He'd had a lot of practice over the years.

Thinking fast, Max grabbed one of the creature's goat-horns and marched back to his seat, pulling it along. His heart jumped when he realized that to the air marshal, it looked like he was holding something behind his back.

He took his cellphone out of his jacket pocket and sat back down, putting the phone to his ear. "Hello?" he said, the earpiece silent. The phone was still turned off.

"What are you doing, you little shit?" he whispered to the silen.

"Trust is earned," it hissed in some dead language, calmly standing there as Max pretended to talk on the phone. For some reason, you could always understand what they were saying, regardless of it whether it was plain English or what the Mesopotamians spoke to each other two millenia ago. "It is done. Our plans are in motion. You cannot stop it."

"Stop what?" asked Maxwell.

The silen did nothing but grin with those horrible, pointy little Bat-Boy teeth. Max couldn't kill an immortal, but he could sure as hell hurt one. He put the phone down, took an ink pen out of his jacket pocket and bit off the cap, then stuck the point in the corner of the silen's eye.

It jerked at the pressure, but didn't retaliate. Max wasn't worried about that; they couldn't be killed *or* kill anyone else. That was part of their curse; they lived forever, but there were conditions, and one of them was that they could not end the life of another by their own hand—their own life, or anyone else's.

"The writer's son is in the other-world," it said.

A lady sitting across the aisle gave him a strange look, so Max scooted backward until he was against the wall; his seat was next to two empty ones. He applied more force with the pen, and the silen scrunched that side of his face, trying to back away. Max held him tight.

"What did you do?" asked Max, and the plane began to decelerate. He could hear exclamations of surprise and fear from coach. "You mused the pilot, didn't you?"

"Now you cannot stop us," said the silen. "The Rhetor has won. The boy will die in the other-world, and now—you will die in this one."

The engines, all four of them, started slowing. Soon, they would be still, and the plane and all six hundred people on board would slam into Kansas at terminal velocity.

The silen began to fade, his shape narrowing until all he could

223

see of it was its staring, liquid-gold reptilian eyes and that huge, hideous puppy-teeth grin.

"*Stop you?*" asked Maxwell. "What makes you think I want to stop you? *We had a deal!*"

The silen blinked out of existence with a slap of displaced air, leaving Max with handfuls of nothing.

Vero Nihil Verius

I AWAKENED TO A FIERCE light, snapping to consciousness as soon as the edge of the sunrise knifed through the window and slit open my eyelids. Gosse Read was asleep in a chair at the end of my bed, his feet kicked up and crossed on my footboard. I sat up and his luminous emerald eyes flicked open.

"Bout time you woke up," he said. "Your friends are in the bath-house washing up."

"Were you watching me sleep?"

"Yeah, you real pretty, boy. Get up and go wash, we're gonna go to the bazaar."

"Why?" I asked, confused. I slid to the edge of the bed and shuffled into my trousers, shrugged into my shirt. I was putting on my shoes as Read said, "Because I've been contemplating what you said yesterday, and something occurred to me."

"What would that be?"

"That maybe the Old Ways were right."

The morning was a beautiful beast that romped and shone with a vital spirit, and the very air was like fresh wine, unsullied and intoxicating. The sky was an infinite miracle of deep blue.

I could not hide my astonishment at how good I felt in this other-world after a good night's sleep and a hot meal; my face was locked in a half-grin that refused to leave. Leaving the Vespertine, I crossed the path of a woman carrying a swaddled infant and couldn't help but greet her, which only earned me a confused

226

smile.

The bath-house turned out to be the large cabin I'd seen the day before and mistaken for some sort of a barn, or a warehouse. It was a central feature of the bazaar itself, and I discovered that it served as a social locus for Salt Point. Mornings here were like blackbirds on a power-line, a multitude of bathers milling in and out of the front entrances and lingering in conversation.

I almost had a crisis when I approached, because I couldn't read the signs that indicated which side of the bath-house was for a certain gender; my fears were allayed when I simply chose to enter through the door from which I saw men coming out.

What a peculiar experience: an illiterate writer.

When I walked in, however, I quickly realized that I'd had no reason to be confused after all, because both doors led into the same central bathing chambers. It resembled an Olympic-style lap pool, except it was only waist-deep.

The sides of it were rimmed with a bench where men and women sat talking and sipping pungent coffee out of vase-like ceramic mugs. There was also a square island in the middle with seating; dark green foliage curled out of a planter inside of it.

The entire floor, pool and all, was tiled in pearlescent green, and the enormous windows were painted over with white, which caught the golden sunrise and translated it into a clean, rich glow. This was in turn captured by the steam and made into a glowing mass of vapor that hung over the bath like a star-cloud and smelled of lemons and mint. Indistinct shapes lurked inside of it, talking and laughing.

The second thing I noticed was that no one was wearing any clothes, only a sort of colorless loincloth; it was a single rectangle of linen that one pulled across their straddle like a diaper, wrapped a piece of twine around the waist to affix it, and let the ends dangle from the butt and crotch.

I was mortified to realize that I was by far the palest, flabbiest man in the room. Nearly all of the locals were like fashion models back home, slender, dark, and chiseled by a life spent digging up a living.

I stared myself down in the floor-length mirror in the changing room (which, it seemed, had been indicated by the signs out front: "Changing-Room" on the left and "Coffee" on the right). Between my muffin top, and my darkening shaved head and week-old beard, I looked like I'd grown up in a cave deep underground, in a war with cave-dwelling coelacanths, subsisting on Doritos and a tincture of colloidal silver and flat Sprite.

I went into the coffee room wearing the loincloth, realized that no one else inside was wearing one, and walked right back out with the urge to shoot myself.

I escaped to the pool and stepped straight in, hoping I could use the milky-hot water to camouflage my flab, and had to restrain myself from whooping out loud as the heat shocked me. My skin was immediately spank-pink.

Sawyer and Noreen were in one corner. I duck-walked in their direction and sat next to them. They had both turned as red as lobsters and were drinking coffee out of the flat-bottomed decanters. I was immediately envious, because even though Sawyer was as pale as myself, at least he was thin. Noreen's arms were folded, and she was holding her breasts with her hands.

"This is the weirdest thing I have ever done," said Sawyer in a deadpan tone. "I'm wearing a diaper, I can see at least seven pairs of breasts, and I am drinking coffee out of an urn with the milk of an animal that I've never actually seen."

I agreed. "It's weird, but I think swimming out of an elevator ranked pretty high on my Weird List. How you feeling, Reen?"

She gave me a grateful half-smile and coughed hard, several times. It sounded productive. "I feel a lot better, actually, between the steam and the medicine I'm doing pretty good. You know, Ross, I had no clue that you were such a hairy-ass man."

I looked down at the whorls of dark hair on my chest. "I'm part muskrat."

"Is that so?"

I was about to retort when someone came up to me carrying a decanter of coffee. It was one of the people with peculiar blue-tinted skin and large heads, dressed in one of the loincloths. I noticed that there was a line of large pores along his collarbone that flared intermittently.

I looked into his eyes and *I could see his retina through his pupils.* It was like reading a map through a pair of keyholes.

"Here you are, sera," he said in a breathy voice. The container was too hot to hold by the base, but I found that holding it by its narrow neck kept me from getting burned. It was made of some satiny metal in reds and greens. Feathery designs and rings had been carved into it. "I just wanted to let you know that bathers are not allowed into the kitchen. Wolf protect you."

When I finally looked away from the blue guy (waiter? manservant?), my friends were giving me funny looks.

Noreen arched an eyebrow. "You're not supposed to go in there. Did you go in there in your towel-thing?"

"Uhh . . . ."

"I bet you forgot something to clean with too. Here, you can use mine," said Sawyer, handing me a bar of gritty soap and a long-handled wooden brush. I smelled the soap; that was where the lemons-and-mint smell was coming from. I lathered up with it and scrubbed myself all over with the brush, which turned out to be very soft.

I decided to finally sample my beaker-vase of coffee now that it was cool enough to drink, and I was astonished at the fact that it was some of the best coffee I'd ever had in my life. A little bitter, and the milk made it frothy-thick, but it had that perfect smoky tang and an added mellow fruitiness besides. It was like drinking an overheated Starbucks mocha out of a hollowed coconut.

We finished bathing and Read was waiting for us when we got outside.

"The first orders of business is to get all of you into clothes a little more appropriate for co-mingling with polite society here in Ain," he said in that erudite way, his words a machine-gun spill of perfect syllables.

"We are goina make a shopping trip to . . . the marketplace, and we'll see if we can't find the three of you something to clothe—to put clothes, different clothes, on your bodies."

We went back to the place in the bazaar where we'd seen clothes the previous day; the merchants were very glad to see us again. After I picked out something that looked more Ainean, I came out to the crowd-choked street where a man in a velvet top hat was playing a rousing jig on a hammered dulcimer with yesterday's shirtless minstrel, who was now sawing at a fiddle.

The music took me back to the Renaissance Faires that I'd attended in the past, but I didn't feel like I was *in* one here. The world was more than *authentic*, it was deeply *actual*. It was *vero nihil verius*, the real deal. No one here was someone else at home. No one here drove here from Cincinnati, none of them were selling food made with ingredients purchased at Walmart, there were no candy wrappers on the ground.

The thought was profoundly refreshing.

I lingered, listening to the music. After a few minutes, the man playing the fiddle stopped playing and indicated a hat on the ground with his foot. "Oi-ye, if you like our music, spare us a coin, bout it?"

230

"I'm afraid I'm tapped out, guys," I said, shrugging. "I don't have any money on me."

"Nice new garb. Fair talents for it, I wager? High quality, that Salomon Spearing does. Best clot'ier in the market. You look right handsome."

"Yeah," I said, feeling awkward. "I guess."

"I don't tink you're lickin up what I'm trowin down, you," said the fiddler, "I'm sayin I know you're carryin, and the music deserves a piece of it, don't you tink?"

"I'm sorry. I just don't have it. A friend of mine bought this, I'm serious."

He seemed to think it over, and played a sad little three-note groan on the fiddle.

I felt a tap on my shoulder. Noreen beamed, demonstrating her new sundress, laced corset and boots. As I surveyed her outfit, I felt a swell of affection. She was ethereal, she was gorgeous. "What do you think?"

"You look good. What about me?" I asked, turning in a circle to show off my vest, flat-crowned hat, and slacks.

"Hmm," she said, and rolled my shirtsleeves up high like a Marine. "There, now you look the part."

Sawyer came up behind her and tickled her, making her yell and laugh. She turned and hugged him, then held him at arm's length. He had chosen one of the brown goat-hair ponchos and a Boss-of-the-Plains; a ribbon of colors was embroidered into the edge of the poncho.

"Wow," Noreen grinned. "You look like Clint Eastwood!"

"That was the idea, baby," he said, waggling his eyebrows. I whistled the trill from *The Good, The Bad, and the Ugly,* and they both cracked up laughing.

"Are you folks finished primping and preening? You kids got

231

expensive taste," asked Read, appearing out of the crowd. "The Deon wants to get going as soon as possible, our ride leaves just before lunch and we let you all sleep late."

The boy snapped awake in the dead of night. Something had hit the roof.

He sat there tangled in his dank bedclothes, listening for something else, anything, another noise to tell him it hadn't just been part of his dream. He'd been flying through the clouds over the countryside on the back of a winged creature whose face he could not see.

Several minutes had passed and he was about to lie back down and try to drift off when he smelled acrid smoke. He got up on his knees and looked out the window.

Six men stood in the cull pen. One of them was holding a liquor bottle with a rag stuffed in the neck; as the boy watched, he lit the rag with a match and lobbed the bottle high into the air. It struck the roof with a thump and rolled off with a thin rumble, sliding off into the woodpile by the window, where it broke and turned into a blinding fireball.

"Pack!" shouted his father from somewhere in the farmhouse.

The boy slid out of bed and moved across the room, but as he took hold of the doorhandle, he heard the rip of gunfire.

A body hit the floor.

Pack stood there, frozen with indecision, then turned and opened his closet. He threw himself inside and shut the door, then pried open the hatch in the back and slid into the crawlspace on his belly. He pulled the board back into place and dragged himself to the hole where the pump pipe rose out of the dirt.

He wedged himself into the ditch by the ice-cold pipe and listened, lying on his side in a grimy puddle.

—The Fiddle and the Fire, vol 1 "The Brine and the Bygone"

Bunkers and Battleships

OUR RIDE TURNED OUT TO BE a train, a great seething black behemoth that was still loading up cargo when we arrived. I admired it as we crossed the platform of the modest red-brick train station where Walter Rollins was waiting for us. A throng of passengers ebbed and flowed around us, boarding the train, shouting to hear each other over the hiss of the mechanism. There were a handful of green-armored men strolling up and down the platform, checking tickets and helping the elderly with their luggage.

"It's a beauty, eh?" asked the Deon, one hand on his hip and the other tapping his leg with his hat. "Top of the line chug-bucket." It was a standard old-school steam engine, a bulbous coal-fired locomotive with a smokestack and a brass bell, with an Ainean-language designation painted in white on the conductors' cabin.

Walter put on his Boss and climbed onboard the caboose; we found a private sitting-room on one of the passenger cars and filed onto the bench seats inside. There was another Kingsman gunslinger joining us that I remembered from the *Vociferous*.

His name was Jonty Garrod. He was a short old fellow with big expressive hound-dog eyes, and a thin beard that had yellowed around the mouth from cigarette smoke. He was tapping filler into a rolling paper as we sat down, so I opened the window.

A wind blew in and made his braided pigtails kick out behind him.

"What's a matter, boy? You got tender lungs? Smoke make you sick?" he asked with a tremendous grin, showing off the gap between his two front teeth.

"No," I lied. "It's just such a pretty day, I thought we should have it open."

"Anybody ever tell you that you ain't worth a damn at lyin?"

I wasn't sure what to say, so I sat down across from him and folded my arms. Sawyer and Noreen came in and sat by Garrod, leaving Read and the Deon to fill out the rest of my bench. Jonty packed the cigarette and lit it . . . soon, the private cabin reeked of sweet, pungent smoke.

It didn't smell like any tobacco I'd ever seen, so I asked him what it was. The train sighed heavily and began to move.

"Pear leaves," Garrod said. *Pahr leaves.* "No, it ain't the Acolouthis, so don't ask. Kids always ask me if it's the fucken Acolouthis, and I allaway says *no, it ain't. And no, you can't have any.*"

"What's the Acolouthis?" I asked.

Garrod's face fell. He glanced over to Walter and said, "Where'd you dig this one up?"

"You know where we got them, you old smokey," said the Deon. He had his feet kicked up on the bench across the cab, slumped down in his seat with his hat over his face and his arms crossed. "You were there."

"Kid, you really *are* ignorant as shit like they say."

"It is because they are from the other-world like Lord Eddick was. The one with the skint head is Eddick's bastard. They don't know any better because they are wholly alien to this world."

I was blown away.

I had no idea Rollins had the scoop on us, or that he was even okay with it. What *really* shocked me was that he knew about my father and that he'd come from Zam/Earth. I registered the

235

disbelief on Sawyer and Noreen's faces as well.

Sawyer picked up the Deon's hat, and there was a stern glare underneath it. "You mean you *knew?*"

"I suspected as soon as the bastard told me who he was," said Walter.

"Why didn't you say anything? You knew about his dad?" asked Sawyer, and he let the hat plop back onto Walter's face.

"I didn't know *everything.* I'd heard stories, when I was a boy, from my father. I overheard them late one night, Clayton, Normand, and Eddick, talking about the other-world, where Eddick had come from. I don't suppose that's something that could stay a secret for long between men as thick as they were."

"Why didn't you say anything?" I said, echoing Sawyer.

"It's not exactly common knowledge," said Walter. "The only people that knew about it were Normand, my father, Ardelia Thirion, myself, and perhaps Jonty Garrod here, the Quartermaster of the Southern Kingsmen. After you told Mr. Read here about it, he came to me as I was getting ready for bed last night and informed me. When I told him I already knew . . . well, you've never seen such a fit."

Read grinned sheepishly. I sat back, my mind awhir, and looked out the window.

The train had left the station by now, and we were entering a flat scrubland. The wind had kicked up and was sucking the Quartermaster's smoke out the window. We rode for a little while like that, watching the yellow and brown desert scrub whip past the car.

"Aren't you glad I didn't say anything?" asked Walter. "You know how people get when faced with the unknown. Your weird clothes were enough to set the people on the ship and in Salt Point on edge. If they'd known you three had stepped right out of

236

scripture, they'd peg you for madmen and not have anything to do with you."

He sat up and jabbed a finger in my direction, and at Sawyer and Noreen as well. "You might even be dead by the side of the road, with a highwayman's bullet in your heads. You lucked out, running into us, you did."

I had to agree.

In the next cabin over, there was apparently a traveling band, because presently a raucous music started up with lots of stomping, clapping, singing and swooping of violins; all it took was a sly smile and soon our own cabin had erupted in applause and stomping of feet.

The train wound through the desert for hours, occasionally passing through little hamlets strewn across the hardpan countryside of Ain like pickup sticks. Some of these villages were little more than a collection of pueblos clustered on a hillside.

They were populated by dark-skinned, sheepskin-wearing men that perched squatting on the terraces and at the bases of crumbling walls. Sleek, hulking white elk-beasts milled about grazing on the coarse and rare grasses. Their horns curved in great arcs over their shoulders, tremendous loops of bone like ivory scimitars. Read told me that they were the *Pohtir-nyhmi* beasts they'd mentioned at the Vespertine.

There were also townships along the way, and several of these we stopped at to disgorge passengers and pick up new ones. A bald man in a long green tunic embroidered with golden threads came into our cabin complaining that there was nowhere else to sit, and we all agreed to let him stay with us. I was discomfited by the way his throat swelled like a balloon from time to time like a toad, turning from a pale pink to a translucent white. He was sitting quite close to me and I realized that his eyebrows were not comprised of hair but of tiny quills.

237

When he noticed me staring at him, the man smiled beatifically and I looked out the window, embarrassed.

These larger towns wheeled past in pale panoramas of sandstone edifices, like thousands of sandcastles in succession. I saw blunt, low forts made of massive bricks, their ramparts, towers and corners bulbous and soft-cornered. At a distance, those looked like tall sand dunes with windows cut into them.

There were also tall and majestic cathedrals with spindly towers, all covered in honey-comb mosaics of sea-colored tiles and limned with gold etchings of fantastic beasts that writhed and rampaged across their sides and over their keystones.

Long lines of storefronts displaying all manner of crude wares stretched for miles, overshadowed by brick mezzanines, their faces a panoply of dizzying geometric patterns and designs. There were also many damaged buildings, great swaths of destruction where I didn't see many people milling about. Gaping holes yawned in the eaves and sides of structures, open to the elements, rimmed with teeth of shattered masonry.

"The War," said Sawyer, when I asked him about it.

I gave him a look of confusion.

"Oh right," he said, glancing at the Aineans in the carriage and leaning in to speak in a conspiratorial tone, "The climactic battle in the last book took place here. Several No-Men walked across the floor of the Aemev Ocean from K-Set. They came ashore near Salt Point, and proceeded to march across Ain toward Council City Ostlyn, leaving a trail of death and carnage. They were put down by Normand Kaliburn, Clayton Rollins, and the Griever Ardelia Thirion.

"I think," he said, after a beat, "Ed never finished that one."

A few minutes after we'd passed the outskirts of the town, we came into a heathered valley and then out into an arid meadow of brush, wavy with rolling hillocks. In the distance, I could see something that looked like a mangled battleship lying on its side, rusting in the sun.

Someone had built a shack in the shadow of it, and that someone sat in a chair out front watching the train pass. He waved.

"That's a No-Man," said Read. "The first one to be defeated. That was what demonstrated to Normand and his lot that they could indeed be killed. The Swordwives were instrumental in their victory."

I marveled at the massive steel homunculus. It was bigger than anything I'd imagined.

It resembled a sort of battleship with great hind legs like a dinosaur, and the front of it bristled with guns, long turrets with polka-dot coolant holes. In my mind I'd held images of the wing-armed robot-men from old Superman cartoons, something cartoonishly antagonistic and just a few meters tall. Instead, I found them to be nothing short of nightmarish. A robot monster out of an H. P. Lovecraft story. I couldn't fathom how an army could stand up to them, much less two pistol-packing cowboys and a sword-wielding Calamity Jane.

The sun was low in the west, and gray mountains had come into being to the east when I noticed that we were passing into a place of sand dunes. They stood taller than the train itself, mountainous hillocks comprised of what appeared to be dark green sand like crushed soda bottles.

The sunset reflected itself in trillions of sparkling flakes; the rose-colored light swept up the sides of the dunes over and over in satin-silver crescents, like fireworks that never dreamed of dying, and burst into oblivion at the top of every one of them. Monumental buttes of pale green, like oxidized bronze, jutted out of the dunes.

This must have been the Emerald Desert I'd seen described in

Ed's notes, an expanse of sedimentary chromium-mica pulverized and deposited here by a long-dry river analogous to the Mississippi. It certainly glittered like emeralds.

As we flickered through the deeper moss shadows of the dune-valleys, we heard a knock at the door.

It was a refreshments cart, pushed through the train cars by another one of the small blue-skinned people. This one was a small, childish woman in a watercolor sarong; she had no shirt on because she had no need of one, having no breasts. The tiny holes along her collarbone irised endlessly, like the shutter of a camera that never stopped taking pictures.

The fine wrinkles around her eyes and the gray in her hair told me she was older than she appeared. She spoke to us and it dawned on me that she had no nostrils—her nose was merely a ridge in the center of her face. "Thurgm, mihe?"

The man in the green tunic smiled to her, and handed her a few of the Council Talent coins. "D'nerg ayo, ert nihim-e cuddci mylid'nurk iq-dhe wy ayo."

The blue girl tried to refuse, but he wouldn't let her. "Ry, u serry'd degi d'nimi."

"U urmum'd," said the man. "Degi d'nilh u zucc pi y'wirtit."

She handed out little cakes and cookies with fruits and nuts baked into them, and wooden cups of some sweet, cool water that reminded me at once of both coconuts and honeysuckle nectar. I sipped it, trying to savor it and make it last.

I spied a tray of pastries that looked like turnovers on the cart and asked for one. It turned out to be a sort of savory herb falafel, wrapped in flatbread, and it was delicious. The smell of fennel and coriander made my stomach knot up and growl.

"So what do you do?" I asked the man in green.

He smiled, the toad-goiter swelling and subsiding. "I am a

240

trader, young man. And yourself?"

"I'm an . . . artist, I guess."

"You guess?" he asked. "You don't know what you are?"

"Sometimes I think I do. Some days I just don't know."

"Sounds like you need a change of scenery!" croaked the trader.

It was my turn to smile. I glanced at Sawyer and Noreen when I said, "I think I found it."

"I am very glad to hear that," said the trader. "Where are you heading now?"

"To Maplenesse. My friends and I . . . I guess you could say we're visiting family."

"Well," he remarked. "You could do worse than to travel with Kingsmen. You are as safe as you could possibly be."

The bottle-green sands of the Emerald Desert faded with the day, and the evening brought rolling foothills crested with heather and milkweed that swayed in the breeze. Ancient fenceposts jutted up from the hilltops like memorials. The double moons of Destin had just risen when we reached Geary Pass, a tiny mining village in the mountains southwest of Maplenesse.

"It's only about an hour's ride from here," said Walter, as we got off the train. We all had to piss, and no matter how many times I offered to hold her hands, I couldn't convince Noreen to hang her ass off the back of the caboose and water the tracks.

"Good," said Sawyer. "I'm looking forward to a hot meal and a good night's sleep."

"I don't know how much sleep you're going to get," said Read. "Mokehlyr's going full-sail this week, startin' yesterday. Huge festival. Shenanigans and drunken carousing every night."

I snorted a chuckle. "Sounds like my kind of party, then."

"Who are you kidding?" asked Walter. "You're a wallflower if ever I saw one."

Waffle-Eaters and Doppelgängers

WE COULD SEE THE lights of Maplenesse as we came down the other side of the mountain a little while later. The urban heart of the city framed a small body of water; the lake in turn was nestled in the belly of a deep, wide valley. Curving streets filled with electric lamps and oil lanterns made the valley into a bowl of glittering night-life.

It was a tremendous horseshoe built around the lake, and each semi-circle described successive rings of buildings that became more and more rural as one climbed the walls of the valley.

The south end of the massive box canyon faded into a deep forest of maples bisected by the river that fed the lake, and as we came out of the pass and wound our way down the side of the ridge into the city center, I got a distant glimpse of wooden buckets hanging from the trees for sap-collecting.

The train slid out from behind a copse of maples and past the end of an alleyway; we were greeted with the dazzling sight of paper lanterns strung from the eaves and people dancing on the balconies overhead.

Maplenesse was a beautiful city. As the train encircled it on a great arcing track, it reminded me both of Mexican and Mediterranean architecture in ways I couldn't quite define.

The sand-colored buildings were rarely less than two stories tall, and all the roofs were made of the same saltillo tile as Salt Point, but in a hundred more colors. Many of the walls were painted with colorful murals, scenes of merriment and derring-do, and most of the people wore flowing knit ponchos and tabards in brown and blue sea-colors.

The station abruptly enveloped us in darkness, muffling the chaos of celebration. Electric lanterns slid into view, filling the windows with amber light. The throng of passengers disembarking turned the platform into a shadowy, crowded labyrinth of dark strangers.

Noreen was beaming as we stepped off of the train.

"You must be feeling much better," I said. "Do you know anything about this festival?"

"Oh yes," she said, clutching Sawyer's elbow. "This is the spring maple harvest festival of the Tekyr. They're the blue people with the air-holes on their necks. I can't believe we're just in time for this year's Mokehlyr!"

"I hope you like waffles," said Sawyer, with a smirk. "Especially corn waffles. They're the local delicacy this time of year."

"Corn waffles? Like, cornmeal?"

"Yup."

I looked at Noreen. "Are waffles normally made out of cornmeal?"

"No, Ross."

"So it's spring here?" I asked. "It's coming up on November back home. That's funny. I wonder if they celebrate some sort of Christmas kind of holiday here."

"There's no Christ. No Bible. Why would there be a Christmas? There's not even a Santa Claus."

"That's a crying shame," I said, feeling like an idiot.

"Nah," said Noreen. "There are plenty of other holidays, just as awesome."

Walter came out of the car behind us, hefting a duffel bag over one shoulder. He was grinning. "This is what I came home for, children! How could I stand myself if I were to miss my hometown's biggest harvest fair? Come, bastard, let us party until the sun rises wool-headed and aching."

He took my arm and guided me to the station entrance as if he were kidnapping a blind man, then shoved me out into the street, where I almost collided with a Tekyr man, who spun in surprise and handed me a wooden flask. "Thurg, thurg, z'nudi ler! Sici phedi zud'n om!"

"I don't know what you just said," I yelled over the commotion, trying to make him understand me. He simply grinned and clapped me on the arm, and went back to dancing. Another Tekyr man sat on a stoop nearby in a robe and a huge woven hat with maple leaves tied into it, playing some steel instrument that looked like a cross between a banjo and a lute.

Walter took off his hat and did a little jig with a Tekyr woman and two human women. They were applauding his fancy footwork as he asided to me, smirking and shaking his head, "Don't worry about it! Just enjoy yourself for now! We'll be going to Ostlyn soon to speak with my father and the King!"

*　*　*

I surprised myself by having a very good time. Children hooted on little wooden whistles and shook rattles, while men strummed lutes and blew trumpets, while women wheezed alongside with garish accordions and pitter-pattered on big booming bongos, blending into a great big bacchanalia of what sounded like merengue and zydeco.

After I finished the rather strong drink the Tekyr man gave

246

me, I couldn't help but join the square dance going on around a huge fountain by the wharf. Sawyer and Noreen and I joined hands with a line of people whose skin ranged a dozen shades of a dozen colors, and I learned that my two (now very sweaty) best friends knew how to jitterbug.

The look in their eyes, as they careened through the crowd matching each other step for step and smile for smile, could have melted a thousand glaciers.

At one point I ended up in a waffle-eating contest with three other people: an unusually tall and skinny Tekyr man with braided hair named Furmyr Hirwyhi, the trader in green from the train (whose name turned out to be Lennox Thackeray), and a very beefy young man named Josh who looked like he would win handily.

Maplenessian waffles, I discovered, were like silver dollar pancakes: small, and round, and toasted, so that they were like fluffy cakes with griddle designs embossed in them, and a crusty exterior that held up to the toppings that were piled on them.

And they did pile: scoops of sweet cream, drizzles of maple syrup, with bits of a fruit that looked like a blue pomegranate, had flesh like an apple, and tasted like a cross between a lime and a strawberry. The tangy, refreshing *culipihha* was surprisingly well-suited to the task.

Thackeray and I made the initial mistake of trying to eat them with a fork; Josh and Furmyr reached right into the pile and ate them with their hands like sandwiches, cramming the waffles ass-over-teakettle into their faces. It wasn't even half a minute before their chests and faces were plastered in a slime of cream and syrup.

We put down our forks, glanced at each other, and did the same.

To our benefit, we "won" the contest by forfeit when one of the children replenished our opponents' waffles with some that had

247

been preloaded with firecrackers, so that when they reached for the next load the stack exploded in their faces, throwing a geyser of syrup and culipihha all over the plaza.

Josh let out a shrill scream, threw his waffle sandwich over his shoulder, and leapt atop the table growling, "I'm gonna *kill* you little shits!" then ran into the crowd covered from head to toe in food.

To our shock, the customary method for getting cleaned up after the waffle-eating contest was to be picked up by the audience and crowd-surfed to the quay, where you were flung into the lake. Josh showed up with a pair of little boys tucked under his arms like footballs and ran right off the end of the dock into the water, regardless of the boys' protests.

Since nobody *really* won the contest, all four of us were hoisted into the air and carried through the streets, Josh holding the trophy over his head, which turned out to be a sort of tiki or a fertility statue, carved out of a maple log.

*　　*　　*

I found my feet somewhere at the end of a road, in the shadow of a long row of balconies overlooking the celebration. I stumbled out into the street behind the crowd as it surged around the corner, and caught my heel on the rough cobblestones, pinwheeling my arms and falling over on my ass.

I lay on my back in the street, my brain pinwheeling, soaked to the bone, trying to regain my faculties.

I opened my eyes and saw an eerily familiar face looking down at me from one of the balconies. There was a man leaning on the wrought-iron railing, and when he saw me, his smile vanished as fast as my own.

He was gone before I could say anything, and it took me too long to recognize him.

The only time I'd ever seen that face . . . was in a mirror.

I scrambled to my feet and ran into the building just in time to see my *doppelgänger* round the bottom of a stairwell and shove through a door into the night. I was standing in the dim lobby of a hostel, a bookshelf to my left, the clerk's counter to my right.

I plunged through behind him. Luckily, the cold water of the lake had sobered me enough that I managed not to tumble headlong to my death. I emerged into an alleyway just in time to see the other-me run sidelong up a wall and pirouette over a fence like an Olympic ice-skater doing a triple-axle.

His overcoat slipped over the edge and he was gone. Like *magic*. Really, really *athletic* magic.

"You gotta be shittin me," I said to myself.

I grabbed the top of the fence, hauled myself atop it like a sack of grain, and toppled off onto the other side. I landed on my shoulder in a wheeled cart, which tipped over and dumped me onto the street.

The other-me was several meters ahead, about to duck into a crowd of revelers. As the cart fell with a thud, he paused to glance at me, and I him.

We locked eyes and he ran. I struggled to my feet and gave chase. He was gone in an instant.

I shoved my way into the onlookers and through, yelling excuses and apologies the entire way. We were in an intersection between the alley and three long thoroughfares. I stood on a chair to see above the crowd and saw him hauling ass into a long strip of marketplace stalls.

I grew more and more amazed as I pursued him; the other-me seemed to be rather good at dodging and weaving, finding the best

249

way through every obstacle.

He came to a thick knot of people and angled to the right, diving under a table, somersaulting, and coming out the other side at a run. I knew I would never be able to do that, so I jumped onto the table and ran across the top of it.

Unfortunately it was laden with fruit, so my footing was less than optimal.

I burst through a rack of hanging clothes and slipped on a pile of something, sprawling headlong onto the cobblestones on the other end under a pile of shirts.

I heard several people gasp at my injury; I ignored them, astonished that I hadn't knocked my teeth out on the street, and launched myself back into the chase. Someone asked me if I was all right, someone else asked me what the devil I thought I was doing.

The other-me took two lunging steps, ran up a wall, grabbed the rim of the balcony overhead, and lifted himself up onto it.

I missed snatching his ankles by about two-tenths of a second.

He looked over the edge at me and ran away. I ducked into the building he had gone into; it turned out to be a haberdashery. The man behind the counter railed at me. "What are you doing, *ulpisuci?* My shop is not a playground!"

I apologized and ran through a door in the back into a short hallway; I found the end of it and an exit door that led to a serviceway.

I looked up and saw a ribbon of stars two stories up. Someone jumped over the gap.

The end of the serviceway opened onto a steep hill leading up to the next terrace, a fence at the top. The other-me sailed off the roof, kicking and flailing; he landed in an awkward crouch on the rim of the board fence and twisted an ankle. I heard him swear out loud in the night as I scrambled up the embankment and found a place where the planks had been pried loose.

I lifted them and dove through the hole.

Other-Me was lying on his back in the dirt, at the edge of a large garden. He rolled over and pulled one of the tines of a tomato cage out of his forearm with a choked scream of anguish, then threw it at me and ran the other direction, the heels of his boots floundering in the loose soil.

"*Stop!*" I flinched, and threw up my arms to bat the cage away. A drop of his blood hit my bottom lip.

"Wasn't me!" he cried, drawing a pistol and firing it.

I screamed like a little girl and dropped, scrambling backwards. Someone ran at me from behind; I turned to confront him and saw it was Walter Rollins. He had revolvers in his hands.

"Who are you chasing, bastard?"

"I think Sardis Bridger," I panted. "Stop calling me bastard."

"It's better than what I *could* be calling you," said the Deon, and he took off running after the Other-Me.

*   *   *

Far from the riotous merry-making of the celebration, two people sat on a veranda set into the roof of the Rollins' house. The lights of the city sprawled down the hill from them, as if they sat on the dark shore of an ocean filled with light. A few empty glass flutes sat on the table with a half-bottle of wine from the Rollins' cellar, uncorked by one of the house staff.

"It's nice to finally have a moment away from everybody," said Noreen. "We've been on the go since Ross ran into me at the coffee shop."

"Yeah," said Sawyer. The spring night air promised warmer

251

days, a draft just the cold side of comfortable. It didn't faze them, though, because they were together, and they were always warm when they were together; ever since they'd huddled for warmth on the raft in the frigid trial of the Aemev.

That was the first time they'd truly held each other, and neither of them could keep it out of their minds for long, especially not him.

"I love this place," said Noreen.

Sawyer nodded, half to himself, half to her. "Me too."

After a hesitant pause, he elbowed her softly and said, "Not as much as I love you, though." As he said it, his heart seemed to swell, and his face rushed with heat.

She gave him a coy smile and pretended to hide her face behind her outstretched arm, her hands clasped in front of her on the tabletop. "I do declare you're getting sweet on me, Mr. Winton."

He thought about scooting a little closer to her, and then he did, and put an arm around her as well.

Noreen put her hand in his, interlacing their fingers. "Thank you for taking care of me when I was sick. I don't think I ever thanked you for that."

"You didn't have to thank me," said Sawyer. "You don't have to thank me for anything ever."

She canted her head quizzically.

"I knew from the second you kissed me in the parking lot at the hotel that I'd do anything in the world for you," he said. "You stole my heart that day. I didn't know then that I'd end up following you into another world, but I'm glad I did."

Noreen made a noise of contentment.

"I'd follow you to the ends of the Earth and another world besides," he said. He reached up and swept her bangs out of her face, pulling her close to kiss her on the forehead. The closeness of her skin and the smell of her platinum-blonde hair made his heart flash again.

He lingered for a second, inhaling her with a sigh, so he could remember the smell; the floral scent of the bath-house soap and the salt of the ocean that still remained even days later.

Startling him a bit, she reached up and took his rough jawline in the palms of her hands, and kissed him on the lips.

He settled into her soothing proximity, her familiarity, and cupped the back of her neck, striving into the kiss, savoring the silky texture of her tongue and her nose pressing against the side of his own. Their teeth grazed against each other, and he could taste the mellow sweetness of the *culipihha* wine.

He was struck with a sudden alarum by the power of his feelings for her, and it faded away, replaced by an ironclad sense of devotion.

She pulled away and looked up into his eyes. "Not that we had any choice, but if I'm going to be dragged into an unreal place like this, I wouldn't want anybody else here with me. I'm glad you're here," she said, and caressed his face, sweeping a hand down his temple. "I love you too, Fred."

"Fred?!" asked Sawyer. "What? Who is Fred?"

"You know, Fred, from *Scooby-Doo*. You call Ross Scooby, so I get to call you Fred."

"I don't have to wear the scarf, do I?"

"Yes. You must wear the scarf."

"Looks like I'm making a trip to the bazaar tomorrow, then," he said. "You know this means I get to call you Daphne, right?"

"I don't *think* so," said Noreen, swerving her head. She held up a finger in warning and said, "Bitch, I'm Velma, one hundred percent. I'm *all* nerd. You better *recognize*."

Sawyer snorted. He was still smiling as he pushed her hair behind her ear and kissed her on the cheek, and then the corner of her eye. She climbed into his lap and he continued kissing her face, and then her throat.

She kissed him on the mouth; this time he expected it, and returned it with a new ferocity. He reached into the kiss as his jaw worked, as if he were eating the last, sweetest apple in existence.

That's how he felt; he couldn't get enough, and wanted it all for himself. He breathed deeply of her, and wrapped his arms around her slender frame. She was intoxicating, every inch and every scent of her; it felt like he had fallen into quicksand, and there was no hope of escape. He couldn't fathom the idea of turning away from her at this point.

By the way she returned his desperate, starving kisses, it didn't seem like she wanted to either. They lunged and gulped at each other, panting deeply through their noses.

The girl bit him softly on the earlobe and purred in his ear, "Take me to my room, *plee-uhz.*"

Normand looked up at the dark god's glass mask. Figures perched in the rafters, clothed in tattered shadows, their white faces fixed on him like a loft full of barn owls. Dozens of them, just waiting for him to make a move.

"I solved your riddles, ghost," said the gunslinger. "Now call off your hounds."

"We never shook on the deal," said the kindly voice from a grille in the front of the cell.

Normand pulled something out of his jacket pocket. It was the stick of dynamite he'd taken off of Roger's corpse, with one of the rubber washers pushed onto the end. He walked over to the flat thing that the god had produced out of the machine earlier and dropped it into the hole in the middle. The washer kept it from falling through.

He lit the fuse and stepped away. The tray tried to slide back into the wall with a whine of clockwork, but the dynamite was in the way. It tried several more times.

"What are you doing?" asked the god. "What is that?"

"Shake on that," said Normand, and he ran for the door, clamping his hat onto his head.

With a choir of shrieking, the Wilders descended on him; he threw open the door and the room upended itself with a noise like a planet tearing itself in half.

—The Fiddle and the Fire, vol 7 (unfinished) "The Gunslinger and the Giant"

Ed's Other Life

As soon as I awoke I slid out of the four-poster bed and stood in the middle of the guest bedroom, teetering, my mouth tasting of cat shit and my head full of bees. It took half a minute of standing there in my underwear to realize that I had no fresh clothes to put on.

The outfit I'd bought in Salt Point was gone, and just as well, because it was a mess. My fingers smelled like pancakes.

I went to the window, drew the curtain with sticky hands, and winced at the lance of pain in the back of my head. The sun sat on the mountaintops like a giant golden eagle egg, sending spears of white into the misty gorge.

Tendrils of fog rolled up from the lake, encompassing the world and making a mystery of it. I could see sleek sand-colored *dhows* cutting through the silver water, made of some paper-smooth wood and pulled by kites.

Men and women bustled here and there about their business, milling up and down the road outside.

I was in a wing of the manor that faced the front lane, where traffic between the town market and the fertile upper steppes was in full force. Despite my misery, I opened the window and waved to some of the passersby that happened to notice me.

From her perch on the bench seat of a haycart, a sweet-faced little Tekyr girl waved enthusiastically back. I smiled and she grinned, lifting my spirits, calling, "Kiet lyh-rurk!"

256

I echoed it right back, whatever it meant. I closed the window and heard a knock at the door.

It was a matronly woman in a gray wool frock, holding my laundered clothes. "Good morning, ser," she said. "Oh! I'm already impressed with you. You don't seem remotely as ruined as the Deon is. It's nice to have a man about the house that can hold his liquor for a change."

I was grateful to see that the suite had its own bathtub, and it even had hot running water. I lathered up and soaked until the water was tepid and my hands were wrinkled. The crisp morning light and impeccably clean bathroom made my morning ritual into a process of paradise. Once I was dressed, I wandered into the manor proper.

The Rollins house was a sprawling complex in the same Mexi-Medi style as the rest of Maplenesse, albeit in a much better condition than the pastel-colored barrios I'd sprinted through last night. The walls were pueblo as most inland buildings here, and paintings of Ainean calligraphy and watercolor scenes hung in simple frames over ornate, fragile-looking wooden furniture.

I found Walter and Garrod sitting at a large, heavy table in an equally large dining room. A crude, unlit candle chandelier dangled over their heads, and the Deon looked like a puppet with his strings cut. He slumped in his seat with his hat pulled low over his eyes and a deep frown on his face.

Quartermaster Garrod was sipping a cup of coffee and had no shirt on, gracing us all with an unobstructed view of his leathery belly and thatch of gray chest hair.

The table itself was laden with a good number of platters arrayed with an orchard's worth of fruits (including the apple-potato things I'd taken to referring to as "applotatoes"); bean-and-bacon falafel balls; savory-looking prosciutto and pancetta marbled with white fat; crusty croissants; fluffy, crisp-edged waffles; grilled

257

flatbreads layered with waxen white cheese, cilantro, and dried tomatoes; spongy spinach quiche; lemon-zest madeleines. I also saw what turned out to be brioche stuffed with salmon coulibiac and brioche filled with boiled cabbage and sausage.

I'm approximating most of this, by the way. There are very few analogs between Earth and Destin when it comes to culture, but culinary dishes seemed to be one thing that I was able to recognize. I knew what prosciutto and pancetta were from eating NATO chow, but don't ask me how I knew what a "brioche" was.

I sat at the table by Walter's right hand and said, "Good morning."

That hand had a fork in it, which tilted toward me. "It is entirely possible to murder a man with eating utensils. Lower your voice, bastard, or you will witness the definition of agony."

I silenced myself with a smile of pursed lips. A Tekyr attendant appeared and poured me a cup of coffee.

"And you," Walter said, pointing the fork at Garrod. He coughed lightly after a moment; Garrod looked down at his naked chest and took another sip of coffee from his dainty teacup.

"No shirt, no shoes, no service," I said.

Walter speared the cabbage brioche on his plate and left the fork standing up in it. "No shit."

Garrod grunted, closed up his robe and cinched it with a sash. He was wearing a cherry-red silken robe with embroidered birds, which looked very feminine on such a coarse-looking old man.

The Tekyr attendant brought me a plate with an enormous omelet, with bacon crumbled over the top of it. She spoke to me in a long string of nonsense syllables I recognized as Tekyrian. She accented several of the words by hooting through the airholes along her neck.

I winced in apology, shrugging. She repeated herself so that I could understand her. "After last night's feast, I thought you would appreciate something other than waffles."

"Oh. Umm—how do you say *thank you very much* in your language?"

"D'nerg ayo fiha los'n."

I recited it back to her, which earned me a flustered smirk. "Very good," she said, and went away again.

"I was unable to detain Sardis," mumbled Walter, as I tucked into my breakfast. "He escaped into the hills before I could lay hand to him."

Noreen and Sawyer shuffled out of a doorway holding hands, and joined us at the table. Neither of them looked as ill as I felt; they were in fact joined at the hip, murmuring animatedly to each other. As I talked to Walter, they grazed off of the platters in front of them.

The Tekyr came back with cups of coffee; it wasn't the rich coco-mocha coffee like the bath-house in Salt Point, but it was delicious nonetheless. I took a croissant, pulled the middle out by one end and ate it, then rolled up a piece of pancetta and plugged the hole with it.

As I chewed the improvised sandwich, I said, "The last thing Sardis said was, 'Wasn't me.'"

"Pure, unadulterated lies," said the Deon. "Sardis was the last person to see Lord Eddick alive. He continues to evade the authorities even now. If he isn't responsible for Eddick's disappearance, then where *is he*? Has Eddick fled to Zam?"

"According to his literary agent Maxwell Bayard, my father was murdered."

"I just realized something," said Noreen. "Your names are two sides of the same coin."

"What do you mean?"

"His name is *Sardis*. Your first and middle names are *Sidney Ross*. *Sardis . . . Sid Ross*. Maybe this guy's your brother or something. I figure you two have the same father and different mothers."

"Murdered, then," said Walter. "With his own guns, no doubt. They are not in his lodge on the hill. I expect that Sardis has taken them."

"His father had guns?" asked Sawyer.

"Eddick was a gunslinger," said the Deon. "Obviously not in the same realm of acumen as my father and I, and especially not as skilled or as fearless as Normand Kaliburn, but he was one of us, yes. Does that surprise you?"

"It does," I admitted.

"Whorin' and shootin'," said Quartermaster Garrod, chuckling through a mouthful of food. "Sounds like you didn't know your father as well as you thought you did."

"He died in our world. Bayard didn't say how he died, or how he got out of Destin."

"Strange."

A man came in with a lyre, tuning it as he entered. "Music to aid the digestion, sera."

Walter raised his butterknife over his head by the blade, preparing to throw it. The man turned around without even slowing and walked right back out.

"I expect you'd like to take a look at Lord Eddick's cottage before we strike out for Ostlyn," he said, glaring at the lyrist as he left. "Perhaps you'll be able to find some clue as to why your would-be brother assassinated your father."

*   *   *

260

The trek was a short but winding hike up the side of the ridge, into the treeline behind the Rollins house. The picturesque path was little more than a dirt trail through tall grass, trod barren by years of passing feet. To our left was a steep slope shadowed in tall pine trees; to our right was a neck-breaker of an incline, slippery with pine needles.

Over the sparse trees marching down the wash, we could see the distant horseshoe of Maplenesse framing the lake as it glittered in the morning sun.

My two friends were all over each other on the walk up to Ed's cottage like a couple of handsy teenagers.

"Looks like you two had a good Mokehlyr last night," I said.

Noreen smiled sheepishly and pretended that she hadn't heard me. Sawyer grinned, focusing on his feet.

I left it at that.

My father's house turned out to be a two-story weaver's cottage tucked back into a sun-dappled glen. A widow's walk extended from the second floor, serving as a roof for a little porch with a pair of wicker chairs and a glass-topped table. A symphony of birdsong serenaded our approach.

I spied a chessboard facedown on the floor behind one of the chairs, and chess pieces were scattered all over the porch. "Odd," I said, pushing the door open.

My breath was stolen as soon as I entered the cottage.

The walls were arrayed with a catalog's worth of artifacts and paraphernalia from Ed's adventures in Destin. Baskets hung from chains affixed to hooks in the ceiling, filled with coins, bullets, oddly-shaped stones, marbles, and other bric-a-brac. Mismatched pieces of battle-worn armor dangled from nails in the plaster walls, from scrollworked steel morions and pauldrons to the sleek green

261

June-bug armor from K-Set.

Parchment sketches of posing people and scenes of action were nailed up alongside antique shields, with the faces of wolves etched into them. The mounted heads of exotic wildlife stared blandly from their wooden plaques, between shelves displaying dishes on which scenes and creatures had been painted with intricate goldleaf and brilliant colors.

All the things I had expected at his cold, unlived-in house in Blackfield. *This* was his true house.

A large desk dominated one end of the room, looking out through the front window onto the hill and the spectacular view of the city. On it was a manual typewriter and a ceramic stein full of pencils and fountain pens, along with an inkwell and several knick-knacks. A little turtle hewn from soft green jade, and a stainless steel whiskey flask with a bullet lodged in one broad side of it.

I also saw a notepad with the simple word "NO" scribbled on it and a furious underline.

A chill coursed over my skin, and my eyes silvered with long-held tears at the trove of things Edward Brigham had collected on his travels. This is when it hit me; this was why my father never had much to do with me. He'd never had much to do with our world at all. I bit my lips and tried to keep the tears welling in my eyes from sliding down my cheeks.

Sawyer finally said what I was thinking. "Ed wasn't a recluse after all, was he?"

My face darkened with the effort it took to hold myself together.

I found myself conflicted. "Why was this world so great that he didn't want to stay in ours? He could've brought me here. He didn't have to come here and have another family, another son. I would've been glad to grow up here."

262

I felt a hand on my shoulder. It was Noreen with an empathetic expression.

I couldn't articulate to myself what I was feeling at knowing we had only seen the tip of my father's iceberg. He had retreated into a fantasy world and left my mother and I behind, leaving only a ghost of himself in his place. I wondered if this was why they'd divorced.

That raised the question *did my mother know?* Did my mother know about this world, this place, my "brother" and *his* mother?

I voiced my question to my friends, not looking away from the things on the walls, which reminded me at length of the restaurants on Earth that nailed farm implements to the walls to give the place a rustic feel.

"I think you answered your own question, Scooby," said Sawyer.

"What do you mean?"

"Well, look at this place," he said, gesturing expansively. He showed me the outside, visible through the front door. "Look at this world. You just said that you would have been glad to grow up here. Not that I would ever condone abandoning yourse—" he faltered and corrected, "—your family, but hell, he had the chance to go to a world that has—it has sea-serpents, and Avatar Snorks, and festivals for pancake syrup, and metal giants, and green deserts, and guys that settle shit at high noon. Any one of us, any one of his fans, would have jumped at the chance to come here. He found it, and he took it."

He shook his head, looking around, and let his hand drop to his side. "Can you blame him, honestly?"

"I guess not."

"And look at what happened to him, Ross," said Noreen. "This place may be great, but I'm sure he thought he was keeping you safe by leaving you behind. Is a boring life better—"

"—Than no life at all?" I asked. "Is it?"

The second epiphany I had after walking into Ed's house was one that revealed to me the nature of my own dissatisfaction at life. Coupled with the events of the past week, it forced me to recognize that ever since I'd stepped into that elevator, I'd felt more alive than at any prior point in my existence.

I looked sadly around the room and acknowledged how right Sawyer was.

We went upstairs; the bedroom was as decorated as the den, with calligraphy paintings like the ones from Walter's house, and shelf after shelf of Ainean literature. A huge, snakelike face as large as a horse's greeted us at the top of the stairs, hanging from the ceiling by a string; it was a startling dragon-kite made to look like the Saoshoma.

The rest of the tremendous facsimile was also tied up, encircling the room with paper and sticks as if it were flying a circle around the bed. The creature's multi-hued hide was a watercolor painting, with blotchy swirls of blue, green, red, and brown. I looked closer and saw that some sort of glittery pigment had been mixed into the paint, which made the monster sparkle in the sunbeams.

The widows-walk was through a French door at the foot of the bed, and a spyglass was mounted on a bracket bolted to the railing. Noreen looked through it and remarked, "Wow, I can see all the way to the marina."

While they lingered on the deck, I went back into the bedroom and looked down at the bed. There was a hand-sized bloodstain on the duvet, partially underneath the pillow. On closer inspection, I noticed a hole in the cover; I pulled the pillow out of the way and folded back the bedclothes. The hole went straight through the mattress.

264

I flipped the mattress, which sent the Saoshoma kite to clattering. The bedframe was a simple, short-legged wooden table on which the mattress lay; I kicked this frame out of the way and looked at the floor, and there I found what I wanted, which was the bullet that killed my father. It was lodged in the boards.

I got one of the artisan knives down off the wall and used it to pry the bullet out. When I had retrieved it, Noreen and Sawyer were standing over me.

"My brother shot him in his sleep," I said, showing them the deformed lump of metal. "The cowardly son of a bitch came in here while my dad was in the bed and shot him."

I put the bullet in my vest pocket and we went back downstairs.

I took a moment to examine the trophies my father displayed on the walls, and took as many of the coins in the baskets as I could carry. I didn't know how much I had, but they looked like they could pay for a few meals, at least. I also took a small leather satchel with the Kingsman shield embossed on the front flap, and dropped the coins inside.

"Hey, check this out," said Noreen. We gathered around her at the typewriter.

Something was typed on the sheet of paper resting behind the daisywheel.

TOTEM DRAGONSLAYER

"What do you think it means?" asked Sawyer.

"I have no idea," I said, taking out the sheet of paper. It was basic Earth A4 paper; the rest of it was in a sheaf in one of the desk's drawers.

—The drawers! I rifled through them, but there was nothing in them of use: pens, ink ribbons, more coins. A little planner-style journal that I tucked away into my satchel for perusal later. The

265

words were in Ainean and I couldn't read them.

Walter Rollins appeared in the doorway. He seemed to have regained his default good humor; I suspected it was a symptom of the hair of the dog. He had put on his clothes, finally; he had on a brown overcoat that billowed behind him in a fragile manner as he walked. A scarf in a dozen oceanic hues dangled from his neck.

"I see you've discovered your father's strange writing-machine," he said. "Hurry up, you lot. I've a surprise for you."

I showed him the paper. "Do you have any idea what this means?"

"Not a clue. Are you finished?"

"I guess."

Sawyer and Noreen were playfighting with a pair of swords, fencing and giggling behind me. My heart warmed at the sound of their childish laughter. It was good to see Noreen in better health again. "There can be only one!" hissed Sawyer, in his best Christopher Lambert impression.

"Good. Come on. We're leaving for Ostlyn in the morning. I need to send him word of our impending arrival; I also want to treat you before we leave."

The road that passed the Rollins house dwindled to a trail scratched into the mountainside; it curled in lazy loops up the ridge to a stone keep. As we drew near I could see gnarly little maple trees growing out of the stone exterior, as if the tower had arms and was using them to shake pom-poms in the air.

In fact, I saw as we neared the top of the mountain that the larger trees had given way to a forest of miniature maples, much like the Japanese maples back on Earth, but the leaves on these were a breathtaking shade of indigo. Birds flew in and out of large, open windows in the top of the keep, calling and singing.

A strange idea came to me as we climbed the stairs: I used to

266

think I was addicted to the internet. I would endlessly procrastinate at work, looking at this or that, reading Twitter as if I were leafing through an old National Geographic at the doctor's office. But since I'd come here, I had barely thought about it at all. I didn't miss it in the least.

The random thought comforted me.

The aerie at the top of the tower was staffed by two men, a Tekyr and a tall green-eyed Iznoki, like Gosse Read. The Iznoki was lanky, and when we crested the stairs and met him, his broad shoulders were a flock of birds. They were large and resembled ravens, except for that they were a fervent shade of blood red, with copper-colored eyes, and had crests like parakeets with white down underneath.

"Rymmu tyyn, j'naastamehk," said the Iznoki. I surprised myself by noticing that he was speaking a language other than Tekyr.

"Kuaea suna, juam fykdan. Rua-ec zo j'ytik?" said Walter.

Sawyer threw up his hands. "All right, all right. So our Iznok is a little rusty, give us a break, here."

The green-eyed man laughed kindly. "My name is Obike Setaro. My friend here is Ytur. It is nice to meet friends of the Deon. He does not have many of them."

"Oh, har har. I'm here to send a message, you skinny old cage-kicker," said Walter. He handed Obike a wooden capsule about the size of his thumb. The bird-keeper attached it to the leg of one of the red ravens and tossed it out the window, then turned to his customer and rasped his thumb and forefinger together.

Walter put a couple of Council Talents into the palm of his hand. "Don't spend it all in one bar, Beaky."

Obike smirked. "This coming from the Man with the Paper Gullet."

267

"I'll throw you in jail."

"I'll throw you out the window."

They laughed and embraced each other, and we were walking back down the path when the Deon said to us, "He's a long-time friend of the family; his ma used to look after me when my father was in the army."

"So what's this treat?" asked Noreen as we came back down the mountain into the town proper. In the morning sun, Maplenesse seemed less festive and looked more like a favela. We walked through the hustle and bustle of people getting back to work; Mokehlyr would be back in full swing tonight, but while the sun was up, the citizens were all about business.

The medievality of Ain came back to me as I watched the crowds of merchants and visitors surge through the marketplace . . . there were crude electrical setups for lights, reverse-engineered from K-Set salvage and ostensibly powered by the windmills in the mountains overlooking Maplenesse, but I got that sense of *vero nihil verius* again.

This wasn't a theme park, no matter how much my mind wanted to make it into one; it was the real deal.

Walter took us to the town bath-house, a large cabin that opened onto the town common where we'd danced the night before. It was getting late in the morning, so the usual crowd had dwindled to a trickle.

We weren't there for another round of happy happy naked co-ed coffee time, this time; the Deon took us to a little salon off the lobby where we signed our names into a ledger and sat on a wooden futon. From where I was sitting I could see into the room accessible through a beaded curtain off the right-hand side; there was a man getting his hair cut.

A woman came out of the left-hand door and checked the

ledger, then turned to us and summoned Walter and myself into a room divided in half by a partition. She told us to strip down to our underwear and lie down on the tables, then bustled back out.

I did as I was told, warmed by a huge metal firebox at the end of the room.

A woman came in, her rich mocha skin mottled with the dark, branching lightning-bolt striations that reminded me of x-rays of lungs. "Good morning."

I looked over at her and had the startling realization that she had four arms; her shoulders split at the neck and became four distinct limbs, each one half the breadth of normal human arms. The foremost arms fit into the inner contour of the rear arms, and each hand had two fingers and a thumb.

Her hair also wasn't hair; it was a backswept membrane, reminiscent of the wings of a bat, that dangled from her skull like a head-dress and draped capelike across her shoulders.

Her appearance creeped me out somewhat, but her demeanor was so pleasant and professional I couldn't hold a grudge. She gave me a massage all over, starting at the calves and working her way up my back until she was palpating my scalp; then she directed me to roll over and she rubbed everything but my groin, even going so far as to rub my face, tug on my arms, and pull all my fingers.

When she was done, I could do nothing but lie on the table like a roast turkey, soaking up the warmth of the fire and glowing in relaxation. I didn't even notice she'd left; when she returned I was so wiped out and mellow that I was trying to remember how to put my clothes back on.

"That was a very good idea," I asided to Sawyer as we traded places.

I went outside to bake in the sun like a lizard, sitting on a bench by the fountain, leaning back with my feet crossed straight

269

out in front of me. Walter came out and sat down beside me.

"I start all my journeys this way," he said. "Much easier to weather a long trip when you start off as relaxed as you can possibly be."

"I can dig it," I said.

I let my head settle against the bench-back and folded my arms, closing my eyes. The sun lit up my eyelids with orange fire.

"I have a query for you," Walter asked.

"Shoot."

"I always wanted to ask Eddick what your world was like, but I'm not sure I ever really believed that he was from Zam. I guess I always simply assumed that they were making a joke about Eddick's eccentric personality or something."

I peered at him from between my eyelids.

"What *is* your world like?"

I thought about it. "A lot like this one, but a lot dirtier and a lot more boring. We go around in machines instead of riding on *po-timir nefertiti* or whatever, nobody really carries a gun, and trains mostly just carry freight.

"Everything is too convenient. Nothing is an adventure anymore. If I want something to drink, I can just pop down to the shop and grab something, I don't have to pump water out of a well. If I want to talk to my friend in another country, I don't have to send him a bird and wait for a reply in a week or three weeks; I can just send him a message on my electric writing-machine and he'll see it in seconds. If I'm cold, I don't have to go out and gather firewood and chop it into little pieces; I can just get off the couch and turn up the heat machine."

"I should like to see your world one day," he said. "I bet it's not as boring as you think it is. You are just used to it. It sounds amazing."

270

"I guess. Here everything seems imbued with importance. The effort it takes to survive here makes every day so much more meaningful." I paused in thought. "Here's an example. Back on our world, I was a soldier."

"A soldier? Really? Pale, doughy you?"

"Yeah, believe it or not. Thanks so much for the vote of confidence."

Walter bit back a smile. "My apologies. Please, continue."

"Anyway, our world has . . . wars going on. I don't know if you would really call them *wars*. That's a whole 'nother can of worms. But when I went to the front lines, I was a long way from my home and all the conveniences there. And in the desert, in the middle of nowhere, milk is *very* hard to come by.

"I had to get together a team, get my hands on some method of travel, and drive several miles to another encampment for milk. And it was warm and thick, and came in little boxes you could store dry on the shelf. I craved milk like a son of a bitch. I couldn't get enough of it. I would walk out of the barracks mess hall with it hidden in my pockets. I couldn't wait to get back to my camp with it, and I would save it, stretch my ration as far as I could.

"But when I got home from the war, I could buy all the milk I wanted. I just had to go to the marketplace and I had all the cold, fresh milk I wanted. I could have mopped the floor with it if I wanted. And suddenly, well, milk didn't seem so great anymore."

We sat there sprawled on the bench, waiting for our friends to come out of the bath-house, watching the crowd swarm and surge around us. I could smell the tantalizing aroma of a man sizzling meat on a charcoal grill in a kiosk at the edge of the square. He probably slaughtered that meat himself. I wondered what kind of animal it came from.

A few minutes later, Walter turned to me. "On second

271

thought . . . I think I can see why you like our world so much more."

The Whirlwind

THE MAPLE FESTIVAL JUST seemed to *happen* once the sun went down; Sawyer, Noreen and I were sitting in a little cafe eating bacon sandwiches when the drums started up. I didn't know if it was just this way tonight or if I just hadn't noticed it the first night, but they had a tribal, unsettling urgency I didn't like. I didn't want to go outside this time. I voiced my reticence to my friends.

"Me neither," said Noreen.

Sawyer agreed. He made to look at his watch, and seemed to remember he wasn't wearing one. "I think I might just head to Walt's house and hit the hay. We've probably got an early morning ahead of us."

"Sounds like a plan."

I'd been sitting there at the table listening to the drums for a while, lost in my thoughts, before I noticed my friends had left. I wondered if we'd exchanged good-nights.

I got up, feeling a little guilty, wadded the last bite of my sandwich in my mouth, and wandered out into the chaos.

The square's activity was too much for me tonight, for some reason. The lights were too bright and the people were too noisy. I aimed myself away from the whirling center of that frenzy and delved deeper into the alien city, so familiar in its flavor, yet so different in its mien.

I was troubled. I knew if I went back to my room, I wouldn't be able to sleep, so I settled on walking around Maplenesse until I felt like going home. The farther I walked, the more déjà visité I experienced, until I stopped even paying attention to what was going on around me and just watched my feet eat up the cobblestones.

I didn't hear her call until the third time she said something. "Kyt ifirurk, md'herkih."

A slender Tekyr, taller than most I'd seen, leaned on the second-story railing of a walkup, holding vigil over the street. She wore a dangling droop of necklaces that covered her bare chest and a thin chain around her waist from which hung a delicate white silken panel that stopped just short of the platform she stood on. On the panel was embroidered a strange sort of catlike creature I didn't recognize.

"I'm sorry," I said, looking up at her. "I don't know any Tekyrian."

"I said, 'good evening, stranger'," she said, smiling. Her voice had a sensual rasp that reminded me of cats' purrs and late-night radio DJs. "Welcome to Leb Cirimmi."

"Good evening. And thank you."

"My name is Memne. What is yours?"

"Ross."

"Rosh," she said. "I like that. It is the name of a warrior."

"Thanks," I replied, rubbing my overgrown buzzcut. "I guess."

"Why don't you come up and listen to the music with me, *la cyfi?*" asked Memne. "I am not so much for the dancing and the singing and the lebci-zuri. The drunken men, thorgeht'm, they are too crazy, they cannot leave me be. I am up here all by myself."

As she spoke, she traced the cords of her necklaces with one light finger. She spoke Ainean/English with a faint Tekyrian accent, which sounded eerily like a Russian's trill of Rs and

275

stringing of Es. Something peculiar occurred to me as I looked up at her, something about the speaking of English, but at the sight of her sweet, fine-featured face, I couldn't quite get a lock on the feeling.

I hefted the little leather satchel I'd found in Ed's cottage. I listened to the jingle of money inside.

At the top of the stairs, Memne cat-crept over to me on bare feet and smiled up at me. I could see her retinas globing gold through the glassy pupils of her eyes, like the man at the bathhouse, as if there was a tiny star hiding in her skull; she took my hand and I was comforted by the warmth.

I'm not sure what I expected. Her fingertips were warm and soft, yet scaly in a subtle way, like the belly of a snake, and the pale cerulean surface of her arms was covered in a fine, plush peach-fuzz. She looked to me like the Egyptian goddess Bast, bestial and lethally beautiful.

I wanted to tell her I didn't have much money, but I didn't want to offend her by being wrong about what she was. I contented myself with simply standing at the railing with her, listening to the distant bands play their muffled, cacophonous rendition of Latinized zydeco.

I could hear the warble of childrens' whistles and then a shooting scream, and a swirling streamer sailed high into the sky, exploding in a burst of light with a cracking *BOOM;* it resolved into a nebula of blue and gold sparks, fading as it fell.

I leaned against the banister, the Tekyr girl between my arms, her downy, vulpine left ear against my right cheek. She was nearly a foot shorter than myself. Her hair was long and raven-black, cool and down-soft against my face, tumbling down her shoulder-blades. She smelled tropical and floral, like coconuts and tulips.

An obscure rumbling came from deep within her; she was actually purring through the Tekyr blowholes on her chest. I didn't know what to say, and I was happy just being within arms' reach of a woman for the first time in almost two years.

Her sweet closeness was more than enough for me.

My heart beat lightly in my chest, a faint stirring inside of me that radiated throughout my body and made me profoundly aware of my physical self. The cool breeze beat against the heat of my face. A sourceless welling of adrenaline told me to move my hand just *this much* . . . and caress the velvet of her arm.

She nuzzled my cheekbone with that exotic nasal ridge she had in place of a nose. I took this as approval, and closed my arms around her slight frame.

She turned and the nasal ridge brushed against my cheek again, and she caressed my lips with her own. I smelled the citrus tang before I tasted it when she kissed me. Her smooth, sharp tongue was a nimble explorer; and then Memne had leaned back against the wrought-iron bar and she was grinning.

She took her bottom lip between her teeth, her eyes alternating between my mouth and my eyes.

I reached into my shirt and took out the simple gold chain that had been hanging around my neck the last three years. It was looped through a gold circle like Frodo bearing the One Ring. I pulled the chain until it broke, shattering into three pieces.

I hesitated for a moment in consideration and doubt, just long enough to see the gold catch the light, glittering, and then I let the ring slide out of my hand. A hundred memories hung in the air, spilling through my mind, dragging regret, panic, relief behind them like a needle and thread as I watched my old wedding band slip away.

I still don't know where it fell.

She put her tiny three-fingered hands on my now-ungilded chest and guided me backwards through a doorway, where I gladly

277

spent half the money in my satchel. I didn't think Ed would begrudge me the use of his coin collection in a situation like this.

For a night, at least, I loved somebody with all my heart again.

*   *   *

I got back to my room and slept for four hours, slept like a dead rock at the bottom of a well. I woke up to the sound of knocking at the door and found Sawyer on the other side of it. As soon as he saw my face, he broke into a tremendous grin and walked away.

I called after him, "Shut up," and closed the door to take a much-needed bath, still redolent of Memne's scent. I lay in the hot water, grinning like an idiot and feeling like Captain Kirk.

Yesterday's buffet was a banquet compared to today, just a platter of croissants and pancetta sitting on the island in the Rollins' modest kitchen. Walter had filled a metal thermos with coffee and we were out the door. I was still eating my breakfast as we wound down the foothill into the valley.

We didn't have to pay for tickets since we were with the Deon and he was on business; Walter, Noreen, Sawyer and I boarded the train and took our seats. I sat down, put my feet up on the seat across the cabin, and the warming morning breeze knocked me out as easy as a haymaker.

Sometime later, I jerked awake, my heart slamming. "What the hell was that?"

"The hell was what?" asked Noreen. They were eating what looked like jam on toast points. I looked out the window. The sun was directly overhead; I'd been asleep for at least three hours. "I heard a voice."

I shut the window so I could hear better. A rasp in my head,

(rammatica, my name is hel grammat)

278

words whispered into the center of my brain like creme

(can only talk to you like this a few time)

injected into a Twinkie. I stood up and walked out of the private cabin, into the hallway, where I leaned against the wall to steady myself as the train rocked from side to side. Noreen came outside and took my arm. Her touch was reassuring. She didn't ask me about myself like I'd asked after her so much the past week, but I knew from the concern on her face.

"I don't know," I said. "Something—somebody's talking to me. In my head."

I leaned against a nearby railing, facing the windows that ran the length of the exterior corridor.

"Maybe you need more sleep, Ross. Maybe you're hallucinating. Who knows what it could do to your mind, what we've done, what we've been through?"

"I don't think that's it."

"Just come back in and sit down. Or lie down," she said, gently tugging my elbow. "You can lie down and put your legs in our lap."

It dawned on me that it had gotten considerably darker in the room, very quickly. I put my face against the cold window and looked outside at the clouds. In other circumstances, the dark, billowing anvil in the sky would have simply foretold the coming of rain. However, I knew that it was something else.

I pointed at the funnel cloud spiralling down from the stormclouds and said, my heart racing, "Something is coming."

I pulled Noreen back into the private sitting-room, leaving the door open. Everybody was immediately alarmed by my expression. Walter pulled his hat off and looked at me, his face growing dark. "What is it?"

"Something is coming," I said again.

A panic crawled into my system and began to take me over. I felt a furious listlessness and my eyes cut back and forth, looking for safety. Whatever was outside was serious business, and I didn't need the voice in my head to tell me so. I could feel the evil emanating from the tornado-sapling worming down from the air when I saw it.

In the few seconds I'd lingered at the window, watching the cottony blackness whip itself into a funnel, I took a sinister inspiration from the sight of it, felt the malice inside of it like a snake in a stocking.

It wasn't natural; it was threaded through with a *wrongness* that threatened the reality around it like a glitched video game or damaged tape cassette.

We stepped back into the corridor and surveyed the coming tempest.

It had reached the ground by now and what filled me with dread was to see that it did not pull dirt into the air and throw it around; instead, the darkness of the tornado seemed to infiltrate and devour the *real* around it in an ink-blot sort of insidious way, billowing, seeping, eating, taking away.

It was not an agitator, it was not a destroyer. It was a *subtractor*.

"That's not good," said Sawyer.

The twisting oblivion raced toward the track, promising to cut the train off as it went.

"We need to get off this train," said Walter, and he pushed through us, moving to the rear of the car. He opened the door and went outside; we followed him. There was only room for the two of us on the coupling outside.

Beyond the car door, the wind was deafening, but the swirling maelstrom in front of the train made no noise except for the high-pitched electronic whistle one might hear when a television is turned on in another room. It was the song of nothing, the eulogy of logic.

Walter looked down at the desert blurring past the platform under our feet.

"It's too fast," he said.

I agreed. "Yeah, if we jump we'll break our legs and necks."

He shoved past me and back into the car. I followed him again, and we raced into the next room, which was the dining car.

As soon as we entered, I knew something was wrong.

No one seemed to be alarmed by the sight of the tornado outside, clearly visible through the large port-side windows; there were at least two dozen people here, and they sat calmly at their tables, their eating utensils in their hands, gazing straight ahead, their food half-eaten and untouched. I waved my hands in their faces, to no avail.

I slapped one of them and he said, "Mickey, Mickey, two four nine," and a woman behind me said, "Two four nine twelve ten oh five," and then the entire car erupted in one single riotous, "HEY MICKEY!"

The surreality of it made me sick with confusion, as if my brain was backwards in my skull.

The two of us surged forward, and I noticed that the rest of our party had joined us. I glanced back and saw them looking at the diners with concern.

The next car was as bizarre as the last, a simple passenger carriage with face-to-face booth seating. The people here were as preoccupied as the others. Walter did not bother trying to rouse them from their stupor and neither did I; we simply kept racing toward the engine.

When we reached the penultimate car, the Deon tried to wrench the door open, but it was shut tight. His eyes were bright and wide.

"It's locked. It's locked," he said as if he couldn't believe it, and drew one of his enormous, exotic revolvers, using the butt to pistol-whip the glass pane out of the door's window.

Sawyer and Noreen spilled into the room, staggering with the train's worsening rocking. The noise of the wind seemed to be falling away, replaced by the clattering-chugging of the train's engine and the hateful silence of the devouring wind outside. Walter had put his arm through the window-hole, feeling for the handle.

Noreen panted, "What is that out there, Ross? Do you know? You said you heard a voice. Did it tell you? Did it tell you what that is?"

"It said its name was 'Hel Grammatica'," I offered.

"The tornado?" asked Sawyer.

"No, the . . . person that the voice was coming from. His name is Hel. He said . . . he said that the 'man is coming'. I don't know what that is."

"The door is chained shut," said the Deon. "There's a padlock."

I looked through the window in the forward wall of the car; I could see the conductor standing in front of the steam engine's coal furnace. He was motionless, facing the rear of the train, swaying with the motion of it, staring at the floor, the bill of his cap obscuring his eyes.

I pounded on the wall, yelling, "Hey! Hey you! Open the door! You've got to stop the train! We're about to—"

The locomotive pierced the veil of seething, roiling black, plunging us into a void of silence; the wall of the tornado raced the length of the train in a sequential rush. Pebbles and dirt clattered against the walls and slowed in mid-air, disintegrating before my eyes.

Even as I watched, the engine itself seemed to shred into individual molecules and helixed fading into the ether, from the back to the front. The last thing I saw before I tore myself away from the window was the conductor's skin slipping from his musculature like a raincoat, and it chipped itself into atoms, leaving a gruesome Mr. Goodbody standing there grinning maniacally at us without lips or eyelids.

"We gotta go now," I said and ran at my friends, taking their shirts in my hands as I went.

They turned and pursued me. I took a last look over my shoulder at them and saw that the forward end of the car was unraveling itself like a bad sweater, shattering and fading behind us. Oblivion chased us from car to car, sucking-windmilling-chewing brain-dead passengers into the heart of obscurity.

We finally made it to the caboose, which turned out to be the mail car. Steamer trunks and crates were piled against the walls and along the floor in long, orderly rows. Noreen slammed the rear door open to reveal the sand and brittlebush shooting away from us, the track arrowing into a dark horizon.

A mail clerk was sitting on a trunk playing solitaire.

"What's going on?" cried the clerk. "You're not supposed to be in here!"

As he stood up, the forward door of the mail car was sucked out of the frame, and all that was visible through the hole was darkness and wind. The wall began to come apart and vaporize.

The mail clerk abandoned all pretense and shoved Noreen out of the way, leaping through the back door. The dust was beaten out of the man as he ragdolled along the tracks behind the train.

We all traded glances and silently agreed that the mail clerk's plan was less than optimal.

283

Walter overturned a steamer trunk, dumping half the envelopes out, and righted it again. He marched over to me, grabbed my vest, and manhandled me over to the trunk, shoving me inside. I clouted the back of my head on the rim of the box and cried out in surprise and pain.

"You are meant for great things," said the Deon. "I see that now. Someone wants you dead."

He slammed the lid shut and I felt-heard the hiss of him pushing the trunk toward the back door. "It is your duty to survive."

The floor fell away as the gunslinger shoved me out into the desert. The trunk hit the track with a teeth-rattling slam and my head bounced off the inside of it, setting off a bottle-rocket in my brain. Luckily, the parcels still inside the box with me buffered me against the worst of the fall.

I found when I stopped rolling that the hasp had fallen shut. I was lying on my back in a trunk I couldn't open.

All around me, the unbelievable grinding roar of the whirlwind howled outside the box, making sounds of uncanny sentient rage. It was looking for me.

The sound of the train shushing down the rails lessened and then petered away into nothing.

The whirlwind faded until I was bathed in silence.

I hugged my knees and pressed my toes against the lid, then shuffled them toward my face until my feet were flat against the inside, and pushed as hard as I could. The wood crackled and lights sparkled in my eyes in the dark, but the hasp held tight. It opened just wide enough to let a hair-thin crack of daylight through.

Shit.

I tried again, and failed again. I felt something pop in my back, just above my ass, and relaxed.

The air was starting to get close, hot, damp. I was running out of oxygen. My head spun free of its axis and twirled for miles in my tiny prison. Then I got an idea. I held the lid up and grabbed an envelope, then stuck it in the crack between the lid and trunk, used it to prod the hasp open.

The lid flew open, flooding the compartment with cool, dusty air. I shot up and took stock of my environment, inviting a spear of agony through my skull.

The tornado and the train were gone, but the sky remained dark and woolen. From here I could see that the track ended in a tangle of iron some quarter of a mile away, bent double and twisted by the force of the devouring black funnel. I climbed out of the trunk and swiveled in every direction, a frantic meerkat in the dust cloud, looking for some evidence that my friends had survived, some obvious clue to their continued existence.

The breeze swept the dust away, revealing an unbroken landscape of flat, scrubby desolation as far as the eye could see. The only thing that remained of Sawyer, Noreen, the Kingsmen, the passengers and the conductor was a short trail of debris and litter strewn across the tracks. Envelopes fluttered in the wind, hats rolled in the sand, scarves whipped and waved at me, beckoning me to them.

I tore one of them off, a silken blue one, and tied it around my neck, and bent to collect a small leather pouch; it was the one I had taken from my father's cottage in Maplenesse. Inside were the coins, and inside of an inner pocket was a sample of strange dry fungus, mired in some sort of gray matter that looked like Spanish moss. Also, I found a fountain pen and a pair of spectacles.

I looked down at the shield and its crossed revolvers, the spear bisecting the center of the crest, the wolf-face carved into the shield itself, and I was overcome with despair. A barb of wet, dull silver pain lanced my ribs and all the strength went out of my legs.

I fell into the dust at the feet of a dozen tall tufts of sagebrush and wept hard.

I pulled it from the rabbit-hole deep in myself where it cowered, I pulled it all out in anger, I scraped the guilt out of me with a trowel of rage, slathered myself with it until I was hollow like a cheap chocolate Easter bunny.

I bellowed into the dust between my knees, inhaling it, panting, and reveled in the breaking of my heart. I deserved this, but Sawyer and Noreen didn't, Walter didn't, no one but myself.

(get up)

The voice in my head spoke to me again, his tone urgent.

(eep another day, but right now y)

I held my breath, canting my head like a curious dog, and the powdery desert clung to the tear-tracks on my face. A familiar shadow fell across me from the west, the same aura of pure, crystallized apathy I'd felt from the tornado. I found my legs, got to my feet, and looked into the dying sun.

The unremembered man.

(got to run, get away fr)

The distant silhouette was walking toward me, and I could feel the laser-burn of his gaze even from here. I picked up the pouch and threw the strap of the leather satchel around me, and fled across the desert.

Pack sat on the bench, his lanky ankles in chains, listening to the crowd in the stands upstairs. The boy sitting next to him, also shackled to the pole under the bench, leaned into him and muttered, "I bet you're glad you hid in that box now, aren't you? Now you know what they do to stowaways."

A filthy-faced man came down the stairs into the ready-room and assessed them. He smelled like pickles.

When he came to Pack, he paused to glare down his nose at the boy's tall, sinewy, raw-boned frame. "You look like a real fighter. What's your name, boy?"

"Normand. Normand Kaliburn. My da called me Pack."

"Well, Pack," said the slaver, "It's your lucky day. Welcome to Finback Fathoms. You get to take a whack at Cutty for a few rounds. I hope your da been feedin you good."

—The Fiddle and the Fire, vol 2 "The Cape and the Castle"

Dry Leaves

NIGHT IN THE LONELY heart of the desert is a damp and creeping thing, a thin cold rope that comes out of the east and twists itself around your middle, cutting off your feet and hands from your heart until there is no place you want to be. The surprise, after the anger of the sun, is what makes it so bad. It ambushes you.

The sky was dead and gone, glittering with strange unfeeling constellations, and all I could see of the desert was the faint blue of the warm sand holding the thirsty echo of the giant moon overhead. I knew tomorrow would be a scorcher, so I forced myself to find shelter before the sun rose.

I searched the wilderness behind me, but I could not see my pursuer. I knew he was there because I could still feel his looming emptiness, as if he were an abandoned city in the distance, glowing the underside of the clouds with streetlights that no one ever thought to turn off. *The lights are on, but nobody's home.*

I stumbled through the black hours, following the tracks, the brush clawing at my new trousers. I sang songs that cartwheeled through my subconscious over and over, trying to keep my mind occupied so I wouldn't think about my friends again.

The lyrics trickled out of my mouth in a fearful whisper, gravelled by my lowest, muttering register. Johnny Cash's "Folsom Prison" and "One Piece at a Time", Charlie Daniels' "The Devil Came Down to Georgia", Chad Kroeger's "Hero" (I had memorized "Hero" about the time Sam Raimi's *Spider-Man* came out, so sue me. It's technically not Nickelback).

My mind circled back around to my life prior to this and I wondered if I was ever going to get back. Did it matter? I found myself uncaring, unwilling to contemplate it. For that matter, whenever I thought about going back, I managed to let Sawyer and Noreen back into my head, which threatened to break my heart all over.

I cracked again and again, until the tears' tracks overlaid each other in the dirt on my face, a rainbow of shades of brown.

I stopped walking several times out of despair—sometimes out of rage, planning on stomping back the way I came to confront the Presence—but always, my dread urged me on, my fear greater than my sadness or my anger.

Halfway through another attempt at "Ring of Fire" (I'd lost count), I spied a dark blob on the eastern edge of the world, a scrim of non-color slightly less dark than the sky.

I thought about a hundred different things. I thought about stupid things. Accumulated years of stupid things that I discovered didn't mean shit. Pop culture. Man, to hell with pop culture. It took being stranded in the desert alone with my gray matter to make me acknowledge just how full of bullshit my head was.

I hated it. I zeroed in on the hate, to give me something to think about that wouldn't break me or make me crazy.

I broke off pieces of brush as I shuffled by them until I eventually had a bundle of brittle twigs, which I stuck in the pocket of my new vest. I took them out and snapped them into tiny methodical pieces, a half-inch at a time, until I ran out of sticks. I gathered more sticks and broke those into little pieces too.

When I got close to the town, I decided to follow the track right to the train station, because I had an irrational fear that if I strayed from the track, I'd never find my way back. There were no lights, but I could see by the luminescent moon the cluster of clapboard buildings jostled together like dead teeth in the loose gums of the sand.

A half-kilometer out, I perceived a broad swath of movement in the corner of my left eye. I didn't pay it any attention at first because I was so tired, but then the sheer size of it meant that I couldn't ignore it any longer.

It was a column of sand, rolling out of the newborn dawn, as tall as a four-story building.

I did not have the strength to run. My knees, hips, and feet were in agony, and every step felt like I was walking on the severed stumps of my ankles. I tugged the scarf over my face.

The sandstorm steam-rollered me with a soft, unchallenging grandiosity that evolved as the wind blew until it was throwing handful after howling handful of grit into my eyes and piling it in my left ear. The world became a dim, amorphous netherworld of blurry outlines. I didn't see the train station platform until I almost ran into it.

I put out a hand and followed the edge like a blind man until I encountered a flight of stairs that creaked as I climbed them onto the loading stage. The train station was a simple affair, clapboard like the rest of what I now understood to be a ghost town, some habitation that had withered up and died years ago.

I wrestled the door open, slid inside, and jerked on the door, scraping it across the floorboards, until it was shut again.

I was awash in shadows, the only visible part of the world around me being the dim gray rectangles that looked out onto the sandstorm. The sound of the sand striking the glass panes reminded me of the soft ticking of falling snow.

I felt my way deeper into the train station, barked my shin on a bench, stepped around it, found a wall, and followed that until I found a ticket window.

I had the crazy suspicion that if I accidentally put my hand into the semi-circle hole at the bottom, some gnobbly gray twig of a hand would close itself over mine and drag me screaming into the ticket office. My imagination painted a grim vision of mummified corpses, stacked against the walls like the postal trunks in the train's mail car.

My friends. Not my friends. My brain, mired in exhaustion, fought to bifurcate reality, to distinguish between what I knew and what I feared.

I managed to not choke up as I stood there in front of the window in the dark. I shuddered at the thought of the mummies again. I pictured them dragging their rigored bodies across the floor with their cool, dry scarecrow's stick-hands, reaching for my legs, yawning, unbreathing, long teeth and black gums.

The fear was keeping me sane.

I shuffled on down the wall, exploring with my hands until I found not the door I expected but a ladder. I started climbing it, tugged the rungs to test my weight, and ascended them into a spacious attic.

There, I swept aside dry leaves and laid down on the boards to listen to the building clatter and complain.

*　　*　　*

I awoke some time later to the loud flapping-banging of the wind ripping at the roof. The sunlight was still brown and grainy against the attic window, a cinnamon-swirl of sand. When I opened my eyes and sat up, I had a bad shock.

One entire end of the attic was occupied by a hulking insect nest, a blob of layered gray paper as big as an automobile, a hole in the side I could fit my head into. All around me were the carcasses of at least a hundred piss-yellow hornets, each one the size of my

291

fist. They lay on their backs, their legs bowed up in knots of death, clouds in eyes the size of thumbnails.

I recoiled, trembling, and scrambled down the ladder in terror.

My stomach growled as I stepped out of the depot and surveyed the time-scoured ghost town around me. The day had come in full, coloring the world a burnt rust-orange with the sandstorm. A sign by the front door of the station building told me that the once-town's name was "Synecdoche", but someone had painted over it: "WELCOME TO THE STICKS".

I pulled my scarf up over my mouth and nose, and walked down the front steps into the dirt cul-de-sac.

My boots clanked on the loose planks of the boardwalk flanking the main street; tired death-rattles toyed with the shutters, aspirating dust through broken windows. A sign in Ainean dangled sideways from a single chain in front of a large cabin with a wraparound porch.

I could have been on any abandoned western movie set, if not for the looping, flowing script painted on boards and murals that reminded me so much of Persian calligraphy.

I sat on the stoop of a shop and stared at the awkward sign as it twisted and flapped, trying to will the words to make sense. Dark, gaping glassless windows gazed back at me from across the street. I sat there long enough that the sandstorm finally started to peter out; the sun began to slip through a crack in the air.

The building the sign was attached to turned out to be a saloon. The wind had coated everything in a layer of dust. There was no furniture inside, not counting the busted debris littering the floor, which included the shattered remnants of the chandelier, a wrought-iron ribcage in the middle of the room. Dry, broken bottles lingered behind the bar shimmering in the dull honey light.

The door behind the bar led to a pantry stocked with ancient mouse turds. Something skittered away from my foot into the shadows and I jerked backwards, my heel colliding with a solid object on the floor.

I toppled against the wall, righted myself, and saw that I'd tripped over a padlock.

It was slipped into a hasp, which was bolted into a trapdoor in the floor. A stone was sufficient to break the lock. I opened the hatch, wary about what might be inside, but nothing leapt up the ladder at me. It was too dark to see, though, so I went back to the bar and found a candle rolling around in a drawer underneath the countertop, half-melted, the wick black.

There were no matches. I took off my satchel and looked through it, none there either.

The spectacles inside were clean and polished. I took them outside and tried to use the sun to make the wicks ignite, but it was useless.

I had saved the broken-up brush twigs. I took them out and piled them on the saloon's porch, using the lens to light them. That didn't work either, so I used a stone to grind some of them into fiber and then focused the solar laser on it.

Soon I was fanning sweet-smelling smoke, and then the chaff caught and I held the tip of one of the twig pieces in it, used that to light the candle. I stood the candle in the neck of a broken beer bottle so that it resembled an Olympic torch, and carried it into the cellar of the saloon.

It was a cramped space, surrounded on all sides by shelves. A few cans gleamed dully at the edge of my light. I gathered as many as I could hold and took them topside.

There was no can opener in the saloon, but the chandelier had daggerlike prongs curling up from the main post of it, wrought-iron filigree leaves with sharp points. It took a couple of swings to pierce the can. I used it to work the end open, slopping some of the contents all over the floorboards. It held some sort of stew, a conglomerate sludge of potatoes, green vegetables . . . perhaps some sort of roast.

I spooned it out with the mangled lid, wolfing down the tasteless slop in gratitude.

A spout behind the blacksmith's stable provided me with water to wash it down with. I didn't even mind that it was dirty. I pumped a bucketful and let the sediment settle, and gulped in all the warm water I could hold.

When I finished, I went upstairs to the saloon's inn rooms to see if there was anywhere to sleep later. The mattresses were ripped to shreds, but someone had left blankets in a dresser. I would need to rest for a day or so before continuing, providing the mysterious presence that had chased me here didn't show up first.

When I thought about him, I could feel him, like a cold aurora from the west that flickered at the outermost edge of my mind, a subthought St. Elmo's Fire.

He had lost me in the sandstorm, but he would find me soon enough.

Bad Juju

I HAD TAKEN OFF my shirt and vest to let the sweat dry, and I was lying on the saloon's front porch in the afternoon sun daydreaming about the Tekyr escort from Maplenesse when the first quiver hit. I sat up and immediately regretted it as a wave of dizziness and nausea overtook me, and salty saliva filled my mouth.

I walked down to the end of the block and vomited several times into the weeds, a torrent of bilious slush. I swore, struggling to breathe, my balls and guts aching. I walked back to the smithy with tears in my eyes, drank a handful of the pump's water and sat by the forge, sweating bullets and shaking.

The sandstorm was just a memory; the sun had become an unrelenting hammer from a hard cobalt sky. I leaned back on my elbows, spat again, and let my head tip back.

When I looked up again, I noticed movement on the dark scar of the horizon.

Three figures were following the train track. They were riding some sort of animal, but I couldn't understand the look of it at this distance.

Rising slowly, so as not to draw attention to myself, I got up and slid behind the far corner of the abandoned smithy shop. From there I made my way across the backsides of the clapboard structures lining the main avenue, jogged across the street, and entered the saloon at a run.

I snatched up the leather satchel with the Kingsman crest and

296

ran outside, where I wriggled underneath the porch.

A few minutes later, I could hear voices. The three men came sauntering around the corner at the far end of Synecdoche (WELCOME TO THE STICKS!) and up the main drag, talking and laughing, generally cutting up. They were riding on the white beasts with heavy bodies and slender faces, with their great curving scimitar-horns that arced backwards over the riders' legs.

The man in the middle seemed to be the brains, the mediator. Once, one of them shoved the other and they started arguing; Brains separated them and warned them to stop.

I could see the pistols at their hips, and one of them was carrying a rifle.

They clunked across the porch into the saloon and explored the building, lamenting the absence of alcohol. I heard a crunch as one of them stepped on the spectacles.

"Cannit believe there's nothin tall in here, no liquor what," said the red-headed one. He was sinewy and lanky, and walked like a bicycle with square wheels. The other guy, shorter and darker, in a green doublet and bowler hat, I could hear him creaking down the ladder into the cellar pantry.

"There's some tins of food down here, but I figure it's gone off, aye."

"Someone's been into em," said Brains. "Look here. Tat's a mess."

Red chuckled. "Say he cut the tin open with the iron spike here, he did. Not been goon long."

"Where d'you think he went?" asked Bowler.

"Prolly still here, I expect," said Brains. "If he's got any smarts, he won't be in here, where he could be run into. He'll be larkin' in one of t'ese periffery parts of town, might even have a roll tossed out on a roof to keep off the street. Migh even have a rifle.

297

If you go back outside, keep an eye on the roofline."

"Think it's a Kingsman?"

"I hope not."

The fact that no one called him out on his cowardice struck me as relevant.

"Spread out and look ferrim," said Brains. "I want to stage here. The shipment will be along in a couple of days, and I want to get set up. I doon't want any extra angles, any wildcards, to have to worry about when the time comes, savvy?"

A scorpion the size of a hamster scuttled across the dirt in front of me. I managed not to react.

"Man, what makes you think that train's not going to have any of Kaliburn's boys on it? I feel like we rode all the way out here for nothing."

"I got my saurces," said Brains, and I could hear him walking up the stairs to the second floor, leaving Red and Bowler with me. I took off my crested satchel and left it in the shadows under the front porch, then belly-crawled to the corner of the building and selected a stone from the narrow ditch under the rainspout.

Red and Bowler both jerked in surprise when a window across the street shattered.

"The fuck?" said Red.

"Go see what it was," Brains called from upstairs.

I heard Bowler draw a revolver and the both of them started toward the front door as I went around the side, but then Bowler said, "Uhh, no. You go check that out. He could be out there waiting to pick us off."

"Oramoz damn you both," said Red, and he loped out the front.

Where I crouched at the back corner of the saloon, I could

see him kick up dust on the road as he went over and stepped onto the boardwalk. He raised the rifle and pie-cut the doorway, then stepped inside, aiming to his severe right, and moved in, fading into the darkened interior.

That was battle tactic. They were not rookies.

I went around to the back door, which was already hanging off the hinges, and grabbed the leg of a table from a pile of smashed furniture out back.

I crept into the bar from the rear. Stepping inside the back door, I was in the pantry behind the bar, the trap door open at my feet. I slammed it shut and danced backwards into the shadows of the windowless little room, turning sideways to hide behind a narrow shelf.

Bowler stormed into the pantry, flung open the hatch, and fired a round into the tin cellar, shouting, "Come out of there, you son of a bitch!"

You ever been poked in the face with a ball bat?

I came around the shelf and leapt at the man in one fluid motion, spearing him in the forehead with the end of the table leg as he looked up at me. The bowler hat flew straight up like Donald Duck doing a double-take and his legs crumpled; he fell onto his knees and swore in a venomous hiss.

Before he could recover and shoot me, I clubbed the gun out of his hand, sending it clattering into the cellar.

He snarled in pain and swung at me; I wasn't fast enough to dodge the punch and he clipped my eyebrow. My head bounced off his knuckles, the world stepped seven inches to the left, and I lost my bearings just long enough for him to snatch the table leg out of my hands and throw it on the floor. For a split second I could smell the pain.

I tried to punch him back, but he caught it and tried to twist my arm.

I stomped his foot and attempted to hip-toss him but since I was already standing on his toe, this only resulted in me collapsing and him falling on top of me like two turtles fucking. We grappled on the floor for a few seconds, grunting and crawling around, and then I managed to grab his lapels and get behind him.

I used the leverage to put my arm around his throat and my legs around his waist, tightened my grip, and tried to pull off his head with the crook of my elbow.

The man began to choke and spit, and tried to shout but all that came out was a strangled *"Ffffcccck ynnn!"*

I held on until he went limp.

His face was a horrible shade of magenta, and the veins on his forehead were swollen.

I tipped his unconscious body toward the trap door and he collapsed like a Slinky into the cellar, tumbling loudly down the ladder, landing at the bottom in a heap of limbs. I bent to grab his revolver off the floor and a loud bang startled me. A bullet hit the wall in front of me, flicking splinters against my face.

I didn't look to see who fired. I ran out the back door and cut to the right.

I was standing next to the stoop when Red came running out.

As soon as the rifle barrel cleared the doorframe I grabbed it and shot him in the face with his friend's pistol. A hole the size of a dime appeared next to the bridge of his nose and the wall behind him was splashed with a fine spray of blood and brain matter.

His inertia carried him the rest of the way down the stairs—he took two more steps and dove bonelessly into the dirt.

I'd never shot a man before. It wasn't what I expected.

I couldn't afford to stand around and get messed up over it. I took his rifle away and ran back to the corner of the saloon, meaning to hide under the porch again and snipe Brains when he came out to look for me.

Somehow he'd expected something of that ilk. A pistol round traveled the clapboard siding next to my face with an insectile whir and I ducked, doubling back, jumping over Red's corpse. I felt a hot thump on my right shoulder like I'd been slapped with the flat of a hot sword.

Luckily, the saloon was only flanked by an alley on one side; the other side was flush up against the structure next door.

I hurdled a fence, almost twisting my knee, and ran as hard as I could.

Brains cursed as he turned the corner, ran across the back of the block, and caught up with me, but unless he was particularly imaginative, he would never find me where I was hiding.

I peered through a crack in the wood panels. He was no more than ten feet away from me.

"Where did you go, Kingsman?" he bellowed into the desert afternoon, staggering to a stop. He panted, looking around, checked the rounds in his chamber, and slapped the cylinder shut.

He stood there for several minutes, listening, waiting for his breathing to slow.

About the time I got tired of watching him listen for me, he turned and walked the way he'd come. I remained where I was, however, unwilling to give him the chance to trick me, and grateful that the outhouse I was currently hiding underneath hadn't been used in a very long time.

I looked down at the dried shit-mud pit I was standing in and vomited again, croaking up a mouthful of bile as quietly as I could manage.

*   *   *

I waited until I hadn't heard anything from the outlaw for a couple of hours or so, and then lifted myself out of the latrine, clambering out of the seat-hole. I looked at my bare arm, sleeved in a grimy craquelure of blood. I needed to get back to my shirt and vest, and rinse the cut on my shoulder where his bullet had grazed me.

The sun was low and fat on the western horizon, the shadows were tall and stringy, and the shredded clouds were tinged with the bruise-purple of settled blood.

I couldn't get the image out of my mind of shooting the other man in the face, the rangy red-headed man, couldn't stop thinking about him. I'd never shot anyone before, not even during my time overseas.

I wondered if he had family. Children.

The thought transfixed me, had paralyzed me while I sat in the dried-out shitpit in the dark, sweating my ass off. I could see him in my mind's eye, stiffening facedown in the dirt as bugs explored his motionless body.

Did someone somewhere love that dead man?

I wondered if the guy in the cellar that I'd clubbed was still alive. If he was, he couldn't be a happy camper at all. I thought about checking on him, but the idea seemed counterproductive. If he was still conscious, he'd for sure have a broken neck. He'd landed on his head when he went into the hole.

It was heartless, but I put it out of my mind.

He would have killed me if given the chance.

There was no reason to trouble myself over it, let the guilt eat at me, or get myself into a situation where I had to fish a broken man out of the cellar and force myself to worry about taking care of him. I told myself that he was an outlaw, probably a wanted man. I had prevented a train robbery.

The knowledge that I'd killed a man rooted me to the spot; the revelation that I'd prevented a serious crime released me.

I sat in the outhouse, listening, trying to ignore my arm, waiting for the boot-scuff that would tell me Brains was waiting for me, waiting to see where I was, where I had been hiding.

I tried to calm myself and pass the time with thoughts of Memne, tried to reminisce about her smell, the peculiar feel of her soft skin, but nothing seemed to work.

I abandoned the tactic. I didn't want to taint my memories by trying to use them here in this place of death and stink.

I crooked my neck so I could see the oblong hole in my upper arm, a divot the size of a spoon-head. Looked like someone had taken a bite out of me, but it wasn't as bad as it felt.

Once I'd had time to calm down, the adrenaline drained from my system and the cut felt like someone was holding a branding iron to my skin. I tried to put it out of my mind, but everything I did aggravated it.

I checked both Red's rifle and Bowler's pistol; the former was empty, but the latter had four rounds out of seven chambers. I would have to make do with the pistol, but if I wanted to use the rifle, I would have to go check Red for more ammo.

I crept around the side of the saloon and retrieved the satchel from where I'd hidden it behind one of the support columns under the front porch. The contents were still there and intact.

I put the fountain pen in my trouser pocket (I did not want the fungus touching me), looped the strap of the bag over my shoulder, and went back to the rear door of the saloon where Red was lying on his belly in a pool of congealing blood. I turned him over and massaged his shirt and jacket, looking for ammo, and found several cartridges tucked into the loops on his belt.

As I was slipping them out, the world crackled in a flash of

303

light and I heard a dull boom of thunder that shook the dust off my boots.

I fell over next to the corpse, and the last thing I remember thinking was that I'd forgotten my umbrella.

It couldn't be helped; the No-Man had forced him to seek refuge in the strange cave. He could still hear the incredible thunder of it walking around on the street above, looking for him. Normand threw a sheet of metal out of the way and descended into the dark burrow. Someone had crafted a stairway, and even lined it with tile, like a bath-house.

A sign on the wall in the Etudaen language told him where he was going, but he couldn't understand it.

Several times he had to crawl on his belly or climb through junk to get past the wreckage, but once he was in the pit, he felt better. Safer.

He took out the Etudaen device and depressed the button on the side, illuminating his surroundings with the weak lamplight. Roaches scattered from his presence, scuttling out of sight. He was in a large sort of atrium, and gates barred his progress. He climbed over them, hoisting his exhausted body through the wreckage, and picked his way down another flight of stairs until he found another unnatural cavern.

At the foot of a tiled platform, an eldritch tunnel extended to the left and right.

He went left. He lowered himself down onto the tunnel floor and found a set of railroad tracks! The familiar sight comforted him. An underground train! Incredible!

—The Fiddle and the Fire, vol 7 (unfinished) "The Gunslinger and the Giant"

I Remember You

I REGAINED CONSCIOUSNESS WITH a tremendous headache, a terrifying, piercing agony like I had an arrow through my face. I was sitting in a barber chair in a dark room, and by the light of an oil lamp I could see my reflection in a mirror on the wall. My beard was a scratchy mask of black felt, oiled with crimson. My scalp and arm were plastered in sheets of blood; I looked like I'd been shot in the head.

I flexed, trying to free myself, but it was useless. The sheets from the saloon's bedrooms were twisted as tight as ropes, and looped around my arms and legs and waist. I was completely immobile.

Someone was standing behind me.

Brains cupped my left cheekbone with the palm of his hand, pressing a straight-razor against my throat. He leaned in and whispered in my ear.

"If you're a Kingsman, you're a stupid one." *Stewwwwped one.*

"What are you talking about?" I asked.

He laid the flat of the razor against the hole in my shoulder and a lance of hot iron rocketed down my arm. The room pixelated for an instant.

"You must've taught I was a dumbass, boy," he said, and came around in front of me. He braced his hands on the chair's arms and tapped the blade on my face. Brains was not a pretty man; he was balding on top, with long greasy wrestler hair and a

306

face like Pete Postlethwaite, thuggish-thick, with beady, twitchy eyes. "You mighta took out me friends, but tey were just kids, like you. Tey ain't been playin ta game as long as I have."

The man gave my face a couple of light slaps and smiled. "You doon't remember me, do you? I remember you."

"What?"

He pointed to a fiddle lying on a table in the corner.

"Does that jog your memory, ya greasy miser?"

The fiddler from Salt Point that asked me for money at the bazaar. He sucked the drool out of the corner of his mouth and shook something in my face. It was the leather satchel.

"At first, after I knocked your ass out with that rock where I was sittin on the roof, when you came back to loot Mr. Rennell, I was like, *Ain't no way this dumb shit is a gunslinger,* but then I saw this bag, and look what I found in it!" Brains plunged his hand into the satchel and shook it off onto the floor.

In his hand was the weird gray fungus, which he jammed against my upper lip. I expected a musty smell, but all I could catch was the penny-scent of my own blood.

"If you ain't a Kingsman, what are you doing with the Acolouthis?" he asked.

He drew the twisted thing under his own nose, taking in the aroma of it like a fine Cuban cigar. It looked like a mummified penis, a stretched and withered finger with a knob on the end.

"I don't know what that is," I said, truthfully. "I've never seen it before in my life."

"Anybody ever tell you you're a shitty liar?" he asked, and punched me in the stomach. I bellowed in his face, my lungs emptying of air.

I answered him with a miserable grunt. *"Yeaaaaahhhhnnnnnn."*

307

He made a face and laughed. "Smells like that tin o ruint food didn't agree with you, did it?"

All I could do was fight to breathe, sweat loosening the blood on my forehead. It trickled down my face. I tried to spit on him, but all I could do was a weak *pfuh* that misted my bare chest with red. I glared at him, trying to brush off the burning knot in my guts. I wanted to puke again, but there was nothing left in me.

"I've never had any of this," said the fiddler. "The slingers and the Grievers keep it pretty locked up. Tey all say it's too dangerous for most people. That only a few people have the intestinal farditude that it takes to survive eatin it. Is tat true?"

"I don't know what you're talking about."

"Actually, it's a funny ting. I might believe you. I don't tink yer a Kingsman gunslinger tall. You're just some stupid spoilt kid. I kinda want to see what I can get out of yer parents for ye. How old are you, anyway?"

"Thirty."

"Tearty yares? Are ye serious? You look twenteh, at t'most."

"I hear that a lot."

"Is tat so? Clean livin, I guess. Why, I ain't got but a few yares on ye."

"Clean living, yes. My body is a temple—that's why I leave my shoes on the outside."

The fiddler threw his head back and laughed at that, great cawing laughs that filled the room.

"My parents are dead, anyway," I said, once his braying had tapered off. It was only half the truth, of course, but hopefully enough to put him off of that idea, at least. "So that's a no-go."

"A *no-go*," said Brains. "Never haerd that befare. I like it. Do you mind if I steal it?"

"Go right ahead."

"Very kind of ye. I like to expand my vocabulary when I can."

"Glad I could help," I said, and spat in his face.

He flinched, closed his eyes, was completely unprepared for it. I'd saved it up while he was talking to me, rolled a blob of saliva at the tip of my tongue and blew it out like a sneeze, shotgunned it all over him in a fine mist.

The fiddler stepped off of my lap and wiped the moisture out of his rheumy eyes, spat my saliva on the floor, and punched me in the jaw as hard as he could. My head dipped down and whipped backwards at the same time. I developed a headache, a dull, twisting agony at the base of my skull.

Surprisingly, my jawbone didn't break. Must've been all the milk I drank growing up. The room swam for a moment, a sea of crawling stars.

He held up the Acolouthis.

"You look like a haingry man," he said, shaking it. He snapped off the fungal cap and held it in his thumb and forefinger like a numismatist inspecting a silver dollar. "I bet yer starvin, aintcha? After pukin up that tin a soup, I bet yer just cavin in at the middle! I bet your arsehole is rubbin a sore on the back o yer navel! Well, *guess what!*"

I looked away from him, but he grabbed my aching jaw and whipped my head back around.

"I'm gonna feed you dinner," he said, and tried to open my mouth like a purse, using my chin and forehead as handles. That made it hard to put the cap against my lips, so he went around behind me and tried to brace my forehead with his armpit and hold my head like a football. He smelled like pickles.

"My treat. I want to see what tis ting does to a man befare I make a decision. Do I want to try it myself and maybe die? Or do I

309

wanna sell it?"

I kept my mouth shut, even as he pulled my right eyebrow up with the heel of his hand, holding my eye open. His breath was the fetid, shitty, cesspool swampiness of a man who'd never brushed his teeth. Ever.

He came back around in front of me, took out his revolver, and put the barrel against my temple.

"Eat it, shit-arse!" he screamed, flinging spittle. *"Eat it or I'll cheese yer thinkin-meat!"*

I couldn't help it, I laughed at that like I used to laugh at *Full Metal Jacket*, but I did it through clenched teeth.

The fiddler aimed his pistol straight-armed to the side and fired all seven cartridges into the wall; one of them hit the mirror and broke it all to pieces.

My ears were ringing when he finally pulled the trigger on an empty chamber. He showed me the gun like he was giving me the A-OK sign, and then put the piping-hot muzzle against the filthy, ragged hole in my shoulder. The nerves in my arm instantly transformed into concertina-wire being dragged through my veins.

The pain sent me into an atavistic, reptilian place I had no idea existed, a raw and crazy corner of my head where the air was purple and up was wet. A night sky of stars exploded in my eyes. I lost myself, reared my head back, and loosed a howl from the depths of everything I had ever been.

The fiddler dropped the Acolouthis cap onto my tongue, tossed the pistol, and clamped my jaw shut.

Walkin on the Moon

IT WASN'T THAT BAD, actually—a bit like having a fishing bobber in my mouth, a bland little ball. The fiddler gazed into my eyes expectantly, like an idiotic lover. I don't know what he wanted.

Did he think I was going to start convulsing underneath him? Explode out of my restraints and start whirling around the room like the Tasmanian Devil, or blow the chair to pieces like Popeye?

"Chew it," he said. I glared at him over the edge of his hand. "Chew it! Swallow it!"

I shook my head, thought about biting him, but then I remembered the extra bullets in his belt. He raised a hand and threatened to slap me in my wound, eliciting a preparatory wince. The memory of the pain of being burned was, of course, still fresh in my mind, so I obeyed without delay.

It was very fibrous, like chewing a styrofoam ball full of hair. Once I started, the bitterness came out, mixed with the saliva, trickled down my throat. I choked a bit, coughed through my nose. My sinuses burned.

He waited until I'd given it a good work-over, then told me to swallow it.

"Hmm-mmph," I said, shaking my head.

He answered that by putting his hand against my throat and pushing my neck against the chair, his thumb and index finger pressed deeply into the flesh under my jawbone. He was cutting off my carotid and jugular. I could feel my heart beating under his grip, and my face began to feel swollen, my eyes bulging.

"Swallow it or choke. Your choice."

I forced it down, gagging at the coppery, acrid feel of the mush on the back of my tongue. He tilted my chin down so that my mouth opened and he could see inside. "Say *ahhhhhhh!*"

"Ahhhhhhhgo fuck yourself."

"You tink you're funny, do ya?" asked the fiddler, getting off of me. He picked up the revolver and tilted the cylinder open, then started loading more rounds into it. "You'll tink you're hilarious once that Acolouthis kicks in. I wonder what it really does."

"Like I told you, I have no idea. I'm as ignorant as you are. Well—not *quite* as ignorant as you, that'd be a feat."

He patted me on the wound with the back of his hand, a friendly gesture that would have been genial in more positive circumstance. A shock of pain rippled from my deltoid.

"I guess we'll just see what happens," he said, smiling. "I hear tat some of the people tat take t'Sacrament, tey come back from the desert with the smarts to *outwit time itself.* Too remarkable, innit?"

The concept evaded me, but I didn't say anything, just sat and watched Brains play jaw music.

"But den some of the people tat take it, tey go out into the wilds and never come back. I hear tey go out tere and der brains just can't take it, tey can't handle the visions and epiphanies. Dey go mad and die, der skulls just crack open from the pressure of the madness. Tey find em out in t'dunes, bled out from t'eyes and nose, chewed up by d'animals. Annatsa looky ones."

"Epiphany?" I asked. "That's a nice big word from your *vo-cab-u-lary,* isn't it?"

"Aye, I told you! I got lots of words up here," he said, tapping his head with the end of the pistol's barrel. The rounds inside it clicked appreciatively. "It's too bad here in about a half an hour you'll forget all of yours."

He laughed uproariously at that. He slapped the cylinder back into the gun, and sat in a nearby chair. He tossed one foot up on his knee, leaned back, and tucked a hand into his armpit. The other dangled across his legs, tapping the revolver against his thigh.

Several minutes passed. My headache got worse. I sniffed and winced at the lamplight, squinting. It felt like my heart was pumping molasses.

"Do you know how long this is supposed to take?" I asked.

The fiddler didn't say anything.

I looked up at the oil lamp on the counter and noticed something odd; instead of softly flickering as it had been, now it seemed to be licking up from the wick in slow, tidal movements, curling up like solar prominence loops and evaporating in the glass bell. The steady hiss had become the low, muffled exhalation of a distant jet engine. It felt like staring into hell.

I cut back to Brains, and he was staring right at me.

He opened his mouth, gradually, and his eyelids slid downwards, covering his baby blues. Then a sound came out of his mouth that reminded me of the Tyrannosaurs from *Jurassic Park*, a deep, warbling-trumpeting vocalization from some Cthulean place deep in his throat that sent thrills of amazed horror through me.

"WWWWAAAAAAAA—"

His eyes slid open again; his eyeballs had been rolled back in his head while they were shut, and now they were falling back into place, great glassy orbs rivered with red veins.

The effect was an ordeal of terrific proportions.

I couldn't handle his face. He was a living nightmare, and his weird roaring was intolerable.

My heart contracted like a fist and sent a slow wave of

314

pressure across my body. I realized it seemed to be beating every ten seconds, a languid, tidal metronome that made my circulatory system vacillate between turgid cold and feverish emptiness.

I looked around the room for something I could focus on to help me ignore the bizarre trip I was experiencing. I'd never had hallucinogens before in my life. I wondered if I was going to be like this until the day I died, which was undoubtedly going to be soon.

I hated it, couldn't understand for the life of me why anyone would willingly go through this. Something was definitely wrong with me.

I looked down. Instead of a naked chest covered in curls of coarse black hair, there was a hinged hatch, and it was open. Inside I could see circuitboards, loops of red and yellow wires, hard-drives with clickety-clackety arms twitching back and forth like the mandibles of ants, so many ants, they were migrating up my legs and into the hatch to pull the wires loose.

Some of them had wings, and they were *hornets*, they were the giant hornets I'd seen in the train station attic, as big as my thumbs.

"—*AAAAAA*—", the fiddler was warbling, and when I looked up at him he was grimacing with those grimy butter-colored teeth, one of them crooked like a mismatched gravestone. He looked like he was about to get out of his chair.

"*Geeet theeese fuuuckiiing thiiings ooooff meee!*" I yodeled, struggling against my bonds, feeling my vocal cords undulate like the strings of a stand-up bass. The hornets tumbled from my lap like derailed train cars, rolling down my legs in slow-motion.

My feet tingled, my hands were sparkling pins and needles, I felt like I weighed a thousand pounds. My legs were made of iron. It was all I could do to move them. I had become a bobblehead figurine, my giant noggin unwieldy on my insubstantial neck. I could feel the numb skin of my face following my skull like an ill-fitting mask.

I couldn't breathe. I sucked at the air with greedy lungs, I opened my innermost self to make room for it but it refused to come into me fast enough. When I finally got enough of it, I was helplessly inflated with it, a solid mass of oxygen and nitrogen occupying my torso, bloating me like a pool toy.

I forced it out into the fiddler's face; it looked like Superman's ice breath as it came out, a blast of white tousling his hair, breaking across the bridge of his nose as he crooned his frightening foghorn song.

"—*TTAAAAAAAAFFFFFFF*—"

The sheets tied around my ankles were loose enough that I could piston my tree-trunk legs up and down under them. I got one foot free and kicked the twisted sheet off.

I remembered something that I'd seen when I was a teenager, where a man had come to my school to show us tricks based in physics. At the moment, I couldn't remember any of the others, but the one that came to mind was where he stood on a turntable that rotated freely to and fro. He had a bicycle wheel in his hands—when he spun it, he could somehow use the spinning wheel to rotate himself on the turntable by canting it to the left or the right.

"—*FFFFFFFUUUUUUUUUUU*—"

I got it into my head that I could do something similar by kicking my legs up, leaning to the left, and bicycling my burdensome feet. And somehow, it seemed to be working. The barber chair began to turn on its pneumatic shaft, and Brains eased out of sight off the right side of my vision. He was now behind me.

My heart was a slamming bank-vault door in my rib cage, thundering over and over. A hand came into sight and gripped the armrest at my left.

I hunkered down in the chair and stretched out my foot,

down, down, and found the pedal underneath the seat. I stood on it and the column loosed a sinister blast of air, causing the seat to sink, which released the tension on the sheet binding my arms.

"—*UUUUUUUUUUUCK*" said Brains, pulling the chair. I swiveled around to face him, slithering one arm out of the sheets.

I took careful aim, slung my arm back like a ten-pound sledgehammer, and planted a blow on the left corner of his jawbone with my fist.

His cheeks rippled at the force of it and white spittle constellated from his flapping lips. I actually saw his eyeballs wobble, billiard balls in a Jello mold. While he coasted away from the impact, spraying a swath of saliva, I freed my other arm and pushed myself out of the chair feet-first.

I cruised forward like a leaden missile and hovered there for what felt like half a minute at the top of an arc. I was backwinging to a landing on the floorboards when Brains held his arm out to the side, the straight-razor in his hand.

The razor swung open with a sibilant *sssssssssssslick,* and he turned toward me, trailing the arm, the blade gleaming in the warped lava-lamp light of the oil lantern. I leaned backward and his arm whipped from his shoulder like a steel chain.

The razor sang through the air where my throat had been.

I took advantage of his follow-through and hoisted one foot into the air, got behind it, and jammed my heel into his shoulder-blade. It was like hitting a walrus with a car. The satisfying weight of his mass carried his feet off the floor and he sailed backwards.

I turned and tried to run, but my body was too slow, too heavy to respond to my demands. It was like a dream, I couldn't move fast enough. I leaned forward, threw out one foot to catch the boards, and basically clawed across the floor alternating with my toes like two frogs pulling a helium balloon.

317

My hand closed on the doorknob and I twisted it, shoved myself against the door. At first, it was like plowing into a wall, but then it gave way and I went tumbling into the night.

One of the recruits was standing in front of the platoon when he came back to the company area, talking animatedly. Normand stood in the shadows under the risers and let him talk. "What does this man know of wilders and metal giants? He's nothing but a poke, from the nowheres," the young man was saying. "And a reformed outlaw, at that. A common criminal!"

Another recruit was trying to get his attention.

"What?" snapped the first.

"'E's back there, larkin in them shadoos. Best watch—"

"What's your name, man?" asked Normand, strolling out of his hiding-place with his hands in the pockets of his dungarees. He spoke with geniality, opting not to come at him with the same barbed hostility as the officers. The recruit spun to face him, and stumbled over his words at first. "Rollins, serah, Clay Rollins. Clayton. That is, Trooper Clayton Rollins."

"Well, Trooper Rollins, how would you like to be my porter and confidant for a while? You talk like quite the diplomat. You get to have a front-row seat for these things I know nothing of."

—The Fiddle and the Fire, vol 3 "The Rope and the Riddle"

319

The Man Comes Around

THE FIDDLER SLID DOWN the wall and landed on his ass as the gibbering maniac shoved the door open and flung himself through it. Julian scrambled to his feet and gave chase, jumping out into the street. By the time he got in line for a good shot, the old boy had already high-stepped it to the end of the block and was rounding the corner, running in that goofy way, mincing into the sunset like a crazed nancy-boy.

Julian fired off a shot, but it was just a formality at this point. The bullet went wide.

He snarled and threw the gun into the dirt, but then remembered that the wanna-be was going to die out there anyway. This thought consoled him, the mental image of him lying on his back out in the sands, blood drying in his teeth as a carrion-bird plucked out his eyes.

He bent to pick up the gun, breathing hard, and sat on the edge of the barber's porch. It had been a long week, and now it was going to get longer.

He'd come out here to the middle of nowhere and scoped out the abandoned town after he'd heard about the rail shipment of K-Set imports, then gone back to Salt Point to recruit a couple of helpers. It was supposed to be a simple job, but the kid had ruined all of it.

He considered taking a walk in the morning to make sure he was dead, to look for the body and put a couple of bullets into it for good measure.

320

Whatever Julian Clines expected the Acolouthis to do, it wasn't the result he got. He'd sat there in the chair for the better part of an hour, watching the kid get sweatier and sweatier, until finally the wannabe had whispered something unintelligible, then started freaking out.

Julian had sworn and gotten out of his chair, but by the time he was on his feet, the kid had fought his way out of the sheets and started pinwheeling his feet. Afraid of having his teeth kicked out, Julian grabbed him and spun him around, and got a haymaker in the face instead.

The fiddler looked down at the withered fungus-finger in his hand.

He'd come out on top this way, at least. A sample of the Acolouthis would rake in a pretty penny out at Finback Fathoms.

He trembled at a chill wind and pulled his jacket tighter at the neck, hugging his elbows to his sides. The desert had grown cool fast.

He was sitting on the porch thinking about what he could buy with the money he was going to get for it when a man came up and stood over him, his boots crunching in the dirt and gravel. Julian looked up at him and stowed the mushroom in a jacket pocket.

"Can I help you, sera?" he asked, searching the shadows for the man's eyes.

The stranger was unusually tall and whip-thin, his arms dangling at his thighs . . . his overcoat, the lifeless yellow of dead hair and old bones, twitched in the breeze like a shroud, as if it were made of cobwebs. He reached into his vest and took out a gold pocket watch with long white fingers.

They were long, so long, too many fingers and too many joints, like a hand molded by a sculptor who'd never seen one and didn't understand their use. They reminded Julian of bird feet and

321

the great big wolf-spiders that lived in his Aunt Marda's cottage out in Callahan.

He thought about the time he'd seen one of those monsters in the cellar, a great bulbous black thing with fingers scuttling gingerly across the floor like a silk glove with a hand inside it. He was twelve, he had just come in from picking okra in the garden. When he saw the spider, he lost his shit and tried to crush it with the basket he was holding, but as the wicker fell across the creature, hundreds and thousands of seed-tiny spiders came streaming out from underneath it.

He jumped on them and tried to stomp as many as he could, but they were nimble, and bit him on the feet.

Julian still thought about those pinprick bites some days. He made a subconscious effort to kill every insect he saw, and shook out his boots every single time he put them on.

"Iqsomilikyytmuhuelcyygurkwyhesihdeururtufutoec," the man said, his voice a throaty whisper. The gibberish whipped out of him all at once, a string of nonsense syllables snatched from the reel of a fishing rod.

The gold pocket watch was huge, the size of a teacup saucer. The ticking of the clockwork inside was incongruously delicate, the soft, crystallic tapping of snowfall. Julian felt like he'd taken some of the Acolouthis himself.

"What?"

He looked up at the man's face, framed in a keyhole of light coming from the dentist's office. He gasped at what he saw there and started to scramble backwards in purest terror.

"What *are* you?" he asked, or at least would have, had he found his voice and had the nerve to use it.

"When you came home last night at two, I was waiting there for you—" the stranger said. He reached down with that eerie cellar-spider

322

hand and covered Julian's nose and mouth. It was surprisingly strong, and his skin was cool and damp.

The arachnid white hand gripped Julian's head and lifted him off the ground as easily as if he were an empty jacket, drawing him close until his hat brushed Julian's forehead. Before the fiddler lost his name, his eyes watered, widening in deepest fear and awe.

He's got no face, he thought. It was just a broad, blank wither, like a water-logged thumb. Under the hat's brim there existed only a wizened plane of pale skin.

"—but when you looked behind the curtain, I wasn't there, for certain."

The man once known as Julian Clines collapsed into the dust and lay still.

"Come away, come away," mumbled the unremembered man as he walked away into the darkening east, *"And see what's behind the door...."*

The House of Water

I HURTLED THROUGH A maze of haunted houses, an unending city of dark-eyed monoliths that clustered close and made the road into a deep valley of paper shadows. A gigantic clap of thunder coughed behind me and something slowly cut the air in my way; it was a torpedo the size of a snow pea, dragging a wobbling, glassy icicle of vacuum behind it. As I passed it, the torpedo hit a wall and starburst into a flowering nebula of tumbling splinters.

The Big Bang, I thought. I kept running.

I wasn't sure what I was running from: my own deteriorated mental condition, or the man with the gun.

I was deep into the desert by the time I realized I couldn't outrun my own mind. I jounced to a stop like a fat man, stumbling in the dirt as my legs rippled from my attempts to stop myself. I fell to my knees in the sagebrush and dry-heaved, but this time, nothing came up.

I wanted to scrape the "Sacrament" out of me, I wanted to stop the madness. I scratched at my tongue with my grimy fingernails and stuck my fingers down my throat, but I couldn't get it out.

After a long while I spat; it did not hang in the air in front of my face, but hit the ground with a soft *thump*. It seemed the Acolouthis was beginning to wear off. Perhaps I had survived it after all. I stood up, pushing myself straight with my hands on my knees, and looked around, shivering sweaty in the breeze.

I was alone, in a flat cool wasteland that bristled with sparse sagebrush. The night sky was a rippling black dome ten feet over my head, like a plastic tent shotgunned with a trillion holes through which I could see an unspeakable light. I couldn't say that it was beautiful.

There was an ineffable malice to it that I could not place, as if there was something back there with that light, something on the outside watching me through those holes.

They twinkled that way because there was someone outside the sky walking back and forth trying to get a better look at me.

I didn't want to be watched anymore. I hated being out in the open.

I got down and groveled in the dirt, thought about digging to China, then crawled into the bushes, trying to find a place to hide from that terrible sky-warden.

Claws of grass scraped at my face and naked back as I found my way through it, cutting and bruising my knees, pushing sprays of rattling thistle out of my path. I fought to understand, to feel the right way in the darkness.

In my searching I put my hand on something that moved away from me with a growl. I recoiled, and kept moving.

I must have crawled a mile.

I looked up, over my shoulder, through the cottony milkweed and realized the moon(s) was still in the sky. I wiped drool from my chin with my forearm, wiped it on my filth-caked pants. When had the moon(s) ever not been there?

I found a break in the brush and dragged myself out into a clearing. As I emerged, a scraggly hand of bristle raked across the hole in my arm and a kaleidoscope grenade went off next to my face. I fell over and screamed into the many-colored ripple trilling from my thirty-two-flavor Crayola wound.

The riot of shades evaporated as something rustled in the desert grass. Something big.

I paused, unmoving, my breath held, listening through the scuff of the wind.

"Who's there?"

I was answered with silence.

The suspense was killing me. I stood up and, glancing at the trash-bag sky, peered over the brush.

I was surprised to see a lantern bobbing in the darkness. It dangled from the end of a chain, attached to a pike held aloft by a man in a monk-brown robe. He looked like an angler that had reeled in one of the stars.

"Hello?" I asked, feeling a slow panic rise up within me. "Hello? Could you help me? I'm really—"

The monk turned and left, the lantern swinging as he walked. I ran through the briars and I ran through the brambles to catch up, careless in dagger-thorns where a rabbit couldn't go. Their tips stung my skin as I crashed through them, my hand clasped gently over my wound to protect it.

I approached him and explained myself. My voice sounded like a death rattle; I was doing little more than whispering. "Friend, sir, you don't know me but I'm in a bit of trouble."

The monk said nothing, simply kept walking. I met his pace and walked alongside him.

"I've been drugged, and my friends are gone."

We wandered for a while across the desert floor like deep-sea divers, he in the lead, holding the swaying lantern out like a Catholic censer. I considered several times trying to make small talk, but his hood obscured his face. The thought of conversating with him unnerved me. One question was eating at me, though.

"Where are we going?" I asked, waving away a fly.

326

He still did not answer.

We walked for a very long time. We passed a butte, tunneling through the semisolid shadow of the gargantuan rock formation with his teetering light. We crossed several dry riverbeds, sliding down into the arroyo and trudging back up the other side, knocking loose rocks down the bank. The robed man traveled like a mountain goat, negotiating the precarious land with ease and grace.

I noticed by and by that something had been painted on the back of his coarse linen robe. It was the stylized head of a bull, the snout protruding down to his buttocks, the broad horns hooking across his shoulder blades.

The eastern horizon was beginning to lighten as the coarse sands gave way to rocky soil and great expanses of heather and wheatgrass listing in sideways air. I could see a monolithic structure on a rise at the other end of a colossal field, silhouetted by the coming day.

As we got closer, wading through a landscape furred with the color of pennies and hoared by the soaking frost of the morning, I began to recognize it as a house. It was a familiar house, two stories, white, with a roomy porch and leggy Roman columns that went all the way up to the topmost roof.

The monk walked up the stoop and onto the porch. He hung the lantern from a hook and leaned the pole against the wall, then produced a key, unlocked the door, and went inside.

He left the door open; I entered the house and closed it behind me, shutting out the distant sighing of the sea.

I was standing in a grand two-story foyer, looking up at the mezzanine of the second floor. There was no furniture; the floor was bone-pale wood planks, the walls unpainted sheetrock. Plastic sheeting was nailed over the windows to keep the draft out. A massive chandelier hung over my head like the sword of Damocles

327

refracted into a thousand blades of cloudy ice.

The sheer whiteness caught the light from the windows and made a drafty, wintry tomb out of the house. I could've said the house had never been lived in, that it was new, except for the cobwebs in the corners and the unmistakable sickly-sweet yeasty smell of old age.

The floor looked so washed-out because it was covered in a carpet of dust. To my left, there were eight spots of clean floor: one big square indicated by four clean spots, and a smaller rectangle that abutted the square, visible the same way.

I looked around for the monk, and wandered through a bare living room into a kitchen.

There were cabinets, and nothing in them. The fridge, though it was running (better catch it!), was hollow as well. I climbed the sweeping staircase in the foyer and found the monk in an austere study, standing in front of a window that overlooked the field in front of the house.

He gazed through the opening of his hood at the tousled grain, and the sparse boulders that threw tall, sharp purple shadows across the ocean of copper.

I stood beside him, but I still couldn't see his face. He spoke.

"Welcome to the House of Water."

"Who are you?" I asked.

"I am whoever you need me to be."

"Are you a hallucination?"

"That depends," said the monk-robed figure, "Are you?"

"What's that supposed to mean?" I asked. The only other thing in the room was a fold-up card table with an old record-player on it; it looked just a few years newer than an antique phonograph.

The bay window flooded the room with a diffuse white light that seeped into the gray floorboards and wall joists, pulling woolen blue shadows from secret places. The high vaulted ceiling was crosshatched with beams and buttresses.

"That's the question," he said.

I sighed. I could see this turning into an Abbott and Costello skit. "Yes, it is, that why I'm asking you it."

"He's coming."

"Who's coming?"

"Exactly. And you'd better come up with an answer before he gets here. This house won't protect you from him forever."

"Who is he?" I asked. "You're talking about the—the man, the one that brought the whirlwind. The man that followed me."

"The man goin' round taking names."

I stood there with him staring out the window. I looked down at the rug we were standing on; it was a big rectangle of Persian carpet, busy with red and blue curlicues, paisley tadpoles, and gold mandalas. Eventually I realized that the darkened west was obscuring the faint anti-glow I'd felt in the sticks of Synecdoche. He was out there.

"He comes not for what you need, but for what you do not want," said the monk. "He is the unremembered man. He is the shadow, not the shadow-caster. He is the shadow of forgotten things, of neglect and of apathy and of lost cities. He is the end of all stories. He was the end of mine."

The monk reached up and tossed off his hood.

Ed Brigham (Lord Eddick Bridger) smiled at me.

He said, "You have come here to show him that he will not be finishing this one."

I backed away from him in fright and surprise. "You're a

hallucination," I said. "You can't be real. I came to your funeral. I saw you dead in your coffin."

Ed gave me a sort of sad smirk. "You don't sound happy to see this old face."

"I am—I guess. It's just . . . a shock. You can't be real."

He turned back to the window. "I'm real, believe me. I'm just not your father."

"What?"

"I've been around a long time," said the robed man. "A long, long, *long* time. I don't remember who I am, but I am not your father; he remains yet interred. Some call me the Mariner. Some called me the Duke of the Field. You may call me Ink, if you like. It's the only name I remember."

"Okay," I said, stepping closer to get a better look at his face.

When I was close to him, he glanced at me over the rim of his spectacles, which had whited over with the glare from the window, and smiled kindly.

At this distance, I could tell that there was something odd about his face; there were moments when it felt as if I were looking at someone else through a pane of glass with Ed Brigham painted on it. Occasionally a ripple of vagueness would flicker across his features, rendering them indistinct for an instant.

"Once," he said, "I used to be much more than the useless old man you see before you. Men prostrated themselves before me in a bid for mercy and compassion. Temples were erected in my honor."

He let the sentiment linger, then turned to me in a stage-aside and said, "I was a big shot, in other words," and chuckled. "Then he came and took it all away as punishment for my hubris. What they say is definitely true: you don't know what you got until it's gone. All that I had gained, all that should have been important to me, wasn't. And I lost it.

"He took my very face," he said, softly raking his fingertips across his face. The gesture distorted his features only long enough for me to blink, and then he was my father again.

"She couldn't—*wouldn't*—give me back who I once was, but she gave me a new face and a new lease on existence. The face of the Father. In exchange, I agreed to stay here, in the Void-Between-The-Worlds, and serve as a guide, a signpost for all those who are lost. The keeper of the lighthouse, the House of Water, at the edge of the boundless sea."

Dead ladybugs lay in a scarce pile where the window met the floor, dozens of tiny orange-and-black marbles. As I noticed them, I also caught sight of the rosebushes lining the front porch. They were a lush blood-crimson.

"The face of the Father," I said. "Everyone's father."

"You catch on quick. Edward must have been very proud of you. I'm glad you have not forgotten his face."

When I looked away from him, the Mariner, in the corner of my eye, was not Ed. He was something wholly outside of *familiar*, it was the visage of something unimaginably ancient and scarred. Looking at him was like looking at a pterodactyl and seeing only a sparrow.

"I didn't see him much. I don't really know how he felt about me."

"A broken family . . . story as old as time."

"You said *she*. Who is She?"

"She has many names in many lands, on many worlds, as I once did, but in Destin she is called the Wolf."

"Oramoz," I said. "The Wolf, who cut the Dragon in two and rendered Behest into the twin worlds Zam and Destin."

"An allegory for the truth. It is different in every world, in

331

every culture. Turtles all the way down!" the Mariner laughed, and then he squinted at me.

"You are different. You have passed through here before. Most of your kind coming from Destin are the young men and women that come here of their own volition, seeking the truth that will enlighten them so that they can go home as warriors, not drained of fear, and no longer possessed by it, but armed with it."

"I'm here from Zam," I said. "Believe me, I am not here of my own free will. I was force-fed a hallucinogen."

"Is that so?" chortled the Mariner. "Have you considered the fact that you may have been given a key?"

"A key?"

"It takes many forms in many worlds. In Destin, it is the Acolouthis, the Sacrament, used by both the Grievers and the Kingsmen as a rite of passage. The origin is always different, but the destination is always the same. Those who are here, are here to seek something. Not all of them survive the seeking. Not all seekings happen by accident."

"What am I here to find?" I asked.

"Don't ask me," said the Mariner, in his friendly Ed-voice, so much like a Jimmy Buffett version of Santa Claus that I couldn't shake the feeling that I had stepped into a theatrical showing of *Miracle on 34th Street* with the reel spliced into *The Endless Summer.* I'd forgotten how charismatic my father could be. Or was that the Duke of the Field? "I am merely the horse that brought you here. It is you that must drink."

I wanted to tell him that his cryptic magic-surfer bullshit was beginning to stir my ire, but the sight of him at the periphery of my vision was prohibitively startling. Whatever he was and whatever he looked like, the mariner Ink, the Duke of the Field, was not my father.

"You said that what the shadow took from you was of importance," I said.

"It was," said the Mariner. "I wasted it. All of it. He takes away everything extraneous about you. He strips you away, strips you of your strength, your identity, your love, your hate, until there is nothing left but the core of you, and then—when he's got the last bit of you over a barrel, when there's nothing left of you but your will—he'll crush it. A fate I narrowly avoided myself. If you do not treasure it, he will take it. He is the ultimate thief, the thief of hubris."

I took his words and pondered them. I noticed a thin sheaf of paper on the fold-up card table. There was also a chair, tucked neatly up under it, a wooden one with a wicker seat and slat back. It seemed very brittle as I pulled it out, and creaked when I sat on it.

"He took my friends," I said. "Does that mean I didn't treasure my friends?"

Ink-Ed stood silently by the glass, staring out at the meadow. When I'd sat down, I'd noticed a rigid object in my pocket. I pulled it out and discovered the fountain pen from the satchel. Digging in my pocket made my shoulder hurt like hell. "Hey, is there any way I can patch up my arm? It's killing me."

He spoke without turning. "The bathroom."

I found the bathroom down the hall, just where I expected it to be. There was no curtain in the shower. I ran the tap over my wound, wincing until the cold water and the dopamine dulled the pain. When I opened the medicine cabinet, there was a roll of gauze inside, some clean cloth, and a bottle of alcohol so old the label was flaking off.

I steeled myself and poured the alcohol over my shoulder. I could hear it hissing, but then the pain rumbled in, so powerful I swore, and had to lash out and kick the clawfoot bathtub with a bellish *bonnnnnng.*

When I returned to the study in my new dressings, the Mariner gave me a sidelong glance. "Sounded like it hurt."

"Yeah, you could say that. So what am I supposed to be doing here?"

"The voo-doo that you-do so well."

"Voo-doo?"

"You do."

"Do what?"

"Remind me of the *babe* . . . ."

I sat down at the card table again. "I can't believe you just made a *Labyrinth* and a *Blazing Saddles* joke."

"You'd be surprised what an old pair of TV rabbit-ears can catch here."

"After the week I've had," I said, picking up the pen, "There's not a lot that surprises me lately."

I contemplated the joke, taking into consideration the sheaf of paper on the table in front of me. I was so hungry I had reached that gnawing, hollow stage where your mouth runs over with saliva at every thought of food. The food poisoning had worked itself out of my system, but I knew there was nothing in the fridge downstairs. What did Ink eat?

Voo-doo, I thought. *Concentrate on the task at hand. You're here to do your voo-doo. What is my voo-doo? What is the voo-doo that I do so well?*

"He's here," said Ed-Ink.

I meant to get up, but he waved me back into the chair. Somewhere he had procured a glass tumbler of some milky liquid and was drinking it. A droplet of condensation slid off of the tumbler and landed on the toe of one of his roper boots with a tap.

"What is that?" I asked.

"What is what?"

He knew very well what I was referring to. "The glass in your hand."

The Mariner smacked his lips and held the drink up to the morning light. "I think it's Swarovski."

"Where the hell would you get—" I began, getting up to join him at the window.

The Mariner wheeled on me. "I thought I told you to stay put. You need to focus. The fear will come soon enough."

The sky was a panoply of storm-iron, darkening at the horizon and rising to a dusky rust color overhead, making it feel as if we were inside of a giant spool of brown yarn. It scrolled by at a blistering pace like the walls of a hurricane.

There was someone standing in the wind-swept grass of the meadow, so far away that I could only determine that he was dressed in a pale yellow overcoat and Stetson. From here he looked like the Marlboro Man as imagined by Stephen Gammell. The wind tugged at the tail of the man's jacket like a little boy trying to get his mother's attention.

He took something out of his vest with a bone-white hand and examined it.

I was going to ask Ink about his mention of fear, but I had no need anymore.

"Wherefore gird up the loins of your mind," he recited, "—be sober, and hope to the end."

I went back to the table and sat down. I was supposed to be doing something, but what? Writing? I had paper and pen. Drawing? As I thought about it, the Mariner took a sip and gestured to me with his glass. The tinkle-crackle of his ice settling punctuated his question.

"What was the first thing Sawyer Winton ever said directly to

335

you?"

(I felt a hand on my shoulder. It was Sawyer, and his eyes were like scalpel blades. "I've read some of your stuff, man. You're not as bad as you think you are.")

"Think about it."

I sighed and picked up the fountain pen, and put it on the page. A blot of ink seeped into the paper. I lifted it again and looked at the nib in the light; a droplet of black hung on the point of it like a drop of blood on the end of a hypodermic needle.

"Writing is voo-doo," I said dreamily.

"And what does voo-doo do, class? Come on, don't make me spoon-feed you. You're too smart for this crap. Use your noodle, here."

"Voo-doo brings back the dead."

The doorbell rang like a game-show bell. *Winner, winner, chicken dinner.*

I dove to the fray, and started writing.

As the boy and the gunslinger sat on the battlement watching the guards stroll back and forth, the sun settled on the horizon like a great golden egg. It glinted through the cords of great rusted-out ruins, a labyrinth of tumbledown spindles assembled to the east. The last vestige of the Etudaen.

Pack hoped he'd never have to go back out into that alien wilderness ever again, but he knew one day he'd have to. He couldn't stay here forever.

The old man sitting by his side looked up from the culipihha he was peeling. "No one ever accomplished anything by dreaming, ulpisuci," he said, handing him a piece of the sickly-sweet fruit. Pack looked down at it. It was an aging windfall, barely edible. Harwell was the master of his own kind of ruin, he thought, and slipped the browning sliver into his mouth. It didn't even crunch.

Harwell squinted into the sunrise. "One day you got to wake up and go get that dream."

—The Fiddle and the Fire, vol 2 "The Cape and the Castle"

The Prosaic Rope

NOREEN AWAKENS IN a cold black place and hears the clattering of falling water, muffled and remote, as if through a wall. She sits up, guarding her face with her hands, expecting to bang her head on some unseen rock or pipe, but nothing presents itself.

She remains, listening carefully to the splashing, and once the shock of her circumstance has worn off, she picks herself up off the concrete floor and begins to feel about in the suffocating wet-velvet darkness.

She finds a wall, tiled in sweaty porcelain, and follows it around to a corner, and that to a large aluminum mop-basin. The sink is full of cold, cloudy water and stinks of age and stagnation.

Clots of matter float in it, like dishwater. She moves on.

Further on she discovers a light switch. She flicks it several times, and after her patience has begun to wear thin, a wan glow flashes overhead, illuminating the room for a second, and then it returns, fading into being, illuminating her environment.

She is in a large, filthy room several meters to an end, strewn with all manner of disgusting debris and matter.

It looks like a long-disused industrial kitchen of the sort one would see in a prison, or a school. Long, wavy ribbons of some silken black fiber are arrayed across the floor like electrical cables, entangled in corroded rebar and waterlogged bits of plaster.

The fiber looks very much like hair.

"Sawyer?" she calls. "Are you here?"

Her voice is thin and weak, but it carries, if only to echo back at her from the cavelike walls, flat and metallic, the whisper of a lifeless robot.

The water in the sink gurgles.

I paused, lifted the pen, and set the sheet of paper aside. The ink had bled through a bit, but it was nothing serious; the paper was a rich, sturdy texture, almost like cardstock.

Was this dark place real? The words flowing from the pen came unbidden, a stream of consciousness more than mere inspiration, and less than the manipulation of the muses. I wanted to marvel over it, the first real writing I'd done in years, but I was too tired, too hungry, too afraid. I honestly don't know how I could find the strength.

"Do not pause," said the Mariner.

I heard a low, muffled, bass-string voice that seemed to come from right next to me. I gasped, jerked away from where I perceived it to be.

This is a fool's errand, child, it said. *No one comes back from the abyss. Let me in.*

"Do not listen to him. He knows what you're trying to do, and he means to stop you," said the Mariner, staring intensely at me, drilling into me with Ed's piercing eyes. "Don't even listen to me. We're both distracting you. You're pulling these words from a deep place. The Sileni feed you stories, but you don't need them now. You are with me, at the shores of the Vur Ukasha."

I glanced at him, locked gazes again, and turned back to the paper, picking up the pen. His eyes reminded me of shore meeting sea, the core of his irises the pale ecru of sand, the limbic ring an aquatic blue.

Even though I could still feel the floorboards of the House of

Water beneath my feet and see the paper before me, I began to feel as if I were standing on the dismal beach of an ocean. It stretched into the horizon and beyond that, ever and ever. The sky over that coast was a non-thing, the electric gray of blindness.

As the surf rolled up to my feet, the susurrance of the tides was a crescendo of whispering voices, millions of them, that flowed and ebbed.

I was in three places at once.

I knelt and scooped up a handful of the sand, letting it trickle through my fingers. When it was gone, I found that I was holding a rope. The rope trailed into the ocean.

"Relax. Keep pulling up that bucket."

Noreen creeps closer to the dark, rippling water, drawn by the sound. Bubbles of air are rising to the surface.

Something emerges from the water. It's a white hand, as white as milk, as white as death, with five long fingers that curl into wizened claws and grip the edge of the sink. She can hear the drain gurgle as the water begins to drain out of it.

A white face breaks the surface, screaming as it breaches.

Speechless with terror, Noreen flees through a nearby doorway, slamming it shut.

A sickly greenish-blue light falls out of a crevice high in the ceiling, but fades before it can do much more than give shape and texture to the slick, stony floor below. She can see that she is in a large cavern, and a network of ruined, swollen timber beams comprise a grid of ribs that encircle the space like a bird cage and serve as a support structure for the rock.

She becomes aware of a constant, undulating noise emanating from the crevice, a rippling binaural tone that might drive her mad if she has to endure it much longer. It is like the steady drone of some vast machine, a thing of grinding black cogs greased with unspeakable ichors.

There are anonymous figures hanging from long ropes tied to some point high overhead.

They are draped in mildewed sackcloth so that only their gray, bloated feet are visible, and their nooses over that, so that their heads are hidden by hoods of taut burlap.

Water runs down them and drips from their black toenails, into puddles below.

The beam of turquoise light streams down their bodies; their shadows make them look as if they are standing atop columns of darkness.

A timid voice, muffled by the kitchen door, whispers, "Why did you leave?"

In a space between the timbers on the other side of the cavern, a hole appears. The stone seems to crumple backwards in measured, square increments, like paper being folded into origami, sliding into itself and out of sight. After several seconds of the whirring-grinding-scraping noise of it, there is a misshapen rectangle of empty space as large as a doorway.

The voice from the kitchen says, "You're not supposed to leave."

Noreen notices movement and looks up at the hanged figures. They seem to have been alarmed by the sound of the transforming stone, and are now fighting and thrashing as if trying to escape their nooses, swinging, pendulous.

Foul water drizzles from their kicking feet. She screams and runs, throwing herself into the hole in the wall.

She runs, her socks squelching in her boots, her boots knocking against the stone as she ventures deeper into what turns out to be a tunnel, as round as the inside of a pipe and just tall

341

enough that she can stand up in it. The light behind her is less and less until she has to slow down, afraid that she might slam into a wall or step off into a pit.

The darkness becomes oppressive, weighing her down the farther she walks, ramping up the gravity as if the very air itself has metamorphosed into lead. Soon the tunnel is invisible and Noreen is reduced to crawling along, scraping her palms and bruising her knees on the rough limestone.

The dark presses her into the floor, more and more.

She pulls herself along on her belly, reaching ahead, dragging her logy body to each handhold, pushing in turn with her feet.

Some force conspires to draw her backward, and she inches along, clutching the stones under her, making her way deeper into the tunnel, fighting the pull that threatens to send her howling and flailing back into the place with the dead things.

Something resists her, does not want her to leave. Soon it's even stronger than gravity itself, and she's clinging to the floor.

A light breeze courses over her exhausted body; escape is near.

The next time she reaches for a handhold, Noreen finds nothing.

She is lying on the floor of the tunnel's end, where it opens into a void so vast that her voice doesn't echo back to her when she calls for Sawyer again. It is simply swallowed up, muffled by emptiness.

She can hear something, though. It is the rushing of trees in the wind.

There is a light coming from somewhere below; she can see the stone around her now. She pulls herself to the edge and looks down, and sees a strange forest sprouting out of the wall around the end of the tunnel.

The light is coming from the intermittent flashing of a nearby neon sign; it says KING'S INN in giant yellow cursive, the second word much larger than the first. Next to it is a stylized image of a bearded man wearing a crown, also made of luminescent tubes. Below that is the word "VACANCY".

It is then that Noreen realizes that she is climbing out of a well.

She grips the rim of the well and hauls herself out, tumbling down from the wall of the cistern and onto the ground where she rests, gulping air. At this angle she can see the sky . . . it is an empty, eternal black, shot through at a dozen places, leaving holes through which that same turquoise light shines in on her.

It only pierces the night, each beam swording downward into eventual dissolution.

That same swelling, swerving mechanical drone rains down from the sky, fainter this time but still enough to make her skin crawl.

She finally rolls over and gets up again, and starts walking toward the sign.

I was startled by a pair of headphones. The Mariner had plugged a pair of stereo cup headphones into the record player, and put them on me. The strains of big-band music wafted out of the turntable . . . Glenn Miller, the Inkspots . . . and the voice I had been trying to ignore faded into the background. A man sang a lilting song about setting the world on fire.

"Maybe that'll help," I heard Ink say through the cups. "The motel sign, that was him poisoning the water. Keep doing your voo-doo, and I'll do what I can to keep him out. I can't last forever, but maybe I can hold him off just long enough."

The Mariner looked away, his shoreline eyes searching the

room. He had a thoughtful look on his face as if he were listening for something.

"He's just outside, looking for the chink in our armor, looking for an unlocked window. He hasn't seen your friend yet. The unremembered man is merely the avatar, the reaching hand, the representative, of the grand horror lurking in the abyss your friend now traverses underneath the Sea of Dreams. Pray she isn't discovered. Keep hauling."

I looked down at my sand-dusted hands.

The rope had become the ink-pen.

The closer Noreen gets to the neon sign, the fiercer it buzzes, and the brighter it becomes, until she is feverish and her head aches. The neon tubing thrums with power until she is afraid that at any moment it is going to burst and shower her with burning plasma.

She recoils as the neon king's eyes shift.

The electricity flicks from one tube-iris to the other, and suddenly . . . he is looking at her.

The sense of idiot madness, of antithetical malice welling from that stare is more than she can bear. It is enough to quail the trees and stones and earth itself with its sourceless hatred.

It is like staring into the guileless, unfeeling eye of a hurricane.

Noreen's heart surges in her chest, and she breaks for the treeline. Only they aren't trees, they are corroded girders standing up out of the soil at sharp, jostling angles, a graveyard of rusty swords. The soil underneath is a roiling black loam infused with an eternity of garbage.

The forest is not a forest at all, but a junkyard of forgotten things.

Tumbleweeds of crumpled paper and Christmas lights drift across the unending wasteland, clattering over heaps of dissected baby dolls and coffee filters, shattered glass and bent candlebra, scraps of car tires, crumbled statues.

A path has been cut in the refuse, and this is what she races along, pushing her tired body as hard as she can, pistoning legs carrying her forward. On the horizon of this hateful hell is a tremendous dark tower of filth and rust spindling upwards out of the desolation.

That must be where she must go.

She is no more than ten steps into this wretched place when the ground shifts underneath her feet.

The world spins madly up and down and in and out, as if perception itself has become a clockwork puppet show.

The trees wheel away, the ceiling heaves down at her until it is so close she can almost touch it, and the dirt sifts away through cracks in tile, as if the grout is a sieve.

Craggy, toothlike boulders punch up through the tile, and Noreen stumbles, flailing, into a shallow pool of dank water. Eyeless white fish scatter, writhing, from the splash. She groans and picks herself up.

She is in a sort of tremendous labyrinth, constructed from bottle-green castlestone. Before her and behind her stretches a corridor devised of what appears to be an infinity of bookshelves. These are filled with ancient tomes, their crumbling spines fractal with rot and mildew, their pages swollen with dank water.

Aquatic light shimmers down from holes in the ceiling, giving vague shape to her environment, guttering with that same mad binaural beat as before. Something behind the light shifts, curling protectively from her acknowledgement.

Noreen finally sees that this place does not conform to the whims of logic.

It is a nightmare outside of reality, beholden to neither time nor space, its laws fluid and rudimentary. It's a non-place where dead dreams settle to the bottom and decay like dead fish on the floor of the universe.

(you're almost th)

The girl looks up at the sound of a voice.

I've heard it too. I recognize it as Hel Grammatica, the silen that spoke to me on the train. It fades in and out as before, like the bad reception of a broken radio. I write it down so Noreen can hear it.

(m here. i am in the void. keep moving! he knows you are h)

"Who is that?" she asks, fearful. Then, she understands. She understands because I understand.

(it's going to take a concerted effort here), says the silen. His voice comes from far away, but it is closer and more intimate than pillow-talk. It originates in the center of our heads, an erudite and muffled intonation.

The stone floor vibrates with a whirring-thudding-scraping; Noreen looks over her shoulder and senses something moving, a vast writhing that billows in the darkness like the shadow of a whale deep underwater. She can hear a leathery creaking, and a metallic rattling, underscored by the constant rumble of unseen machinery.

Then, as she is rooted in terror, staring into the black, a brilliant yellow eye opens back there, a neon mandala that twitches from wall to wall and then locks onto the trembling girl.

The hovering golden iris is easily the size of an automobile.

Without a word, Noreen darts in the other direction, sprinting at top speed, the puddles spraying at her footsteps.

The eye gives chase. The floor shakes.

She comes to an intersection and takes the ~~left-hand path,~~

(NO!)

the right-hand path, and a shelf full of rotten books disgorges its contents at her. The pile of slush-paper and book backings vomits out onto the floor. Noreen slows down just enough to keep from sliding in it, and clears the obstacle.

The dark behind her is rent in twain by the sudden appearance of the eye, as it comes around the corner in pursuit.

(now go left)

We heeded the voice in unison, and I was writing and editing and writing and editing as Noreen hurled herself through the maze. I drew inspiration from the Vur Ukasha hand over fist as I stood on the shores of inspiration, altering it according to Hel Grammatica's advice even as the prose led her ever closer to our imprisoned friends and the possibility of freedom.

My hand cramped as I furiously scribbled forth, changing and rewording, several times editing Noreen out of lethal mistakes and situations.

At length I was unsure if I was describing things as they happened outside of my control, or if I was setting events into motion with every word I transcribed.

The "past" and the "future" were irrelevant.

The three of us became one, the silen's broken advice filtering the dream-water as I drew it and poured it onto the page, trying to ignore the insidious whispers from the grim, cold face pressed against the second-story window in front of me.

The unremembered man hovered there just beyond the glass, his yellow coat bat-winging around him in the air.

He floated like a drowned man, his greasy black hair haloing around his terrifying featureless face. He looked like something that had never been born and would never die. He was a half-assed facsimile of a man made by something that hated men. I wanted to scream just look

(forget that guy, listen to me kid)

ing at him. The Mariner turned up the stereo and

STOP WRITING. STOP WHAT YOU ARE DOING. GET OUT

OF THE HOUSE OR

(keep pulling up the water)

YOU ARE GOING TO DIE. .EID OT GNIOG ERA UOY

I AM GOING TO KILL YOU.

I put the pen's nib to the paper and

I AM GOING TO RIP YOU IN HALF AND FUCK YOUR RAW GUTS.

tried to write. Judy Garland's soulful, haunting voice was drilling "Over the Rainbow" into my head from the sides, and the yellow-coat man was drilling from the front, and this Hel guy was drilling from the back,

(left, right, left, left, no, left)

I AM GOING TO DRAG YOU INTO THE DEEP AND THE DEAD AND THE DARK

"Some*wheeeeerrrrre* over the rainbow . . . ."

AND LICK YOUR WET RED BONES WHILE EVERYONE FORGETS

YOU EVER EXISTED.

"Where skies *are bluuue* . . . ."

The tunnel begins to rotate, or perhaps it is gravity getting more comfortable, and the water pours across the bookshelves as Noreen finds herself running across the spines of water-fat tomes.

The rushing cavewater threatens to sweep her feet out from under her.

The thing that is the true form of the unremembered man looms behind her, the Nameless Feaster, gazing down at her with that blazing-hot electric Sauron eye, that great swinging backburner sun.

The shelf, the books, the walls and all come to an abrupt end. Noreen is running straight at the precipice of a waterfall.

There is no time to hesitate.

She leaps without pausing from the edge, and a gargantuan maw slops shut where she had just been. Unspeakably foul ichor splatters across her back.

YOU CANNOT WIN.

She lands on her knees and then her stomach, on a steel catwalk brown with age, one leg dangling into space. Blood drips from a deep scrape, a thin flap of skin fileted from her left knee.

She scrambles to her feet and bolts forward again. The tears in her eyes—she is weeping with terror—stream out of their corners and trickle backwards across her temples.

Ahead is that citadel again, a misshapen spindle of refuse reaching into the beams of blue-green light that buzz down from holes in the void ceiling.

She redoubles her efforts even as the catwalk begins to twist in midair.

The Feaster is devouring it in her wake, the steel screaming, scraping, and spiraling into the nothing beyond the Eye.

The railing and the grating come off in sections and whirl away like playing cards in the wind.

The vacuum of the thing pulls gently at her hair and clothes as she runs, it is so close. The constant trilling drone from the cave-sky is being drowned out now, by the sucking-roaring of the

Feaster behind Noreen.

She is now mere seconds from entering the Spindle. The entrance gapes before her. She can hear her boots echoing inside.

And then—sorry Charlie, the door slams shut.

The Tower of Silence

LUCKILY, NOREEN IS ON the inside of the door as it shuts. At first, she didn't make it, and I had to go back and edit her through it, but the words didn't seem to want to be edited. Something was pulling the other end of the rope, and it was pulling hard.

Even as I crossed out words and wrote new ones, I found myself writing the same words again, and having to cross them out again. Several times I realized I was scribbling gibberish and had to mark that out as well.

I looked up at the ghoulish spectre outside the window and shouted, "Stop! Get the hell away from me!"

He laughed.

It was a terrible sound, a grating, grinding vibrato that reminded me of bad transmissions and subway trains. EVERYTHING DIES, he said. YOU DIE WE DIE WE ALL DIE FOR ICE CREAM. AHAHAHAHA

His hideous face fell, and he said with a deadly seriousness, YOU ARE SHIT. YOU ARE A SHIT WRITER AND A SHIT ARTIST. YOU ARE WASTING

YOUR TIME. THIS ISN'T

EVEN

REAL.

Unbidden, I got a mental image of myself lying curled into the fetal position, somewhere out in the desert all alone. He/I was shaking and drooling a thick foam, his/my sightless eyes gazing at the backs of his/my upper eyelids. The sun had risen in full, and was beginning to turn the hardpan sand into a griddle.

Even then, sitting there at the card table in the House of Water, I could feel the heat of it. Sweat sheeted down my face and back, funnelling into the crack of my ass and hanging from the tip of my nose.

FORGOTTEN AND ALONE.

You try so hard to be the strong one, boy. You always have.

You push the world away, neglecting your friends and loved ones, you self-serving, condescending piece of shit, and you break yourself trying to prove you're better than what you think your family, your friends see in you.

You think you're a "lone wolf", but all you are is a scared little boy trying to tell himself that since his daddy didn't need him, nobody needs him.

For what? Cry it out, bitch.

It all comes to naught in the end. Give up and walk away.

You don't have to be strong anymore. You will be forgotten no matter how hard you work . . . no matter how hard you try.

(I am your father's muse, Ross. Listen to me,) said Hel Grammatica. The silen's raspy voice was as clear as a bell. *(Ignore him. I can't keep this up for long; I'm really pushing)*

BE GONE, WATER-CARRIER, roared the other, the Unremembered Man, the Feaster. His voice was like a roach on a wedding cake.

(my voice to you right now, but if you can get her to the top of the tower of silence, everything will be okay. I'm down here waiting. I've got the others with me, Sawyer and Walter, they're okay. You can't save everybody but if you can

The house around me shimmered, and I could see through the walls into a bright and rainless expanse. The Formica of the table under my forearms began to disintegrate and grow gritty with sand, and also hot. I could hear the rustling of wind-blown desert brush over the Sea of Dreams.

The rope in my hands slipped, and I panicked, reaching for it.

A terrifying, ripping screech startled me. A blotch appeared on the paper.

I hadn't even realized the Mariner had changed the vinyl on the turntable; the strains of The Beatles' "Come Together" thumped out of the headphones. The sweat-drop on my nose fell on the bottom end of the paper like a signature, blurring the ink-spot (set the world on fire!).

The desert reeled away from me like a drop of dish-soap in a bowl of pepper and water, leaving me sitting at the table with my feet (in wet sand / on floorboards).

I used the song's rotary-phone backbeat as a handle to anchor myself and put the pen to the paper again.

The inside of the spindle is a depthless black, only pierced by a shimmering shaft of light, the blue-green of the ocean, that comes down through a hole in a low ceiling. It's so dark in here that the column is almost a solid thing, a rotating obelisk of ice confined to the space in the center of the round room.

The pulsating thrum is unbearable here. It emanates from the light, a wheedling, harrowing drumbeat that reverberates in the massive room, rolling around the hollow walls like a New Year's Eve noisemaker.

It is nothing compared to the stench permeating the air, a filthy, raunchy smell that reminds Noreen of both french fries and roadkill.

It is nothing compared to the constant metallic creaking and snapping thundering from the walls as they groan in the agony of stress.

The entire tower sounds as if it is being slowly twisted to pieces.

She feels instinctively for a light switch, and she's touched the wall before it occurs to her what an exercise in futility that is. She finds the unmistakable smooth surface of polished metal, and for some reason, it is *greasy*, as if coated in lard.

The floor is a catwalk of steel grating, as slimy as the wall but the texture of the grill provides grip.

She feels her way around the room, keeping her eyes on the light for perspective. It spills through a deep funnel in the center of the floor, and grows stronger as Noreen circumnavigates the wall.

When she returns to the side where she came in, she freezes in terror and confusion.

The door is gone.

That's when she sees that the floor has become the same smooth steel as the walls. Her second epiphany is that the tower is rotating, very slowly, like a gigantic auger drilling into the floor of the void, and she is walking up the thread of the auger's screw.

She is climbing the inside of a huge screw-conveyor, and it is moving in reverse, drilling into the rock like an oil-platform.

Bones lay in haphazard sorts across the floor here. Some of them are locked into restraining cuffs mounted on the wall like tools on a pegboard. As she watches, a human skull buzzes across the steel, carried by the vibrations of the tower, and topples clattering into the hole in the middle of the room.

Another bone follows it—a long, knobby femur—and then another, a curving rib-bone. A skirl of terror whips through

Noreen as she understands, setting her scalp on edge.

The walls are greasy because they are dripping with adipocere.

Corpse-fat.

A pelvis falls from the hole in the ceiling and strikes the side of the pit, shattering like a ceramic gravy-boat. The shards flash white and then they're gone into the deep and the dark.

She follows the curve of the climb with her eyes, and she's able to make out human skeletons locked into cuffs. They are queued endlessly around the interior wall into the darkness at the apex of the curve, gradually shaken apart at the joints as they make their way downward into the depths of the abyss.

They swing free on bands of rotten ligament and tumble like pickup sticks into the pit.

"Oh Jesus God," says Noreen, wiping her hands on her clothes.

She keeps talking to herself, mumbling ecclesiastical names as she ventures onward and upward into the upper reaches of the Tower of Silence.

As she goes, the bones lining the walls become less and less defined.

Blow-flies crawl across ragged strips of leathery fiber. Grinning skulls gradually turn into the gaping, gore-eyed Edvard Munch screams of train-station mummies, their taut skin shrink-wrapped by death and thirst.

Each corpse is less deteriorated than the last, but only just.

The longer Noreen walks, the brighter the light gets, until the room is the frigid blue of sunlight filtering through the non-Euclidean frozen shapes of Arctic waters. It's as if she is walking around and around the inside of a Zoroastrian dakhma hermetically sealed under the North Atlantic ice.

An hour into the climb, the parade of shackled bones

356

encircling her become shriveled and hoary bags of bulbous angles. Their desiccated brown eyeballs dangle in sockets like olives in knot-holes; their arms are drawn to their chests, some as if they died begging, some in protective affect.

She keeps her face averted. Tears have begun to stream down her face in earnest.

She can hear groans from somewhere up above. Most of them are in a language Noreen doesn't speak; gutteral, exhausted, nonsensical rambling, barely audible over the beating-fluttering pulsation of the spindle.

The sounds of life stir her out of her anguish, propel her up the fat-slimed metal spiral, past the motionless scarecrows . . . until she sees the first of them. A man hangs from the wall-shackles, bristling with long locks of grimy, gray-gone hair.

His eyes glitter in the pits of his eye-sockets, and his sunken cheeks cling to his greening teeth.

"Help," he says, matter-of-factly. "Please."

A woman dangling next to him hears, and gazes at Noreen with rheumy eyes. "Per favore, lasciami uscire."

I sat back in the chair and pressed the heels of my hands to my eyes, my temples throbbing. The Sea of Dreams washed ashore before me, inky and thick, like the cast-off of an oil-spill. Even the words from the ink pen stood up from the paper. As it dried, I could run my fingertips across it and feel the ink protruding from the paper, like Braille.

"What is this?"

The Mariner lifted one of my headphones and said, "Keep your pen on the page and your eyes on the sea. Keep pulling."

"What's going on?" I asked, looking up at his seashore eyes.

"You have found her, now go and get her," sang the Beatles.

His face was grim. "He's in the house with us."

Normand chanced a fire. The smoke curled from the half-dead embers, mixing with the eternal fog that engulfed this cursed land. He looked around at the ruins surrounding him, a building that had once been sleek and utilitarian. Even in ancient disrepair, it was obvious that in its own time, the structure had been exponentially more advanced and comfortable than anything in Ain.

He was beginning to understand just how long the Antargata k-Setra had been here, dying in this half-sunned netherworld. Whole civilizations had come and gone before he and everything he'd known had even been born.

He curled up on the demolished sofa and tried to catch some sleep before continuing, but his thoughts were, as always, plagued with worry about the events taking place back home. He hoped he was not too late.

—The Fiddle and the Fire, vol 7 (unfinished) "The Gunslinger and the Giant"

The Goat-Fish

SHE PICKS UP A femur and hammers the man's shackles with it, trying to break them. The left one's cotterpin cracks in half and slides out; his arm free, the emaciated prisoner sets to freeing his other arm and then the woman next to him.

Before Noreen can pardon any of the others, however, she hears one last burst from the voice in our heads.

(It's harsh, but you're going to have to leave them to their own devices. We may not be able to save them, but if we can get out, we can prevent the Feaster from bringing any more of them down here. Just get yourself to the—)

The girl understands, even though the transmission fails. She starts running.

The floor is no longer slick with decay, so there's no more reason to be cautious. The men and women cuffed to the wall cry out for release in a hundred different languages as she sprints past them, but there's nothing she can do but hope they can free themselves. The regret is a swelling knot in her chest.

Not all of the shackled are human; some of them seem to be Tekyr, some of them are Iznoki, some of them are even the shadowy, white-masked Bemo-Epneme of K-Set. Some of them are of some species Noreen doesn't even recognize, and they plead in languages she's never known; she realizes that they are the citizens of other worlds alien even to Destin.

The Tower of Silence is a place of sacrifice, she can see now; it is filled with abductees from myriad planes of existence,

360

thousands of people from a hundred storied worlds fed rotting to the unseen thing under the rock.

There is something going on here, deeper and larger than she'd ever expected. The Feaster's master schemes to devour the whole of existence, and someone—or something—is giving it the leeway to do so.

Her mind is occupied with deduction when she hears a voice and halts in her tracks.

"Baby!" exclaims Sawyer.

He is cuffed to the inner wall of the tower; just above, the top of the massive dakhma opens onto the dark elements. A dazzling beam of blue-green light swords down from some point high above, filling the tower with luminescence.

She can see over the parapet and it chills her to realize that the other beams of light she has been seeing since emerging from the well end in towers just like this one. It is an endless dark forest of neglect and obscurity. Spearing up from the shadowscape are thousands of black death-spires screwing into the rock, feeding forgotten people from countless worlds to the Feaster's ancient master.

In this instant, she understands what's happening.

She is underneath the Vur Ukasha, in the Void-Between-The-Worlds, and something—the thing suckling at the towers as they drill the dead through the rock—is down here, waiting, preparing itself, getting ready to surface.

"It's about time," someone says, snapping her out of her reverie.

Noreen turns to see a short little man, half her own height, and slender, with pink skin and piercing golden eyes. Tiny goat-horns jut from the crown of his bald head, and he's grinning. Tiny puppy-teeth shine white in the glow of the beam.

361

"Nice to meet you," says Hel Grammatica, the silen and muse of Edward Richard Brigham. "Normie's gonna be ecstatic that you're all three in Destin. Remind me to send Ross a Christmas card. Now could you kindly get us out of these cuffs?"

The study door slammed shut with a hollow bang; I spun in my chair to see the Mariner leaning against it. Tendrils of shadow snaked around the edges of the door, licking like tongues of black flame, and I could hear it rattling softly in the frame. Ink's Swarovski crystal glass glittered with sweat on the windowsill.

I turned back to my task, but I could hear him cursing the being behind the door.

Looking down at the pen-rope, I got an idea.

I let go of it, and it began to wash back into the Sea of Dreams.

Noreen smashes the cuff with the knob of the femur. To her dismay and shock, they both break into pieces at the same time. Hel swings free, dangling by one pink wrist.

"Well, it's a start," he says, and grabs his forearm with his free hand. The tattered gray robe tied around his waist flutters in the breeze as he braces himself and sticks one of his goat-horns into the keyhole of his remaining shackle.

The shimmering light extinguishes, and then flares to life again.

They look up and see that clouding overhead is an obscene stormfront of writhing black feelers, and at the forefront of that clicking-billowing-thrashing is the burning yellow god-Eye.

It stares down at them with an unblinking, all-seeing fury.

Hel pries at the cuff with the horn-point and finally, with a crackle of sparks, it breaks. He tumbles onto the floor in a spill of arrows and is instantly back on his feet.

They look up at the Feaster and Walter Rollins shouts, "No!"

A throng of freed people are barreling up the ramp into the open air, blinking blindly at the bright beam from above. The silen is trying to free Walter and Sawyer from their shackles, but the longer it takes, the more people cluster around them trying to escape.

There are at least twenty people in the small space atop the tower, and more are trying to force their way into the apex, crying and wailing in unintelligible languages.

Walter is free.

He takes a skull away from one of the refugees and starts beating on Sawyer's cuffs, knocking the teeth out of it.

"We've got to get the hell off of this thing before—" the Deon starts to say, but someone elbows him in the ear. He's gotten one of Sawyer's hands free, so Walter hands him the skull and shoves the refugee backwards.

Something tumbles out of the light. A rope clatters to the floor at her feet and Noreen grabs it. "Goddamnit, get off me!" she screams. The people from the tower are beginning to fight; the cluster is turning into a riot. Starved, dying people tumble from the parapet and hurtle, screaming, into the darkness.

The Feaster squids closer, watching the chaos.

Black tendrils venture in and pluck screaming people from the growing crowd, drawing them into its amorphous mass, dropping some of them. They bounce off the side of the tower and plummet, flailing, out of sight.

Noreen peers into the crowd surging up the ramp and sees a familiar face, but it confuses and exhilarates and terrifies her all at once.

Standing on the other side of the thinning crowd is Ross

Brigham.

I heard a voice behind me, but I couldn't afford to look. The Mariner was roaring something in a language I didn't know; his voice had changed, become deeper, and hoarse. Even though I was standing on the shore of the Sea of Dreams, I could still hear the study door rattling.

"Edin na zu, emuqa!" he was shouting, "Barra, idimmu, edin na zu emuqa!"

How the hell could I be down there when I'm up here?

This other-Ross is not the man Noreen knows; he is leaner, darker-complected, with sharp, hungry eyes. He strides purposefully up the ramp, followed by another of the silen, like Hel. This one, however, is taller, as tall as a man, and has skin the fiery orange of burnished bronze.

His nacreous horns branch from his gleaming skull like the antlers of a deer. A battle-skirt of leather pennants sweeps the floor around his boots as he walks. His torso is a finely-chiseled bas-relief of perfect musculature.

In the other-Ross's hands is a strange object that Noreen only thinks of as a sword because it has the conceptual *shape* of a sword. It seems to flicker precariously from form to form, as if the thing itself isn't sure what it wants to be. The blade shimmers like oil on water, a broadsword one second and a *no-dachi* the next.

It obviously pains Sardis to wield the thing, as blood continuously drips from his hands, and Noreen can see tears standing in his eyes.

"Rhetor Logos," growls Hel Grammatica, turning to meet the not-Ross and the other silen. "Getting Ed's murderer to do even more dirty work for you? Was giving up on the Water Covenant

364

and endangering existence not enough for you?"

The Rhetor smiles.

His teeth would be needle-sharp if they weren't so rotten. As he speaks, they bend in the gums like an angler-fish. His eyes burn with ten thousand years of bottled malice. "I expect you know what this is," he says, indicating the not-Ross and his bizarre amorphous sword.

Sardis gibbers, "Walla walla bing-bang."

"You're not going to get away with this," says Hel. "Even with the Datdimra."

"Hey!" says the Rhetor. His voice is bell-deep, sinister, and as oily as his skin. "I can shit out a cliché too! How's this: *I've already gotten away with it.*"

"Immortality wasn't the reward part of the Covenant, you cowardly son of a bitch," says Hel. "Your reward and your honor was the chance to become carriers of the Water. You're not fulfilling your duty anymore. You pervert your gift, you tell men to do horrific things to each other."

The Rhetor laughs. "Yes, and it's hilarious, isn't it? Who needs cable TV when I can tell a man to shoot up a school with an assault rifle? Or drive a bus through the front of a restaurant? It's better than anything on your precious internet. You're half-right. The entire pact we made with the Creator is a curse.

"We deserve the rest of death. We all deserve one final bow. We've done our part a million times over since the dawn of man. No more next chapters, no more sequels, no more self-important liars like Brigham pulling whole worlds out of his ass and making people suffer for entertainment.

"For the last thousand years, I've been going from world to world hiding and destroying the First Sword of every civilization," says the Rhetor, indicating Sardis and the dubious sword in his hands. "Excalibur, Dabutai, Ik-simmor, Windrender. All of them. The Datdimra here is the final facet of the First Sword: the First Sword of Destin. Now we'll make *all* the worlds suffer, not just the fictional ones. We'll have our fun before we finally fade away."

"The Keyworlds will die without the water of the Vur Ukasha, Master Rhetor," says Hel. "They'll dry up and waste away, the system will fall apart, and—"

The Rhetor crooks his head like a curious dog. "Now you're catching on. It's time for the end of all stories, water-carrier. And I'm here to make sure we all die happily ever after."

"I'm sorry," says not-Ross, his voice strained and sad.

He plunges the sword-point into Hel's chest, groaning, "Purple monkey dishwasher."

I grinned at the weight on the other end of the rope. *Hold on tight,* I thought, looping it around my arms for grip. *I'm getting you guys out of there.* The study seemed to melt away around me, becoming transparent, as if the rope had pulled me out of the house. The card table blew out from under me like ashes in the wind, and then I was standing in sand, cold ocean-water lapping around my boots.

I hauled up another two feet of rope, digging my heels into the sand, and reached for more. It felt like I was pulling a shipwreck out of the sea. My arms and hands cramped with exertion, and my back ached from neck to hip.

"I am the Duke of the Field," growled Ink. I heard the sibilance of a sword being drawn from a sheath.

The ocean fell quiet; I felt the rope go slack in my hands.

Noreen, Sawyer, and Walter swing precariously over the Tower of Silence at the end of the prosaic rope. The burning neon eye of the Feaster is close enough to them that they can feel the heat of its gaze like a bonfire. Protuberances snake out of the blackness and threaten to envelop them.

As he lies dying at the feet of the Rhetor and Sardis Bridger, Hel Grammatica calls up to them, "Find the First Sword! It's the only thing that can kill—"

Ink the Mariner's voice erupts from the light like a peal of thunder. "I AM THE LORD OF TRIALS, THE KEEPER OF FEARS AND SECRETS! I AM THE *GOAT-FISH OF THE VUR UKASHA AND THE STEWARD OF THE HOUSE OF WATER,* AND *THIS IS WHERE YOU END!"*

At the same time, with a wince, Sardis lifts the infinitely-sharp blade of the Datdimra, known to the Kingsmen as the Timecutter, known to the Tekyr as the Dragonslayer, and brings it down on Hel's throat.

I hazarded a glance over my shoulder and saw two things:

The first was a door standing on end in the sand, alone, with no wall around it; it was ajar and some slender, terrifying figure was moving through it. I had a sense of cold fire, wreathed in darkness.

The other was that the Mariner—or what I knew of him—was gone.

In his place was a beautiful warrior, armored in golden plates that glittered as though the light came from within him.

Bovine white horns as big around as a man's calves curled from the temples of his helmet. His skin was a deathly blue-white and his eyes were as those of a hooved animal: gray, his pupils ragged and gaping. His tattered, faded red cape billowed in the gale as he pulled the blade of a gleaming cutlass out of the scabbard at his hip.

The ocean seemed to inhale, then, and grew silent.

The tip of the sword came from the scabbard, and an arc of

water leapt out of the tide like a sheet on a fish-hook. It trailed the cutlass as the Duke of the Field swept it across the study door, following the cut of his blade, and the Unremembered Man was flung backwards into the dark doorway.

The door itself was cleft clean in half.

The sea, dark with a nameless poison, swelled behind me and disgorged itself onto the beach in a stunning deluge, as if it were vomiting up the influence of the ancient being underneath it.

The rope came at me in twirling curls of hemp and hit me in the face. I was knocked off my feet and submerged in the singing-chanting-whispering tsunami. Shadowy figures approached me, thrown by the water, and I thought I recognized one of them.

Having cleansed itself, the ocean ebbed, diminishing back into itself and taking us with it.

I heard a muffled crash of glass as the study window exploded and I was washed through the hole into something that resembled a galaxy—not of stars but of a million trillion stories, and just as many wishes.

I peered through the murky glass of the tide and saw that each point of light was another place and time, another unending tale containing another storyteller containing a tale, and so on, each inside the other like a Russian stacking doll crafted by M.C. Escher.

I could read each bright star as easily as signs on a road. *This is the water of the Sea of Dreams*, I thought to myself, as I sank toward a cluster of light somewhere in a farflung arm of the gargantuan spiral. I was adrift in the collective creative consciousness of every storyteller that ever lived and ever would live, the drinking-font of every God-thing that gathered around a campfire with his own ladle of fables.

I soared through this green-black liquid aether; the akashic records wheeled for light-centuries underneath me, a infinitely large compendium of love and hate, war and peace, hope and regret. It was a great grand library shaped into something that looked like the Milky Way.

I could see dark shapes hovering in it and as I tumbled past them, they resolved into multicolored creatures that resembled whales. Sleek, gargantuan paunches loomed from the darkness, trailed by iridescent ribbons as long as lifetimes. They stared at me as I passed, with a hundred tiny silver eyes, and I saw members of the Sileni clinging to their dirigible hides like horned remora.

I hurtled through this secret universe, gaining speed, the gurgling roar of liquid rushing past my ears.

I heard a low whistling, like the steam-whistle of a train, and found myself orbiting a Jovian sphere made of white-chrome light, inscribed with so many words I couldn't possibly ever hope to read them all.

Shades of pink and teal darkled across its surface like koi swimming in milk, refracted by cracks where something had broken it. The tectonic shards drifted, slow and massive.

Floating next to it, I must have looked like an ant on a bowling ball.

What I did see, and understand, showed me pieces of our story I'd never been privy to. I saw Noreen and Sawyer lying together in Maplenesse. I saw Maxwell Bayard talking to the silen on the doomed plane. I saw the Unremembered Man take Julian Clines' name and leave him a soulless shell in the sands of the abandoned town in the desert.

I even saw my father materializing in the trees behind his house on Earth, splashing facefirst into the stream with a fresh hole in his neck from Sardis' Ainean bullet.

All of this took place in the theater of my mind's eye as I scanned the words.

I reached out and touched the glowing sentences with one quivering finger, and fell through the sphere's blinding surface.

I didn't even have a chance to scream.

The Second Verse, Just Like the First

I HAD THE DISTINCT sensation of speeding backwards, reeling and tumbling through open space, and of things being reassembled. Angular movements of reconstruction and realignment slid past each other, pieces of the past interlocking to create panoramas of happenstance that, suddenly, were never broken to begin with. Moments unshattered in tumbling fragments, seconds becoming minutes becoming hours becoming days.

The sphere was being repaired by someone or something I could not see. A mural of narrative rebuilt itself before my eyes, feeding itself into the darkness behind me as I hurtled toward the end of it.

I felt like I was inside of a nucleus, racing down a track made of DNA.

My memory flashed on a time in high school when my mom used to paint ceramics; she loved her hobby with all the ferocity of a new passion, and churned them out as fast as they could kiln them at the pottery store in town. She had meticulously painted a Santa Claus one week, and I had accidentally knocked it off a shelf and broke it into three dozen pieces. The paint wasn't even two days dry.

I had stayed up all night gluing that ceramic statue back together, my heart aching at how hard she'd cried at seeing that broken Santa figurine. It turned out good as new, and I'd even painted over the cracks. My mind recalled that now, with that same sense of broken things being seamlessly put back together.

372

The abrupt feeling of being dropped into my rightful place came to me, as if I were a video tape being pushed into a VCR. Time slowed and garbled words coalesced into real things: the smell of smoke and of sweat, the sound of wind rustling in grass.

Lucidity came at me from every angle, a silent flock of doves converging on my confusion, and I clustered into a diamond focus. I opened my eyes.

The low whistle I'd been hearing resolved into the hollow hoot of the wind in eaves. I was sitting on a cushioned seat in darkness.

To my left was a rectangle only slightly lighter than the room I was in, looking out onto dim, moonlit colors. There a cool, thin wind caressed a gently rippling meadow of wildflowers: crimson clover, and blue gay-feathers. In the distance loomed a great purple mountain. I heard a loon out there, or something like it yodeling over a chorus of night-bugs.

As I stared open-mouthed at the scenery, I heard furtive movement to my right. Someone struck a match and a face flickered into view.

It was the Deon of the Southern Kingsmen. He held out the flame, and I saw Sawyer's and Noreen's faces glowing in the shade. We were sitting in our car back on the train out of Maplenesse. Tears laced my vision at the sight of my friends; I saw the firelight in their own welling eyes just before Walter swore and shook the match out.

He lit another one and used it to light an oil sconce on the wall. The compartment brightened again and Noreen leapt at me without a word, throwing her arms around my neck. To my surprise, so did Sawyer.

I held them at arms' length and appreciated them: Sawyer's narrow face, large, expressive mouth, patchy week-old beard, and intense gray eyes . . . Noreen's heart-shaped face and fine features, her platinum-blonde hair; I couldn't help but be infatuated with the curve of her cupid's-bow lips.

It was like meeting them all over again. I burned their faces into my brain: the dogged, steely guile that never left Sawyer's eyes even when he was laughing . . . his easy confidence . . . Noreen's eternally fairy-serene smile . . . the way she stuck her tongue through her teeth as she cackled at our jokes. The way her hair smelled as I embraced them; like tulips and sea-breeze.

"You guys," I gushed, and broke down. I hugged them again, and wept on someone's shirt.

I didn't know what else to say—something about how they'd been with me all this way, and sentiments about loyalty and brotherhood and such, and how glad I was to have them back, but in the end I didn't have to find the words—because it was Sawyer that did me the favor with one concise phrase.

"Ditto, Scooby."

I suddenly realized that my shoulder was unmarked. I looked at the sleeve and pulled my collar back in astonishment. The hole was gone; it was as if the fiddler's bullet had never hit me.

"I can't believe it," said Walter, clapping slowly and softly. "Congratulations, Mr. Bridger. I don't know what happened and I don't know how you fixed it, but bravo."

"It was the Acolouthis," I said.

"The Acolouthis?" asked Walter. "You took the Sacrament?"

"Some guy tied me to a chair and fed it to me after you guys and the train disappeared. I wandered across the desert all that night until some guy called the Mariner found me," I said, and briefly recounted my adventures since losing them to the Feaster.

"So the tales were true," said Walter. "The Sea of Dreams exists."

"You met the Mariner?" asked Noreen.

374

"You know who that is?"

"He's in the books."

"Every gunslinger knows him," said Walter. "We all take the Sacrament; it's a rite of passage for the gunslingers of Destin, even your father many years ago. The Mariner waits at the House of Water to help us to cleanse ourselves of failure and self-doubt, and to overcome the parts of ourselves that keep us from greatness. He is the Lord of Trials.

"No one knows if he is real or simply an illusion of the Acolouthis; though, in light of the events that have just transpired, it would appear that there is more than a grain of veracity to his existence."

"The gods of Destin aren't quite as hands-off as the one back home," said Noreen. "Taking the Sacrament is like a Native American going on a vision quest. Only, the Acolouthis is a *little* stronger than peyote."

"Not everyone survives the hallucinations," said Walter. "The Acolouthis doesn't simply alter your perceptions, it alters your very reality. It works from the outside in, not the inside out, and opens a doorway in your head. The wastelands of Ain are littered with the bones of the men and women that tried and failed to overcome their worst fears and flaws.

"I'm exceedingly glad to find that you were able to succeed where so many others have not. We might not have come back from wherever we were."

"Speaking of that . . . place," said Sawyer, "What the hell was up with that? I thought I saw Ross down there with another silen."

"That wasn't me," I said. "That was my brother Sardis."

"He looks that much like you?"

"I guess he does."

"The last thing this Hel creature said was to find the

375

Datdimra," said Walter. "I'm assuming that was the weapon Sardis Bridger killed it with."

"What is the Datdimra?" I asked.

"A sword. A legend. A child's story, an old spinsters' tale. It is said that the sword is the blade the Wolf Oramoz used to cut the Time Dragon in half. No one knows where it came from or what became of it, though there are certainly enough stories handed down through the centuries that tell of other heroes wielding it in the name of whatever kingdom was in vogue at the time."

Noreen patted my knee. "Ross, do you still have that piece of paper from Ed's cottage?"

I thought about it and shook my head. "No, I put it in my dad's satchel, and I don't have it anymore. The fiddler took it."

"Do you remember what it said?"

"Something about a Dragonslayer."

Walter folded his arms and leaned back in his seat. "That's another name of the Datdimra. It's also known as the Timecutter. Who do you suppose put that there?"

"Well, since there wasn't any blood in the house except for in the bed where he was shot," I said, "I don't suppose my dad did it, so that leaves Sardis himself. But why would he do that?"

Sawyer said, "Did you hear what he said when he stabbed Hel Grammatica with the Dragonslayer? He was talking gibberish."

"Glossolalia," said Noreen. "Divine inspiration. I'll bet your brother was being influenced by the silen Hel called 'Rhetor Logos'."

"I'm grateful for the creature's involvement there at the last moment," said Walter. "At least now we know what's going on. I wonder why they felt the need to murder Lord Eddick, though."

"Maybe he knew too much. Hel was his muse, after all. I'm sure Ed heard more from him than stories about Normand."

"Of the King," said Walter, "I believe we would do well to go to Normand with our questions. No doubt he and my father may be more informed than we on these matters. And if Eddick was slain for knowing too much, they may be next on the Rhetor's list."

"I wonder what Sardis was trying to tell us," said Sawyer. "Maybe he was trying to tell us where the Datdimra is going to be hidden. But why?"

Walter told him, "He is obviously not acting of his own volition. I recall what transpired during the Mokehlyr celebration when Ross spotted him in the crowd and gave chase. He denied involvement, but fled."

"I don't figure he wanted to be locked up or interrogated," said Sawyer. "Probably even afraid of this Rhetor guy."

"I remember the other word on the paper was *Totem*," I said. "Sardis killed Hel with the Datdimra. Maybe he wanted us to know it can be used on the Rhetor."

"Totem. The word is meaningless to me," said Walter. "Like I've proposed; if anyone is better equipped with knowledge than ourselves, it would be Eddick's confidants Normand Kaliburn and my father. Let us continue to Ostlyn and see if he knows anything about Eddick's death and this 'Totem'. We must warn them of the Rhetor's machinations as well. Let's pray we aren't too late."

The Deon tamped pear leaves into a pipe and searched himself for a match. As he was lighting his pipe, he reached into his jacket and unholstered one of his Kingsman pistols. He handed it to me. "Now that you've been through the Trial of the Sacrament, that makes you a Kingsman—well, a fledgling, at any rate. I wager you didn't even know, did you?"

"What?" I asked in astonishment, looking down at the battle-worn revolver. It was long and the barrel was grooved with etchings in the exotic Ainean script.

377

Sawyer and Noreen were beaming. "That's awesome, man!" said Sawyer. "Congratulations? I guess?"

"It's an honor," I said to Walter. "Both the pistol and the promotion."

"Bravery is not the absence of fear," said Walter. "—That's what it says. On the pistol. I gather you can't read Ainean."

"Afraid not."

"Hold onto that, until we can get your father's guns back from your brother. It may come in handy at some point."

"Will do," I said. "What does the other one say, by the way?"

"Mercy is not the absence of strength."

We sat there for a moment before we all realized the train wasn't going anywhere. I got up and went out into the dark hallway, and went from room to room looking for other passengers. There was no one in our car; there was no one in the adjacent cars either. As I was coming back from the dining car, I met Walter.

"We are alone, I take it," he said. "As I expected. The other passengers are regrettably still down there in that tower."

"Oh, God," I said, feeling my heart drop into my stomach. "All those people."

He put a gentle hand on my chest and gave me a steely glare. "Don't you dare blame yourself. You could only do so much with what you were given. You barely rescued us; you never would have been able to haul all those thousands of people out as well. Tens of thousands, even, perhaps. You are no superhuman, Ross."

I made note of the fact that he had called me by my name, instead of *bastard.* I had crossed some kind of threshold. I felt the flush of embarrassed pride.

"You couldn't save them all, but maybe you can keep more people from ending up down there. Maybe we can even save some of the ones already down there. Now that we've won the battle, it is time to address the war." His lips pursed at the sight of my worried face, and he cupped the back of my neck with his hand. "Are you with me? Now is not the time to falter or doubt yourself."

I stood there, gazing into the sword-edge of his eyes, and gradually calmed down. I felt a hand on my shoulder and saw that Noreen was standing behind me.

"He's right," she said. "Now we've seen the whites of their eyes. It's time to take the fight to them."

I considered their supportive words, and touched her hand in gratitude.

"Now what?" I asked, once I felt confident again.

Walter flung the door open, bathing us in moonlight. "Now? We start walking."

* * *

The world lay bare before us, a meadow of spring-born wildflowers that unfurled to the distance like a giant quilt. Motes of white drifted up from the undergrowth as we walked, kicked up from the weeds mingling with the red and blue blossoms. They made the night look as if snow were falling into the sky, where the double moons hung logy and ponderous among the too-bright stars. Moonlight gave the fibrous white matter an unearthly pearlescent-green glow, and each tuft sparkled like satin as it turned, rising, in the air.

"The mothweed blooms," said Walter, as we made our way toward a fervent red glow on the horizon. He sneezed. "Late spring gives me fits."

"Do you know where we are?" asked Sawyer.

379

"Judging by the flora and the mountains, I'd say somewhere outside of the village of Teg White, just on the other side of the Longmarch."

"That puts us a day's walk to the Weatherhead, then," Sawyer said, and pointed at the warm red glow on the northern horizon, saying to me, "That's what that glow is, Ross—Council City Ostlyn."

"What an odd place to end up," said Noreen.

Walter gestured with his pipe and said, "Girl, if there's one thing I've learned in my life—recently, in particular—it's never to look a gift steed in the mouth."

"That's a saying back where we come from too. What a co-inky-dink!"

The Deon fell quiet and grim as we walked. I held the pistol in both my hands, studying its mechanisms and etchings, my feet mindlessly eating up the ground in front of me. —Eating! Damn, I was hungry. Even as I acknowledged it, my stomach growled in anticipation. The gnawing hunger hit me all at once, as if it had been lying in wait to ambush me.

I put the pistol in my pocket and took off my knapsack; I had found it searching the train for provisions, and filled it with stuff from the train's galley. Miraculously, the lifeless train had still been stocked with fresh food as if we'd stepped right off the *Mary Celeste*.

Okay, it was a lady's handbag, but I'm going to call it a knapsack.

I was ravenously violating some sort of fruitcake when Noreen saw me and asked me for the sack. Soon we were all cramming our faces. I said around a mouthful of cake, "I wonder if this is what happened to all those ghost-ships and explorer expeditions. The mysterious disappearances."

"Whaf?" asked Sawyer, his own mouth packed. "Dint

380

ungastan you."

I chewed up the cake and swallowed it, then repeated myself. "Like the *Mary Celeste*. Amelia Earhart. Ambrose Bierce."

Noreen hesitated, then said, "I was going to say that's a bit farfetched, but I don't find anything farfetched anymore."

After what felt like an hour of walking, we began to see a cluster of buildings at the other end of the meadow, under a heavy, stormcloud-like canopy of oak trees.

The distant shapes were cloaked by the night in angles of cold blue and black . . . I could just make out the warm orange lights in the windows: tiny, bright squares in the dark. As we approached the little village, I realized that they were tents, erected in a clearing in the sparse undergrowth.

They were cylindrical and at least two stories tall, with walls of stiff hide that barely moved in the breeze. The upper floors were tied off to the trees with a web of ropes, and the bottom rooms were tied to stakes in the ground.

We came around the side of a tent, picking our way through the stake-ropes so as not to trip, when we saw a campfire. The man that had been tending it stood up and aimed a muzzle-loader at us. I could see that he was an Iznoki, dressed in a loose, flowing tunic and sandals.

His eyes glowed a lambent green in the firelight. "Zui um vair zed tyir va nui?"

"Lyirui pigylli'ht ziim rui, yrm um f'huirti." said Walter, holding up his hands. "Yrm um rid hiumukih'm."

The last word reminded me of the Dari language. *Hee-oo-moo-kee-um.*

"Ig um 'r Kingsman."

The Iznoki lowered the rifle and spoke in a language we could understand. "Welcome to our camp, Kingsman. Please sit and

381

spend my watch at my fire with me."

Walter went to him and gave him the shield-bow salute, and we all sat down on logs and rocks around the flickering embers. The Iznoki dropped another log on the flames, which erupted in a spiraling cloud of crimson glitter. The breeze carried the sparks into the treetops, where they faded away into ash.

While we needed to be on the move, I appreciated the opportunity to rest and get something more substantial to eat than cakes and cold pastries.

"My name is Kabma," said the Iznoki, tossing a hand at the pot hanging over the fire. "Have some soup. There is plenty to go around."

"Peui tergui," said Sawyer.

There was a stack of empty tin cups next to the pot frame; he picked one up and ladled a smoking helping of soup into the cup, handing it to Noreen, then went back for a cup himself.

She smiled up at him, "I didn't know you knew how to speak Iznok."

"All I know is *thank you,*" he said with a smirk.

Once we'd gotten settled in, Kabma asked, "What brings you into the foothills?"

I blew on my soup. I thought about telling him some sort of convoluted story about our train getting ambushed, but I decided to take an honest tack and said, "We were heading to Ostlyn on a train when we were ambushed by an otherworldly being and my friends here were thrown into the Void-Between-The-Worlds."

I continued to talk, and told him the whole story in a brief tale, interrupting myself a few times to slurp my soup. It was satisfying and onion-pungent, with a tart lemon bite. Something like water chestnuts floated in it with boiled cabbage. When I was done talking, Kabma stared at us wordlessly for a beat, then burst into loud laughter.

"Sounds like you've had a very productive day," he said in a doubtful, if amused, tone. "If you were looking for a place to tell a tall tale, there is no better place than a campfire, eh?"

"Part of the road we were on slid down a hill," said Walter. "Our stagecoach overturned; one of our *pohtir* broke a leg and the other one ran away. We've been walking all evening. I can't tell you how glad we were to see you out here. I for one am ecstatic for the chance to rest before we head over the pass into Council City."

Kabma kept chuckling and said, "Well it is nice to meet such heroes in the dead of night such as this. I am honored to sup with men who will no doubt be legends by summer. You, boy, you should make a living of being a storyteller."

I smiled at my friends. "I'm strongly considering it."

We huddled over our cups of soup by the fire. I could feel the heat pouring into my bones and radiating through my body; my face felt taut and my eyes got grainy. I slid down off the rock I was sitting on and leaned against it, dozing off and on at the fire's edge, lulled by the crickets and treefrogs trilling their obdurate, fragile sonnets through the vaults of the forest.

I had a brief dream in which I was wading through a dark, ominous swamp, carrying a inflatable pool toy, a large and vividly-colored unicorn.

It was Kabma who woke me up a while later when he told us he was trading watch with another man. He got up and walked away; I went to sip my soup again but it was tepid. I poured it into the fire and dipped another cup, looking around with raw eyes. Sawyer and Noreen were asleep; Walter had taken both of his pistols apart and was cleaning them by the embers' dull light.

I sat down next to him again.

"You said you were a soldier," he said.

"That's right."

"I'm guessing—nay, hoping—that means you have at least a passing familiarity with these in Zam."

"Well," I said, "we don't generally use revolvers there . . . we have gas-operated self-repeating rifles. The bolt's on a spring. The cap firing in the cartridge pushes the bolt back, the casing flies out, the bolt rides forward and pushes another round into the chamber."

"Semi-automatic rifles?" asked the Deon.

I felt like an idiot. "Uhh, yeah—you have those here?"

"There are rudimentary experiments here and there, but few successes. The next time you meet a man with missing fingers, you should ask him about his career trying to perfect the gas repeater."

"I see."

"You should send someone back home a letter and ask for a few of those. We may need them."

"Aye aye, skipper."

He glanced up at me, unsmiling. "I ask because at some point in the near future, we are probably going to have to do some shooting. You strike me as a man that hasn't done much of that. At other people."

My mind's eye flashed back on the sight of watching my bullet go through Red's face back in the ghost town, his brains and flecks of skull spraying across the saloon's back wall.

I closed my eyes for a second and it didn't help, because then I saw him lying on his face in the dirt and scrub. It hadn't figured to me until now to admit that I'd seen the smoking red crater in the back of his head, a deep hole the size of a cueball, oozing with red-gray foam and thin, yellow curds of fat like runny scrambled eggs.

I shuddered and scalded my mouth with a sip of soup I don't remember tasting.

Walter must have recognized the expression on my face, because he didn't say anything else for a while.

"I'm better with a pistol than I am with a rifle," I said, finally. "I usually got like thirty, thirty-two out of forty at the qualification range with the rifle, but almost perfect at the M9 range, give or take a shot or two. I'm shit at *Call of Duty*."

"Whatever that is, I'm not particularly worried about your aim," said the gunslinger. "I'm worried about your nerve."

My silence betrayed me.

"I need to know that I can count on you when people start yelling. Because around here, yelling often precedes shooting."

"I'm good at yelling."

"You know what I mean."

"Yeah."

"When we get to Ostlyn," said the Deon, "I want you to stay near the King. Can you do that?"

"Why's that?" I asked. "So I can protect Old Man Normand?"

"By the Wolf, *no*," said Walter, and the corner of his mouth curled up in a half-smile. "So Old Man Normand can protect *you*."

Ardelia hammered the glowing steel rod into shape, the embers reflecting in the sweat on her brow. She could feel the heat against her bare arms, and even through her thick gloves. Her perfect sword existed wholly in her mind right now, but soon she would give it life. The Ancress would see to that. She would eat, sleep, and bathe right here in the Forge until the blade was completed.

She looked up at the hooded Griever standing in the archway, her arms folded, unmoving, unspeaking.

"So what's your name?" Ardelia asked.

There was no answer. There never would be an answer, not until she had become one of them.

—The Fiddle and the Fire, vol 5 "The Blade and the Bone"

Ostlyn City Limits

WE AWOKE IN THE late morning. The sun was a tempered ball of gold high over the eastern horizon, and the sunrise clouds had already burned away to reveal a pale indigo sky. The Iznoki traders were packing up their tents and getting ready to move on.

Burly white *pohtir-nyhmi* chuffed and kicked restlessly in the yokes of low-slung canvas carriages, their silvery crescent horns draped with leather reins. Pots and pans and buntings made of string and beads dangled from the panels of the wagons; the canvas coverings were painted with garish figures that threatened each other with javelins and recurved bows.

We waved to them as we left, and passed Kabma on the way out of the encampment.

He said to us, "M'digdi ur vyo hium, Kingsman. Be careful in Ostlyn. Word is there are fomenters of dissent in the city. I hear whispers of rally and rout. This is why we are leaving for Fi Himdet so early in the month. My family and I want to be out of the way in case of insurrection."

"Understandable," said Walter, shooting us a grim look as we left the caravan. "Take care, Kabma, and thanks for the warning. May your journey be more than its end."

The Iznoki rifleman tipped his hat as the forest enveloped us in birdsong and solitude. "May it be, friends."

The arid-lands continued even here, making for hours of hiking across a sparse timberland. Massive gray oaks stood at spacious distances from each other, leaving great gaping holes in the canopy that spilled in hot white sunlight and flat, reaching meadows.

Standing among the oaks were lanky, towering pine trees with needle-branches only at the very top, which made them resemble giant chimneysweeps stood on end. The pines carpeted the ground with dry, crunchy brown needles through which punched berry-bushes and green-leafed briars. There were also swaying bobble-headed sunflowers, and fat clumps of hairy mothweed that looked like patches of bread-mold.

At one point I saw a stand of foliage that looked like fiddlehead fern, but when I went to touch one of the fronds, instead of curling up protectively it spread its leaves so that it looked like a mimosa branch and tried to lick my hand.

We came to the base of the mountain range that stood between us and Ostlyn, and started up a broad, shallow grade where it seemed someone or something had burned out a good deal of undergrowth. The woodland had thinned out until we were ants under a magnifying glass, and the birdsong faded until we were only accompanied by the constant rush of wind. Intimidating raptors perched in the treetops: brown barrel-bodied birds that focused on us with the unblinking intensity of their golden gimlet eyes.

The red-brown soil was layered in a fine black char that stained our boots and trouser legs. The few remaining pines ended not in greenery, but gray ember-spikes that crumbled under our hands. Squat, knobby joshua-trees competed for moisture with jackalberry trees that reached into the razor-blue sky with dozens of lightning-fork fingers.

Ominous black thistle-bushes offered us berries, served on sawblade leaves. Hulking boulders of shale and granite made for a labyrinth of black-smeared obstacles. Several times I spied little brown reptiles on them, scuttling out of sight.

Looking back the way we came, we had climbed above the treetops; behind us was a sea of green and gray that did not seem to move in the wind, but hissed at us just the same, a constant, dry rasping rush that sounded like a waterfall.

Our path led up the seared mountainside into a deep divot between two wide buttes, like a pair of gapped teeth. As we got closer, and pushed through a stand of tamarind trees, I realized that the pass actually wound through a crack in a plateau. The trail lay at the bottom of a smooth-walled crevice so deep that the light struggled to reach us. Tufts of green jutted from holes in the cavern sides, serving as beards to the curved cheeks of weathered stone that swelled and ebbed like sideways sand-dunes. The further we walked, the darker it got until we were moving through honey-colored shade that took our shadows away. The ground was flat and soft with powdery red dirt and the walls bulged inward, making low, deep places filled with darkness.

We alarmed some furry creature that got up and bounded deeper into the chasm; after another few minutes we encountered it as it lay sprawled on a rock ledge some five or six meters overhead. It was a slender mountain cat, with salt and pepper fur like an Australian shepherd dog and a lush mane of silver hair. It watched us with unnerving, judicious eyes that glinted like nickels in the artificial gloom. I recognized it as the cat that had been embroidered on Memne's clothes, and thoughts of her gave me comfort. I wondered if I'd ever see her again.

The Deon walked a little closer with me. "Before we reach the City, I feel I must address with you a certain effect produced in a man who survives exposure to the Acolouthis. It is the secret to the prowess of the gunslingers of Ain."

I holstered the pistol. "I'm listening."

"I can probably explain it in terms he's more familiar with, if you don't mind, Deon," said Noreen. Our voices reverberated tightly in the narrow corridor. "I've done a bit of personal research into the things Ed described in his . . . records."

Walter tossed a shoulder. "By all means, mis'ra."

"Basically, the Acolouthis is a nootropic hallucinogen."

"Well, you've lost me already," I said.

"Where did I lose you?"

"Is."

"What?"

"You lost me at the word *is*."

"Oh."

"I'm kidding. Continue."

Noreen shot me an evil squint, and started speaking again. "The Acolouthis is a nootropic hallucinogen. The most powerful in all of human history; back home it wouldn't even have a street value. It would be priceless. Even the supply here is very limited. One of the stipulations of becoming King is that you have to undertake a voyage to find new growths of the fungus and bring them to Ostlyn. You can be nominated for coronation, but that's just a formality unless you can retrieve some of the Sacrament.

"That's another story altogether. In addition to altering your personal reality—in effect opening a doorway and pushing you through it—it also alters your brain chemistry. In order to make the changes to your personal reality-fabric, it has to ramp up the efficiency of your mental system in order to make you process what you're seeing. And see what you are processing."

Sawyer added, "Otherwise, the hallucinations would just fry your neurons and put you into catatonic shock. To put it into technical terms, the Sacrament installs a brand-new video card into your computer-brain so it can run the newest game—your hallucination. Otherwise your brain will crash."

"Right," said Noreen.

"That explains the slow-motion freakout I had back in Synecdoche. Welcome to the sticks!"

They looked at me in confusion. I looked at my feet and pretended I hadn't said anything.

"And now you'll have that high-powered graphics card in your head until the day you die. To break it down Mickey-Mouse-style—" said Noreen, "—that stuff made your brain chemistry so powerful it was able to temporarily rearrange a large enough piece of time and space to let you through. For about six hours, you were a demi-god."

"*Holy shit.*"

"Basically you are now the proud new owner of an extremely overclocked brain. And now every time you get a big enough hit of adrenaline?"

"Yeah?"

"That supercognitive time-dilation *comes back.*"

Walter was packing his pipe as he walked. "I'm afraid I didn't understand any of that explanation myself, friends," he said. "But it all sounded very legitimate and knowledgeable and did the trick. Good show. However, you forget one key point."

"What's that?" I asked.

"It is nigh useless without a certain level of preparation and training. You've got to learn to *control* the Sacrament before it can use you."

I had a little trouble wrapping my head around the connotations of what they were telling me. I had no trouble understanding the technical aspects of it, right, but . . . "Before it can use me?"

"You didn't think you were the one in the driver's seat, did you?" asked Walter, grinning. "You are merely the conduit through

392

which the Sacrament delivers the justice of the Kingsmen. We are in service to the power of the Acolouthis. We are the righteous hand of the Acolouthis. You will do well to respect it. The Sacrament abides us, not the other way around."

"The Dude abides."

"Eh?"

"Nothing."

"There's another thing you should be aware of," said Sawyer. "Remember the overclocked-brain analogy?"

I nodded.

"The same thing applies here. If you overexpose yourself to the effects . . . use the Acolouthis Effect too much at one time . . . you'll burn out your brain. You have to moderate yourself, you'll have to practice being calm. Meditation, maybe. Zen shit."

"Zen shit does vat?" I said in a bad German accent.

"Very funny, Frau Blucher."

Noreen whinnied like a horse.

"Maybe I'll start a rock garden and rake sand when I get too excited," I said. "I don't turn green or anything, do I?"

"No, Ross. You don't turn green."

"Good. So you were saying: I'll burn out my brain if I let it happen too much?"

"Your memory will be mush. You turn into a deranged madman," said Walter. "You'll forget who you are. You'll forget your friends. You won't know your arse from a gopher-hole."

Noreen said, "Lord Seymour Bennett from *The Fiddle and the Fire* is a burned-out gunslinger. He wore the same outfit every day—his mother's wedding dress—for the last six years of his exile in Ormont, and slept in a hamper with a jar of crickets."

Walter scoffed, a humorless chuckle. "You want to know

something funny, though? Seymour is the best shot that's ever earned a place on the walls of Ostlyn. Even after he went mad, he could still knock a cigarette out of a man's mouth at two hundred paces with a pistol. Some say going mad made him an even *better* shot."

"He's still alive?" asked Sawyer.

"Oh, yeah," said the Deon. "He's been living in Council City Ostlyn for years. He's the son of Councilman Thaddeus Bennett. Normand agreed to let him live there with Thaddeus as long as nobody let him get within reach of a firearm."

Half an hour later the shadows did not reel back into their hiding places, but the blue light of day brightened our path again. We came to the end of the trail at the bottom of the crack and pushed through a stand of brush. As soon as we emerged from the hidden pass, the sudden, outright majesty of Council City Ostlyn nearly knocked me down.

At first, I thought the city was on fire and I felt an instant of panic. The longer I looked, however, I realized that what I was seeing were hundreds of red jacaranda trees peeking over the ramparts, blazing brightly in the mid-day sun. They rippled, teasing the sky, like unending bonfires.

Ostlyn lay draped over a dome-shaped mountain like a gargantuan ziggurat, its protective battlements carved from the very rock itself. The dark gray walls, several meters high, formed concentric circles successively higher up the mountain, enclosing rising sections of the city like a vast conical bulls-eye.

Deep bas-reliefs of seated figures, like three-dimensional hieroglyphics, formed an unbroken band that ran just below the top of each wall, all the way around the city. Each figure faced outward: thousands of silent sentinels, gazing at the cottages, farms, and gardens that formed the patchwork Ainean countryside surrounding Ostlyn.

"Each statue you see on the walls," said Walter, coming up behind us, as we stood at the mouth of the pass in abject awe, "— is the likeness of a gunslinger that came before. We honor our fallen that way because none of us are allowed to have gravestones. We must be buried in unmarked graves, to foil graverobbers. The bones of a Kingsman are a highly lucrative business opportunity."

Saltillo-tile roofs in a thousand colors filled the open space between each protective wall, and I could see that these tight streets were a winding labyrinth of switchbacks, leading visitors to the peak that stood in the center. On that flattened apex stood the Weatherhead, a dark cathedral with no discernible face.

It consisted of a central pineapple-shaped spire; slim walls drooped down the sides, radiating outward to seven rook-style keeps. The craggy mosaic surface of the Weatherhead glittered in the sun like rock candy, lending the black-green malachite structure the sheen of a wet fish. Silvery angles and scrollworks decorated its edges and lines.

"The entire city is round, to facilitate constant three-hundred-and-sixty-degree vigilance," said Walter, as we picked our way down the crumbling shale mountainside. We were heading toward a rutted road that meandered through the rural outskirts. Wagons and pedestrians trundled along it in a slow, straggling parade.

"Gunslingers always sit with their backs against a wall, but Ostlyn stands alone. The only way to sit against a wall, when there are no walls big enough, is to not have a back."

The Uncomfortable Solace of Madness

WE MINGLED WITH THE traffic and spotted a hay wagon bumping and jangling along the rutted road; sitting on the back was Lennox Thackeray, cutting slices from a baguette of some dark-rinded bread and eating them. He wore a voluminous green robe and a peaked cap, all of it trimmed in gold piping and braided velvet cords, and as he sat on the backboard, he kicked his feet like a little boy.

His toadish goiter swelled and ebbed when he saw us, and he made a *BRRRROB* sound that I wasn't sure was a belch or a frog-noise. "Good morning, friends! It is nice to see you again! What a small world it is!"

"It's nice to see a familiar face," I said.

We walked along behind the wagon, talking to the trader as the ruts jostled him. For a man that ate as much as he did, he was surprisingly slender. He had very short legs and small feet, and his arms were very long; he almost seemed to have monkey-like proportions. The robe gave him a curious bell-shape.

"I have to agree," said Walter. "Still moving on the plans to help your brother run his shop here in the City that Sleeps with One Eye Open?"

"I am, I am!" said Thackeray, chortling to himself. His nictitating eyelids blinked, the membranes filming over his eyes for an instant, and he added, "You guys must have had one hell of a trip. You look worn-out. Here," he interrupted himself, scooting over, "Have a seat, take a load off."

396

Sawyer and Noreen piled on with him; as there was no room left, Walter and I continued walking. "It's a long story," I said. "Maybe I'll tell it to you sometime. Maybe I'll even write a book about it. Who the hell knows."

"Let me know when you do!" said Thackeray. "I want a signed copy!"

I smiled. "Absolutely."

The gates of Ostlyn soared over the road in a grand arc, carved to look like a pair of majestic eagles facing away from each other. Their wings stretched out behind them and touched in the middle, forming an archway of stone feathers wide enough for forty men abreast and four meters higher than the tallest carriage.

As we entered the city, I looked up at the stoic faces of long-dead heroes and heroines carved into the outermost wall. The life-sized statues stared into the distance, some of them with their arms crossed over their chests, some of them peering from under the brim of a hat.

We slipped through the gate and I saw that doorways in the eagles' backs led into their hollow interiors, which served as gatehouses. Thin archer-slit windows in the eagles' necks provided visibility and protection.

"Heaven help me," said Noreen, her eyes wandering the tremendous edifice above us. "This is amazing."

The chills coursing along my scalp had never left me; indeed, as we entered Ostlyn, they had grown progressively stronger until I had trouble remembering to breathe; my chest swelled with amazed euphoria. We bid Thackeray farewell and started off on foot.

The first circle of the labyrinth was comprised of perhaps a hundred shops, taverns, and boutiques. I could just see their wares through their mullioned windows: glittering chainmail, satiny tunics and tabards, colored bottles filled with foaming and sparkling concoctions, tooled-leather longcoats and flat-crowned hats. The goldleaf fonts of their signs mirrored the morning sun, throwing italic sun-cats across the shops' white stucco walls.

Men and women of a dozen nationalities and colors sat at tables outside of quiet pubs and raucous taverns, sipping steins of lager or mugs of coffee. They chattered with each other in exotic languages, dressed in shimmering finery and tailed jackets dusty from travel. My stomach complained to me as I spied crusty sandwiches piled with tender meats and colorful vegetables, and smelled the hearty spices of pot pies.

"I'm going to be three hundred pounds by the time we get out of here," said Sawyer.

"Damn skippy," I said.

We had barely walked a half-mile when Walter stepped into a tavern and made a bee-line for the kitchen door. I only had the time to glance at the people sitting at the rough-hewn tables before we were crossing the fire-lit galley and coming out of a service door. The piano music faded as we went down an alleyway and came out in the second inner circle of the city.

Here, the ramparts were lined with cozy half-timbered brownstones; residents sat on the stoops eating breakfast and conversing. Several times, men recognized Walter and waved to him with broad smiles. "May it be, m'Deon," they called.

"May the end never come," he called back.

The Deon cut down into a narrow alleyway and climbed a steep staircase to a wooden catwalk behind one of the brownstones, then climbed a short ladder to the top of a rampart. Deeply-weathered memorial statues watched the day with bland, regal faces as we ascended past them to the battlement.

The breeze off the plains was rather fierce on top of the labyrinth wall, ripping at our clothes and threatening to throw my hat away. Noreen's sundress flapped at her hips as we threaded down the narrow walkway between the crenelated parapets, the gigantic Weatherhead looming over us in the middle distance. Rifle-wielding armored men patrolling the walls paused at the sight of civilians on their level, but recognized the Deon when he waved to them.

Walter led us through several more shadowy, convoluted secret passages before we finally came round a corner and started up a sloping meadow carpeted with crimson poppies. They swayed in the air, creating a mesmerizing, roiling texture that captured the eye.

Our road cut through the middle of it, leading to a gate in the innermost wall. This was indeed the oldest rampart in Ostlyn. The sentinels' statues here were beaten almost faceless by the centuries, the blades of their stone swords broken and blunt and their chests and arms pitted by the elements.

Through the gates was a wide staircase of mountain-stone. Dozens of steps led up, narrowing, into the wide-open mouth of the central temple; to either side of them stood a flaming jacaranda tree. A wide portico served as the entrance to the great pineapple-shaped dome.

As we crested the stairs with burning legs, I saw a man lying on the floor. He was on his belly with his ear to the cool travertine slab, dressed in embroidered jeans and a black frock coat florid with curlicues. "May it be," he said, without looking up. He seemed to be a good ten years older than us, his greasy hair dangling lank around his face.

"May it be, Seymour," said Walter. "It is good to see you again."

Seymour looked up at us from his prostrations. "I wish I could say the same, William," he said, his voice low and introspective, a furtive croak. He reminded me of a dog that'd been kicked one too many times.

"You're not glad to see me, old friend?"

"You only visit when something is wrong," said Seymour. He licked his lips and asided to us in all seriousness, making odd, indicative gestures with his hands like a magician, "He doesn't like the Council very much. The feeling is mutual, but they put up with each other because of the Chiral."

Noreen knelt by the Councilman's son and laid a soft hand on the shoulder of his silken coat. "Hello there. It's nice to meet you, Lord Seymour."

The man sat up and smiled. "You're very pretty," he said, tucking his tongue into his cheek and regarding her with narrowed eyes. "What's your name?"

"Thank you very much. My name is Noreen. This is my . . . boyfriend Sawyer," she said, glancing at Sawyer as she said it. He smiled broadly back at her. She touched my knee to indicate me. "And this is Ross, Lord Eddick's son."

"I'm so sorry for your loss," said Seymour, putting his ear to the floor again. He seemed to have finished the conversation, at least on his end.

I put my hands in my pockets. "It's . . . okay now, I guess. I've had a little time to cope."

"I wasn't talking to you."

I blinked in confusion. "What do you mean?"

He put his finger to his lips and shushed me. "I must ask you to lower your voices. I'm listening to the vibrations. This is very important. And by important, I mean breakfast."

Noreen shrugged and stood up.

"What did you mean, Seymour?" I asked. "Whose loss?"

"Ssshhhh," said the mad gunslinger, pressing his palms against the stone and flexing his fingers in frustration. I could see shiny pink scars crisscrossing the backs of his hands. Another one cut a shallow divot across the back of his crown where his hairline had receded. Bullet-cuts. Near-misses.

I realized he had no fingernails. At some point, they'd been pried out, and they'd never grown back.

"Let us proceed," said Walter. "We are at odds with this one."

A giant ebony door stood open in the dark recesses of the deep portico. Passing through it, I watched the blue sunlight filter in through the portico's pillars and wash over the door's glossy carvings. Ancient Ainean pictographs and pictures of rampant creatures shimmered in the gloom.

Our footsteps clattered as we crossed a polished malachite floor. I marveled at the beautiful, sweeping ribbons of green and black writhing under our boots. It was divided by clean, straight fault-lines into a radial design that resembled a wagon-wheel.

Buttresses ascended upward into a dome of black, at least fifty feet overhead; there were points of light floating in it like stars in the night. It reminded me of the watcher behind the sky that I'd sensed while the Acolouthis was taking hold on me out in the desert, and I grew uneasy looking at it.

"The stars you see above you are just that—stars," said Walter. "Holes in the ceiling in the precise positions of the constellations of the night sky. The circular pattern you see under your feet is a depiction of the continent of Ain. The holes send sunlight and moonlight down onto the floor, and the sun-cats on the floor correspond to the stars in the night sky at that particular time of year."

On the back wall was an actual shield, embossed with the simplified face of Oramoz. A pair of beautiful scrollworked shotguns made a crossbones in the center of the shining steel plate.

Below it, seven thrones stood abreast, all of them empty. They were made of carved ebony with black leather seats, and had tall backs. Each one had an intricate symbol etched into the back and the armrests looked like eagle-heads, but they were otherwise unremarkable. A gunbelt dangled over the back of the middle throne, its holsters empty.

"Somehow I expected something more grandiose from a throne," I said.

"No one ever accused the nation of Ain of affluence," said Walter. "We are far-reaching, but next to the Ersecad, we are a kingdom of mendicants."

"It is not the throne," said Sawyer, "—but who sits in it."

Walter quirked an eyebrow. "Wise words."

"I suppose, then, that it is particularly appropriate that no one is sitting in them," said someone behind us. A heavy-set old man stood in one of the doorways that led out of this round room. He looked stately in a black cassock and pointed riding boots. He looked fresh, well-fed, and dewy; age and sun had not ravaged his face like so many other Aineans I had seen.

"May it be, Deon South," he said. He seemed warm-mannered, if a bit harried.

"And yourself, Councilman," said Walter.

"It is, as usual, an honor. I see you've finally made some friends. See? Miracles *do* come true."

Walter smirked. "I'd like to introduce you to a very special visitor, Councilman. This is Lord Bridger's other son, Ross. Friends, this is Seymour's father, Thaddeus Bennett."

"Councilman of Lands," said Sawyer, doing the shield-bow thing. "May it be."

"How polite! May it never end," said Bennett, mopping at his forehead with a handkerchief. "What brings you to Ostlyn on such

402

short notice? I was under the impression that you were undertaking a search for the assassin Sardis, not this presumably much more agreeable fellow."

"I was on my way back from seeking Sardis in Finback Fathoms when I found these three floating on a raft in the Aemev. Ahh . . . I suppose they were on their way here from the Antargata k-Setra when their ship was capsized by the sea-beast."

"Dreadful creature," said Bennett. "I'm glad to see you've survived your encounter. —As well as your excursion to the Fathoms: a most discouraging place, to put it mildly."

Walter nodded. "It's a wonderful place for getting things one ought not to have, and for being robbed of all one's spending money. Meanwhile," he said, "—we're looking for my father and the King. Have you seen them about?"

"The Chiral is out taking his mid-day repast. You might find him at the barracks. Normand is speaking with an envoy from Cice Jiunad."

Walter seemed to consider this, then said, "Faced with the choice, I think I'll remain here and wait for the King. My father may not be entirely coherent when he returns from irrigating his innards."

"I know you feel the Chiral does not favor you as much as he favors his vices," said Bennett, "But he mellows in his old age. If you visited more than once a year, you might know this, m'Deon."

"Maybe," said Walter. He went back outside without a word and we followed him back to the portico. I had meant to ask Seymour about his strange consolations earlier, but he was gone. We sat halfway down the steps and basked in the sun, listening to the jacarandas cackle softly in the wind. None of us really said anything; we were too tired to really have much to talk about.

Finally, Walter spoke to us. His voice was a clipped mutter.

"When we've spoken to the King and let him know we're here, we'll get a room at a little place I know of down the hill. They have good food."

After a time, Noreen said, "So what's going on with you and your father, if you don't mind me asking?"

Walter seemed to appraise her for a moment, but looked down at the steps. "I'd rather not speak about it, if it's all the same."

"I understand," she said. "But if you get the notion to talk, let me know?"

"You will be the first to have your ear bent, Misera Mears."

The broad ebony door opened and a man came out, dressed in a gray hooded tabard that came down to his knees. The front of it depicted a large red sword-shaped emblem that made him resemble a Templar, but the gunbelt around his waist marked him as no knight.

"In any case," he was saying, "they have been pledged, serah. You have the word of the Ersecad. May it be."

"Consider me at ease, then. May it never," said a rumbling voice from beyond the doorway. We stood up as the envoy passed; he jogged down the stairs without a word and disappeared through the front gate of the courtyard.

The owner of the brass pipes stepped into the dim blue light of the distant day.

The world seemed to hang silent as Normand Kaliburn the King of Ain came out of the Weatherhead to greet us. A prickling chill trickled up my ribs and across my scalp at the sight of such a tall and aged man.

He reminded me of the actor Clancy Brown, but also somehow of Clint Walker as Cheyenne Bodie in *Cheyenne*. The decades had not stooped or bent him in the least—he was at least

404

two meters lean and a few inches above that, standing ramrod-straight, his broad shoulders squared back.

His face was long and careworn with deep crisscrossing lines, like a map made of old leather. His hair was lush and silvery-blonde, tousled in sickle-blade locks. Somehow I'd expected a wizardly beard, like Merlin, or Dumbledore or Gandalf, but instead Normand had cultivated a horseshoe mustache of silver-white that matched his eyebrows.

The lack of a beard took nothing away from his strong, square jaw. He wore a spotless doublet, jeans, and pointed riding boots—all black. A length of cape concealed his left arm, hanging from a chain through the passant of his right shoulder. Normand spoke again, his gravelly voice reverberating in the portico.

"Afternoon, Deon," he said, clapping Walter on the shoulder. "I've been waiting for quite some time for the lot of you. Come in. We've got a lot to talk about."

I couldn't imagine how Sawyer and Noreen felt, staring open-mouthed at the protagonist of the novels they'd grown up reading. My friends knew almost everything there was to know about this man—or at least what Ed had recorded.

Normand ushered us into the council chambers and we followed him across the room to the line of thrones at the back. They sat on a gently curved dais. A pair of men in dark green longcoats flanked the nearest doorway; the King ordered them into it but to linger within earshot of a shout.

"I don't know who you *are,*" he said slowly, measuredly, his warm smile directed at Sawyer and Noreen. "But I have the distinct feeling that you know very much who *I* am."

Noreen was the first to speak. "Yeah. —Yes, yessir. We do."

The old man chuckled. It was like stones scraping together. "I know—I know *you* know. Eddie told me all about his books about my life and adventures growing up. He told me about all the boys and girls that read them back in his world—in your world. Back on Earth. I never knew what to think of it, but he was very proud that he could do that."

"We were there from the beginning, sir," said Sawyer. "We were always at your side. Cheering you on when you fell, crying when you cried, bleeding when you bled. From that day Tem Lucas attacked Oriensligne—"

"—To the day you stowed away on the *Warrior Tide* and sailed to the Antargata k-Setra," cut in Noreen. "Through the fights and beatings in the Fathoms. To the day you were almost killed by the No-Men on the frontier, and saved by the separatist rebel Lord Harwell."

"We were all there with you, all of us, every step of the way, believing in you. All the way through the war, up to the Battle of Ostlyn," said Sawyer. "But that was the last book Mr. Brigham was working on—he never published it. We weren't there for that."

Noreen almost—it seemed as if she wanted to reach out and touch the old man, whether for his comfort or her own, I wasn't sure. I saw her hand twitch.

So did Normand, it seemed, and he took the initiative instead, taking her hand in his weathered own and covering it with his other one. When I looked up at his face, I realized that there were tears standing in the rims of his pale blue eyes.

"I'm sorry we weren't there at the end, sir," she said.

He blinked, and smiled; his mustache quivered and he said, his eyes intense, "Don't you worry about that, young lady. You got me just far enough."

They held the moment long enough for the sentiment to ebb, and Normand looked away. He appeared to suddenly notice the Council thrones behind him and he stepped aside, resting one hand on the armrest of the center chair.

"Why don't you have a seat?" he asked, his voice hoarse with emotion. "You three look like you've come a very long way."

"Really?" asked Sawyer.

"Us?"

I couldn't help but smile. They were like kids in a candy store. Sawyer stood aside and let Noreen sit on the throne. She seemed uncomfortable and nervous, as if it were an ejector seat primed to launch her through the ceiling.

"Relax, my dear," said Normand. "Now—you know who *I* am. I would be most honored to learn the names of the long-unmet companions of my life."

"My name is Noreen Elizabeth Mears and I was born and raised in Florida. I've been reading Ed Brigham's novels ever since I was a little girl. My mother wasn't . . . wasn't a very nice person, and my father might as well have not been there, as much as he was gone on business. She had a lot of things she'd rather do than deal with me, and she'd never really wanted me to begin with."

She sighed. "So I spent a lot of time in my room with the door locked from the inside. I lost myself in *The Fiddle and the Fire* and I've been hooked ever since. You got me through a lot of hard and lonely times, Mr. Kaliburn."

She looked down at her hands.

"It is most pleasing to see that I could be there for you as well," he said, and paused to let it resonate. "Please, call me Normand. Mr. Kaliburn was my father. It is also good to see that you appear to be none the worse for wear. To all appearances you have grown to become quite the young lady. I'm very sorry that I couldn't do more for you than sit on a page between a pair of covers."

"Thank you," she said.

"And you?" he asked, his eyes settling on Sawyer.

Sawyer gave up his name, and then related the insight he'd given me at the funeral the first night we'd met, about how he'd been deprived of a father, and how a certain teacher had given him the first book in the series. In retrospect, now I understood why she went out of her way to be so kind to an obviously troubled little boy.

"I grew up on the poor side of town, in south Georgia," he said. "I'm sure you don't know what video games are, but I didn't get to have all the newest ones like the other kids, so I was raised on books. After my dad died, we didn't have much money for things like that."

"Tutelage is not merely the instilling of knowledge," said Normand. "The best tutor is the one that seeds a love of learning. And it is a truly portentous childhood when it is filled with books."

He turned to me and grasped my shoulder. "And at last we come to you," he said, squeezing the muscle. He had a grip like an iron clamp. "The prodigal son. We all four of us—Clayton, Ardelia, Edward, myself—knew you would come here one day. We just didn't know it would be under such troubling auspice. Welcome to the city of Ostlyn, boy. It's good to see you."

"How?" I asked. "How did you know?"

"We'll jaw about it later," said Normand. "Right now we must arrange a convention of the Council. I've been hearing dark things as of late, and I fear that what you're here for will be no less ominous."

"Wait one minute here," said Walter, putting up a hand. "I'm not entirely sure I'm fully grasping the bag of what you've all been talking about. Are you trying to tell me that your life thus far is a bauble of fiction on Zam?"

Normand chuckled. "Why yes, yes it is, dear boy. It's a long,

long story, about many people, and it even includes you. It's very popular, or so I hear."

"What? You mean I'm in this book too?"

"I suppose you are, at that."

Noreen seemed to have relaxed on the throne, even leaning back and tossing a leg over one knee. "You are, Deon, but as far as Ed's written it, you were still a kid."

"I was going to ask you if any followers of the books idolize me, but I guess it's a moot point, then."

"No, but if Ross continues the series, I'm certain you'll have a rabid cult of Walterites."

"I'm going to pretend that's a good thing."

I regarded Normand with something not quite suspicion. His odd allusions and tone of voice—not to mention his prescient knowledge of our arrival—chewed at the edges of my awareness.

He saw it in my eyes, I think. The old man turned and called the green-coated retainers back into the room. "Please go and arrange for a *hyupyt m'gebbih*, please. Three of them, dispatched to our absent Council members. I need them here as quickly as they can get here."

To the man that remained, he said, "I will require the remaining three members at midday tomorrow; please go and deliver this delayed summons as best you can."

"Most haste," he said to them as they nodded in assent and marched out of the room. "Now," he said, sitting on the edge of the dais at Noreen's feet and speaking to all of us with that same intensely warm and trailworn smile, "My lovely princess, and my loyal men, please tell me what has brought you to Destin on such urgent business."

"Are you aware of the Sileni?" asked Sawyer.

"Ah, yes, yes," said Normand. "Edward told me of them.

409

They are the water-carriers of the Sea of Dreams, are they not?"

"It looks like they're tired of being immortal muses. They've turned on the universe," I said.

I told Normand our tale thus far, beginning with my father's death and on through my force-feeding of the Acolouthis and our battle against the Feaster and its corporeal avatar on Destin, the Unremembered Man. I told him what I could recall of the encounter with Hel Grammatica and the silen Hel had called the Rhetor.

I told him about the mysterious entity trapped underneath the dakhmas that littered the Void floor, slowly growing powerful on the souls drilled through the rock. "The Sileni don't just have the ability to tell you what to write," I concluded. "They can tell you what to do. And now they're telling people to do horrific things."

Throughout my recollection, the King's face had grown more and more grim. "Shadowy men, seeding chaos throughout the cosmos as reparation for a millennium of servitude. It seems that things have progressed just as Edward feared. I expect that his knowledge of the coming rebellion was why he was killed.

"With Ed's and Hel Grammatica's help, this Rhetor Logos could have possibly been stopped at some point. To our dismay and misfortune, Edward was murdered before he could be warned of his impending assassination and give you the information you needed. Fortunately for us, we had a hidden wild-card the entire time."

"Eh?"

He pointed to me.

"Me? What do you mean?"

"You are Edward's heir," he said. "As you've already taken upon yourself, you have now assumed the mantle that Edward once wore. The mantle of the Messenger."

410

"The Messenger?"

"Yes. The Sileni do not choose at random who they bring the waters of the Vur Ukasha. Your father was chosen to bring life to the world of Destin, as so many other men were chosen before him to bring other worlds to life. Such men are destined from birth to do so; they are referred to as the Messengers by the muse-creatures. And so, I now see, were you destined to take his place."

I became solemn myself.

Normand reached out and patted me on the knee. "It's good to have you back, boy," he said.

A numb electric chill spread down my body, starting at the crown of my scalp. It took me several seconds to respond with a dry and insubordinate " . . . What?"

"Three," said Clayton, as the midwife bustled back into the other room. He turned to his companions, a broad smile spreading across his face. "My third boy! Walter and Oliver, and now a third! Can you believe it? Oh, by the Wolf, what am I going to name this one?"

The scribe spoke up, adjusting his spectacles. "I have a book here I've been saving for this. I think it's got the perfect name."

—The Fiddle and the Fire, vol 6 "The Feared and the Free"

Trailmates in Time

"ED NEVER TOLD YOU?" said Normand, feigning amused surprise. "Haven't you ever felt like you didn't fit in, no matter where you were? Didn't you feel like you belonged somewhere else? That you were from a different place and time?"

He stroked his mustache. "Why, you are a native of the country of Ain. You and your brother Sardis were born here. You were spirited away to Earth as protection, and your brother was taken by your mother to the land of Cice Jiunad. Given, the man you were being protected from is now gone, but that's all water under the bridge."

My mouth worked, but it took some measure of effort to get words to come out of it. "I was *born* here?"

"Right here in Ostlyn, in fact. Several months before the Great Battle."

"To an Ainean woman?"

"No," said Normand. "To a Cicean. The excommunicated Griever, Ardelia Thirion, the Heroine of Ostlyn. She is who fled to Cice Jiunad with your brother to protect you from Tem Lucas, as I returned from my journey to the heart of the Antargata k-Setra to kill the thing the Wilders called Obelus.

"Edward managed to escape to Earth with you, my daughter Noreen, and Clayton's youngest boy Sawyer, just before Lucas led the No-Men to Ostlyn. The two of them rightly assumed that another plane of existence would be the safest place for you, and, as it turned out, he was right."

Sawyer and Noreen were the epitome of silence. They stood there, slackjawed and unmoving, probably as numb with shock as I was.

"Funny fate," said Normand, and he grinned. What he said next sounded very surreal in that rumbly wise-man voice. "To bring the three of you back to the city where you were born."

The old gunslinger smirked slyly, and said, "Tell me; are you familiar with the term . . . *co-inky-dink?*"

I admit that I sat there, stunned, for what felt like a full minute. All of us did. Before I could regain my bearings, Sawyer seemed to have recovered first. He said, his voice low and accusatory, "Sir . . . this really isn't a very funny joke."

"It's no joke," said Normand. "No joke at all! No jest, no jibe, nor prank or foul."

I didn't even know where to start asking questions. All I could do was stare at him. Suddenly in my confusion, so far away from everything that I'd known, I felt very alone and useless, and put-upon.

"All three of us?" I asked. "How could you possibly know? I mean, myself, yeah, sure, maybe I could get behind that. Is Ed really even my father?"

"Oh, yes," said the King. "Ardelia spent a lot of time alone with Edward, in those days, while I roamed Destin with Clayton, searching for my nemesis. Your father was not always the, ahh— the *robustly-proportioned* fellow he was when he died. He used to be quite the handsome companion, you know. So much so, that he is the reason why she broke her vow to the Forge. She took Sardis with her when she fled Ostlyn to seek reconciliation with the Ancress."

He chuffed soft laughter. "She always did have a fondness for

415

the bookish types. As for how I know who you three truly are; you had names when you were taken to Earth. The names you have now. Besides, you so much resemble your forebears that there's no denying it."

I had to admit that Noreen had inherited Normand's cold blue eyes. She finally snapped out of it and looked down at the old man. "You mean . . . I'm the daughter of Normand Kaliburn?"

"Yes," said the King. "And Sawyer here is Clayton's youngest. The Chiral named him much like his two older brothers, Walter and Oliver. It was actually Eddick that proposed he name his boy after a character from a book he'd brought from Earth: Mark Twain's *Tom Sawyer*. Clayton was fond of using names from Edward's books. He said he thought it destined them for fame."

"I have brothers?" asked Sawyer.

"Yes," said Normand. "Oliver, named after *Oliver Twist*, and Walter here, named after *Walter Mitty*."

"A *fine surprise!*" said Walter, and he grabbed the other, and embraced him in a big bear hug. I was amazed I hadn't noticed the familial resemblance before: they shared the same long face, sharp nose, wide mouth, steely eyes. "A fine surprise indeed! I've lost a brother and now I've gained another! Life has replaced what it has taken away from us. A joyous day all around."

With Walter's olive sun-ripened complexion and wavy black locks versus Sawyer's Earth-pale skin and short hair, it was an easy miss; especially when you've taken your friends for granted as I did.

"Yeah, that's pretty cool," said Sawyer, still looking a bit shell-shocked as Walter let go of him.

"I'm guessing Clayton never actually read *The Secret Life of Walter Mitty*," I said.

Walter's head tilted and he looked at me funny.

I shrugged. "I plead the Fifth."

That's when I realized that the *vero nihil verius* I had been feeling wasn't a product of being in a place where the tabards and tunics weren't mass-produced in China. It was the *absence of homesickness*. I was home, and my heart knew it.

Noreen slid down off the throne and hugged Normand around the neck. He made a noise of alarm and almost fell over, then put an arm around her and held her just as closely. I could see tears on her face before she buried it in his chest. He reached up and stroked her hair with one ancient, scarred hand, and said, "It's good to have all three of you back. Especially you, my little princess."

A faint memory rose to the surface of my mind. "It may not have been pure chance that brought us back together," I said, recalling what Hel had said to Noreen in the tower of silence. "I think Ed's muse has been a busy bee."

"It is unfortunate that he is not here for me to demonstrate my gratitude," said Normand.

"I wonder why we weren't living with Ed . . . or brought back to Destin after you killed Tem Lucas?" asked Sawyer. The expression of dazzled astonishment on his face had become one of hurt confusion. "Why did we have to grow up with strangers?"

Here, Normand pursed his lips in regret and looked at the floor as he spoke. It was an odd gesture of humility from such a legendary figure. "There are reasons for both of your issues. The first one I shall address by allowing Edward a modicum of sympathy in that he simply could not afford to raise three children by himself. It ruined him to do so, but he had to give the two of you up to the authorities, so that you would have a better chance at life."

His eyebrows rose and he tossed up a hand. "It may not have turned out that way, but he thought he was doing the right thing at the time. So it goes; as Ed himself was wont to say, the road to hell is paved with good intentions."

He raised his brow, filling his forehead with worry-lines. "He regretted it until his last breath. Many times in the night he would come to me with apologies and kick himself until I reassured him that the future may yet bring you back to us. And now you know why he drank so much. He could not live with himself for having to give you up."

Suddenly, everything came into focus, and Ed's rampant alcoholism in my childhood made perfect sense. Now I knew why my parents had separated; he was simply unbearable to live with anymore. He was racked with guilt for having to relinquish his friends' children to the adoption system.

It hit me just how intimately kind Hel Grammatica must have been, and how long it had taken him, to track them down.

No—in the end, it wasn't necessary. Ed's death had brought us together. I realized that Noreen's car failure hadn't been an accident. *That* had been Hel's doing. Had it also been the silen that had intentionally scared me into asking Sawyer to investigate Ed's house? Did he know I would call my new friend for backup?

Or did Hel talk me into doing it himself without my knowledge? I smiled to myself. The manipulative little shit.

"Your second point," said Normand, "I've already answered it, and I imagine you've already surmised the gist of it. From what Ed told me, the orphanages on Earth do not easily restore custody of children to their original guardians. He was unable to retrieve you after having to give you up."

Noreen sat back down on the throne. I had to admit, she looked very regal sitting on it.

"Enough wailing and gnashing," said the King, a warm yet commanding presence returning to his bronzy voice. I could see where the loyalty of the Kingsmen came from; the man filled the room with himself just by speaking. Back home, they called orators like Normand 'phonebook actors'. They could sell out a theater by sitting on a stage and reading a phonebook.

"You are home, and that's what is important. We will confer on any further injuries and injustices later; right now you all look as if you've spent the last week lying in a ditch being worked over by buzzards. I love you all, but you smell like the dark end of a dawnbound *pohtir.*"

*   *   *

This late in the day, we had the dark bath-house to ourselves. There was no coffee to be served, but the water was still hot enough to raise goosebumps. We slid into the soap-milky water and relaxed. The uptown Ostlyn bath was set into the side of the hill so there were no windows, but a soaped skylight overhead dropped dim light onto the fog and created a heavenly glow. It looked like the set of an Indiana Jones movie.

We rested in silence, letting the heat soak in. I didn't even know what to say even if I'd felt like being talkative.

Noreen broke the quiet solitude. "I still can't wrap my mind around it."

"It's going to take a while to get used to, I imagine," said Walter. He was sitting on the end of a wooden chaise lounge smoking a cigarette, a towel around his waist. He stubbed it out into a little metal cymbal dish and stepped into the bath with us. "I'm still coming to terms with the fact that I now have a brother I never knew. What I've learned today explains so much."

"Same here," said Sawyer. "I've never had a brother before."

"I would be honored to have you by my side as a Kingsman one day, yeah?"

"Seriously?" asked Sawyer. "Wait—this means my last name is actually Rollins, isn't it?"

"I expect so."

"Sawyer Rollins," he said. "I like it."

"Do you know anything about gunplay? Were you a soldier in your world like Ross?"

"No. I don't own a gun, I've never even fired one. Never could afford it. Hell, the road trip to attend Ed's funeral broke me. If I hadn't ended up here, I'd be freezing my ass off in my apartment living on Ramen noodles."

"I'll tell you what," said Walter. "We'll see if Normand's got anything Ross can use and you can have my other pistol. Two of a kind, us! The Rollins brothers!"

"I see how it is!" I said, smirking. "Somebody new comes along and you forget all about me!"

"You jest, but King Normand's got quite the armory. You're getting the better end of the deal, savvy. You forget who runs the gun show around here."

Noreen dunked her head underwater to wet her hair and started lathering it up. I took this as a cue to shave my beard, getting out of the water. I got a bucket from a stack leaning against the wall and dipped some of the water out of the bath, and started scraping my face and head with the straight razor Normand had lent us.

I grievously wounded myself with it several times, but managed to get most of the hair off without outright killing myself.

The tan I'd gotten and the weight I'd lost after the whirlwind ambush had been undone by the reparation of the narrative, after I'd been washed into the Vur Ukasha. I wasn't bothered. I was home. I'd have plenty of time to get healthy again.

"We've been faffing about long enough," said Walter, getting out of the water and drying off. "When you're done here, meet me at Weatherhead, on the portico. It's time we started preparing. This Rhetor character knows we're topside and now he understands that after Ross rewrote reality, that we might be a force to be reckoned with.

"We don't want to be standing around with our puds in our hands when the immortal and his brainwashed lackeys show up looking for a fight. The warriors of Destin do not expire easily. I want to make sure that when he gets here, all he finds are warriors."

*   *   *

When we caught up with Walter, he was arguing with a man. I assume it was a man, at any rate, because the closer we got to him the bigger he seemed. He wasn't even as tall as his son, but Chiral Clayton was twice as big on the horizontal and looked like a bearded tree stump. The man was a brick shithouse. I could tell his sons got their looks from their mother and I'd never even seen the woman.

"I'm tellin you, boy—the lad's gone. Eddie Brig couldn't get him back," he was saying when we walked up. "And who might you be?"

"I'm Ed's son, Ross."

"These are the ones I was telling you about," said Walter.

Clayton looked like a craggier, meaner, balder, older Teddy Roosevelt. He was clad in a leather vest, corduroy trousers, and a collared shirt with the sleeves rolled up Marine-style. He looked very much like the quintessential Rough Rider.

He stepped toward us and tugged down his spectacles, inspecting me in the early evening sun over the rims of the lenses.

Then he looked at Sawyer, and would have turned away if Noreen hadn't caught his eye. He took his glasses off and put them in his vest pocket, took her shoulders in his bear-paw hands and squinted down his nose at her.

"I'll be hung out to dry," he said. He looked at Sawyer again, then me. "—and folded up neat. It is you. It *is* you!"

He guffawed laughter and hugged the girl hard enough to make her grunt. She wriggled her nose at the old man's briny aura. He was obviously more given to spending his coin at the tavern than the bath-house.

He reached over and took all three of us up in an embrace, clapping Sawyer on the back. He held his long-lost son at arms' length and smiled. "Dear me, dear me, dear me," he said. "Boy, it's an amazin thing. I scarce understand it, but I'm glad to see you all back where you belong. By the Wolf, you've got Rollins blood, you do. I see it in ye. I see Normand in the girl, too. She's got his spark in her eyes."

Sawyer returned the smile half-heartedly. I could tell he was still spooked by the revelation.

"How did you get back from Zam?" asked Clayton.

"It was the silen's doing," I said. "It might—"

Clayton resumed talking; he seemed not to have heard me. "Well, no matter how you got here, I'm happy to have you back."

"Thank you, sir," said Sawyer.

"What's this *sir* shit? Call me Father, or Pa, or Da, or something."

"Okay."

The moment seemed to hesitate in the air. I got a weird vibe from the old man, who glanced at Sawyer out of the corner of his eye and pretended to notice something on his lapel and brush it off. He said at Walter, "So what's going on? I'm gettin that feelin again, like you got somethin on the edge of your tongue."

Walter stared back at him wordlessly for several long seconds and then said, "We are in dire circumstances. Ross was about to tell you about it before you interrupted him."

"Oh," said Clayton. "I thought he was done talkin. Shoot, boy, out with it. Give us what you got."

"The silen is dead," I said. "By my brother's hand, the same man that murdered my father. He is under the control of another silen, an evil being called the Rhetor who looks to kill a hell of a lot more people. We came here to warn Normand and yourself in case he comes here to kill you, and to look for help dealing with the Sileni."

"Not that it is of any concern to you," said Walter. "We have business to attend—"

"Not that—" Clayton sputtered, getting flustered. "—any concern—I'll scrape your hide, boy. Who are *you* talking to? I ain't your kennel-boys down to the lake."

"This conversation is over," said Walter. He walked away with a swirl of longcoat. "Please follow me, friends."

Kennel-boys? I sighed, glanced at Sawyer, and at Clayton, whose face was beginning to resemble an heirloom tomato. We siphoned away onto Walter, who was crossing the portico to a smaller door tucked into the shadows in the corner. He opened it; a stairway led down into darkness.

"Where are *you* going in such a hurry?" snarled Clayton.

Walter said nothing. I could tell he was the kind of man that got quieter as he got angrier. Sawyer said, "We need to get ready."

"Get ready, he says," said Clayton. "I'll come spectate. If you boys are spoilin for a fight with somebody, you best have an audience that knows what it looks like when a man knows how to handle a gun."

The stairwell led down into a long hallway with a polished floor pitted with marks and cracks, and ended in an iron grille that resembled a jail cell door, which Walter unlocked with a key. The armory was a vault at the bottom of the stairs and the end of a long stone hallway.

We walked into a large room that was wall-to-wall shelving, illuminated from above by a series of skylights. Rows of simple six-shooters lined the shelves, inset in velveted brackets. Entire racks of them were missing, presumably issued to the lesser armored gunslingers that served as the Ainean militia under the Kingsmen.

Upright racks held shotguns and rifles, short repeaters and long-barreled breech-loaders with soda-bottle scopes. In a corner was a pile of fearsome-looking heater shields, made of banded steel. Each one had leather loops on the backside of them for ammo, and a pistol holster.

Clayton stood by the entrance as Walter handed us pistols and gave us each a box of loose cartridges. "I'll meet you out there," he said, as we were leaving. "I'll just be a few minutes."

"Suit yourself," said the Deon, holstering a pair of sixguns.

Home on the Range

IT WAS A LONG walk out to the range, an open pasture out in the countryside. On the way, I had the opportunity to ask Walter about the 'kennel-boys' Clayton had mentioned. "Do you guys keep working dogs for the—"

"No," he said, cutting me off. "It's nothing you should be concerned with. It is a matter between my father and I."

"All . . . right."

We passed through shadowed lanes between hedgerows and down dirt roads, through neighborhoods of splintery farmhouses and under the shade of towering crabapple trees. We emerged from a narrow break in a wall of honeysuckle thicket onto a long trail that wound alongside several dozen freshly-tilled acres.

A man was leading a team of mules down the field, pulling a plow in the distance; as he recognized us, he took off his hat and swatted at us with it. We all took off our own hats and waved back.

The range was on the other side of a large graveyard; we came out on top of a tall hill studded with worn gravestones. The trail trickled in terraced zigzags down through the graves to a fence overgrown by brambles and kudzu. Lush green trees stood sentinel over the barrier. I tried to read the stones as we walked through them, but they were all in weather-scoured Ainean.

"Someone is going to have to teach me how to read this stuff," I said. "It's frustrating not knowing what anything says."

"You're in good company," said Noreen. "Large parts of the

426

population are illiterate."

"I'm not sure that reassures me."

"We'll figure something out later, though. Maybe after we've . . . done whatever it is that needs to be done."

Sawyer kicked a rock. "What *are* we doing, anyway?"

"What do you mean?" I asked.

"I mean, what are we supposed to be doing?" he asked. "It just seems like we're being reactive. We're turtling up and waiting for something to happen. We should be looking for this guy. We should be helping those people down there in those towers."

"Patience," said Walter. "I understand your frustration, but we've got to focus. To begin with, we don't even know where to look yet."

I said, "That reminds me. I need to ask Normand if he knows anything about Totem."

We slipped through the fence where the barbed wire had been cut long ago, and hiked out to a patch of pea gravel where someone had left a wooden picnic table, an empty crate, and some large bin with an oilcloth tarp thrown over it.

The sky was a dark swelling thing overhead, darker than the trees, littered with shreds of damp, bulging clouds that threatened us with their blue and orange bellies. I could see the Weatherhead from here, a cathedral at the top of a huge ziggurat of city districts.

It was bleached pale by the miles and the low clouds, but I could still just make out the birds chasing each other around the council keeps. The sun, low and fiery on the western horizon, picked them out for me. I could also see a dozen windmill columns in the distance, their needle-thin props turning in great slow circles.

The Deon sat down at the table and patted its grainy, scarred surface. "Sit. I don't bite."

We sat down and plopped the ammo boxes down in front of

427

us.

"This is my favorite part," said Walter. "Loading up. Take out your guns."

We did so. He took out his own and tipped the cylinder open, spilling the rounds inside on the table with a clatter. He scooped them back up and held them loosely, like a handful of pebbles. He manipulated them until one was pincered between his thumb and forefinger, and slid it into one of the chambers in the cylinder of his pistol.

"Next to cleaning them, this is one of the most meditative things a man can do. Go ahead, load up."

He continued to slip the cartridges into the pistol with slow, meticulous gestures, rolling them in his hand like Baoding balls as he did so. They tinkled softly in the evening silence. We were each carrying one pistol, so we each loaded six rounds—Sawyer and Walter twenty-one, since Walter had two seven-shot—one breaktop and one swingout, and Sawyer had his other seven-shot swingout, the one with the inscription.

We took our time. Walter was right, it was a calming, mindless task, and it reminded me of loading magazines for qualification day in the Army. I knew we would probably be cleaning the pistols when we got done. The thought made me instinctively glance around the table for my old cleaning kit.

When I looked up from the revolver, I saw the man-shaped wooden silhouettes standing out in the pasture. They were spaced out at long intervals, bunny-hopping to the left and right in a staggered line, out to a berm at the treeline three hundred meters downrange.

He huddled us together by the table. I stood to the side, my weight on one foot, the heels of my palms resting on the butt of my pistol as it rested in my drop-leg holster.

428

"Since there are only three of you, I'll put you up one at a time. Saw first, milady second, and since he's got a bit of experience with a firearm, Ross third if he wants to go."

I told him I'd worry about it later. The Deon took out one of his pistols and aimed it in the general direction of the silhouettes. "I'm going to start from the ground up with you two, then," he said. "Look at me, and watch what I am doing."

He put his arms out straight, almost locking his elbows. The pistol rested at the apex of the triangle formed from his hands and his shoulders. "Don't take them out unless you're going to either fire them, hand them to someone, or clean them. Never, ever point them at anything you do not intend to kill. And do not put your finger inside the trigger-well unless you intend to kill."

"Gunspinning like the movies is bullshit," I said. "It'll get you killed. Leave it to the rodeo stars and Walter."

He looked over his shoulder at us and added, "Some people would like to tell you that they are nothing more than instruments of brutality, weapons of senseless destruction; *we* know that they are tools of defense and propriety. In responsible hands, they can be a signpost on the way to civilized behavior. Sometimes all it takes is intimidation to turn a tenuous situation into a placid one. It is a wise gunman that knows a battle is best won without a shot fired, or even a weapon drawn."

I thought about the bullet-hole in Red's face, the exit wound in the back of his skull. I got a mental image of a bottle-fly crawling around on his exposed brain. I imagined the sound of buzzing flies, and it made me ill.

I knelt down to look at the clover at my feet, occupying my mind by looking for a lucky four-leaf clover. I knew Walter had paused to wonder why I had stopped paying attention and give me a funny look, but I also knew he recognized the faraway look in my eyes because he continued talking.

"Sometimes we stand like this, and sometimes we stand like *this,*" he was saying. I knew he was demonstrating the difference between the Isosceles and Weaver shooting stances by the way he was shifting back and forth. "Most of the soldiers do it this way so they don't expose the flank, see? Their armor doesn't have side-plates, so if you lean *this* way, you could get shot in the ribs, perhaps puncture a lung or hit the heart if the angle is strong enough. And you *sure* don't want a bullet bouncing around under your armor."

I looked up at him as he canted to the side, putting his strong foot back and bending his left elbow in the Weaver style. "Kingsmen don't normally wear armor or have need of it, as you probably already know. It weighs us down and makes it hard to maneuver. So we shoot like this for the most part, unless—"

"Unless shit gets *real,*" said Sawyer.

"Err, yes—you might say that," said Walter. "When 'shit gets real', then you shoot with whatever hand your gun happens to be in." He squinted at them. "You two seem knowledgeable about our world . . . I'm guessing that you've read the books that Lord Eddick wrote? And, you are aware of the limitations and the abilities of the Kingsmen and the Grievers?"

"Yes," said Noreen.

"Perhaps at some point we will see about putting you both through the ceremony of the Acolouthis, if that is what you wish."

"That would be pretty great," said Sawyer. "I already know that's what I want to do. I—"

He seemed to pause, and a curious look passed across his face, an expression that made him look as if he were trying to remember where he'd misplaced something. He seemed to be scanning the clover underfoot, and his eyes passed across mine. He blinked at the eye contact.

"What is it, babe?" asked Noreen.

"I was about to say *I'm done with my other life,*" he said, and his brow furrowed. "That made me remember I actually *have* another life. An *old* life, I guess."

"Is *this* your new life?"

Walter let his pistol sink to his side. "No one blames you for being homesick or regretful, brother. You were meant to come here one day, I think. You aren't betraying anyone. And you will be able to go back one day, I'm sure, even if it's just to visit because . . . . Well, don't lose hope of seeing loved ones again."

"I realized I don't feel the way I *used* to feel anymore. Not completely. I've always felt out of place, like I was on the wrong bus in the wrong part of town," said Sawyer. "I don't know. Did I *have* a life back there?

He looked into Noreen's eyes. "I feel like I actually *have* one here. I had acquaintances there. I have *friends* here. I had a job *there*. I feel like I have a duty *here*. I don't feel *trapped* anymore. I feel like I'm *supposed* to be here."

Walter gestured at him with his empty off-hand. "It's that feeling of duty that will keep you going when shit gets *real*. Despair and uselessness will kill a man just as dead as any bullet."

"It's getting to you, isn't it?" I said. "*Vero nihil verius*. Nothing truer than truth. It's true. It's real. And you're feeling the importance of scarcity. Everything matters more here. You feel like *you* matter more here."

"Yeah, yeah," said Sawyer. "I do. Back on Zam—Earth, I mean—I was just going through the motions. Some people say they feel like everybody else got an instruction manual for life and they didn't . . . but I felt like all I was doing, was following the instruction manual. Putting my life together by the numbers, like Ikea furniture. Here I'm just playing it by ear. And it feels good."

"The air is sweeter, huh?" I asked. I plucked a four-leaf clover and handed it to him. "For good luck."

"Thanks, I guess," he said, with a half-smile. He tucked it into the band of his hat.

"Anyway, from what you've said of the Sacrament and since I know you've read of our adventures from Eddick's books, I'm assuming you know something of how it is to be in the grip of it," said Walter, holstering his pistol. "Those of us accustomed to the effects of the Sacrament experience gunfighting in a much different way. We will worry about that when it comes to it—Ross, I will address your training soon—but for right now I want you other two to able to defend yourselves with the fundamentals."

He beckoned Sawyer up and bid him take out a pistol. "Since you'll be wearing the soldiers' armor until the ceremony, I want you to stand square to front. Don't expose your sides. Like I said, the armor protects your front and back, but not your ribs. Okay, extend your arms all the way out and point the pistol down the field. There you go, hold it that way, overlap your other fingers. You can hold it that way for now, we'll worry about using the hammer later, when you're more comfortable."

Walter stood beside him, one hand on his shoulder blade and the other on Sawyer's hands.

"Now, I want you to look down the ironsights and center the front sight on one of the silhouettes. Without moving the pistol, I want you to close your right eye."

He did so.

"The sight is no longer on the cutout, correct?"

"Yep. I mean, no—no, it isn't."

"Now close your left and open your right. Now it's on the cutout?"

"Yes."

432

"Then that's your dominant eye," said Walter. "To begin with, you'll want to aim with that eye. With time and practice, you won't need to close either of your eyes. Aiming and shooting will be as natural as throwing a stone or pointing your finger."

He slid his fingertips from Sawyer's shoulder, down his arm, all the way to the tip of the barrel. "The gunslinger's pistol is part of his body. Part of his soul, even. It is the end of your arm, the tool at your hip, and the dragon-fire in your throat."

He noticed someone standing behind him and turned to find Noreen standing there, her own pistol extended.

"I'm gonna get in on this," she said. *"If you don't mind."*

"Not at all, Mis'ra—" He paused.

Noreen's brow crinkled. "I guess I'm not a Mears, am I?" she asked. "I'm a Kaliburn."

"You are who you always were," said Walter.

Sawyer said, smiling at her over his shoulder, "A rose by any other name, hon."

"Okay, let's get on with it. There will be time for that later," said Walter. "Now, what you want to do is put the front sight in the middle of the silhouette's chest. Focus on the cutout and allow the front sight to blur. Breathe. Breathe steadily, breathe slowly, breathe with your stomach, not your chest. Pay attention to your heartbeat. Squeeze the trigger *between* the beats. In time, you will learn to delay your heartbeat to give yourself more time with a steady hand, but for now—"

"Delay my heartbeat?" asked Sawyer. "I didn't know that was possible."

"Oh, it very much is. It takes focus and conditioning, but it's possible. Here, holster your weapon and give me your hand."

He put away the revolver and put his wrist in the Deon's open hand. Walter curled back Sawyer's smallest two fingers and pressed his index and middle finger to the softest part of his own throat, between his larynx and neck muscle, where blood pulsed through the carotid artery.

Walter took a few deep breaths and shallowed his respiration until I could barely see his chest moving. *Thump. Thump. Thump. Thump. . . . Thump.*

"Oh!" said Sawyer. "I guess so! It was only, like, a half-second."

"In a gunfight, a half-second can save your life."

"That's pretty incredible," said Noreen. "Is that all you can do?"

"I can also stop my own hiccups, if that matters a pence."

"Interesting. You'll have to show me that some time."

"We are digressing!" grinned Walter. "We needs must apply ourselves. Listen; I say to squeeze the trigger when you fire—oh, take out your pistol again, there you go—squeeze the trigger, don't pull it. If you pull, you will turn the sight to the left a bit . . . and by the time the round gets to its target, that *little bit* will have become a miss by a meter or more."

As he spoke, he showed them his hand, holding an imaginary pistol. He bent his index finger in several times.

"Think of it as a gas pedal," I said. "If you stomp the pedal, what happens?"

"The car hauls ass," said Noreen. "The tires squeal."

"Right. So you want to apply even, steady pressure. The round going off in your hand should always be a surprise."

"Very good," said Walter. "I may have underestimated you, bastard. Yes, don't anticipate the shot. Just focus on steadying your breathing, keeping the sight steady on the target, and drawing back the trigger. And when you do that, use the crook of the smallest joint of your pointer finger, and only really bend this second

434

knuckle joint here. Don't curl your finger; that turns the gun to the inside."

He curled his finger in a hook shape. "If you do it right, you should be pointing the pistol directly at the target when the action lets go, the hammer hits, and the cap-strike surprises you."

He stepped away from them and sat on the edge of the table. "All right. This is just a simple test of your abilities as of today. I want you each, in turn, to fire five rounds into the wooden cutout closest to you. Lady Kaliburn—"

Noreen smiled over her shoulder at the sound of her new surname.

"—You will be first."

She stepped up to the firing line, delineated from the rest of the field by a line of wooden beams lying on the ground. She stood straight with her feet shoulder-width apart and pushed the pistol out in front of her.

"If your arms get tired," said Walter, "—keep your hands together and the pistol pointing out there, but bring your arms closer to your chest to rest, as if you were praying. Actually, go ahead and do that right now."

"Okay."

"At the count of five, I want you to very calmly extend your arms to length, sight down the barrel of the pistol, and fire five rounds into the cutout. Try to remember what I've told you. Dominant eye, sight on the chest, breathing, squeeze, surprise."

He took off his hat and combed his fingers through his long hair, then laid it on the table and put a rock in it to keep it from blowing away. "Five . . . four . . . three . . . two . . . one."

Noreen put out the gun, hesitated long enough to look at the front sight, and the gun went off with a deafening *crack*. Several seconds later, it fired again . . . and again. I saw a puff of dust stand up from one of the cutouts and roll away, fading into the air. Twice more, and she was done.

"Holster the pistol, and we'll go down and see how you did. When you holster it, make sure your finger is outside the trigger well. Believe me, you don't want to shoot yourself in the foot. That's why the Quartermaster walks with a limp."

The Deon whipped the oilcloth off of the box by the table and uncovered a pile of cutout men. He picked one up and we went down to Noreen's cutout—I'd say it was about twenty-five, thirty yards away—and looked for bullet-holes in the splintered wood and flaking paint. Someone had painted a smiley-face on it and a pair of hands holding a gun.

I saw four holes—one in the right cheek, one in the left shoulder, one in the gut, and one on the edge of the right arm, about where the elbow would be. "Not horrendous," said Walter. "Not astounding. There's potential. You need to work on your breathing and trigger squeeze."

We were discussing the cutout when Clayton came up behind us. I hadn't even noticed him coming across the field; he was stealthy for such a big man.

"How's it going so far?"

"I've only gotten Normand's daughter up," Walter said as we went back to the gear table. "She didn't do too bad. I still have to put up Sawyer and Eddick's boy."

"Well, let's see how he does. Sounds like I've shown up just in the nick of time. You're up, kid!"

Sawyer got up and sauntered over to the firing line cross-ties, the heels of his hands on his pistol grips. I couldn't help but notice just how much he was beginning to look like a real Ainean.

"You got this in the bag, desperado," I said, and sang the Eagles' eponymous *"Deees-peraaado!"*

He looked back and grinned, and drew a pistol, aiming it downrange. He had elected to use the Weaver stance, angling himself so that his right foot was back. Walter told him that he was holding the gun too close to his face, so he pushed it out a little bit.

"You don't want that thing to kick back and hit you in the mouth."

"You're too pretty," said Noreen.

"Thanks," said Sawyer.

Walter cleared his throat. "You remember everything I told you, correct? Dominant eye, sight on the chest, breathing, squeeze, surprise. Just aim with your eye, and shoot with your mind."

"Kill with your heart," I piped in, though I wasn't sure where I'd heard it before.

"I like it," said Walt. "Yes, you want to do it all in your head. Your head is the locus of battle. When you aim your gun, let everything else fall to the wayside. Draw a curtain around yourself and shut the world away, focus on your target. In that last instant, you and your opponent are all that exist. *You* are the one that will continue to exist. You are the bullet. You are the god of death. Smite him and move on to the next."

"Five, four, three, two, one," said Noreen.

Unbidden memories of a loudspeaker voice came to me and I said, "It's your lane. Five shots."

Sawyer lifted the pistol and sighted down the barrel. Two seconds later, the round went off. I saw a clot of dust whip from a cutout and fade away, leaving a bullethole in the silhouette's face.

"Nice one," said Clayton.

The pistol erupted again and a cutout to the left wobbled. I could see a clean hole in the shape's left chest: the heart area. Clayton whistled.

Bang! A cutout some several dozen yards distant jerked,

437

halfway up the field. I couldn't see the hole from here, but it must have been a good shot to make it move like that, better than a glancing blow. I looked over at Walter; his head turned and he nodded appreciatively to me, his eyebrows high.

"Don't get fancy," he said to Saw, "You don't have to shoot all the targets out there."

Bang! A silhouette to the right shook; I could see the woodline through the hole in its belly.

Sawyer rolled his shoulders, bringing the pistol back and up to his nose, resting his arms. Refreshed, he extended it again and took aim. This time, he took a little longer. I could tell he was having trouble getting it to stay center-mass. He was overreaching himself, trying to shoot targets too far away.

I thought about getting up and saying something, but I don't like surprising people holding firearms.

The gunshot whipcracked and rolled up the valley; I didn't see any cutouts move. The echo soared back to us through air pungent with cordite.

"I don't think that one hit," said Walter. "Come on, let's go see how you did."

"Damn," said Sawyer.

The last one turned out to have been a near-miss; Clayton found a notch where the bullet had hit the very edge of the wood plate, at the point where the left shoulder sloped down into the upper arm of the man-shape.

On the way back to the table, I said to Walter, "I think you should put a few rounds down-range before we leave."

"I like the way you think," he said.

We sat back down at the table, and Walter went over to the firing line in his sauntering, loosey-goosey walk of his. He stood straight, staring down the field, and tugged the brim of his hat.

438

"Count to five, and don't stop," he said, his hands hovering over the handles of his pistols. His fingertips tappled the sandalwood grips in a soft rattle.

"One—" said Noreen.

He snatched up the left-hand gun, his thumb on the recoil guard, and fanned the hammer with the blade of his right hand for six shots, *bang-bang-bang-bangbangbang*.

She continued counting, "—two, three, four—"

He holstered it—drawing the other as he did so—and fanned the trigger with his left hand for seven shots. I squinted and tried to make out the holes in the cutout he'd been shooting at, but all I could see in the bluing dusk was a hole in the silhouette's left clavicle the size of my fist. He'd been splitting his own arrows.

"—six."

"Shit!" Walter said, holstering the pistol. "I'm rusty!"

"Rusty my ass!" cawed Clayton, throwing his head back with laughter. "You're just *slow*, fancy-pants!"

We dumped our casings and unexpended ammo and started back to town. The last of the sunlight was slipping down below the roofs and treetops, immersing us in deep purple shadow. The night-bugs were beginning to sing, and the air had taken on a cool sweetness, flavored by the honeysuckle and grass. I took a deep breath and caught some heavy, musky scent.

"I don't think I ever want to leave here," Noreen said, after nearly twenty minutes of silent walking.

"What, Ostlyn?" asked Sawyer.

"No, Destin. I don't—I don't think I want to go back."

"I do," said Sawyer. "I want to tell my . . . my 'Earth mom'? I want to tell her where I am and that I'm doing okay. And tell her the truth, maybe. You know, I bet she's worried sick."

439

"Yeah."

"What's wrong?"

"I don't think anybody misses me back home—on Earth, I mean. My dad, maybe. My Earth dad."

"You never told me his name," said Sawyer.

"Rick. Short for Richard. He's a district manager for Wells Fargo."

"What's that?" asked Walter.

I said, "It's a bank."

"A bank!" said Clayton. "Banks in the other-world too? I guess evil is universal, innit?"

That made me think about the towers of silence again, and the people languishing in them. I had been thinking about them off and on since we got off the train. Worrying. I wondered if they existed while I wasn't writing about them. I wondered if they ever existed at all.

I looked at Sawyer and Noreen's faces, and Walter's, and wondered what they'd seen down there. Had they even been down there at all? Were their minds filled with visions I'd poured into them? Was the whole thing in my head? Had the hallucinations been wholly manufactured for my benefit? For their benefit? Did I manufacture them? Were my *friends* hallucinations?

My mind felt like it was about to split at the seams trying to distinguish reality from fiction. I tried not to think about it.

Sawyer must have noticed how grim and thoughtful I was, because as we passed through the front gate of Ostlyn proper, he elbowed me. The crowd had tapered off significantly since the sun had gone down, and we went the long way, walking the main street unmolested. Ostlyn was not a party-town like Maplenesse.

"You okay, Scooby?"

440

"Yeah—I guess. I can't stop thinking about what happened."

"The towers? The Mariner? The rope?" he asked.

I wondered if I was actually drooling in a mental hospital somewhere, strapped to a bed, dreaming all of this. Maybe the gunshot in the shoulder I'd suffered back in that ghost town had been a hypodermic syringe full of Thorazine. I couldn't imagine what the nurses were thinking about my one-sided conversations with gunslingers they couldn't see.

"Yeah. I'm having trouble reconciling it all. I've been feeling a little crazy all day."

"I hear ya, man. I don't feel like I'm all here either. It doesn't feel real, does it?"

"No," I said, maybe a little curtly.

"You know what they say, Scoob. Truth is stranger than fiction."

The two men walked around each other in lazy circles, their hands resting on their gunbutts. The Redbird stroked his lush gray beard and pulled the collar of his shirt loose.

"It's been a long time comin, Pack boy," said Lucas. His voice was a raspy whiskey buzzsaw.

"It has," said Normand.

"Why'd it take you so long?" asked the older man. "It ain't like I've been laid up all this time. I been movin and shakin too. I been watchin you. I know all about your exploits. You coulda come gunnin for me at any time."

"Waiting. And watching."

"Waitin for what?"

Normand licked his lips. His fingertips traced the contours of the pistol in his hip holster with almost erotic grace. He was a coiled snake. "I never could settle on how I wanted to watch you die. And then after a while, it hit me like a bolt from the blue—I didn't want to watch you die so bad anymore."

"Oh?" asked Lucas. "Why's that?"

"I realized some time ago . . . I had become partial to the anticipation."

Lucas smiled. It was a warm smile, but his eyes were dead and cold. "I see. You've become a hunter. Didn't anyone ever tell you it's rude to play with your food?"

Normand simply stood there, crow's-feet in the corners of his tight eyes.

The smile dropped like a hot potato. "Without the chase, you ain't nothin no more. You're a hollow hunter, Kaliburn. Full of vengeance and nothing else. Whoever ends this today, it don't matter. You'll die either way!"

Lucas broke into uproarious laughter, giving Normand the half-second he needed to draw first.

—The Fiddle and the Fire, vol 7 (unfinished) "The Gunslinger and the Giant"

Dreaming in Technicolor

CLAYTON TREATED US TO a huge dinner at a little restaurant in the first tier of the city. Well, I say restaurant, but it was more of a roach coach; we ordered our food from a little window in the side of a drawn carriage and sat at one of a half-dozen tables by the street to wait for our orders.

The fare was decidedly less seaside and more upscale than Salt Point, and more meat-and-potatoes than Maplenesse. Several other carriages were lined up next to that one, each one of them touting different dishes and desserts.

I ordered something that looked like an open-faced chili-burger: crumbled ground meat in a bowl made of a crusty heel of bread, covered in something like a cross between chili and curry.

It had beans but looked milky and had peppers julienned into it. The bread's crust was as hard as a rock, and the stuff piled on was hot enough to strip the paint off of a Cadillac, but the whole thing was amazing. I ate it with a fork in one hand and a sweaty napkin in the other.

I got the feeling Clayton fed us less out of generosity, and more out of a need to flaunt his financial plumage. He seemed to have warmed up to the idea that his youngest son was back in Destin, and asked Sawyer questions about himself between gulps of beer. The more he drank, the friendlier he became. I sensed that this was a trend.

"So what do ye do for a livin, back in Zam?" asked the old man. He smoothed out his salt-and-pepper mustache with his

444

thumb and forefinger. It struck me how often I'd seen Maxwell Bayard do that.

Sawyer was eating some sort of flatbread club sandwich. It smelled like chicken. "I'm going to school. I'm a student."

"A student, eh? A scholar?" said Clayton. He leaned back, his belly pressing against the table. "What are you studying?"

I decided that it was dubious whether fame and affluence had been good to the Chiral. I wondered what he was like when he and Normand were young. It suddenly occured to me that I hadn't seen any copies of the *Fiddle* series lying around in either of my father's houses.

"Making movies."

"Movies?" asked Clayton. "What are those?"

Sawyer seemed to be confused, then he remembered who he was talking to and where he was. "They're like . . . a combination of books and stage plays. They're like a stage play you can take home and watch whenever you like."

"Oh!" said Walter, squinting through his smoke. He tapped ashes into an ashtray, sneaking fried potatoes out of Sawyer's basket. "Picture shows. We have those. Well, something like them, I suppose. I guess if you had the equipment you could take it home and watch it."

"Are you serious?" asked Sawyer.

"Oh, yeah," said Clayton. "They been around for a good ten or fifteen year'n. They were invented by an Iznok named Atanaz . . . . Atanzas . . . see-jee . . . whatever the hell his name was. I used to know the guy. Real good sort, charitable chap."

Sawyer took a huge bite of his sandwich, and said through it, "Can we go look at it when we're done here?"

"Why not."

"I'll be," said Clayton. He threw back his head and barked

445

laughter. "My youngest is a picture-show maker. Not what I expected, but there are . . . worse things a man could do with his life. What kind of picture shows d'you make, boy?" He pretended to fondle his own nipples and wobbled in his chair. "The ones with dancin women in em?"

Walter dropped his face into his palm.

Sawyer grinned. "No. I used to want to be a nature filmmaker, but I got into a project with a friend of mine and got hooked on making horror movies."

"Nature?" asked Clayton. "What's that, you take pictures of the woods?"

"Ahh, sort of. It's kind of like hunting, but instead of killing animals, you make picture shows of animals in faraway places that most people wouldn't get to see up close. And then later you record someone talking about the animals, and put it with the picture show so people can learn about them."

"Oh, okay then. Well, that's certainly charitable of ye. There ain't a many farmer in Ain get to leave his farm for too long, what with his work and all. It's mighty nice you make it so they can see the world."

"I like to think so. It's a good career. Lots of famous filmmakers."

"What's a horror movie?"

"It's a picture show with . . . scary things in it. Some people back on Earth like to be scared, I guess. There isn't much to be scared of there, so people like to get a thrill seeing spooky things."

"I get what you're saying, I get you, I get you," said Clayton. "We don't cert need that here, I figure. There's plenty to be scared of here. You want a thrill? I know where to take you and show you things that would make you piss your pants. And the next guy's pants."

446

"I believe it. I've seen plenty of scary things since I've been here."

I noticed that Noreen seemed quiet and introspective. She was picking at some sort of chowder in a big spun-clay bowl, absent-mindedly dipping a breadstick in and nibbling on it.

"What's up, buttercup?" I asked her, dipping a breadstick into the chowder and leaving it there.

"I wish Normand could be here," she said. "I want to hang out with him."

My heart ached. "Awww. I bet you do. He probably doesn't come out too often these days, though. He'd probably get mobbed or something like Brad Pitt at a McDonald's."

"Yeah," said Noreen, staring into her food as if she were trying to scry her father in it.

After we ate, Clayton broke off and went back to Weatherhead, while the four of us strolled up the main avenue, enjoying the dry, cool evening. The streetlights were short steel lamps, squat like fire hydrants, with conical shades. They gave off a soft and indirect electric light that I found very comfortable.

Next to the half-timbered shops and boutiques, and the fact that there were so many slat benches, the lamps made me feel as if I were in an inside-out house. The sky full of stars I saw now was more familiar, faded by the light-pollution of sprawling Ostlyn.

"Why is this city laid out like this?" I asked. "This big round maze is a pain in the ass."

Noreen took a deep breath, her head tilting back and her eyes scanning the tops of the protective walls. "Mainly for siege purposes. The longer it takes invaders to get to the center of the city, the more time the troopers have to attack them from the ramparts. The streets are basically great big gauntlets."

"The streetlights are low and soft to keep the battlement

447

patrol in shadow," said Walter. "And to prevent any troopers on the ground from being dazzled in a gunfight."

We found the picture show in a stucco-sided cabin in the crook of the first switchback. Inside was a dark room full of wooden folding chairs. Upturned faces watched a flickering movie projected over their heads onto a white sheet stretched taut across the far wall.

The image was of a man in chaps and a hat, wearing dark eyeliner and gripping an oversized six-shooter, creeping up to a doorway. Beyond, three men were lasciviously counting a pile of shiny coins on a heavy pub table, by candlelight.

"Oh!" I murmured. "It looks like the little theater from *The Green Mile* where they take John Coffey to see a Fred Astaire movie."

"It's a silent movie," said Noreen, the herky-jerky image dancing across her eyes. "Just like the old Charlie Chaplin films."

Sawyer was beaming. "I feel like I've gone back in time to see the birth of cinema. Like I could turn around and see Georges Méliès running the projector."

There were a few empty seats in the back row; we sat down and settled into the droopy canvas seats.

On the screen, the man in the chaps and hat had gotten the drop on the others, and they were taunting each other. Script cards popped up between each line, but they were in Ainean and mostly illegible to me. I leaned back, folded my arms, and relaxed in the cool moviehouse.

I recall wishing I had a box of Junior Mints, and then I was sitting in a dark study, slumped in a Victorian wingback chair. A nearby window flickered with faint firelight, giving me enough visibility to see that the place was tastefully furnished. I recognized the titles and authors of the books arranged on the shelves:

Dickens, Antoine de Saint-Exupéry, Jean-Paul Sartre.

I got up out of the chair and went over to the window. The scene that awaited me was one of total devastation; the ruined shells of a peaceful neighborhood lay scattered all over the place, flaming and crumbling. The night sky held not stars but a goose-flock of airplanes. I could hear the drone of their engines.

I looked down on this Boschian hell from a third-floor window. Someone was standing in the street. I opened the window and called out, though I don't remember having a voice.

The figure turned around. He was wearing a yellow longcoat.

Embers danced across the brim of his weatherbeaten black Boss; I couldn't discern his face because of the hat, but I already knew what I would see. He had taken out a gold pocket watch and was looking down at it.

He snapped it shut and slipped it into a pocket. He walked toward the window, and into the entrance of the building.

I ran for the door and closed it, not with a slam, but softly. As soon as it clicked, I hid in the footwell of the broad mahogany desk by the window, hugging my knees. I pulled the chair in with me.

I waited. The oblivious ticking of a grandfather clock reminded me of the passage of time, sounding out a bat-like sonar that ricocheted off the passing seconds. I heard faraway thunder, muffled by the walls of the house. No—not thunder. Bombs. The planes I'd seen were dropping bombs.

Tick. Tick. Tick. Where the hell was I?

My legs began to cramp. Maybe the front door was locked. Maybe he couldn't get in at me. I pushed the chair out of the kickspace and slid out, unfolding myself. I stood like that for a moment, my hands on my knees, stretching my back.

Tick. Tick. Tick . . . .

The clock had stopped. I walked over to it, the floorboards

groaning under my feet, and looked up at the clock face. The arms had ceased to move. I opened the face's glass front and saw a hole just below the arms' center pin; lying on the inside of the frame was a little key. I inserted it and started winding the clock up.

The loud ratcheting of the clockwork startled me as I worked. I tried to turn it a little softer, but it was impossible, so I just turned it slower.

A searing pain crept into my hand. I snatched it away. "Ow."

The key was red-hot, glowing in the shadows. I licked my fingertips and blew on them. *What on Earth?*

The paper clock-face caught on fire. A trickle of flames licked up from the bottom and started chewing up the sand-colored backing. I could see orange metal inside, as if the gears themselves were connected to some power source.

I backed away as the paper burned. Tiny ashes floated out of the clock like snow; as I remained there, the face's backing was obliterated by a ring of glowing hot metal inside. It was like the eye of a electric stove. The arms drooped and fell off, and oozed down the front of the clock like slugs.

I saw movement out of the corner of my eye. Something was next to the piano.

I looked down and perceived a shape in the dark, a dimmer, hunched figure. It shuffled toward me and uncoiled as it moved, writhing open like a newborn fawn and reaching upward with long, angled arms and hands like empty black gloves.

It groaned and stood up on lank legs, and the shadow turned toward the clock. It reached up with those empty hands and took the glowing ring of metal down from the mechanism inside, and put it on like a mask.

The Feaster turned toward me, that eye burning through the night, and those slender, lightless arms crooked toward me like spider-legs. It opened those glove-hands and took hold of me. I could feel the heat of it through my shirt.

"It's over," it said, and I screamed.

I heard polite laughter from the last stragglers leaving the movie-house. Noreen was shaking my shoulder to wake me up. She covered her mouth with her hand to stifle her own chuckling. "Hey, the movie is over. Did you have a nightmare?"

"I guess I did," I said, and got out of my chair, stiff and mortified. My heart was still pounding.

A little boy filed past, clutching his mother's hand. He looked up at me and said, "Are you all right, serah?"

"Yeah, yeah, I am. Yeah."

"It's all right," he said, smiling, as she pulled him into the crowd. Just before he was swallowed by the throng, he added, "He scares me too."

Walter took us to a comfortable little inn down the hill from the Weatherhead and set us up with cozy digs, since there were no guest quarters at Normand's keep. The furnishings were rustic but top-notch: aromatic, unfinished cedar bed-frames from the mountains west of Ostlyn, blue flannel sheets to stem the spring chill, and handmade quilts.

Someone had started a fire in the pot-belly stove in the corner, and the dry heat permeated the room with a sooty effulgence that made my head swimmy and scattered my thoughts. Noreen excused herself to go see if the King was still awake, and left us to our devices.

As Sawyer and I were getting ready for bed, Chiral Clayton showed up with a pair of bulging gunny sacks.

"You'll be needin this," he said, dumping them out on the floor. The vespine green K-Set armor inside cascaded out in a muffled clatter. The two of us didn't pick any of it up, just sat on our beds with grainy eyes, dully taking in the old man as he stood there, the sacks hanging empty from his hands. "Well? Go ahead and try it on, see if it fits."

Sawyer looked as if he wanted to protest, but the Chiral's piercing eyes made that seem like an unwise choice. I could tell he was a night-owl. I used to be, before I began my life spending all my time running from otherworldly beings and walking for hours across prairies.

After a brief hesitation meant to drop the hint that we didn't particularly appreciate the intrusion, we slid out of bed and started putting on the pieces. There were greaves, cuirasses, gauntlets, shoulder-protectors, helmets that looked like a prop from *Robocop* or *Judge Dredd.*

I had never really gotten a good look at anything but the gauntlet Gosse Read had handed to me on the *Vociferous* our first week here. I was astonished to realize that the retaining straps that hadn't dry-rotted, fallen off, and been replaced with leather belts— why, they were made of elastic webbing!

"Are you seeing what I'm seeing?" I asked Sawyer as I put the pieces on. "This is Spandex. Look, it's even got Velcro. It's wore the hell out and doesn't stick to itself anymore, but it's Velcro, all right."

"Yeah," he said. "The inside looks like neoprene, too. Those Etudaen really knew their stuff, huh? I hate to say *co-inky-dink,* but—hey, I dunno."

We stood straight and modeled the armor for Clayton. He nodded appreciatively, and we started taking it back off and putting it back into the bags.

"I'm just glad we don't have to fill out a hand receipt for this crap," I said.

"Hey, boy," said Clayton, his nostrils flaring. "That *crap* will save your life one day. Believe it."

I didn't know how he would react if I called him *sir*, so I just focused on removing the pieces. I unbuckled the cuirass and slid it over my head; on the way out of the bottom, something caught my eye. I carried the chestpiece over to the pot belly stove and angled it so that I could see the inside of the plate by the light of the fire.

It was the same icon I'd seen stenciled on the lightning-gun on the steamship, only this was in much better condition. A symbolic eagle in rampant, his wings spread and his head in profile, like a medieval coat of arms. It was a label, printed on the lining of the chestpiece.

Underneath it were two words that sent the deepest chill up my spine that I'd felt since surfacing in the Aemev—again, as when I'd first heard about "Lord Eddick", the world seemed to jar loose from its moorings. Sawyer came over and I showed him as well. I saw him get the same feeling of existential horror. He tore his eyes away from the symbol and looked at me. "Do you think Ed knew about this?"

"I don't know," I said, "But I think I know who needs to know about it."

I looked down at the printed symbol and words.

NEVADA ORGANON

Noreen and the King

SHE CREPT UP THE grand staircase, as cat-quiet and furtive as Dorothy heading into the palace of the Wizard of Oz. Only this time, the heroine's beloved Tin Man, Cowardly Lion, and Scarecrow were away sawing logs. The stone steps held the heat of the day, radiating it into the cooling night air. The two moons of Destin swelled in the sky like celestial Chinese lanterns, one as white as bone and the other a livid red.

A gunslinger trooper was pacing back and forth on the torch-lit portico, serving as the night's council retainer. Noreen could see a gun on her hip. "Well met, mis'ra. What brings you to the Weatherhead at such an hour? The Council doesn't take visitors this late, I'm afraid."

"I came to see my father before I went to bed for the night."

One gunslinger? That seemed peculiar, Noreen thought, but then it was evident that nothing really ever happened to warrant heightened security in Ostlyn these days. She hoped that trend would continue.

"Your father?" asked the retainer. She tossed her longcoat back, casually making room for a draw. The sleek green armor reflected the firelight as a faint, sparkling pearlescent sheen. Noreen couldn't see her face inside the swarthy K-Set armor; she wore something that resembled a motorcycle helmet with a grille visor and looked for all the world like a grinning green demon.

"Yes. Do you know if he's still awake?"

"Who is your father, that I may know who to disturb?"

"Ahh—" said Noreen, and swallowed. "King Normand."

"Is that so?" asked the retainer. "I'll have you know I'm the daughter of Ancress Momerren."

"Really?"

"Uhh . . . no."

"Oh."

"I was being coy. Who are you in fact?"

"Noreen Kaliburn, princess of the nation of Ain," said a voice in the darkness.

They both looked in that direction and saw a flare of light as Clayton lit a cigarette, cupping the flame with his hands. He shook out the match and evaporated into the shadows again. "We're all learning to adapt to sudden circumstances. No harm, no foul, Meadow, but if I were you, I'd let er pass."

The army gunslinger seemed to regard her with new eyes.

"My apologies, milady. May it be," Meadow said, bowing low over her fist.

Noreen blinked in Clayton's direction and frowned slightly at Meadow. "It's all good. Everybody makes mistakes. I only just arrived today."

"It is my job not to make mistakes, milady," said Meadow.

Noreen wasn't sure what to say. She tried to think of several wise aphorisms, something appropriate and sly and princess-clever, but came up with nothing but trite bullshit that felt lame in her mouth. In the end, she said in a confidential tone, "Then this will just be between the three of us."

"Yes, milady," said Meadows, pacing into the limits of the firelight.

Noreen pulled the door open and went into the council

455

chamber, giving Sawyer's father a last glance, but she could see nothing there but an inky pool of night.

Her father and another man were standing by one of the ancillary doorways, conversing when she entered.

"Well met," said Normand, noticing her. He was wearing a night-robe with a subtle, elaborate pattern and a pair of canvas shoes. "What a delightful surprise. August, I'd like you to meet someone very special to me."

He beckoned her over and put an arm around her, enveloping her shoulder in one of his ancient, rough hands. She felt very small and fragile, in a juvenile sort of way. *Is this what fathers are supposed to make you feel?* "My dear, this is August Armistead, the Councilman of the Kingdom. I'm sure you probably already know what August does here."

"I do," she said, and Noreen realized that over the course of her life reading the *Fiddle* series, she had been privy to many secret indiscretions and questionable aspects of the people she was now meeting. She knew of some of the morally dubious things the Councilman had done in his career, and it pained her to act courteous toward him.

Indeed, she experienced the urge to blurt out the things she'd seen him do on the page, but she stifled it. They seemed amicable enough. She didn't want to rock that boat if the need hadn't presented itself.

An epiphany, broad and startling, slowly came to her as she nodded her head in deference, but it was tantalizingly out of her grasp.

"May it be, Councilman Armistead," she said.

Armistead was a solid figure, barrel-chested, with a squeaking-bald scalp, a short, woolly beard, and the perpetual scowl of a vulture. He handled matters of diplomacy and served much as a

456

Secretary of State. In Ain, that usually meant dealing with two political entities: Cice Jiunad, a nation to the southeast and home of the Griever cult, and the Antargata k-Setra, which over time had evolved from a colony into a distinct—but not wholly autonomous—government all its own.

"May it be, young lady," said Armistead. His voice was grave and erudite, like a fine cameo carved out of granite, but he spoke in refreshingly clipped tones. He was like a gnarly sea captain that spent his Saturdays at the bookstore reading legal thrillers over a soy latte.

Normand winced a smile at her and winked. "This is my daughter, Noreen."

"Daughter?" said Armistead. "I was aware of no such thing! I look away, and she appears while my back is turned! You work fast, old man. But seriously . . . ."

"It involves the matter of importance that I've summoned the council to discuss. Goddard and Eleanor should arrive in two days' time, and then we will convene," said Normand.

"I understand. I do know how you hate to repeat yourself." Armistead asided to Noreen loud enough for the King to hear, "You will learn, he can be a man of few words."

The old gunslinger shook his head in disapproval, but the ghost of a smile still remained under his chopped mustache.

The Councilman bowed. "I'm afraid it's getting late for me. I must retire to my quarters; there is a crisp new tome and a slice of lemon cake, and I can hear them chanting my name from here. I will leave you two be. I trust I will know much more about this lovely surprise in two days, then?"

"That you will," said Normand. "Sleep well."

He disappeared through one of the doors. The girl and the old man were alone.

Normand smiled down at her; even as warm as it was, she couldn't help but feel uncomfortable. They were warm, scratchy, fatherly hands to be sure, but she had been along for a very long and very dark ride. They were bloody hands.

The smile was genuine and affectionate, but his blue eyes, like the skies over the tallest mountain in the world, were cold and distant. In this instant, she saw a flicker of regret in the back of her heart, like a fleeting glimpse of some rare animal. Suddenly she felt vulnerable and very, very alone.

He finally said, "So what brings you up to see this old stranger, milady?"

She didn't know what to say. She caught herself staring at him and let out the breath she'd been holding, blinking. Her eyes were dry with fatigue.

"Just wanted to come up and see me before bed? Spend a few minutes with this wore-out old bandit?"

She nodded. Normand's smile faltered, metamorphosed seemingly without moving from guileless and happy to wistful. "I get the feeling I'm not entirely what you expected," he said. His voice had lost some of that baritone edge.

"No," Noreen said. She rummaged for the words. "You're what—what I *should've* expected, I think."

Normand appeared to understand that she was cryptic out of necessity, out of a fundamental inability to put herself into tenable words. He turned and walked over to the doorway nearest to the dais, opening it. "Perhaps it might help to . . . well, just come with me."

She chewed her lip. "Okay."

She came over; expected him to take her hand in his, but he passed through the doorway into a dim, narrow corridor. She followed him down it. As they walked through the gloom toward

458

the dancing light of a torch, the gunslinger said, "You are afraid of me."

Noreen said nothing, but she had no need to.

"I understand your reticence," he said. "You've been privy to every last thing I've had to do in my life. I am in an unusual position, you must know. It's not every father whose life has been laid bare to his children. Most men, at least, have the advantage of omission. I at least have the advantage of tardiness, I suppose. I cannot teach you what not to do, because you've already done it."

They came to a tall wooden door. Normand unlocked it with a key and pushed both sides open. The door split in the middle and swung apart; a breeze flowed in to take their place. A rich, warm light filled the hallway around his lean silhouette.

The room they entered was a round parlor twenty paces across. In the center of a round wooden table was a hurricane lantern. A half-dozen books lay scattered around it, half of which were well-thumbed volumes of *The Fiddle and the Fire*. Others were treatises on war, poetry anthologies, and nature encyclopedias.

A cool copper teapot stood among them, along with an empty teacup that had a tiny Saoshoma writhing along its rim. More books stood in teetering stacks around the room, at least a hundred or more of them. Mired somewhere in that forest of literature was a plush red wingback chair with cherrywood lion-feet.

Paintings and mounted game heads hung from the walls, the former in various states of tilt and the latter draped with all manner of accoutrements. A roebuck gawped at nothing, a multicolored scarf dangling from its antlers like bunting. An off-kilter frame held an oil painting of a woman. A bird that looked like a pale brown turkey perched on a lacquered log that had a hat hanging from one end of it.

A staircase followed the curvature of the wall up the left-hand side to the second floor. It all looked very Merlinesque, and

Noreen surprised herself by feeling more at ease.

"I've found myself in many dark situations, doing dark things," Normand said in a slow gravelly tone, his fingertips brushing the surfaces of Ed's books. He pulled out one of the table's diamondwood chairs and sat down in it with a sigh, picking up one of the *Fiddle* books and indicating it. "But I am not an evil man." He punctuated the sentiment by looking up at her across the table, his brow crinkling.

Am I?, his face seemed to say.

Noreen sat in the red armchair and slipped out of her boots, pulled her feet up under her. They sat like this for a long moment, basking in each others' presence like lizards on a too-hot rock. The rough fabric of the chair felt good on her bare feet, contrasting against the uncomfortable silence.

Normand started to speak, and stopped himself—and then said, "Would you like some coffee?"

"No," said the girl. She smoothed out her sundress, and picked little knots off where the fabric was pilling. "You're not."

"Hmm?" he said, and paused in the middle of getting up.

She looked up at him with his own arctic eyes. "You're not evil."

"Ahh," he said, and stood up. He seemed to hesitate, then went through a nearby door. She could hear him rooting around in a kitchen, banging pots together, pouring water.

She slid out of the chair and padded into the kitchen. It was a surprisingly cramped space, little more than an oven, a pantry, and a horseshoe-shaped counter with wall cupboards. A chopping-block island stood in the middle, and he tended to bump it with his hip when he wasn't paying attention as he moved around the rough slate floor.

"I run into this thing all the time," he said. "I'm surprised it

460

hasn't fallen over."

"It's a very small kitchen."

"It's all it must be. We usually have an attendant around during the day for breakfast and midday meals, but after the sun goes down, we're on our own. Just as well," Normand said, crinkling his crow's-feet. "I don't eat much."

He put a kettle on the stove to boil and turned around, leaning against the counter and folding his arms.

"So—have you made a decision on whether you're going to stay here, or . . . go back to Earth? For good, I mean."

"It's not etched in stone yet," she said, "but I think I want to stay here."

The gunslinger nodded, staring down at the chopping block. "I really am glad you're here. I'd— If it's all right with you, I'd like to have you around. Around here, you know—I'd like to get to know you. I don't know how you feel about that."

Noreen went to put her hands in the pockets of her jacket, but she wasn't wearing it anymore. She clasped them behind her back.

"I can see you've had a little time to think about it all," said the King.

"Yeah."

"Taking you to Earth wasn't my idea, you know. Wasn't even my call. I wasn't even here for it. Not to say he did the wrong thing, or made the wrong call, but it was all Ed. In retrospect, I'm glad he did it. —Took you away from here. I wasn't here to protect you, and at the time, you needed it."

He anxiously twirled the corner of his mustache and added, "I'd like a second chance to do that. To take care of you. If you want to stick around with this old man. My house always has been, and forever will be, your house."

Noreen pursed her lips together and felt the sting of tears burn her sinuses. She fought to contain them and nodded, smiling, her brows knitting together.

He tossed a thumb over his shoulder. "I'm making tea, if you'd like some of that. Maybe you aren't a coffee drinker."

"Okay," she said, her voice breaking.

"That sound good?"

"Yeah. Yeah, I think I'd like that."

"W'go get that teapot sitting in there on the table so I can wash it out."

She did just that. When she returned, Normand was lathering up a rag in the basin. "Oh," he said, and turned, wiping his hands with a towel. He took the teapot off her hands and put it on the stove, but to his surprise, the girl stepped in against him, hugging herself, and he understood what she meant to do without being told.

She laid her ear on his chest, her hair tickling his nose, and the old man put his arms around her. One of his ursine hands cupped her head against the silky robe and he kissed her on the part of her blonde hair.

"You said earlier that you were always there with me," he said. "All the way back to the beginning. I've been thinking; maybe I always knew you were there. *All* of you, but especially my Noreen. Even then. Perhaps your brave little heart is what kept me going. What kept me from giving up."

"Maybe," she said, her arms and hands clasped to her chest. His robe smelled of wood-smoke and the cloying-sweet smell of the jacarandas. She stepped back and he beheld her at arms' length.

"You may have my eyes, but you've your mother's face."

"My mother . . . ." she said. "Who is my mother? Is . . . ."

"The kindest, toughest, smartest lady I've ever known in my

462

life. Lucas . . . took her life while I was overseas. It was . . . actually the impetus driving Edward's decision to take the three of you to Earth. He knew that if Lucas could take Josephine away from me, he could take any of you."

"That was my mother?" asked Noreen. She squinted up at his weathered face. "Josephine Rose? You finally got together with her?"

"Yes. By the gods, she was really something."

"If what Ed wrote is true, then I liked her. I wish I could have met her; could you tell me about her?"

"I think you two would have gotten along famously," said Normand, as the teapot began to whistle. "I ran into her again about a year before the No-Men came to Ostlyn."

They retired to the sitting room and conversed until their cups were empty and the dregs in the teapot were cold. They talked about a very beautiful woman whose life was taken far before her time. They spoke about the past and they spoke about the future.

And to turn things on their head for a change, a storied old knight sat and listened to a long tale about a lonesome little girl that never once suspected that she was a real princess.

The darkness was rent by a disc of white light. Normand found himself standing in it, as if illuminated from above by a spotlight. "Heyo?" he called into the shadows, the taste of the Sacrament cloying on his dry tongue. "Anybody?"

He realized that his voice was different; squeaky, small, thin. He looked down at his hands and saw the smooth, unmarked hands of a child. When his head rose again, he was standing in his childhood bedroom, draped in the gloom of midnight. He gripped his father's gun tight in the hand that had not been torn by the mountain cats.

A figure lay in his bed, facing the wall.

He approached it and when he touched it, Pack came awake in the bed himself, disoriented and displaced, still holding the pistol. Something had hit the roof. He smelled smoke.

This time he would not let them take his family. Six bullets for six men.

—The Fiddle and the Fire, vol 4 "The Truth and the Trial"

Revelations

SAWYER AND I GOT up and dressed as soon as we awoke and went up to the Weatherhead; Noreen was still dead asleep, having come to bed some time after midnight. The sun hung low over the eastern horizon, mounted on a wall painted in a thousand shades of red. Scrims of purple and orange lay shredded across the sky, dusted with the night's dying stars. The sounds of the waking city drifted to us from the maze unfurling down the mountain like a bride's train.

My mind wandered as we walked, and I became introspective, contemplating the events of the last several days. I realized that I was remembering the train-ride to Ostlyn in an unbroken sequence, as if the whirlwind had never happened. I even recalled getting off the train on the opposite side of the city and missing our run-in with Lennox Thackeray.

Looking back, it felt as if I were looking at two timelines at the same time, and the sheer implausibility of having existed in two simultaneous temporal stretches made my head hurt.

I couldn't quite put the sensation into words, so I decided to wait until we spoke with Normand to bring it up. Perhaps he had some insight that could encapsulate and explain it better than I could. We passed through the innermost rampart and started walking up the stairs to the capitol entrance.

"I need coffee," I said, shivering a little. I carried one of the chestpieces tucked into my armpit like a picture book.

"You *always* need coffee."

466

"I'm not sure what I ate yesterday, but I need you to help me make sure I never eat it again."

"Why?" Sawyer asked.

"I dreamt I was trapped at the bottom of a well with the Golden Girls. The last thing I remember was seeing Estelle Getty bite into a rat like a slice of watermelon, and then I woke up sweating."

He laughed. "Will do."

We'd gotten a great night's sleep—I felt better than I had in a long time—but the last ten steps were still a bit of a trek. When we got to the top, we paused to catch our breath. A gunslinger in green strolled over and greeted us with a ready smile, taking off his hat. He was a thin, handsome fellow, with narrow-set eyes and a beakish nose.

"*Good* mor-ning!" he said. "Welcome to the seat of Ain."

"The home of the Whopper," I said.

"The huh?" said the retainer.

"Nothing. We're here to see the King."

"Is that so!" he said. "Who may I say is calling? The King is in exercises, and normally does not like to be disturbed."

"The Chiral's son," said Sawyer, "—which would be myself, and the scribe's son, which would be this unsmiling savage slouching here." He rapped on my chest as if it were a door.

"Hey," I said. "I smile. When nobody's looking, I smile a whole lot."

"And that's why you're creepy."

The gunslinger bowed over his fist; we did the same. "You must be the individuals we were briefed on this morning. I will go and announce you."

"No, that's all right," said Sawyer. "We'll go in ourselves. No need."

He seemed put off balance by the shirking of custom, but recovered quickly. "Very well, then. Go on ahead."

We went through the ebony door and into the council chamber, which had nobody in it. A door stood open behind the dais, spilling bright golden sunlight across the backs of the thrones standing there.

I looked at Sawyer and he shrugged, going around the chairs and through the archway. I followed him into a large courtyard between two of the seven rook towers; it sprawled atop a plateau of rock carved out of the mountainside that jutted from the back of Weatherhead like a Cadillac's tail fin.

As we walked outside, we passed a stone bench that had a tall metal canister standing on it with a valve spout on the bottom. Steam issued from the top of it and curled from its sides in the chilly early air.

"Oh, coffee," I said. "I wish I had a cup."

We passed a ring of rocks that enclosed a small, crackling campfire. Hanging on a spit was a pot of some bubbling gruel, and a man in a linen suit and suspenders was tending it. He nodded as we passed, and we did the same.

Normand was at the very end of the courtyard where it jutted out in a great arc of stone, looming over the hillside.

If one were to vault the parapet, it was easily a twelve-meter drop to a steep, rocky slope, and a very injurious tumble ending in a head-on crash against Ostlyn's innermost wall. I peered over the edge, imagining this plummet, and leaned back with a wince.

The old man only wore a pair of canvas trousers and roper boots. His bare skin was a biography of pain written on pages of taut glove-leather. Some of the arcing scars marred a tattoo that engulfed his left shoulder, an intricate enigma of lines and symbols

468

that looked like an illustration from a medieval text on the occult.

He was lost in thought as we approached, performing what appeared to be slow, meditative tai-chi katas; I noticed when we got close enough that he had a revolver in either hand.

The polished guns caught the dawn's light and flicked ghostly sun-cats across the floor at our feet. He stepped this way and that, with no wasted movement, light and clever, moving around the balcony in a graceful, sweeping slow-motion waltz. His muscles rolled as he moved, his tendons as fine as guitar strings.

Every time he stopped, whether he had them thrust out straight or tucked under his elbow or behind his back, the pistols were leveled at some invisible opponent. With each pause, I could hear the actions click and the hammers hit empty chambers.

When he saw us watching, Normand turned the weapons with subtle gestures and slid them into his gunbelt. I realized that there were four holsters.

"Good morning, children," he said in that wrought-iron bass-baritone. His long silver hair curtained down his temples; he tossed his head back to clear his face, put down the belt, and took the undershirt draped over the parapet, putting it on.

I have to admit I was impressed and not a little intimidated; the years had been kind to the old man. He had to have been in his early seventies, but he looked like a chiseled statue. A slender, hungry, battle-scarred old wolf. Even his icy eyes looked wolven.

"Good morning, sir," said Sawyer. I echoed the greeting.

"How goes your first day in our fair city?"

"We haven't been up long," said Sawyer, and I handed him the K-Set chestpiece. "We had a few questions and wanted to come see if you had any possible answers."

He strode past us, pulling his suspenders on. "I am an open book, my friends—but if you'll excuse me, I'd like a few minutes to

469

put on my cover and warm my pages. Why don't you come with me and we'll see if Merritt can't rustle you boys up some coffee and something for breakfast."

Merritt was the man in the linen suit tending the campfire. He followed the King into the citadel, and a few minutes later came out with two ceramic decanters, two tin cups, a little pewter boat full of sugar, and a tiny jug of cream.

Sawyer showed me how to use the decanters; apparently, here you don't stir your coffee, you pour it from the carafe into the decanter. Then you add the cream and sugar to the decanter, swirl it around, and pour it into your cup. We sat on the stone bench and sipped coffee while Merritt fried bacon and made omelets over the fire.

When Normand came back, we had just been handed our plates. He was wearing a blue frock coat with leather elbows and a pair of canvas slacks. His gunbelt was on the outside of his doublet. He looked a bit like a Union general as he sat next to Sawyer and the attendant handed him an omelet.

"Now then," Normand said, putting the armor on the ground by the bench. He illuminated his next point by gesturing at the air with his fork, "—let us continue. Good conversation always aids digestion, or so I hear."

"I told you about my hallucination under the influence of the Acolouthis," I said.

The gunslinger cut off a bite and chewed it thoughtfully. "Ahh, so you did. The Sacrament is a powerful experience. It is forever in debate . . . whether the events that take place in that ethereal consciousness are real or imagined. For instance; how do you know you ever even visited that abandoned town by the wayside? The entire thing could have been wholly in your mind."

'That's an unsettling thought."

"You said yourself that you read the sign on the wall in that town. It was in the Earth language. Haven't you asked yourself *why* you could understand it?"

Synecdoche (WELCOME TO THE STICKS!)

It hadn't even occured to me. I'd been in such a state at the time that the fact had completely eluded me.

"I have to admit I haven't." I didn't know what else to say. It was a strange epiphany, one that made me doubt myself. I began to feel a little crazy again, and the sensation was not pleasurable. "Wait—that was *before* the outlaw ever gave me the stuff. How could—"

"Remember what we said yesterday about shifting time and space?" asked Sawyer.

"Not to undermine your senses," Normand said. "I apologize. I do have a fondness for speculating about such things. The sensations one encounters under the Sacrament are not always real, but the insight one gains from the experience is . . . more often than not, rooted deeper in truth than you realize. Some might even call it *clairvoyance.*"

"Maybe the Acolouthis had your brain ramped up so much you were able to understand Ainean," said Sawyer.

"Who needs Rosetta Stone? *Live life incoherently.*"

"Maybe it was so powerful it affected you before you even took it."

I gave him a dazed look. "Anyway, sir, I wanted to ask you about something related to the hallucination."

"Fire away."

"Right before Sardis slew the silen with the Datdimra, the silen said something about *finding* the 'First Sword' . . . he said it's the only thing that can kill—that can kill the Sileni, I'm assuming."

"Yes. Edward mentioned that they were immortal. If anything

471

could kill them, it is the Dragonslayer. But I don't know what the 'First Sword' is."

Sawyer rubbed the bridge of his nose, squinching his eyes shut. "The Rhetor said that he'd been going from world to world hiding the First Sword of each world. He mentioned Excalibur and a few other names, and said that the Datdimra is the First Sword's 'facet' here in Destin. I'm guessing that this First Sword is something that exists singularly, alone, but in all worlds at the same time."

"Kinda like a man standing at the Four Corners in Utah," I piped up. "That's where you can stand in four states at the same time: Arizona, Colorado, New Mexico, and Utah. The Mariner said something similar about the Wolf Oramoz. He said, *She exists in many worlds, with many names.*"

"Yeah. A lot like that, I guess," said Sawyer. "God Christ, I wish Ed were here to explain this shit." He was obviously pained. His food was growing cold in his lap, but he had drained his coffee cup.

"You okay?" I asked.

"Yeah. I just have a headache. I'm . . . remembering things that never happened."

"You too?"

"Yeah. It's like—damn, we need to write this stuff down. I'm forgetting it."

"Forgetting what?" I asked.

"Here, have you got a pen? You lost that paper you found in Ed's cottage, didn't you?"

"I did, it was in the satchel. The only pens around here are fountain pens, Saw. You'll have to go find one."

Sawyer got up and went into the Weatherhead. A moment later, he came back out with a piece of paper and a fountain pen.

472

He put the paper on the stone bench and made a big ugly ink-blot on it. "How the hell——?" he asked, but then he seemed to get used to it.

He wrote, TOTEM DRAGONSLAYER DATDIMRA CAN KILL SILEN on it, then held it up and blew on it to dry the ink. "I feel like I'm forgetting the things we saw and heard down there," he said. "It feels like—like—there was a wound in reality, in time, and now it's closing back up. It's healing. It's replacing the bad part with what *should* have happened."

"Like a skin graft?" I asked.

"Yeah," he said. "A time-graft. When you wrote us out of the Void and fell into the Vur Ukasha, you went down—you went down and put the story back together. I think that's what happened when you went down and saw the giant glowing ball with words all over it."

"You think so? You think I did that?"

Normand looked at the paper. "You are the Messenger now, after all," he said. "The task of bringing life and light to the story of this world has passed from Ed to you. It only makes sense that you would have the capacity for repairing it."

"I thought the Mariner did it."

"The Mariner is only a guide."

Sawyer poured himself another cup of coffee. "He can only lead a horse to water, Ross. He can't make you drink."

I got up and tucked my hand into my armpit, hugging myself. I took a sip of coffee, finishing my cup. Normand smoothed out his mustache, studying the paper, and presently he said, "You know, I think I've *heard* this word before. Totem."

"Have you?" I asked.

"I have. I heard it several times, while I was in the Antargata k-Setra. The Wilders spoke of it."

Sawyer swirled his coffee decanter, pulling his legs up to sit cross-legged. "Yeah? How come it wasn't in *The Cape and the Castle?*"

"Most of what the Wilders said was gibberish," said Normand. "Their gibberish language. Only Lord Harwell, rest his soul, could remotely understand them. I got the feeling, though, that Totem was not a thing. It was a place. They often spoke of it and their god, Obelus, in the same breath. It was probably the ghost-god's home. I didn't talk to Ed about it because I didn't consider it important at the time."

"Hmm," said Sawyer. "*Totem* is an English word. Well, an English loan-word. I wonder why the Wilders would be using English words?"

"What does it mean?" asked Normand.

"I know it came from Native American, but it represents a concept from a lot of Earth societies. I don't really know the definition of the word itself, but I know it has symbolic, spiritual meaning. People back on Earth talk about their 'totem animals'. I think it's a word for something that represents a definition larger than itself—like an icon."

I picked up the armor chestpiece and turned it around so Normand could see the printed label on the inside. "That reminds me. Do you know anything about this?"

"I can't even read it, I'm afraid," said Normand.

"It says *Nevada Organon*," I said. "I don't know what an 'organon' is, but Nevada is a place on Earth. It's one of the United States."

"Peculiar. I do notice, however, that two of those letters look like Ainean letters. The first letters." Normand leaned over and traced the words on the label with his fingertip, indicating the N and the O. "The sweep . . . here, and this is missing a line and a dot, but otherwise they look very similar. Similar to Ainean illuminated capitals, at any rate. I don't see any similarities in these lowercase symbols."

"No," said Sawyer.

"Hmm?"

"—I mean, N. O. I mean, yeah, come on. It's obvious. That must have been where Aarne Hargrave got 'No-Men' in book two. He wasn't saying they weren't men, he wasn't saying there *were* no men, he was talking about something he saw."

I shrugged, making a face.

An armored retainer came out into the courtyard and announced, "S'rah, Councilwoman Noemi has arrived."

He stepped to the side; a lady came out of the central spire and strode straight to Normand as he got up. They embraced briefly and he introduced us to each other. "Friends, this is Councilwoman of Knowledge Eleanor Noemi. Eleanor, these are very special visitors . . . the tall one is the Chiral's youngest, Sawyer, and the one with the shaven pate is Ross, the son of Ardelia Thirion and the scribe Lord Eddick we were so unfortunate to lose recently."

Noemi was slender and stately in a slim robe the gray of dove-down and a modest wide-brimmed hat. She took off the hat to reveal short silver-white hair and beamed with a genuine smile. Her face was friendly and open, and her crystalline-gray eyes completed the grave color scheme.

"The pleasure is all mine," she said. "It's refreshing to see such handsome young men in court for a change. You never quite get used to being around these weatherbeaten old beasts."

"Tactfully tactical as always," guffawed Normand.

Noreen came out of the Weatherhead, Walter behind her. She was wearing a beautiful dress that swirled and capered in the

475

slightest breeze, a white ankle-length dress that looked as if someone had thrown a bucket full of sky at her. Soft shades of dark blue cascaded from her left shoulder in blotches and spatters, trailing down the side in a whorl of droplets.

She went straight over to Sawyer and he set his plate aside. She leaned against his back and draped her arms around his neck, commenting on his dazzled expression. "Mikey likey, huh?"

"It's gorgeous."

"It belonged to my mom," she said. "The King gave it to me last night."

"Oh?" asked Sawyer. "Who is that?"

"Josephine Rose."

"What? Are you for real? The outlaw from book three and book five?"

"The very same," she said. "That's actually where *my* name came from. They put *their* names together."

Eleanor Noemi smirked quizzically. "And who is this bold and beautiful young lady who knows so much about your romantic exploits, dear Normand?"

"That would be my daughter, Eleanor," said Normand. "Noreen, this is Councilwoman—"

"Noemi," Noreen said, coming around the bench to take her hand. The girl did a little curtsey. "I know you from Lord Eddick's books. I'm an admirer, ma'am. I know how hard you fought for your appointment to the head of Ainean scientific society. It's an honor."

Noemi beamed. "And you're as beautiful as your mother was. Too bad, however, that Josephine's tongue wasn't as silver as yours," she said, and turned to the King. "Normand, why haven't I met this dear child years ago? Where in the world have you been hiding her?"

"It's a very long story," he said. "And I plan on recounting it once the rest of the council is here. We've got a lot of planning to do and I want everyone to be on the same page."

"Ah, yes," said Noemi. "I do know how you are loath to repeat yourself."

The Best-Laid Plans

THE REST OF THE day was spent with Walter practicing at the range while Normand and the available council members attended to their usual business. It turned out that—contrary to my own skills—Noreen was far better with a scoped rifle. I like to say that I'm a deft hand with a pistol, but she could lie on the gear table with a falling-block carbine and chew the heads off of the cutouts in the back forty.

The last council members had arrived when we returned from the range that evening. A few of the attendants stayed late to prepare a small feast for us, a cookout that reminded me of backyard barbeques back home. I stood in Normand's little kitchen as they bustled about, enjoying their banter and the smell of the spices they were using, until they ran me out.

I found everyone sitting around Normand's campfire out in the courtyard. The council members had changed out of their upscale riding clothes and dressed down in shirts and slacks. The mad gunslinger Seymour was even in attendance, plucking at a lap-guitar in a languid, dreamy melody, his eyes closed and his face upturned in rapture.

I sat between Noreen and a gawky, weak-chinned old fellow I discovered was the Councilman of the Treasury, Ozazias Harper. He reminded me of the tortoise from the *Looney Tunes* cartoons; he wore a pair of coke-bottle glasses, had a nose like a cowcatcher, and the knot in his throat bobbled when he spoke, which was in a laconic farmer drawl.

Sitting across from me were also Talbot Horn and Goddard Grey, the Councilmen of Merchantry and Justice respectively. Horn was a small, anxious man in a straw porkpie hat and pinstripe jacket. He served as the nation's director of commerce, and liaised between the Council and the traders' union. Hand in hand with Harper, the two of them did what they could to moderate Ain's modest economy.

Grey was a tall bearded man with a heavy, arboreal frame that made him look even bigger than rangy Normand and hands that made me feel like a little girl. He showed up in a wool military dress-suit the olive-green of strained peas and a tyrolean hat the same dulcet color. Councilman Grey ran the Ainean military, which served a dual purpose as the national protector of Ain and as her police force. He also advised Councilman Bennett on matters of state security.

I liked the Council of Ain. I liked Ostlyn itself.

There was a certain Old World backwater grandeur to the place that appealed to me, and the people that ran the country weren't neck-deep in ostentatious bullshit, squabbling over petty issues like the politicians back on Earth. The city itself was ancient, older than anyone in it; the people in charge were like a bunch of old friends that'd stumbled across a set of mythical ruins and decided to run a country out of it.

Which, I suppose, might have even been the case.

We ate steaks grilled over the fire, beans, cornbread (hands down the best I'd ever had, and that's saying something coming from a country boy), and roasted pieces of the apple-potato things on long steel skewers. I finally found out what the "applotatoes" were called: *semefe*.

When we were all packed to the brim and sitting on the low slat benches around the fire, staring into the flames and letting our gluttony digest, Normand spoke up. The chill of the night hung on our backs like capes.

"I had planned on saving this for a more appropriate venue tomorrow, as I don't normally like to mix business with pleasure," he said, and looked up at the sky with beatific eyes like a painting of a pious man. "And this is certainly pleasure. It's been a long, long time since I had the chance to share a good meal with good friends under the stars like this."

"Hear, hear," said Clayton.

"Too right," boomed Grey in his war-drum voice.

Normand continued, "However in light of current events, circumstances dictate haste. Friends, issues have come to light that involve and affect all of us. Destin itself may be in danger."

There was a rumble of alarm in the Council.

"It is time for me to divulge a secret to you which I have been holding for most of my life." He leaned forward, his elbows on his knees, and gazed into the fire as he spoke. I was transfixed; he looked like Gandalf himself peering into a palantír. "The Old Ways, the religions our ancestors abandoned as archaic and obsolete, as it turns out, were not rooted in fiction and myth, but in reality."

The Council members seemed vaguely confused, but otherwise unfazed. I glanced at Sawyer and Noreen; their faces were stoic marble busts, jaws set in stone. They'd never asked to come here, and they'd never asked to be connected to this place, but I loved them for their resolve and acceptance.

"The Destin we know is in fact the brother of another world, the world called Zam. The people that live there call it Earth, but it is the very same land cut away from Behest when the Great Wolf Oramoz cleft the Time Dragon Angr'manu in two."

"Sounds like you've gotten into the larkweed, Normand," said Armistead. "No one told me we were going to tell tall tales around the campfire tonight. I've got a few satisfyingly lewd jokes I've been saving for a time like this, if . . . ?"

Noemi gave the Councilman a deadly glare, but her expression resolved into one of concern as she turned back to the King. "Dear friend, I've always considered you one of the most rational, sound-minded people I know. Where did this come from?"

"Yes, old man," said Grey. "You are the one man I'd least beg flights of fancy."

Harper said simply in his gooble-gobble hillbilly voice, "How do you *know?*"

Normand said without looking away from the fire, "I know because the young lady and two young men sitting with us tonight are from the other-world I've mentioned."

They were taken aback, and made faces of concern and doubt at each other; then they looked at Sawyer, Noreen and I.

"Is this true?" asked Bennett.

"It is," I said. "We were born here in this world, but taken to Zam by my father Lord Eddick to keep us safe from Tem Lucas after the Battle of Ostlyn."

"Interesting."

"What is so special about the scribe?" asked Horn. "I thought he was merely a poet, tagging along with you to write your biography for posterity, and to keep you lot entertained on the road."

"My father was born in the other world."

Normand gave a deep nod and said, "Eddick told me the story one lonely night when we were young. There are beings from outside our worlds who made a pact with the Wolf at the beginning of time. In exchange for immortality, they promised to serve as the water-carriers of the Sea of Dreams, the Vur Ukasha."

"They give stories to storytellers," said Noreen.

481

"My stars and garters," said Noemi. "You're serious, aren't you dearie? This *isn't* a prank."

"The day Normand Kaliburn pulls a prank on a man is the day I turn in my gun," said Grey. "The man's as funny as a baby in a well and twice as cold."

"Deadly serious, dove," Normand said. "Listen to me, friends: these beings are called the Sileni. They are ageless and as dream-bringers, they are imbued with the capacity to talk a man into doing just about anything within the scope of his character. They cannot kill, but they cannot *be* killed, either, except by someone wielding the Timecutter."

"The Timecutter. *Now* I *know* you're spitting wind," said Bennett. "The Datdimra is a nursery tale straight from the old legends."

Normand held up a finger, and swept a hand at us. "If these boys and this girl, these *children* of legends, tell me they've seen it with their own eyes, seen it in the hands of Sardis Bridger himself, then I believe them. Do you trust me?" he asked the council. "Have I ever led you astray? Do you still follow me?"

The moment crouched there like a coiled spring, and then Grey said, "You hain't. Ever."

"Damn straight," said Clayton, puffing a long-stemmed pipe.

"Then trust me when I say that we may have another war on our hands. Some of these Sileni have grown weary of servitude and seek to sow discord and destruction throughout the worlds. And there are many worlds, other worlds than these, old friends, as many worlds as there are stories and storytellers to tell them."

He looked up from the fire. "I know these things because Lord Eddick was an Earthling chosen by the Sileni to tell *our* tale. That man was infinitely more vital than any of you knew, and now he is slain because of what *he* knew."

"And now we know what he knew," I said. "That makes *us* a target."

"If this is true," said Horn, "—why are you telling *us?*"

"Because I am the only man in all of Ain who has traveled as far into the Antargata k-Setra," said Normand. "I alone have been to the place where the Datdimra may now sleep. The Sileni must be stopped before they bring the universe down around our heads, and we need that mythical blade to accomplish that."

He drew a fist and shook it in resolve. "We have the solution, here, in Destin; it is our obligation to fetch this sword and put an end to these machinations. I will be departing the city to lead an expedition into the heart of the Frontier as soon as can be expected. I will be leaving the city in your most capable hands."

"As always, your rhetoric brings a tear to my eye," said Grey. "It all sounds crazy, but count me in, you old son of a bitch."

"I cannot bring you along, old friend. I need you to stay here and maintain order."

"Oh, come *on,*" the general said. He took off his hat and slammed it on the ground at his feet, but then he said, "All right. But you better bring me a souvenir."

"Yes, the ears of our enemies, splendid. I'll have Eleanor make them into a necklace for you."

"I most certainly will not, you disgusting ghouls."

"The expedition will consist of myself, the Chiral, Ross, my daughter Noreen, and the Chiral's two sons Sawyer and Walter," said Normand. "Once we reach the Frontier, we will be departing the presence of the Ainean military contingent and continuing on alone. I want full might retained here in Ostlyn and at Maplenesse, as well as in Fed Panaeg and Fi Himdet, in case our antagonist attempts to lure us away from our destination by attacking our homes."

The guitar melody, which I had forgotten about, ended in a dissonant *twonk*.

Everybody looked over at Seymour, who was staring at Normand. "I'm going with you," he said, and continued playing. "You are going to need me."

"*I'll* be damned," said Councilman Bennett. "You're not going anywhere, son. If this is all true, then the King will have his hands full taking care of you on top of everything else. He doesn't need the burden."

Seymour looked up from the guitar, but didn't stop reeling out the plucky song. "I'm not an idiot, mother, I'm mad. There's a difference."

"Oh! Very well then, it seems I've been schooled here."

"You believe me to be a burden?"

"Err . . . ." began Bennett, " . . . no. No, son, you are not a burden. But if—"

"Then by your logic, I will not hinder the expedition," said Seymour. "Will I?"

The Councilman inhaled, hesitated, and his face grew dark with reluctant concession. He wrung his hands and stared at the fire. "You are a grown man, See. I will not stand in your way."

"I'm glad you agree," said Seymour, and he punctuated the sentiment with a happy flourish of notes.

Normand clasped Bennett's hands with one of his own. "He will be safe with me, Thaddeus."

"Many thanks," said the Councilman, and he remained quiet.

Ozazias Harper had been deep in thought, rubbing his bristly mouth as he watched the conversation. Now he addressed Normand, his thumbs hooked into his suspenders. "Norm, earlier you said there are many other worlds. Perhaps I missed an important point here, but does that mean that there's one of these .

. . Sileni for each world?"

"Ostensibly, yes."

"How are you going to kill all those nasty buggers with one little sword?"

"I've been thinking about that," said Walter, speaking up for the first time. The Deon had been sitting on the parapet at the firelight's edge, the cherry of his cigarette bobbing up and down in the blue night. He got up and stubbed it out, walking over to the gathering.

"From what I can tell," he said, "The silen leading the revolt is a big ugly one called 'The Rhetor'. Now, when I saw him, the silen that had been helping us referred to the Rhetor as 'Master'. I'm assuming this means that the Rhetor is their leader."

Seymour played an ominous note.

"So it goes without saying that these guys are listening to *him*, right? He's obviously got some kind of pull. I'm thinking if we can get to him and take *him* out, maybe the others will straighten out, or give up."

"Sounds like a plan," said Normand. "The best we have right now. Perhaps—"

He was interrupted by a brilliant flash that lit up the sky like an atomic bomb. It was followed by a crash that seemed to echo faintly from some distant point.

"The hell was that?" said Sawyer.

We all leapt from our seats and ran into the Weatherhead. Inside the central chamber, everyone clustered in confusion, looking for the source of the flash.

Grey pointed toward a doorway and said, "Out there. Follow me."

We spilled through into another elevated courtyard, and heard screams from below. It was immediately evident what had

485

happened as soon as we got outside; a hulking, rust-streaked metal shape hung over the outskirts of Ostlyn, suspended from the hips of long saurian legs.

It looked as if someone had torn an aircraft carrier to pieces and cobbled together a Tyrannosaur from them. Even from here, I could hear cable-tendons thrumming and clanking. The *Nevada Organon* eagle was stenciled on its flank.

Noreen's eyes were wide, a deep frown on her face.

"This must be the Rhetor's doing," said Normand. "Those things haven't walked the sands of Ain for decades!"

I broke ahead of the council and was halfway to the parapet when something marred the air in front of me and the wind seemed to solidify. A slender red-shrouded figure materialized from the swirling matter, landing at my feet in a crouch. I backed away in surprise.

It was the cloaked swordswoman that had confronted Sawyer and I in the village beyond the mirror.

The Griever stood up, silhouetted by a stormfront that flickered with heat lightning, and pulled off her banded veil. Ardelia Thirion's silver-blonde hair rippled in the night-breeze, and she was breathtakingly beautiful, fierce and primordial, like a Norse war-goddess.

My mother glanced over her shoulder at the approaching No-Man. She unsheathed the sword at her hip and flourished it with a *whoop* of steel cutting air. Moonlight glittered from her blade.

"Get out of here," she told us, turning to face the lumbering giant. "I'll catch up."

About the Author.

S. A. Hunt lives in Georgia. Although *The Whirlwind in the Thorn Tree* was his first completed novel, he's been writing and producing art for almost twenty years. Short stories and illustrations can be found at his website. Keep an eye out for *Law of the Wolf*, the next book in the Outlaw King series.

http://theusualmadman.net/

https://twitter.com/authorsamhunt

http://gplus.to/samuelhunt

Made in the USA
Las Vegas, NV
19 January 2021

16163604R00272